WORLD OF FIRE

ALSO BY JAMES LOVEGROVE

NOVELS
The Hope • Days
The Foreigners • Untied Kingdom
Worldstorm • Provender Gleed

Co-writing with Peter Crowther
Escardy Gap

The Pantheon series
The Age Of Ra • The Age Of Zeus
The Age Of Odin • Age Of Aztec
Age of Voodoo • Age of Godpunk
Age of Shiva

The Redlaw series
Redlaw • Redlaw: Red Eye

NOVELLAS
How The Other Half Lives • Gig
Age Of Anansi • Age of Satan • Age of Gaia

SHERLOCK HOLMES
The Stuff of Nightmares

COLLECTIONS OF SHORT FICTION
Imagined Slights • Diversifications

FOR YOUNGER READERS
The Web: Computopia • Warsuit 1.0
The Black Phone

FOR RELUCTANT READERS
Wings • The House of Lazarus
Ant God • Cold Keep • Dead Brigade
Kill Swap • Free Runner

The 5 Lords Of Pain series
The Lord Of The Mountain • The Lord Of The Void
The Lord Of Tears • The Lord Of The Typhoon
The Lord Of Fire

WRITING AS JAY AMORY
The Clouded World series
The Fledging Of Az Gabrielson • Pirates Of The Relentless Desert
Darkening For A Fall • Empire Of Chaos

WORLD OF FIRE

A DEV HARMER MISSION

...ng planets.

...Diaspora, continued un...

...ace of artificial intelligence...

...ved a gruelling, decade-lo...

...uneasy truce.

...ce, along the notio...

...dy of men...

JAMES LOVEGROVE

SOLARIS

First published 2014 by Solaris
an imprint of Rebellion Publishing Ltd,
Riverside House, Osney Mead,
Oxford, OX2 0ES, UK

www.solarisbooks.com

ISBN: 978 1 78108 207 2

10 9 8 7 6 5 4 3 2 1

A CIP catalogue record for this book is available from the
British Library.

Designed & typeset by Rebellion Publishing

Printed in the US

In the century after it cast off all religion, humankind flourished and prospered, spreading out beyond Earth, beyond the solar system, to colonise far-flung planets.

This expansion, the Diaspora, continued until it reached the territory of the race of artificial intelligence zealots known as Polis+.

There followed a gruelling, decade-long war that ended eventually in an uneasy truce.

In the years since, along the notional Border Wall between the two empires, a body of men and women – the officers of Interstellar Security Solutions and similar companies – have stood guard against enemy sabotage, sedition and subversion.

One of these agents is Dev Harmer...

1

10101010101011111001101101010011110110101011 00
01101010010100101111010010101010111000010101 01
01010000101001010010110010100100000000101011 01
10101000101001001010010000011111101010101101 01
00100101001001010001100 Dad? Daddy! Don't 0101
10010100100000000101100101001000000000101010 111
01111010101011101000101 01

11101010010100101101010101010101111001101101 0101 0
01111011010101100011010100101001011110100101 01
01011100001010101111010101010001010010100011 11
00100010010101010101111110010110010100100000 0
00101010111010100010010110010100100000000010 101
01110111001110101100010001111101011010 exclusion
from this school 010000

11110101010101011111001101101010011110110101 0
11000110101001010010111101001010101011100001 0
10101111101001101010111001010110010100100000 0
00101010111010100010010110010100100000000101 01
01110101010110010100100011010101010101010010 1
00101010010100100010101111110101111010101011 010

10101111111111111111101011010101010100110010101 alternatives are a spell of detention at a juvenile correctional facility or 00000100111
10010110010100100000000101010111010100010001111
01010101001111011101111101010110101010101001010
1111100101101010011111001010010111010111101001
010101011100001010101 eyes front, Private Harmer
1110101000101
11100111001000000010100010001010100111110010010
010111000001010100011010101010101111100110101
010011110110101011000110101001010010111101001 0
101010111000010110101010011111001010010100111011
01011110010100000111 Frontier War 0010011010101
010011111001010010111010100100101010101010101111
100110110101001111011110101 01
111101010101010101010101010101111100110110101 00
111010100111110010100101111101101010110001101
010010100101111010010101010111000010 Contact!
Contact! Enemy 01001010101010101010101010101010010
100011101011010101
110100011010101011111111111111110101010101101010101
0101010101010101010101011111001101110101010101 scrap
metal
010101010101010101010101011111001101101101010101101
011011010101010101011010000111011110101000011 10
111110101101010100101010101011010010001010101111
101010001100101100101111100101110101010101 01
011111001101101010011110110 10 sustained act of meritorious service and extreme courage under fire
0111100100110000101101000 0
01010101010101010101010101111100110110101011110

011011010100111101101010110001101010010010010
111101001010101011100001110111001010001010 10
Lieutenant, they're all around us, shit, Lieutenant
Harmer 1000111
11010101110101010100100101010101010101010101
01111100110110100010010100000101001010010100
0010101010100100100011111110101010 shoot the
digimentalist bastards in the 11010101010001111010
11110101010100011
1111010101010101110101011011111101100101001011
10 Leather Hill 10101010101010101010101000111010
1010011
00001010010 aaaaaahhhhhhh!!! 10110010100000010
101101010101010101010111110011010111111110101
0100111
0001010110101010100101111111101011100111111
111101111101000 terminal physiological damage
101010011
11010010011 trauma 010001000101010100001010011
10101010101111001101101010011101101010110001
101010010
001011110 regrowth 111001100100 expense 1110100
0011001011110101110111101101001111110011010111
deal
0111111111100110110101001110110101011
Solutions 1001011100011111111001101 skill set
101000101001011101
1001010 consultant 1000001010 contract 0001010100
earn 01101001 phased payment 1010101110 valuable
1000010100 Border Wall 11101010 troubleshoot 110
indenture 10 data 'porting

100101 terms of employment 111010 host forms 00101 Mr Harmer? Mr Harmer?

"Mr Harmer?"

A new voice. Loud. Clear. Not a ghost from his past, not part of his life flashing before him. Real.

"Mr Harmer? You're fully installed in the host form. Ultraspace download via commmplant is one hundred per cent complete. All readings nominal. Feel free to open your eyes."

Dev opened his eyes.

There was the familiar nausea, like a hangover. A tightness in the head, as though he had been squeezed into something he didn't fit – a foot crammed into a shoe a size too small. He felt a swirling in his belly, travel sickness of the mind.

"Please speak to me, Mr Harmer, so that I know the insertion was a success."

"Shit."

"Thank you. How are you feeling?"

"Shit."

"Do you know what your situation is? Are you aware?"

"Shit."

"I'll take that as a yes."

He was a young man, skin white as chalk. Shock of frizzy hair. Eager eyes with pupils that flashed with a weird kind of inner light.

"My name is Junius Bilk," the young man said. "Your ISS liaison."

"Of course you are," said Dev. "What else would you be?"

Bilk detached the transcription matrix from the side of Dev's head. The floatscreens around Dev continued to monitor his heart rate, blood oxygen levels and neural activity. A brain scan revealed the dark bulge of the commplant in the left hemisphere, its dendritic tendrils insinuated into the Broca's and Wernicke's areas.

"Is there anything I can get you?" Bilk enquired. "You look a bit peaky. Maybe you need to vomit. I could fetch a bowl."

"No," said Dev. He did still feel close to puking, but if there had been anything in his digestive tract, it would have come out. "Why's it so bright in here?" The ceiling light was as dazzling as the sun. "Hurts."

"Let me adjust that for you." Junius Bilk rheostatted the light down to a dull throbbing glare. "Sorry. You'll be beginning to appreciate that you now have nocturnal vision – a greater than Terratypical concentration of rods in the retina and, behind the retina, a tapetum lucidum, a reflective layer of tissue that gives the photoreceptor cells an extra chance to absorb light. Like cats have."

"Meow."

"Takes a bit of getting used to, I should think. If you weren't born with it."

Dev blinked up at the kid. How old was he? Seventeen? Eighteen? Was this the best that ISS could do? Were they recruiting straight out of high school?

"Twenty-six," Bilk said, as though reading his mind. "I'm older than I look. We maintain our youthful bloom longer here. It's the absence of UV."

"'Here'?" said Dev. His voice was warming up, losing its virgin roughness. "Where's here?"

"Calder's Edge."

"That's the planet? Never heard of it."

"No, the city. My mistake. I assumed you knew. Assumed they'd have told you in advance."

"Don't assume anything where ISS are concerned, least of all that they're considerate of my welfare. They tell me zilch, just dump me from place to place and expect me to catch up as I go along."

"Iota Draconis C. Also known as Alighieri."

"Alighieri. That's a clue. The poet Dante's surname. Someone has a sense of humour... or thinks he does. Thermoplanet?"

"Extreme thermoplanet, actually, orbiting an evolved giant star just outside the Messier 101 nebula. Point-four on the Earth Similarity Index, and one notch above mercurian. It reaches six hundred degrees Celsius up on the crust. Cooler at night, but not by much."

"Joy."

"It's slightly smaller than Earth, but denser in composition, so the gravity is more or less equivalent. You won't notice any extra buoyancy. Alighieri has a faster rotation, too, so the days are shorter. But again, not so much that you'd notice any difference."

"Okay. Let me see how this feels."

Dev was lying supine on a form-fitting, foam-lined mediplinth. He struggled to a sitting position, then swung his legs over the side to stand. Bilk offered to help, but Dev waved him away.

The body he had been downloaded into was short, heavyset, and muscular. Stumpier than he was accustomed to. As best he remembered, he was several centimetres taller than this.

The hands were pale and hairy, with blunt spatulate fingers. Efficient blue-collar hands, not meant for delicate work.

"How do I look?" he said.

Junius Bilk set one of the floatscreens to display a realtime shot of Dev.

Dev warily studied the face. The face he had been given. The face that wasn't his.

It was coarse and squashed. Rough iron-wool hair peaked from a broad, flat brow. The nose was a squatting frog, the lips chunky. He grinned without humour. Decent teeth, but big.

Not unhandsome, he thought. Puggy, he decided. That was the word for it. Puggy. Like a boxer who'd gone a few too many rounds. The face of a man who liked a scrap, perhaps more than was good for him.

A face he could live with, for however long he had to. Drawn from the colonist DNA bank, so he would be seeing plenty others like it on this world.

He was stark naked, as always on arrival. He glanced down to check how well-endowed, or not, they had made him.

They had been relatively generous this time.

He flexed his arms, articulated his thick, spadelike fingers.

Him, but not him. A new car for the driver that

was Dev Harmer. A new extension of himself. A bespoke temporary home.

"Commplant is operational whenever you want it," said Bilk. "You have clearance for full access to Alighieri's insite and communications network, plus standard bundled features like memo scribing."

Dev thought *On*, and felt the buzz of the commplant booting up, an intracerebral tingle. Within a few seconds the unit was synchronised, initialised and awaiting use. A mental cursor winked. He sensed addresses, social media, shared personal data, contact numbers, all lurking behind a partition, accessible as and when necessary.

He set a firewall password: *leatherhill1000*. Then he powered the commplant down. No point wasting energy. Even idle mode burned calories.

"Clothes," he said, but Bilk had anticipated the request.

The outfit consisted of underwear, an undershirt, and a basic, utilitarian set of dungaree-like overalls, accompanied by thick-soled, sturdy boots. The fabrics were flimsy and breathable. Keeping warm must not be a priority on Alighieri. Likewise fashionability.

"And this." Bilk held out a reinforced cap, similar to a hardhat, made from keratin derivatives.

"Really?"

"Not obligatory, but folks prefer to wear them outdoors. An umbrella in case of rain."

Dev took the cap, but didn't put it on. The impressions he was forming of Alighieri – none of them filled him with delight.

Thermoplanet. Well short of the inner limit of its system's Goldilocks zone, seared by solar radiation. Human-inhospitable surface. Subterranean habitation only. The principal industry, if he didn't miss his guess, would be mining.

It certainly wouldn't be tourism.

Once, just once, couldn't Interstellar Security Solutions send him somewhere that was a solid "1" on the Earth Similarity Index? A place boasting balmy blue skies and gorgeous sugary beaches. A resort planet, perhaps, with five-star hotels, spas, fine wine, and beautiful bored women looking for some uncomplicated, no-strings fun.

He knew the answer already.

Because bad shit didn't happen on nice, cosy resort planets. Bad shit happened on the fringes of the Terran Diaspora, out by the Border Wall, on planets that had covetable natural resources or were of strategic importance.

"Other environment-specific physiological attributes you should be aware of," said Bilk. "Every native-born Alighierian has them, through heritable genes." He counted off on his fingers. "One, haemoglobin with a high oxygen affinity. Good air is at a premium down here. Two, hyper-efficient thermoregulation, with an increased epidermal vasodilation and eccrine gland response."

"Translation?"

"The blood vessels in your skin dilate easily in order to shed heat from your bloodstream through convection, and you sweat a lot."

"Nice."

"Three, lowered body temperature. You won't feel cold, though, because the ambient warmth is so high. As for the sweating, try not to overtax yourself aerobically, drink plenty of fluids, and you'll be fine. Finally, four, your kidneys have been tweaked to produce higher concentrations of the prohormone calcitriol. This counteracts the almost total absence of naturally-synthesised vitamin D due to lack of exposure to sunlight."

"Right," Dev said. He was hungry. Famished, in fact. The host form was pristine. It hadn't been fed yet. Fresh from the growth vat and craving nutrition.

But first things first. Info, then food.

"Briefing," he said.

Bilk nodded. "I was warned you were the straight-down-to-business type. The profile they sent me –"

"Is just some human resources crap. Piece of fiction. Reduces me to a bunch of bullet points and Myers-Briggs personality metrics. Doesn't mean a thing."

"The profile said that's exactly what you would say about it."

"Do you want to get on my wrong side, Mr Bilk?"

"No sir, Mr Harmer."

"Then don't get clever with me. Briefing. Come on. Why have I been inserted here? What's going on that needs the attention of an ISS troubleshooter?"

"Well, it's fairly simple," Bilk began. "Starting just a few weeks back, we've been experiencing –"

The room trembled. The floatscreens flickered, readouts scattering into zigzag lines. Cupboard doors rattled in their frames. Shelves and their contents shook. The already dim lighting dimmed further.

Dev felt a deep vibrato hum through the soles of his feet, a sound with a pulse, like a singer reaching some unfathomably low bass note. He gripped the edge of the gurney. It wasn't that he was going to topple over; more that he found it hard to keep his legs from crumpling.

The noise faded. Stability returned.

"Right on cue," said Bilk with grim relish. "This is exactly the problem. We've been experiencing tremors just like that, and worse, more severe, on a regular basis. No one's sure what's causing them or what they signify. They don't appear to have any natural cause. Calder's Edge doesn't lie in a region of seismic activity. It would never have been built here otherwise. There's been nothing like this in all of Alighieri's known history."

"No geological evidence dating back to pre-colonial times?"

"Not as far as we can determine. It just seems that –"

And then it resumed, like thunder. The room heaved and yawed. Some titanic fist was punching, pounding, pummelling from outside. Walls appeared to flex, solid structures turning to liquid.

Dev and Bilk swayed, helpless as a massive force warped the world around them, seeming to bend the very air itself.

The earthquake – this was no mere tremor – rumbled on for a minute and more, merciless, relentless. Dev heard Junius Bilk screaming in panic, and wanted to join in. He kept reminding himself he had known worse – lived through worse. Some of the things he had seen, some of the things he had endured... By rights, life should have no terrors left in store for him.

But he wanted to scream, like Bilk. It was only through sheer willpower that he didn't.

An ear-splitting *crack* was followed by a tumultuous *crash*.

The ceiling broke and caved in.

An avalanche of rock gushed down from above, right on top of the two of them.

2

Dev OPENED HIS eyes and wondered why he wasn't dead.

The air was filled with dust, dense as fog. He coughed and wiped his eyes.

"Bilk? Bilk?"

No response.

The mediplinth and plain old good luck had saved him. When the ceiling collapsed, Dev had instinctively thrown himself flat on the floor. One end of a support joist had landed on the mediplinth. The rest of the joist had canted at an angle, forming a shelter over him, protecting him from the worst of the falling debris.

He was bruised and battered, but okay.

He hoisted himself up onto all fours, shucking chunks of rubble.

As the dust cleared he saw Bilk, sprawled nearby.

Most of Bilk lay buried under rocks. His head had been crushed. One eyeball was dislodged from its socket. His tongue lolled idiotically. Blood caked his mouth and nostrils.

The transcription matrix had been crushed and ruined, too.

"Ah, damn it," Dev said. "Well, this is a great start."

He got shakily to his feet, took one last look at the dead ISS liaison, then began searching for an exit.

The room, his private arrivals lounge, was half-destroyed. Torn electrical cables sparked. A single floatscreen remained on, suspended in midair at shoulder height. It was desperately trying to function, error messages flashing uncertainly.

The door had been blown open by the pressure of the cave-in. Dev picked his way over to it, feet slithering on shattered rock and pieces of broken equipment.

The corridor beyond was more or less intact, although several ceiling panels hung askew and part of a ventilation duct sagged like a length of disembowelled intestine.

Dev passed an open doorway to a chamber containing an upright plexiglass cylinder large enough to accommodate a person. Large enough, indeed, to have accommodated *him*.

The growth vat. Womb to the artificially engineered host form he was walking around in.

The glass was cracked and the nutrient solution inside was leaking out. A yellowish puddle was spreading, like spilled amniotic fluid. ISS would not be pleased that one of their nightmarishly expensive body-generating machines was trashed. They'd probably be upset about Junius Bilk too, but nowhere near as much. Personnel were more readily replaceable than cutting-edge proprietary technology.

Another door, marked ARMOURY, was code-locked. Bilk would have known the code, but he wasn't giving up any secrets now. Dev had no access to weapons for the time being. A setback, but not insurmountable.

He checked the equipment lockers and found what he was looking for: a backup transcription matrix, intact. That was something. He had a ticket out of here, when the time came. Spaceship flight was always an option, if push came to shove, but data 'porting, ISS's preferred method for relocating their operatives, was swifter and more direct. Unless you were shifting objects of greater mass than an electron stream, ultraspace trumped infraspace every time.

An aftershock shuddered around him.

Time to get going. It was surely safer outdoors than in.

He slipped the keratin-derivative cap on his head, just in case.

He emerged from the front entrance of the ISS outpost, finding himself on a paved esplanade. Citizens of Calder's Edge milled around, conversing anxiously with one another or communing silently via commplant with friends and relatives elsewhere, reassuring their loved ones that they were okay. Alarm and consternation showed on every face, along with an aggrieved weariness.

The outpost was situated hard against one wall of

the cavern, atop a small plateau. The view from here was panoramic and remarkable, and Dev would have paused to take it in but for the fact that he had narrowly escaped death a moment ago and had no wish to hang around near a building left potentially very unstable by the earthquake.

He moved out across the esplanade, still stumbling a little as he acclimatised to the host form's proportions. Only when he reached the railing at the edge did he stop to survey the scenery.

Calder's Edge occupied a cavern as large as any he had ever seen – big enough to have served as a hangar for a billion-ton goods freighter and still leave room for a few long-range gravity-drive gulf cruisers besides. The opposite end of it was almost too distant to see.

Prefab habitats rose in spiral layers on the vast natural columns that vaulted between the cavern's roof and floor. Living quarters, mostly, by the look of them; prefab modular polygons huddling along carved-out tiers.

A maglev rail system curved between them, dual guideway runners perched on support struts. A couple of the tracks traversed a deep chasm, from which fumes softly purled. There was a strong stench of burning in the air, with a sulphurous undernote.

From the roof of the cavern itself, amid jagged stalactites the size of cathedral pillars, hung pyramidal illumination clusters. Their dusky orange glow was weak by Terratypical standards, but more than adequate for the dark-adapted Alighierian eye.

Single-storey buildings were spread out across the cavern floor. These appeared to be business and leisure units, including a number of retail parks. If the column habitats were residential, the floor-based premises were where Calder's Edge citizens shopped and pursued recreation.

Cantilevered out over the lip of the chasm was a binary cycle geothermal power plant, harvesting energy from heat. Not far from it was another huge manufacturing structure whose purpose Dev couldn't immediately fathom. He opened up his commplant and ran a quick search.

> Ionizer anode extractor centre. Uses an electrochemical process to release oxygen from metal oxides. Turns rock into breathable air.

That would account for the three tall chimney vents that crowned it. Here were Alighieri's lungs.

Dev turned round.

It appeared that the earthquake had caused a section of overhang on the cavern wall to shear off and plunge onto the ISS outpost and adjacent buildings. The damage was extensive, though mainly confined to the outpost itself. Windows were broken all along the row of buildings and rooftops scarred, but only the bunker belonging to ISS had actually been flattened.

Chance? Or something else?

Now, somewhat belatedly, Dev noted that there were uniformed individuals among the dazed people on the esplanade, making up a significant proportion of the total. They had high-collared tunics, well-stocked utility belts, and an aura of officiousness that not even an earthquake could put a dent in.

Cops.

Law enforcement was law enforcement wherever you went in the universe. The uniforms varied to some extent, tending towards black fabric and paramilitary styling. The people who wore them, however, were a distinct, unique type. It was in their posture, their stiff-backed bearing.

ISS, in their infinite wisdom, had placed their outpost on Alighieri just a few doors down from the local police headquarters.

With dismay, Dev spotted a couple of the police officers now heading towards him across the esplanade with purposeful strides. Whether their interest in him was concern or suspicion, he couldn't say, but he feared the latter.

He elected to stand his ground. Contact with the local gendarmes might prove useful, especially since his ISS liaison was no longer in any fit state to be of help.

"You," said the higher-ranking of the two officers. She pointed at Dev, then crooked a finger in a curt summons.

"Yes?"

"Saw you sneaking out of the ISS place just now."

"I wasn't sneaking," Dev said.

"Looked like it to me."

"Then you and I have very different definitions of 'sneak,' Officer...?"

"Kahlo. Captain Kahlo. Chief of police."

"Right. Ah. Should I salute, or prostrate myself, or...?"

Kahlo eyed him sidelong, coolly. She had tight-bobbed hair, a jutting jawline, and large, dark eyes set beneath a high forehead. She was not only strikingly pretty, but looked smart and capable, which to Dev were two reasons why he should tread cautiously.

"Who are you?" demanded the other police officer, a younger man, Kahlo's subordinate. "Don't recognise you."

"I'm –"

Kahlo interrupted. "I think, Sergeant Stegman, that this is none other than the ISS so-called 'consultant' whose arrival we were told to expect. Judging by the state of him, all tattered and covered in dust, he only just made it out of that building alive. Where's Junius Bilk?"

"He didn't," Dev said. "Make it out alive, I mean."

"Pity. I liked him. Good kid, though not very bright. Failed the police exams, but he thought ISS was the next best thing. As I say, not very bright. I'm just scribing an internal memo."

Her eyes defocused as she activated her commplant.

"Send someone round to Bilk's parents' place to break the news. Also requesting a coroner's retrieval unit to this location. Okay, done. Now then – name?"

"Harmer. Dev Harmer."

"Welcome to Alighieri, Mr Harmer," Kahlo said with a humourless quirk of her lips. She threw a glance back at the outpost. "I should point out that we don't normally drop several tons of rock on top of everyone who comes here. Just the special guests."

"Glad to hear it."

Her expression hardened. "We also don't take strangers at their word when they tell us who they are. You could be Interstellar Security Solutions; equally, your intentions towards Calder's Edge and its community could be hostile. We won't know until we've checked you out."

This. Dev had been afraid of exactly this. He had seen it coming.

"Sergeant Stegman? Let's take Mr Harmer in for questioning. Cuff him, but keep your mosquito handy in case he resists arrest. He won't, if he's got any sense."

From his utility belt Stegman produced both a pair of smartcuffs and a compressed-air incapacitator gun loaded with tiny soluble neurotoxin darts.

"I'd be obliged if you'd come quietly, sir."

Jurisdictional bullshit. That was all it was. Indigenous police not liking outside agencies on their turf. Feeling that their toes were being trodden on. Wanting to assert who was boss round these parts.

Bilk, were he still alive, could doubtless have smoothed over any difficulties. He at least had been a native, a known quantity, even if he *had* chosen to align himself with a little-loved private security firm. They would have listened to him.

Clearly Dev, in Kahlo's opinion, needed taking down a peg, and she was appointing herself the woman to do it.

Well, two could play at that game.

Besides, this host form needed putting through its paces. Dev had no idea of its limitations, what it was and wasn't capable of.

So he turned and ran.

3

ALMOST IMMEDIATELY HE learned that short legs and dense muscle mass do not a sprinter make. Quite the reverse. Each stride he took was about three quarters as long as he would have liked or hoped, and clumsy. It was more a lope than a run.

At least Kahlo and Stegman were labouring under the same constraints. Neither stood much above five feet tall, and both were broadly built. On paper, they were no faster than him.

The difference was, they were used to their Alighierian physiques, whereas Dev was a novice.

Soon they were gaining on him, Kahlo to the fore. People scattered out of their path.

Dev charged past some sort of municipal ornament, half-sculptural, half-horticultural: an arrangement of gigantic luminous fungi, cultivated with artful precision. Toadstool-shaped, some of them twice the height of a man, the fungi glowed lilac, peppermint and aquamarine.

He swerved behind this, then halted. He found

he was sweating profusely, his mouth dry as a bone.

Less efficient thermoregulation, Bilk had said. *Try not to overtax yourself aerobically.*

Too late to worry about that right now.

Kahlo followed him round the back of the ornament, not expecting to find him waiting. Her reactions were fast but not fast enough. Dev grabbed her wrist and twisted it round, levering her arm up behind her back. Kahlo bent double, forced down by the compliance hold.

An ordinary civilian would have been rendered helpless, but Kahlo had had training. She seized Dev's ankle with her free hand and jerked his foot out from under him. She was startlingly, spectacularly strong.

Thrown off-balance, Dev lost control of the wristlock. Kahlo came up immediately with a palm-heel strike to his chin. He jerked his head aside to evade the blow, but she had anticipated this. In the same movement she brought her arm round the back of his neck and bore down.

Now Dev was the one bent double, and Kahlo was repositioning herself to get her other arm under his throat so that she could choke him into submission.

Dev jabbed an elbow into the back of her knee. Kahlo sagged forward, her grip on his neck loosening a little, just enough for him to tug his head free.

Kahlo went for a shin stamp, a classic but predictable attack, hoping to incapacitate him with pain. He turned his leg so that her instep scraped his calf – unpleasant, but not crippling.

His response was to seize her thumb and turn it back against its base joint, sharply enough to elicit a hiss of pain from her, but stopping short of actually dislocating the digit.

Kahlo refused to be beaten. She lunged, driving her head into Dev's stomach and partially winding him. Dev applied greater pressure to her thumb. He could feel tendons straining, close to snapping. Kahlo merely growled, transmuting pain to fury.

"Let her go."

This was Stegman, who had his mosquito levelled with Dev's neck, just inches away. Point-blank range. He couldn't miss.

"I *said* let the chief go."

Dev kicked out, catching Stegman hard in the thigh, crushing quadriceps muscle against femur. A perfect dead leg. The numbed limb gave way beneath Stegman and he fell to the ground.

The distraction provided Kahlo with an opening, however, and she took it. Gripping Dev round the waist, she propelled the two of them over the rim of the fungus sculpture's pedestal. They tumbled together into soft, loamy growth medium. Kahlo ended up on top, straddling Dev, who had lost his grip on her hand.

Next instant, a teeth-clackingly powerful punch landed on the side of his head. Fireworks exploded in his vision.

He answered by scooping up a handful of mulch and chucking it into Kahlo's face. He'd hoped to blind her temporarily, but, dazed from her punch, he missed her eyes, getting her mouth instead.

Spitting out the damp brown muck, Kahlo torqued Dev's head round with both hands and shoved his face sideways into the loam.

"Tastes like crap," she said. "Try some yourself."

It went up Dev's nose, trickled into his mouth. He blew out hard to prevent himself inhaling fragments of it.

"Stegman! Mosquito!"

The sergeant, propped half upright on the ground, tossed the little dart gun to her. Kahlo caught it smartly, took aim and, without hesitating, pulled the trigger.

A rasping puff of air, and a thorn-like dart stuck Dev in the biceps. It stung like crazy for a couple of seconds, then all at once he could no longer feel his arm. He writhed as though he could fight it, but the lack of sensation spread inexorably to his torso, then his legs, a tide of ice-cold water.

Soon he was immobile, paralysed from head to toe, able only to breathe and blink.

Kahlo clambered off him with a look of profound satisfaction on her face.

"How'd that work out for you?" she said. "You've just joined the Don't Mess With Astrid Kahlo Club. The fees are free. Membership sucks."

4

THEY LEFT HIM on a bunk in a cell for an hour while the effects of the neurotoxin wore off. Then he was taken, smartcuffed, to an interview room, where he was dumped unceremoniously on a chair and told to wait.

He waited for what must have been at least three hours, his stomach growling the whole time. The hunger pangs were all-consuming, his belly cramping. The pulsing ache from the bruise on the side of his head was nothing by comparison.

The smartcuffs were made of a milky orange programmable plastic which moulded to the contours of your wrists and welded themselves in place, forging a bond with your flesh. If you tried to wriggle out of them it would hurt; pull hard enough, and your skin would tear. The standard method of release was the application of a tone-generating 'key' which broke down the plastic's molecular bonds, dissolving the smartcuffs to goo.

Finally, Kahlo deigned to pay a visit.

"Okay, Harmer," she said, seating herself across the table from him. "Let's start again. What was all that about anyway, haring off like you did? What did you hope to achieve? Were you *trying* to look like a criminal?"

"I fancied a bit of a workout. It's good for the health, you know."

"What's good for the health is not running away when two of Calder's Edge PD are in the process of detaining you."

"I realise that now." Dev shrugged a shoulder to indicate the contusion just behind his ear. His hands were resting in his lap, beneath the table, out of sight. "Shall we just say I was engaged in a little experiment?"

"Experimenting with how far you could push me?"

"Something like that."

"Well, you got results. You know what you're dealing with now. So maybe you should play ball. You're ISS?"

"So I'm led to believe."

"Enough of the smart-assery. Are you or are you not an Interstellar Security Solutions consultant?"

"Didn't I prove that to you out there?"

"All you proved is that you're tricky and have some training."

"Some? How's the thumb, by the way?"

Kahlo's hand was partly encased in a clear gel bandage. The ball of her thumb was mottled purple and blue. Analgesics secreted by the gel would be holding the discomfort and inflammation at bay. Dedicated astrocyte cells would be repairing the damage tissue.

"Not bothering me in the slightest," she replied. "How's the head?"

"Gently ringing. Look, is it possible I could get something to eat? I'm starving. Haven't eaten in forever. Literally."

"That so? Funny, because I've just come from the canteen, where I had the best burger ever. Gherkin, relish, bacon, cheese, the works. Oh, and a mound of fries with a ton of ketchup on top. Yum."

Dev's mouth watered. It was almost embarrassing how delicious Kahlo's meal sounded.

He affected nonchalance.

"I'm a steak man myself. Sirloin, flash-fried, seared on the outside, pink and oozing juices in the middle."

"The meat we vat-grow on Alighieri is second to none. Honestly. Guys come here from the core planets and tell us they haven't tasted better. The workforce gets fed well. It's one of the perks."

"Looking forward to sampling some, then."

"*If* I let you out of here."

"*When* you do. No reason you won't. Technically, arresting me and holding me prisoner contravenes federal Diasporan law. ISS immunity supersedes all regional criminal codes. I could have your badge for this."

"You've got me confused with someone who gives a shit. All I know is I'm looking at a man who ran when police officers approached him in the course of their duties. A man, what's more, whose appearance gave me reasonable cause to suspect him of any number of infractions. Vagrancy, for starters. Possible sabotage, too."

Dev cocked an eyebrow. "Interesting. And why would there be saboteurs on Alighieri? Got a terrorism problem on this world, captain?"

"Who's interrogating who, Harmer?"

"Just data mining. I would have put the time you've left me hanging around in this room to good use, checking news feeds and conducting some research, but you've installed interference fields in your police HQ. My commplant's fritzed. All I'm getting is static."

"It's standard procedure. We can't allow crooks unfettered communications access."

"I'm no crook."

"You still haven't convinced me of that."

"I shouldn't need to. By now you'll have verified my credentials. Perhaps before you went to dinner you fired off an information request to ISS Central, and the reply only just pinged back. What's the ultraspace transmission delay between here and Earth? An hour? Hour and a half at most."

Kahlo poker-faced, but that alone told Dev he was right on the money, on every count.

"So," he continued, "you have official confirmation that I'm the consultant who was booked to pay a call. They even sent you an image of my host form. It's beyond doubt. I am who I say I am, and the only reason I'm still in custody is pure spite on your part."

"Or that I don't trust you."

"The feeling is mutual. Already we have something in common; surely we can build on that."

"Say I do let you go, Harmer. You're implying you want CEPD to co-operate with you?"

"It'd make my job easier. Specifically, I'd like *you* to co-operate with me, Captain Kahlo. I don't have an ISS contact any more, and it'd be good to partner up with someone from round these parts who knows the ropes and has some sway. Who better than a senior cop?"

"Out of the question. I'm far too busy."

"Shame. Guess I'll just have to go it alone. By the way..."

He raised his hands from his lap, laying them on the tabletop.

"I've saved you the hassle of uncuffing me."

His wrists were bare, free, showing rings of chafed skin where the smartcuffs had been.

Kahlo's jaw dropped just a fraction before she caught herself and recovered her composure.

"Clever," she said. "I'll bite. How did you manage it?"

"Old trick. If you rub the join between the cuffs up and down against a solid surface – a table leg, for example – you create a vibrational resonance, kind of like strumming a guitar string. Smarts a bit, but once you hit the correct frequency, it acts like the tone-generating key does. Design flaw. The cuffs disintegrate. If you look down by my feet, you'll see what's left of them."

Kahlo glanced down. The floor around Dev's chair was spattered with blobs of sticky milky-orange fluid.

"Polis Plus technology is a speciality of mine," Dev said. "Particularly dismantling it. I hate the fucking stuff."

"The guy monitoring the surveillance feed saw you moving your arms up and down. He assumed you were playing with yourself or had some kind of unfortunate rash." She sighed. "All right. You've made your point. You're Mr Super-Duper-ISS-Man and we should all bow down and give thanks that you've graced us with your presence. I have no option but to release you and send you on your way. As for helping you..."

"I'd be grateful."

"It's out of the question. We're stretched as it is. I can't spare anyone. We need all the manpower we've got."

"ISS would be grateful, too. The kind of grateful that puts credit in a person's bank account."

"Is that some sort of cackhanded attempt at bribery?"

"Just offering you an incentive to do a little moonlighting."

"Mr Harmer," Kahlo said severely. "Unlike you, I work directly and exclusively for TerCon. I'm a public servant, not some freelance mercenary. I'm in receipt of a government salary and proud of it."

"That's fine. I'm sure you earn enough. Or is the job its own reward?"

"You can't put a price on keeping the peace and upholding the law."

"I used to think that too, once."

"Well, whatever changed your mind, I'm sorry for you."

Not as sorry as Dev was.

"Now, if you don't mind," Kahlo said, rising to her feet, "I've a police force to run. Don't waste my time any further. Do what you have to, carry out your mission, but for your own sake, stay out of my –"

The door burst open, and a police officer leaned in.

"Sorry to interrupt, ma'am."

"You're not interrupting anything. What is it?"

"Got an emergency call from the Jansson Crossing township. Something about a train crash. Possible casualties."

"Okay. I presume first responders are en route."

"So I'm told."

"I'll go too. Someone has to supervise."

Kahlo, halfway out of the room, turned to find Dev right behind her.

"What are you doing?" she snapped.

"Tagging along."

"No."

"Why not?"

"Weren't you listening? Didn't I just tell you to stay out of my way?"

"Well, to be honest, you didn't actually finish the sentence. You could have been about to add 'unless you see a pressing need to follow me somewhere.'"

"There isn't any pressing need. This is official business."

"Captain, I'm doing my best to get an overview of what's happening on this planet," said Dev. "Already I know you're having unusual earthquakes. Now a train crash. You raised the issue of potential sabotage earlier. It's all relevant, it all adds up to something, and my job is to work out what and why and put a stop to it. Now, I could travel to this Jansson Crossing on my own, or I could cadge a ride off you. Either way, it's my next destination."

"I'm not going to get rid of you, am I?"

Dev smiled in what he hoped was a winning manner. For all he knew, he was pulling some hideous grimace. A host form's facial muscles were always the hardest to master. Gross motor skills came first, fine motor skills second.

Kahlo rolled her eyes, resigned. "Very well. I suppose I'm better off keeping a close watch on you anyway, rather than letting you blunder around off the leash. You can come with. Just don't get under my feet."

"I won't, trust me."

"We've already established that I don't," said Kahlo. "I'd like to keep it that way, for my own peace of mind."

5

THE POLICE POD shot across the city along the maglev track, accelerating easily to a humming, frictionless 200kph. Kahlo and a driver, Patrolman Utz, were in the front. Dev shared the back seat with Sergeant Stegman, who kept shooting surly, resentful glances at him.

"How long 'til we get there, captain?" Dev enquired.

"You sound like my cousin's seven-year-old," said Kahlo. "'Are we there yet? Are we there yet?'"

"I ask because, if we've time, I'd like you to fill me in about the earthquakes."

"We've got a few minutes."

The pod shimmied slightly as it passed under an enormous arch formed by twin stalactites that descended all the way to the cavern floor. Their size – they were as big as skyscrapers – spoke of millennia of slow growth.

"So...?" Dev prompted.

"They started roughly a month ago," Kahlo said.

"The odd tremor now and then. Nobody thought much of it, at first. Mostly they were centred around the mines, and you do get the occasional rumble there. The digger rigs disturb the rock strata. There's settling, subsidence. Par for the course. Miners call it 'bellyaching.'"

"But it got worse."

"We've had tunnel collapses. Equipment destroyed, some casualties. And it's no longer confined to the mines. The quakes have spread outward, to the inhabited regions – the townships, Calder's Edge itself. Which isn't meant to be possible."

"Because the inhabited regions were specially selected for their stability."

"Exactly."

"How long ago was that?"

"Alighieri was colonised back in the 'forties."

"Part of the second wave of the Diaspora," said Stegman, "when the next-generation Riemann Deviation drives came onstream and reduced infraspace journey times by half."

"Thanks for the history lesson," said Dev.

"Want me to mosquito you again?"

"As I recall, your boss did that last time, not you."

"I'd quite like a turn."

"Zip it, sergeant," said Kahlo. "He's only trying to get a rise out of you."

"He's succeeding."

"So don't let him. Don't give him the satisfaction."

Stegman, cheeks reddening, folded his arms.

Dev said to Kahlo, "Back then there would have

been a colonisation precursor survey, wouldn't there?"

"Yes. Sonar and ground penetrating radar were used to determine which were the safest caverns to build in. Calder's Edge and the outlying townships sit dead centre of a tectonic plate. We're nowhere near any faultlines, and the bedrock surrounding us is pure igneous granite. Solid as a... well, as a rock."

"So why earthquakes all of a sudden?"

"That's the honking great question, isn't it? That, and why are they getting progressively more severe?"

"You think there's a chance some living agency might be responsible? It's perhaps enemy action?"

"Maybe so, maybe not. I've not found any proof as yet, but my gut says it could well be. What I *do* know is that it's got people scared and restless, not least the miners, and they're a hard lot to frighten. Nobody likes going around thinking the world could fall in on their heads at any moment. We've seen a marked upswing in emigration applications and requests to terminate work contracts and ship out early. The next scheduled gulf cruiser isn't due for another six months, but if one put in tomorrow, I reckon we'd wave 'bye-bye to a third of our population."

A passenger train loomed ahead on the track. The pod, being smaller, lighter and faster, had to tuck in behind the tapered end of its rear carriage until a station appeared. The train pulled in at the platform while the pod leapfrogged around it on a passing siding.

"What do you mine here?" Dev asked. "Helium-three would be my guess."

"Bingo," said Kahlo. "Alighieri's got it by the crap-ton. No atmosphere, so there's been nothing to prevent the regolith soaking up solar radiation, for millions of years. The He-three deposits are distributed evenly throughout the crust, extending to a depth of two thousand metres and more."

"Rick pickings. Fusion power for everyone."

And, Dev thought, who was more energy-hungry, more rapacious when it came to power consumption, than Polis+? The artificial-intelligence empire relied not on agriculture, nor on physical labour, but on its machines, and machines guzzled electricity.

Alighieri, blessed with the raw materials to keep thousands of aneutronic nuclear reactors fuelled for centuries to come, was just the sort of world Polis+ coveted and would like to claim for its own.

The pod entered a tunnel bored into the far wall of the Calder's Edge cavern. Outside the windows, ribbons of geological layers rippled up and down. Seams of quartz and feldspar flashed by like horizontal lightning bolts.

"We may be a small planet, but we punch above our weight economically," said Kahlo.

"Any internal troubles? Civil unrest? Radical elements?"

"None to speak of. We have a pretty sensible citizenry, and I keep a tight lid on things. You get folks going on a bender every now and then, and the drying-out tank's never short of occupants.

Sometimes native Alighierians and itinerant workers clash, but it's bar arguments, rowdy neighbours, that level of nuisance, usually. The unions get stroppy from time to time and call a strike, and we have to oversee the picket lines. Nothing we can't cope with."

"People come and go, though."

"Yes. We get migrant miners dropping by to do tours of three or four years. There's a constant turnover. Every gulf cruiser that comes drops off about twenty thousand of them and takes a similar number away. The total mining workforce tops out at a quarter of a million at any time. Another couple of million of us – second- and third-generation Alighierians – are in service industries that support the mining biz, or else in administrative roles. A million more are children or other dependents. That's just Calder's Edge."

"There are other cities?"

"A couple. You've got Xanadu. That's our nearest neighbour, about seven hundred kilometres due west. Then there's Lidenbrock City, way over on the side of the world. We don't have much to do with Lidenbrockers, or them with us."

"Troglodytes," muttered Stegman.

"Uncalled-for, Stegman," Kahlo scolded.

"But it's true."

"Still uncalled-for." She resumed her conversation with Dev. "Unlike with Lidenbrock, relations between Calder's Edge and Xanadu are open and cordial. There's a direct rail link, calling at all the major townships along the way. Lots of Calder's folk have relatives there."

"They having earthquakes, too? Over in Xanadu?"

"None that we've heard about."

"And who runs Calder's Edge?"

"What do you mean?"

"Someone has to be in charge. You have a mayor? A prime minister? A president? Who's top dog?"

Kahlo hesitated briefly, and Dev noticed Patrolman Utz aiming a sidelong look at her, as if intrigued to see how she chose to answer.

"The highest civic political position is governor," she said. "But if you want the honest truth, the mining corporations call the shots. The place wouldn't survive – wouldn't have a reason to exist – without them, and they know it. They say jump, the governor asks how high."

Dev filed all this information away. It might be germane, it might not. He wouldn't know until he had been here a little longer. The first day of any mission was a miasma of acclimatisation and intelligence-gathering. You could scour the local insite via commplant to find out when you needed, but it was usually better to get it first-hand. You learned more from someone with an opinion and an insider's perspective than from 'pedia entries and officially sanctioned publicity material.

Townships whizzed by – smaller caverns than Calder's Edge's, with smatterings of habitats, some forested with lichen outcrops and gargantuan mushrooms. One, Loveville by name, was evidently a self-contained red light district. Huge garish floatscreen signs advertised burlesque revues and lapdance clubs.

"Jansson Crossing," said Utz eventually, and he retracted the police pod's electromagnet array, drawing it away from the propulsion and levitation coils embedded in the track. The vehicle's progress slowed to a gentle glide, and finally the pod coasted to a hovering halt.

The township was centred around a busy, intricate rail intersection. The crash had occurred on a branch line just outside its station. An automated freight shuttle had been involved in a head-on collision with a commuter train. According to the chief rescue officer on the scene, there were two confirmed fatalities: the driver of the train and one of the passengers. There were also several injured, with three people on their way to hospital in critical condition and paramedics attending to the rest.

Freight shuttle and commuter train were locked together like a pair of animals who had died in the throes of feral territorial combat. It was hard to tell where one ended and the other began. A knot of tangled, tormented steel fused them, nose to nose.

Survivors, interviewed by Kahlo, said there had been no warning, just an almighty walloping impact that had hurled them from their seats. They had emerged from the wreckage, shaken and bloodied, glad to be alive.

Kahlo looked baffled. And angry.

"What?" said Dev. "What's the matter?"

"What do you think's the matter?" she snapped. "An accident like this is impossible."

"Accidents happen. There's even a saying about it. It goes: 'accidents happen.'"

She flared at him. "Don't you laugh at this! Don't you dare!" She fell silent for a moment, glaring at him, and he thought she was about to hit him. Then she looked away again. "Anyway, you're wrong. The entire maglev network is computer-regulated. There are failsafes in place to prevent precisely this sort of thing, any number of minimum-distance protocols. One train *cannot* be heading down a track towards another coming the opposite way. Overrides would kick in. Worse come to worst, the power would shut down and they'd brake well before a collision."

"Then there's been a mainframe error. A software glitch."

"Maybe," she said, relenting just a very little. "I'll have one of our techs analyse the records at the central rail control room."

She made the call, think-sending the message over her commplant.

Meanwhile Dev's gaze fell on a vending machine on the station platform, which sold high-protein, glucose-rich energy bars and electrolyte-replenishing drinks. It advertised its wares with the slogan REFRESH YOURSELF! BEAT THE MID-SHIFT SLUMP! and illustrated their effectiveness with clips of burning suns and crashing waterfalls.

He activated his commplant and checked to see if ISS had given him a standard operational slush fund to draw on. They had. Hardly a king's ransom, but enough credit to be getting on with.

He linked to the vending machine and bought himself a fistful of bars and two cans of drink. He tore open the wrapper of one of the bars – mint flavour – and swallowed it nearly in one bite. It tasted like sweet sawdust with a toothpaste top note. The next bar, claiming to be chocolate-raspberry, tasted much the same as the first.

But it was bliss to have some food inside him at last. As his blood sugar level rose, a haze in his mind seemed to clear. The last vestiges of the nausea he had been feeling since arriving on Alighieri were dispelled.

"Harmer!" Kahlo called from the door to the police pod. "You want a lift back to Calder's? Or are you going to stand there all day stuffing your ugly face?"

He climbed aboard, and Utz reversed into a turning siding. Then, remotely triggering the appropriate points, the patrolman manoeuvred the pod out onto the track that ran parallel to the one they had come in on.

Dev proffered an energy bar to Stegman, but he turned his nose up at the humble olive branch.

"Kind of disrespectful. Eating, when people died back there. Everyone else thinking what a tragedy, you only thinking about your stomach."

"Until a few hours ago, my consciousness was just a fizz of electrons zapping through ultraspace, sergeant. And this body was a mindless empty husk floating in a vat of nutrient solution. Cut me some slack."

"Is it weird?" Kahlo said over her shoulder.

"This energy bar? I wouldn't call it that. Then again: ginger and wheatgrass?"

"No. The whole ultraspace travel thing. Your special commute. Data 'porting. Hopping from body to body."

"Don't know," said Dev. "I've been at it so long, it's almost begun to seem normal."

"Has to be pretty tough going. Waking up somewhere else, as someone else, over and over. Like a bad dream. I'm just wondering if it would account for why you're such a thoroughbred douchebag."

"No, that's natural. It's a talent."

A red signal began flashing on the dashboard screen in front of Utz, accompanied by a repeated insistent buzzing.

"Utz?" said Kahlo. "Tell me that's nothing bad."

"It's, uh... the proximity sensor alert."

"The...? Is there an obstruction ahead?"

Utz scanned the readout. "No. Something behind. A freight shuttle. It's joined the track at the junction we just passed."

"So? Why is that a proximity issue?"

Utz was flustered. "Because it's... it's getting closer. And fast. Too fast."

Dev turned round. Through the rear windscreen, he saw the glow of running lights some distance down the tunnel.

"It'll reduce speed," said Kahlo. "Surely. It'll brake to maintain a safe distance. It has to."

"The one at Jansson Crossing didn't," Dev pointed out.

"That was a one-off," said Stegman, although his tone was more hopeful than confident.

The lights behind were getting brighter, and the alert buzzing was becoming louder and more strident.

"This is crazy," said Kahlo. "Another shuttle gone rogue? There must have been some network-wide server crash. That's the only explanation."

"That or somebody is using trains to kill people," Dev said. "Which would be a pity," he added. "I've always liked trains."

6

THE FREIGHT SHUTTLE loomed large in the rear windscreen. Its blunt snout couldn't have been more than thirty metres away, a rectangle of blank, windowless metal, oncoming. It had a terrible, unthinking purposefulness about it, a blind juggernaut with no heed for anything that lay in its path.

The gap between it and the pod was narrowing rapidly.

Utz had accelerated to top speed, in an effort to stay ahead. Kahlo, meanwhile, was contacting the rail network control room. Her brow was furrowed in concentration.

"No good," she said eventually. "I'm not getting through. I've flagged it as a high-priority call. Still nothing. I'm being shut out."

"Maybe they're a bit busy there," Dev suggested, "trying to stop the runaway."

"I'm using police codes. I shouldn't be getting the 'unavailable' tone. Someone should be answering and saying sorry for not picking up sooner."

"Can't we go any faster?" Stegman said, an edge of panic in his voice.

"The limiter says no," Utz replied. "We're at two-fifty kph, the allowable maximum."

"How come a freight shuttle's going quicker than a pod anyway?"

"How should I know? It's heavier. Has momentum. Maybe *its* limiter's been disabled."

"Can't you disable ours too?"

"Tell me how and I will," Utz said acidly. That shut Stegman up.

The tunnel walls were rushing by. A township station flickered and was gone. The pod was shuddering now, as though trying to decide whether to leave the guideway and take flight.

If it and the track parted company, in the tight confines of a tunnel...

Dev tried not to imagine what the result might be. It would make the crash at Jansson Crossing look like a gentle flirtation. Cleanup crews would be scraping parts of the pod's occupants off the rails for weeks.

The freight shuttle had got to within a stone's throw of the pod. The pressure wave it was pushing before it added to the smaller vehicle's instability. Dev could feel the pod being bounced and buffeted. There was a squeal and a spray of sparks as its left-hand flank nudged the guideway. Kahlo swore and Stegman wailed.

Dev looked up. "I've got an idea," he announced, and before anyone could ask what it was, he swivelled round in his seat and began kicking at the rear windscreen.

"Hey!" yelled Stegman. "That's police property."

"Seriously?" said Dev, kicking harder. "That's what you're going with, at a moment like this?"

"You can't vandalise police property. It's an offence."

"I gave you a dead leg. Does that count as vandalising police property too?"

The windscreen glass starred.

"Besides," said Dev, using both feet now, "if that shuttle shunts us, a whole lot worse is going to happen to this pod than a busted window."

The windscreen bowed outward, then all at once broke free of its frame, rubber seal and all. It spiralled into the shuttle's face, exploding to smithereens. Shards hailed along the tunnel.

"Those are gun-stuns, right?" he said to Stegman.

Stegman glanced down at the two chunky rubberised cylinders attached to his utility belt. Police-issue EMP grenades.

"Yeah. So?"

"So give me one of them."

"No."

"Okay, then."

Dev reached over and briskly unclipped one of the gun-stuns. Stegman tried to snatch it back off him, but Dev swatted his hand aside, then levered himself halfway out of the hollowed windscreen frame.

A hurricane tore at his hair and clothing. His ears popped.

The shuttle had neared to a distance of five metres, still remorselessly bearing down on them.

Dev lowered his arm, lining up his hand with the gap between the shuttle's skirt and the inside of the guideway. He primed the grenade, thumbing off the cap and depressing the spring-release trigger. One-second delay. All he had to do was let go of it at just the right moment...

The pod juddered sharply as he released the gun-stun, throwing his aim off. The grenade hit the base of the track, then bounced up the front of the shuttle and over the top. It detonated halfway along the shuttle, over its cargo bay, silently, uselessly.

Dev crawled back inside the pod.

"All right, give me the other one," he said to Stegman.

"Just what the fuck are you up to?"

"What do you think? Gun-stun. Three-metre-radius pulse of electromagnetic energy. Disrupts electronics. Disables non-shielded weapons that rely on circuitry. Also electric motors and electromagnetic fields. And what is that shuttle riding on? A damn great electromagnetic field. I land the thing beside the levitation coils, and the shuttle should flip out."

"Should?" said Kahlo.

"Will. If the grenade goes off in just the right spot."

"That's a stupid plan," said Stegman.

"Do you have a better idea, sergeant?" said Kahlo.

"No, ma'am. Not as such."

"Then give him the other damn gun-stun."

"Thanks," said Dev, as Stegman passed the grenade over. "Now, I'll need you to hold my legs this time, sergeant, so I can lean further out."

Dev crawled out onto the rear of the pod again. He felt Stegman clamp arms around his knees. He teetered over the space between pod and shuttle, which was down to one metre. The track blurred by below him, dizzyingly close.

One shot.

If he missed this time, there wouldn't be another attempt. It would be too late. The shuttle would rear-end the pod, and that would be that. The tunnel walls would be decorated in various shades of human.

The pod shook and leapt. Dev, hanging out the back, was flung around like a wagging tail. If not for Stegman, he would have been thrown loose. The police sergeant was good for something, at least.

Steadying himself against the pod's turbulence, Dev extended his arm. Carefully, with as much precision as the situation allowed, he took aim.

He let go.

The gun-stun was sucked into the gap between the shuttle and the guideway and detonated, unleashing its burst of energy, shutting down the levitation coils in a section of track.

The shuttle was knocked off-course.

Slightly off-course, but that was all it took.

The shuttle's skirt dug into the guideway on the opposite side. There was a shrieking, a rending. Metal curled like potato peel. The entire vehicle trembled, as though in mortal pain.

It veered. It slewed and slithered crazily.

Then it sprang aloft, hitting the tunnel ceiling, and began to disintegrate.

Dev watched from far too close for comfort as the shuttle shredded itself to bits against the tunnel's insides. There was no flame. Nothing combustible in the shuttle's structure. Only coachwork, chassis and electrical mechanism to be destroyed. The train became a bolus of fragments barrelling along the tunnel at breakneck speed, large chunks whittling themselves smaller, a relentless, roaring unravelling.

This torrent of torn, howling metal looked set to overtake and engulf the pod.

But then it began to lose impetus and subside. The pod pulled away, putting the maelstrom of ruined shuttle behind it. Its progress smoothed until it was sailing serenely along the track as though nothing had happened, the terrible near-miss now far behind.

Dev slid back through the windscreen frame, aided by Stegman.

"That was..." – Dev groped for an adjective – "exponential."

"You mad bastard, Harmer," gasped Stegman.

"Coming from you, I'm going to take that as a compliment."

Utz's grip on the pod's acceleration lever loosened, colour returning to his whitened knuckles. "Another five minutes to Calder's Edge. Man, I'll be glad to stop and get out. I don't think I ever want to drive one of these things again. Captain? Oh, sorry, you're making a call."

"Hang on." Kahlo held up a hand. "Right. Done. I've just been informing the rescue crew about the second shuttle. They'll cordon off the tunnel. That should hold things 'til the rail controllers sort their shit out. What is it, Utz?"

"Nothing. Just – earthquakes were bad enough. Now we've got homicidal trains?"

"Quite. This has to stop. It's like the whole of Alighieri is turning against us." She leaned round in her seat. "And the situation has got measurably worse since you showed up, Harmer."

"Whoa, hold on," Dev said. "The implication being that *I'm* responsible somehow? We all nearly just got killed, remember?" He jabbed a finger at his chest for emphasis. "Me included."

"Can you even get killed?"

"Of course I can. What sort of question is that?"

"I mean, you data 'ported in. Can't you just data 'port out again, should you get shot or fatally maimed or whatever?"

"Nope. Not how it works. I don't have the ability to randomly project my consciousness into ultraspace whenever I feel like it. I have to be hooked up to a transcription matrix first and use that as a portal. If I die here, I die; just like you, Utz, Stegman, anyone."

"Oh. I just thought –"

"You just thought an ISS consultant can chuck host forms aside like used tissues. You thought I can unzip my consciousness from one shell and zip it into another like Polis Plussers do. Uh-uh. Not that simple."

"I see."

"And for what it's worth, suicide isn't high on my bucket list. I'm not prepared to kill myself in order to take a target out. This isn't about you, Kahlo. That's what you're thinking, isn't it? You're the highest-ranking person on board this pod, Calder's Edge's chief of police, so you've got to be the target. But what if you're wrong? I think so. I think, if this is about anyone, it's about me."

"What makes you so sure?" said Kahlo.

"Consider the facts. The moment I arrive, a chunk of rock drops onto where I am. Couple of hours later, I accompany local cops to the site of a train crash – a very suspicious incident, just the sort of thing a newly arrived ISS consultant might want to check out – and on the way back I almost get clobbered by another train. Either of those events alone could be happenstance. The two together – that begins to smell nasty."

"You're saying someone knows you're here and is gunning for you."

"That would be the logical conclusion," said Dev. "Someone's unhappy about the presence of active ISS personnel on Alighieri. Someone doesn't want me sniffing around. They're targeting me, and trying to make it look like mishap rather than assassination."

"Assuming that's the case, any ideas who?"

"Too soon to say with any certainty. I've hardly got the lie of the land yet. But I'd like to start pursuing certain avenues of enquiry, and for that I'd like to beg a favour off you, captain."

"I'm not particularly inclined to grant you one," said Kahlo. "If you're right, the three of us almost died because of you."

"But fair's fair, I saved your lives."

"And Bilk *did* die because of you."

"Unfortunate, but he was ISS. He must've realised there's risk attached to that. I'm sure it's mentioned in the welcome pack."

"I don't feel like I owe you anything, if that's what you're hoping. I'm not in your debt."

"No, but do you want these shenanigans to end, or do you want things to get worse? Because, if the first, I'm your guy. Your best bet. Like it or not, it's true."

Kahlo was quiet. The pod rocketed from the tunnel, out into the barely fathomable vastness of the Calder's Edge cavern. It traversed a bridge over the chasm where the geothermal plant was sited. Down below, far down, at the foot of an abyss, a thin line of magma wove its way like a golden thread.

"Not liking it," she said at last. "But I'm willing to give you at least a chance. Benefit of the doubt."

"That's all I ask."

"What do you want me to do?"

7

ROUND UP THE *awkward squad*.

That was Dev's request. Kahlo voiced misgivings, talking about ethics and due process, but eventually relented and put several squads of her officers onto it.

They bulldozed into bars and homes and dragged out the usual suspects: the people who liked a fight, the union firebrands, the habitual drunks, the young rebellious tearaways who were forever falling foul of the law. Anyone, in fact, who had long arrest records for infractions such as affray, public disorder and breach of the peace. The troublemakers.

They brought them back to the police HQ and dumped them in holding cells. It wasn't a hassle-free procedure. There were scuffles. Disgruntled detainees objected; grievances were aired, loudly. These were the sort of people who tended to shout "I've done nothing!" whenever they were collared, and this time, for once, there was truth in their protestations.

Each was brought before Dev in the interview room, one after another. He sat across the table from them, where Kahlo had sat when interrogating him. He spent the first minute simply peering deep into their eyes, saying nothing.

"What are you staring at?"

"Stop looking at me like that."

"What do you want, you perv?"

Dev ignored the comments. He tried to see past the pouting defiance, the resentful glares, the postures of calculated affront...

Tried to see if there was a particular absence behind the eyes.

Something missing.

Uncanny Valley.

Then he asked questions.

Mostly they were about God.

"Do you believe in a supreme being?"

"Do you believe in fate or destiny?"

"Were you created by a divine force, or are you just a random assemblage of molecules?"

"What's going to happen to you after you die?"

The answers varied, but the common thread was incredulity.

"What are you on, man? This is the second century Post-Enlightenment. Are you having a joke?"

"Newsflash. God died. Like, a hundred years ago."

"No heaven, no hell. Just oblivion."

"I haven't heard anything so daft in ages."

"Oh, yeah, there's a God. There are also fairies and unicorns."

Only one person, out of the forty or so Dev spoke to, twigged what was going on. He was Ben Thorne, a miner who headed up one of the more militant unions, the Fair Dues Collective. Thorne led protest rallies calling for higher wages, better benefits packages and more generous pensions. He had clashed with the city's governor several times on social media, branding him a corporate stooge and telling him to pull his head out of the mining companies' backsides.

He was not popular with the Calder's Edge authorities.

He was also fiercely smart.

"You want to know if I'm a Plusser, huh?" Thorne said after Dev had posed a couple of his God questions. "See if you can provoke me by challenging my faith."

"Do you have faith?" Dev said.

"I have faith that you're a chump. Do I look like I'm an AI sentience trying to pass myself off as human? Am I dead behind the eyes? Lights on but nobody home? Uncanny Valley, isn't that what it's called? Do you see that here?"

Dev did not, but he forged on anyway. 'Union activist' would be an ideal cover identity for a Polis+ agitator.

"Are you scared of death, Mr Thorne? Or do you live comforted by the falsehood that, when you pass on, your soul becomes subsumed into the Singularity?"

"Do I go to that big database in the sky when I die? I doubt it."

"The Singularity is bullshit, right?"

"Maybe not to the Plussers, but as far as I'm concerned, yeah."

"It's a fantasy for fanatics. Does it upset you when I say that?"

"What upsets me is that this is illegal arrest," said Thorne. He sat back in his chair with the cocksure aggressiveness of a man who knew his rights. "The cops have just hauled in a bunch of citizens for no good reason whatsoever. That's a lawsuit in the making. Someone, somewhere, will pay for this."

"You didn't answer me."

"I think I did. Pretty well, too. One call when I get out of here, and my union'll sick its best lawyer onto Calder's Edge PD." He rubbed index and middle fingers against thumb. "I smell a big fat compensation claim."

"Do you hate people like me? Just like your nonexistent Singularity tells you to?"

"You're persistent, I'll give you that. Like a moleworm gnawing a scroach. All those trigger words – 'falsehood,' 'bullshit,' 'fantasy.' Designed to make a Polis Plusser lose their cool. Get them to flip out and break role. Military-trained, huh?"

"This isn't about me."

"Couple of my co-workers fought in the war too. They've told me how you're taught to bust Plusser infiltrators and spies. Not easy, but if you push the right buttons hard enough..."

Dev studied the man. If Thorne *was* Polis+, a digital sentience housed in a flesh casing and trying to pass for human, then he was doing a superb job. More likely he was just what he appeared to be. A very cool customer, too.

"You can go," Dev said.

"Oh, thank you, my lord," the miner drawled. "Too kind. Tell the chief of police I'll see her in court."

There was only one other detainee who caught Dev's attention. He was a young unemployed man who, according to Kahlo, was a confirmed user and dealer of illegal homemade pharmaceuticals, and such a frequent offender that they were thinking of installing a revolving door at police headquarters especially for him.

His glazed, watery eyes, with their hugely dilated pupils, gave away little. He was off his face on some sort of psychoactive substance, probably one of the customised opiate alkaloids or partial dopamine agonists he synthesised on a printer in his apartment. His responses were slow and puzzled.

Of course, if you were a Polis+ infiltrator and wanted to pass the Uncanny Valley test, you could do worse than pose as a dull-witted junkie.

Dev spent quarter of an hour with the dopehead – his name was Franz Glazkov – before concluding that it was hopeless carrying on. The kid kept drifting off mid-sentence, or else simply repeated Dev's questions back at him. Drug use had turned his brain into a kind of echo chamber, where sounds reverberated meaninglessly.

Doubts remained, however, even after Dev had dismissed him.

"I'm going to follow Glazkov, see where he goes and what he gets up to," he told Kahlo. "I'd like you to release him from custody first and let the other detainees stew a little longer."

"He's just a junkie. Knowing him, he'll head off somewhere to score or deal, one or the other. Waste of your time."

"Let me be the judge of that."

"Fine." Kahlo shrugged. "Me, I'm off to the rail network HQ. I've managed to get through at last to the controllers."

"They worked out what happened?"

"No clue as yet. All they can tell me is that it was some kind of mass systemic failure. They lost all power to the mainframe, the backups didn't kick in, and they were impotent for about ten minutes, not to mention incommunicado. Blind, deaf and dumb. Couldn't do a thing, not even activate a complete network shutdown. It happened twice. Once around the time of the first crash, and again when the shuttle came after us."

"Have them check for an externally transmitted virus."

"As in a Polis Plus virus?"

"Could be. Just have them run a Polisware scan. They might not have thought of that. They can download the software off the ISS central office hub if they haven't got their own."

"Okay," said Kahlo, "but only because I think it's a good idea. Don't get the impression I'm taking orders from you, Lieutenant Harmer."

"Ahhh. 'Lieutenant.' You've been doing some homework on me, captain. I'm flattered."

"Don't be. I'm thorough, that's all. Lieutenant Dev Harmer of the Ninth Extrasolar Engineers. You were a sapper. Speciality: neutralising and demolishing Polis Plus hardware in the field, mainly mechs. Served all nine and a half years of the Frontier War. Started out as a private, rose rapidly as you racked up the combat hours until you were leading your own platoon. Highly decorated." Narrowing her eyes a smidgeon, she added, "Also, a veteran of the Battle of Leather Hill – or should I say a 'survivor'?"

Dev deflected that last statement as quickly as possible. "Yes, well, before my head swells too large, I should point out that I'm not in the army any more, so strictly speaking I'm not a lieutenant now, and none of those other facts are pertinent. Also, the police hierarchy and the military hierarchy aren't compatible, so you don't outrank me."

"You're a civilian in my city, so I do."

"Fair enough. Good luck with your enquiries. Let me know what you find out."

"If I feel like it," said Kahlo. "Mostly, though, I'm looking forward to tearing someone a new hole."

"Then enjoy."

"Believe me, I'm going to."

8

FRANZ GLAZKOV LEFT CEPD headquarters. Dev followed a little way behind.

Glazkov hopped the first train back to the city centre. Dev lurked in the next carriage along, keeping a surreptitious eye on him through the window of the connecting door. He had a feeling that this would be a fruitless journey, just as Kahlo had said. But as long as there was a chance, however slender, that Glazkov was Polis+, it was worth a shot.

Night was falling over Calder's Edge, the illumination clusters gradually dimming. Crepuscular half-light gave way to an almost total blackness, and in that blackness Dev found he could see...

Everything.

His eyes showed him the world in silvery, pristine definition. There was a sharpness to textures and surfaces that he found disconcerting. The faces of other passengers became agglomerations of smooth planes and creases. The texture of the seat covers was so rough and porous it could have been a lunar landscape.

His own body seemed to glow, unrecognisably. The back of his hand was no longer familiar. He had to wriggle his fingers to remind himself they belonged to him.

He was so distracted by his first true experience of nocturnal vision that he almost failed to notice when Glazkov got off the train. Dev darted out through the doors just as they closed.

"North Three station," said an automated announcement in a seductive female voice that echoed along the platform. "North Three station. The train is now departing. Please stand clear."

The station was in one of the city's seedier areas, judging by its litter-strewn shabbiness and the relatively small number of people alighting there. Just Dev and Glazkov, as it transpired.

Glazkov shambled waywardly to the exit. If he had been in less of a narcotic stupor, he might have noticed that someone was dogging his footsteps. But he didn't even turn round once, and besides, Dev moved with a practised nonchalant stealth, hugging shadows, maintaining a casual air, as though he were just any old Calder's Edger on his way somewhere.

Crossing a plaza, Glazkov headed up a ramp leading to the base tier of one of the towering residential columns. Habitats lined a spiral roadway that wound up and around the rockface like a helter-skelter slide. The roadway was fitted with dual, contra-running travelator belts for pedestrians, although there were also mass-transit elevators for quicker access between tiers.

Glazkov didn't use either. Instead he ducked into an alley between two buildings. At the far end lay a narrow stairwell carved into the core of the column.

Dev, still keeping his distance, tiptoed after him down switchbacking flights of steps, which were slippery underfoot. The air was thick and cloyingly humid.

He detected the thump of a bass beat vibrating up the stairwell. Deeper he went, until he arrived in a kind of vestibule presided over by a doorman built like a stone monolith.

The doorman invited Dev to deposit funds in a specified back account. Shortly afterward, Dev was ushered through into a long low room whose rugged ceiling dripped condensation.

Music roared, all growling low-frequency chord layers and thundering drums. Ultraviolet lamps strobed in darkness, picking out streaks of fluorescent paint on the walls and making them blaze vividly. Bodies cavorted to the rhythm. Hands, also coated in fluorescent paint, flickered to and fro.

Dev recoiled, squinting and flinching. The bass drum boomed like heavy artillery. The flashes of brightly coloured light resembled muon beam weapon discharges. Where the dancers revelled in the sensory overload, he was repulsed by it.

Too many battlefields.

Too many memories.

Too many nightmares.

His gut clenched in fear. His brain was sending out warnings, like flares. *Plussers! Check your six!*

Prioritise threats! Maintain formation! Move!

He told himself he was not in a firefight; he was in a nightclub. There were no enemy mechs advancing on his position, no comrades beside him, no omnipresent terror of death. That life was in the past. Safely in the past.

"You all right?" a stranger asked. It was hard to sound truly, sincerely concerned when you had to scream at the top of your lungs to be heard.

Dev couldn't even nod. It was stupid. Pathetic. Crippled by loud music and lights. Get a grip. He was drawing attention to himself.

He looked up to find Franz Glazkov standing a few metres away. Glazkov had been deep in conversation with a smartly dressed man, conducting some kind of transaction. But now both of them were staring at Dev, as were several other people around them.

Recognition dawned in Glazkov's dulled eyes. He shouted something to the smartly dressed man, gesticulating in alarm. Dev didn't catch what he said, but it was clear that Glazkov was fingering him as an undercover cop or something similar – the guy who had been interrogating him just now at police headquarters.

The smartly dressed man gave a curt, grim nod. His expression slackened briefly as he thought-sent a message.

Dev struggled to shake off the paralysis and regain control of himself. He straightened up, tuning out the auditory and visual assault, focusing on Glazkov.

He lunged forward. Glazkov turned tail.

Someone grabbed Dev's collar and spun him round.

He came face to face with the monolithic doorman. The smartly dressed man was, it seemed, the club owner. He had summoned the doorman to deal with an unwelcome guest.

The doorman yanked Dev off his feet and began escorting – more accurately, dragging – him towards the club entrance.

Out in the vestibule, where the music was marginally more muted, he told Dev that cops weren't welcome at Inferno. It was a private club. All above board, strictly legal, permits paid, paperwork in order. But punters came here to have a good time, to forget their troubles, and that meant, among other things, not having plainclothes law loitering on the dance floor.

"Got it?" he said. "So off you go, nice and quiet, and we'll pretend this never happened. Okay?"

He was genial about it, as though there had been a misunderstanding, that was all. As though Dev had carelessly crossed a line, transgressed some unwritten rule. Least said, soonest mended.

"I want Franz Glazkov," Dev said, sounding just as reasonable. "He's a suspect. Let me back in there to fetch him. I'll only be a moment."

The doorman's massive spherical head oscillated slowly from side to side. "Please don't be awkward, pal. My boss has asked me to help you leave. There's room for interpretation in the word 'help,' if you catch my drift."

"Don't get in my way."

"Don't make me."

"You seem like a decent guy. I wouldn't like to have to hurt you."

"You?" the doorman scoffed. "How?"

"Induced sarcoplasmic hypertrophy, yes?" said Dev, casting an eye over the doorman's excessively muscled bulk. "Desensitised pain receptors. Extra epidermal layers."

"I've had the full suite of professional-security modifications," the doorman confirmed. "Only an idiot would do this job without. Also, I'm –"

Dev's arm shot out, delivering a throat strike with the outer edge of his hand.

"Still tragically vulnerable to a bruised trachea," he said.

The doorman sank, wheezing horribly.

"Try to breathe as normal," Dev advised. "Your windpipe's swelling up, but I gauged the blow so that it won't close altogether. You'll be fine."

The doorman made a feeble, ineffectual grab for Dev's leg as he stepped round him. Dev shook him off.

This time, as he re-entered Inferno, he was mentally prepared. The shock and disorientation were minimised, tolerable.

He searched for Glazkov, but couldn't find him. A hundred or so faces in the club, many of them spaced-out and vacuous, none of them Glazkov's.

The club owner was loitering in one corner, glugging down water from a two-litre bottle.

Even though he wasn't dancing, his face was slick with perspiration. Inferno was like a sauna, and no Alighierian could afford to lose so much sweat without regular rehydration.

He didn't even see Dev until he was down on his knees with his head being forced back at a sharp angle.

Dev upended the bottle and tipped water down the man's throat. The club owner spluttered, gargled and gagged. Water started spilling out of the sides of his mouth and splashing down the front of his silk shirt.

Dev didn't even ask the question. It was obvious.

The club owner, half drowned, still choking, pointed to a back room.

Dev held up the bottle menacingly.

The club owner made a pleading, exaggeratedly sincere face.

Dev let go of him and tossed the bottle neck-first into his lap, soaking the crotch of his trousers.

The backroom was cramped, the floor covered in tumbled mounds of cushions and throw rugs that were patterned with stains from spilled drinks and other less easily identifiable substances. Womb-pink illumination. Mirrored walls. A chill-out area for when the intensity of the music and dancefloor lights became too much.

A stranger was in here with him, image reflected countless times in the mirrors, receding away in infinite recursion.

It took Dev a moment to realise the stranger was himself.

Otherwise, himself aside, the room was empty. Had the club owner lied?

No. One of the mirrors was angled slightly out of true, attached to a section of hinged false wall. A secret door, which Glazkov had left slightly ajar in his hurry to flee the premises.

Dev pried it all the way open to reveal access to the top of a vertical shaft.

An emergency escape route, known only to a favoured few, the owner's inner circle. A back exit for patrons who needed to leave in secret, for whatever reason.

Dev climbed down.

9

HAND OVER HAND Dev scaled down a crude ladder – metal rungs bolted to raw rock. One hundred metres below, he emerged into a low-ceilinged passageway, a natural tunnel.

Patches of bioluminescent slime mould clung to the walls, shedding a spectral blue glow. To Alighierian eyes, this was equivalent to broad daylight.

Dev sensed movement ahead – a rustle of footfalls. He called out Glazkov's name and the footfalls sped up. He hurried after them, bent over to give his head clearance.

The tunnel forked, but Glazkov was not so far ahead that Dev couldn't determine by sound alone which of the two paths he had taken.

"Glazkov! Running's not the answer. I just want to talk to you some more."

"Fuck off, pig," came the reply.

"If you're not Polis Plus, you've nothing to fear."

"Leave me alone."

Dev came to another fork. This time, there were three divergent routes to choose from.

Glazkov, in a sudden fit of cunning, had decided to stand still. Whichever of the three tunnels he had taken, he wasn't going to advertise his position by continuing to run. He was hiding down one of them, just out of sight, staying silent, controlling his breathing.

Dev inspected the entrance to each, looking for a sign, tracks of some sort. The floors were slick with moisture, but solid rock. Not a footprint to be seen.

Guesswork, then. Process of elimination.

He took the left hand tunnel. It descended at a shallow gradient, kinking at an angle every couple of dozen paces. Finally it opened out into a dome-shaped chamber where Dev could once again, to his relief, stand upright.

All around him were encrustations of a fine pale crystal mineral. Some growths were rounded and lumpy, others branched outward in snowflake-like fronds. In the glow cast by patches of slime mould, they sparkled faintly.

This was a giant geode, a cavity formed by a gas bubble rising from Alighieri's molten core and cooling.

It was no dead-end, since a narrow fissure linked it to another, similar geode. Dev squeezed through the crack on his hands and knees, to find that this geode joined on to two more, and on and on. There was a clustered mass of the things, like geological foam, all interconnected.

In all likelihood this was where Glazkov had taken refuge. He seemed to know the layout of these tunnels intimately. He was sneaking through the geode maze, intending either to elude Dev or lead him astray.

Trouble was, it was working. On both counts.

Dev soon realised, to his dismay, that he had ventured too far into the crystal-lined labyrinth for comfort. He had been doing his best to log his progress, memorising the position of each geode relative to its neighbours. At some point, however, he had got muddled up. All at once, his mental map ceased to make sense and became more or less useless.

He doubled back, but the next geode he crawled into wasn't immediately familiar to him. Nor was it *un*familiar. Had he been through this one already or not?

So he returned to the previous one, but here there were two other fissures to choose from, two possible ways out.

Shit.

Brilliant, Dev, he told himself. Just brilliant.

Not only had he lost his quarry, he'd lost his bearings. The damn geodes were all of similar dimensions and hard to tell apart. One set of glittery mineral outcrops looked much like another. He should have taken the precaution of leaving a trail. Markings scratched into the rock. Something so that he would be able to tell which way he had come.

He had been too eager, overconfident. Figuring a junkie like Glazkov wouldn't be about to outwit him.

Now he was a bit fucked.

He reached out via commplant into the Alighierian insite. There would be a proper map cached there somewhere, surely. He couldn't be the first person to have got lost down here. Given a 3D schematic of the geodes, he would be able to navigate back through to the tunnels, using his commplant's GPS.

No service available.

"You what?" Dev exclaimed out loud. The close quarters and the jagged inner surfaces of the geode lent his voice a weird robotic timbre.

There was no signal. He couldn't connect to the insite. He was too deep down, maybe. Out of range. Too much rock in the way. That or the composition of the geodes was somehow interfering.

Dev was not the kind who got easily flustered. He prided himself on that. Nor was he prone to claustrophobia.

Even so, he couldn't help but feel a tingle of anxiety which, if he wasn't careful, might easily escalate into full-blown panic.

It was time to get methodical. He started exploring again. Now he did make sure to mark the fissures, using a small scrap of rock. Little etched Ds that said *Dev came this way*.

Didn't help. The geode maze seemed infinite. Many-layered, too; he was going up and down as well as sideways.

After what was probably an hour, but felt longer,

he stopped for a breather. He sat on his haunches, wrists on knees, and tried to calm himself.

This was stupid. Lost underground. How had he let it happen?

One thing he was adamant about: he was not going to die down here. As long as he kept his head, didn't flap, he would be all right. He would survive.

Think about it sensibly. Kahlo would notice his absence. Perhaps not straight away, but at some point. If not tonight, then tomorrow morning for sure. She would chase it up. She knew he had followed Glazkov. She was bright. Diligent. She would piece it together, work out where he had gone.

There would be a search party. Kahlo would arrange it. Alighieri must have dedicated cave-rescue squads on standby for just this sort of contingency. They would look for him down below Inferno. They would find him.

That was assuming Kahlo was concerned enough. Assuming she cared...

Dev smiled weakly. Kahlo *didn't* care about him. But she cared about her job, her responsibilities. If an ISS consultant went missing, the company would want to know what had become of him, and Kahlo would be the person they leaned on. They'd demand answers from her, explanations. She had to be concerned about him if she valued her career.

Patience was what Dev needed now. The ability to sit tight and wait without succumbing to fear or despair.

He stretched his legs out, rested his hands on the geode floor...

Something under his left palm *moved*.

Dev sprang to his feet.

He had touched something hard. Smooth. Alive.

He looked down to see just about the most disgusting animal he had ever laid eyes on.

10

IT WAS THE size of a small dog, with a rounded shiny carapace and a dozen legs. A segmented tail curved over the top of its abdomen, tipped with a sharp, ugly point. A sting.

It had not liked having a hand placed on it. Now it stood stock still, its stance wary and aggressive. Two thick forelimbs were raised, pincers agape, waiting for Dev to make a move. It was sizing him up with a cluster of black, beady eyes set below a projecting chitinous brow, assessing just how much of a threat he presented. An ominous, rattling hiss issued from its multiple mouth parts.

Dev, too, stood stock still, biting back his revulsion.

The creature gradually, grudgingly, lowered its forelimbs. It trod sideways a few steps, then addressed itself to a patch of the bioluminescent slime mould on the geode wall. A smaller, secondary set of forelimbs extruded just below its stumpy head, like ultra-articulate mandibles, and with these it commenced scooping up the mould and popping it into a dextrous, rippling mouth, almost daintily fastidious.

Every now and then it swivelled towards Dev, tail twitching, and let out another hiss interspersed with soft clicks. This was as if to say: My *slime mould. All mine. Stay away, or else.*

Dev wished he could somehow tell the thing that he didn't want its wretched mould. It could have the stuff all to itself. He didn't want even to go near the animal, and he certainly didn't want to come between it and its feast.

The creature was, he thought, like a cockroach crossed with a scorpion. Two nightmares in one – but bigger.

A moleworm gnawing a scroach.

That was how Thorne, the union leader, had described Dev, paying tribute to his tenacity. Dev had no idea what a 'moleworm' looked like but he would be very surprised if this thing in front of him wasn't a 'scroach.' The name fit it to a T.

He began backing away, moving as slowly as a sloth, laying down one foot toe-to-heel, soundlessly, then the other. Every time the creature – the scroach – paused in its eating and turned towards him, he froze.

Was that sting deadly?

He thought so. Judging by the size of the topmost joint of the scroach's tail, its venom gland had to have a good quarter-pint capacity. That much poison injected in to him would be agonisingly painful at the very least, more likely lethal. The sheer volume alone might trigger fatal anaphylaxis.

As he reached the nearest fissure that led out of the geode, Dev spied a second scroach crawling into view. It scuttled over to join the first beside the slime mould. There was a brief altercation. Forelimbs waved, pincers snapping open and shut. Pugnacious semaphore. Each creature unleashed a volley of irate chittering hisses at the other.

The new arrival was somewhat larger, and in the end the first scroach backed off, going to a smaller patch of mould.

Through the fissure Dev intended to exit by, a third scroach now appeared.

Oh, this was just splendid. Lovely. He was smack dab in the middle of a convention of oversized Alighierian arthropods. How many more of the buggers were there round here?

Pressing himself flat against the wall of the geode, Dev watched the three scroaches circle around one another. Their tails were up and swaying from side to side like cobras, dewdrops of venom glistening at the tips of their stings. Occasionally one of them would charge at one of the other two. A feint. Then another of them would retaliate with a feint of its own.

The hisses they made were now more or less continuous. The noises were raspy and slightly moist, like air escaping from a child's balloon.

A fourth scroach turned up to join in the fun, and a fifth. The geode was beginning to get crowded.

The scroaches had to be coming from somewhere.

And just like that, Dev came up with a plan.

These creatures struck him as solitary rather than

social. When they met up, they found it hard to get along.

Yet to have this many at once in the same place suggested they followed set routes. Feeding trails. They were scavengers who returned again and again to established sources of their yummy slime mould.

Chances were, they might not live in the geode maze at all. They might come from outside.

In which case, if he went in the opposite direction, contrary to the flow of traffic, it might just lead him to freedom.

Dev had to acknowledge that, as plans went, it wasn't the soundest. It definitely wasn't a sure thing. He might just wind up straying into a scroach nest – lair, den, whatever the place was called where Ma and Pa Scroach reared their young.

But it was far preferable to staying put in the geode with five – no, six now – hideous, bad-tempered giant insect beasties all spoiling for a fight.

Dev checked the fissure to see if yet another scroach was on its way through.

Then he dived in and wriggled smartly out the other side.

He loitered in this adjacent geode until a scroach emerged from one of the other fissures.

He wormed through that one too.

He went from geode to geode another three times before taking an enforced hiatus. The procession of scroaches had run out. No more of them coming.

Eventually he heard a faint scuttling from the nearest fissure. He bent cautiously to peer in.

The hugest scroach yet pounced from the crevice, forelimbs extended. Where the others were the size of a spaniel, this one was a full-grown labrador.

Before Dev could react, the creature seized his hand. It felt as though his fingers were trapped in a vice.

Dev reared backwards, trying to wrench himself free. The scroach's pincer was clamped fast. It couldn't bring its sting to bear yet – it was only part way out of the fissure – but all it had to do was advance a couple of steps and its tail would be in the clear.

Dev ignored the pain of the crushing pressure from the pincer. He also ignored – although this took some doing – the loathsome sensation of being touched by the scroach, the hard, slightly clammy feel of its exoskeleton on his skin.

The scroach pressed forward, nothing but deadly implacability in its myriad eyes. Its mouth parts worked furiously as it let out a string of vicious, menacing hisses.

Dev tried shunting it back into the fissure, but it was strong, and with his hand held tight, he couldn't get the necessary leverage. The only tactic left was surprise.

Dev stopped pushing and instead *pulled*.

He yanked the scroach fully out of the fissure. Its feet scrabbled for purchase.

Quick!

Before the scroach could gather its wits and deploy its sting, Dev hauled it off the ground. He seized its tail with his free hand, at the joint just below the top segment.

He swung the monstrous insect against the wall. Once. Twice.

On the third impact the scroach's pincer opened and let go.

Now Dev whirled it by the tail alone, double-handed, slamming the scroach even harder against the geode's crystalline growths. He flailed the thing back and forth, this way, that way, and each time it hit the wall the sound was a little crunchier, a little squishier.

Shards of carapace flew. A foul-smelling custardy ichor spattered – the haemolymph that was the scroach's blood. Slender brittle legs snapped off and fell.

Dev kept smashing and smashing the scroach until just about only the tail was left intact. The rest was a ragged, oozing butchery. Nameless innards and organs clung to the interior of the geode, some dangling in gelatinous dripping ribbons.

Panting hard, and close to puking, Dev tossed the mangled remnants of the insect aside.

"What did you have to go and do *that* for?" demanded an indignant voice behind him.

11

THE MAN WAS dressed in military-surplus protective outerwear, complete with a pair of gauntlets made of artificial spider-silk fibroins, lightweight but virtually impenetrable. His head was encased in mesh helmet not unlike a fencer's. He flipped up the visor and blinked at Dev owlishly.

His face was skinny and slight, with a nose a little like a chicken's beak. His corneas were sheathed in jet-black lenses with an iridescent sheen – image intensification contacts. He had a motion-sensitive tracking device strapped to his forearm.

"You mean kill that scroach?" Dev said, indicating the mess.

"Yes I mean kill that scroach. What did it ever do to you?"

"Er, tried to kill *me*."

"Well, okay. Yes. Well, if it did, that wasn't its fault. You must've alarmed it."

"Not as much as it alarmed me," Dev said. "You should have seen the size of it."

"Mature adult male," said the man, scrutinising the tail. "On his seventh, maybe eighth ecdysis. Which would put his age at about twenty-five. A venerable specimen."

"Ecdysis?"

"The shedding of the cuticula. Moulting. You can't get that big without going through a few exoskeletons."

"You're a scroach expert?" said Dev.

"Not yet, but I aspire to be." The man pulled off a gauntlet and extended a hand. "Ludlow Trundell. Professor of xeno-entomology at the Qatar Institute for Extraterrestrial Sciences."

"Dev Harmer. Amateur scroach squasher. No other relevant qualifications. You'll forgive me if I don't shake." His fingers were sticky with a liberal coating of arthropod juices.

"No, I quite understand," said Professor Trundell, withdrawing and re-gloving his hand. "And I apologise for sounding off at you just now. I'm not happy about what you did, but I can see the rationale. Clearly you don't appreciate what a remarkable, wonderful creature *Dromopoda alighieriensis* is."

"I don't think this one appreciated what a remarkable, wonderful creature *Homo sapiens* is, either. Otherwise we mightn't have had a problem."

"You're in his domain. You're an intruder. What did you expect? He's going to want to defend himself."

"Look, back that-a-way there's a half-dozen more of the things that I *didn't* destroy. I don't think, on balance, that massacring one is too bad."

"Such restraint," said Trundell dryly.

"Listen, Trundle..."

"Trun*dell*. Stress on the second syllable."

"You obviously know your way around these geodes."

"Been spelunking down here for over three months now," said the xeno-entomologist proudly. He showed off his tracking device. "This helps me navigate. It's got a detailed chart of the tunnels programmed in, on which I've marked common scroach migratory routes. But even without it, I doubt I'd get lost. I've become a bit of a tunnel rat during my researches."

"So can you get me out and back up to civilisation?"

"I *can*," said Trundell pedantically. "What you're asking is, would I be *willing* to."

"Would you?"

"I might. I've only just started work this evening, though. Scroaches are more active when they're on Alighieri's night side – my theory is it's something to do with the slight temperature drop – so I've had to become somewhat nocturnal myself. I was planning to study them for another two or three hours."

"I don't want to hang around that long."

"Then we are at an impasse."

Dev restrained an infuriated sigh. "I'll pay you."

"I'm well-funded. My university is generous with its grants. Besides, you can't put a price on pure science."

"How about this, then? Help me or I'll treat you much the same as I did this scroach. Protective gear won't save you."

Trundell gulped and blanched. "I'm not a man of violence."

"Nor am I, unless provoked. The evidence for that is, I'd say, pretty conclusive."

Trundell glanced around the gore-spattered geode.

"Fine," he said. "Your argument is forceful and persuasive. Let's go."

The professor led the way, shuffling through the fissures, Dev close behind. Every so often he paused to consult his tracking device, then carried on.

"Trundle?"

"Trundell."

"If you love scroaches so much, how come you're all togged up in ceramide fibre and tungsten mesh? Don't you trust them?"

"I may admire the scroach, but I'm not crazy. They're temperamental and sometimes unpredictable. Only a fool would get as close to them as I do and not take precautions."

"Ever been attacked?"

"Couple of times. A female tried to sting me once, but her aculeus failed to pierce my clothing. Just. It felt like being rammed hard in the chest with the end of a steel rod. I was bruised for days. I blame myself, though."

"You would."

"No, really. I didn't respect her. She was carrying her infant brood on her back, and I plucked one off to take a closer look. I was going to return it, of course, but she couldn't have known that. Another scroach nearly took a couple of my fingers off with its pincer. Again, *mea culpa. Dromopoda alighieriensis* is a proud beast and doesn't take kindly to insults."

"You were rude to it?"

"By its own lights, yes," said Trundell. "I mimicked the brandishing of its pedipalps incorrectly."

"For shame. It waved its arms at you and you didn't have the courtesy to wave back?"

"I did, but in order to indicate submission you not only have to copy what the other scroach does precisely but you must do so at a marginally slower rate to denote your inferior status. I freely admit I got it wrong. Also, and this is the real issue, I don't have chelicerae."

"Those being..."

"Moveable mouth parts. Scroaches use them to signal to one another in addition to their pedipalps. They exhale through special spiracles set just inside their jaws and modify the sound with the chelicerae. I can hiss too, of course, but not with nearly the same range of modulations and frequencies."

Dev recalled the extensive rattly hissing he had heard from the scroaches. "You're saying they can talk to one another?"

"In a manner of speaking, yes."

"Ugh."

"Why 'ugh'?"

"Because that's freaky. Insects talking."

"No more so than birds chirping or dogs barking, and scroaches are no less intelligent then either of those species. Personally I find it extraordinary and rather beautiful."

"Of course you do."

"In fact I'm thinking of making it my field of specialism – quasi-verbal communication among alien invertebrates. How they manage to convey aggression, announce the desire to mate, familiarise themselves with their young, share warning messages and so forth, by means of a complex system of principally auditory cues."

Dev did not seem to have endeared himself to Trundell by bullying him earlier, but the xeno-entomologist's passion for his subject, however, was overcoming his nerdy resentment. He just couldn't help enthusing about his beloved scroaches to anyone who would listen, and in Dev he had a more or less captive audience.

"We're familiar with Terran insects who use sound to communicate," he went on. "The stridulation of cicadas and grasshoppers, for instance, or the sharp air expulsions of the Fijian long-horned beetle and the Madagascan hissing cockroach. But they operate at a relatively low level of sophistication compared with the scroach. They're either calling to mates, demarcating territory, or trying to repel rivals or predators. That's about all."

"Who needs more than that? I know I don't."

"*Dromopoda alighieriensis*," said Trundell patiently, "has such a variety of hisses, so many intonations and patterns to suit different circumstances, that I can't help but think of it as a language. I haven't found another insect quite so intricately expressive, apart from the so-called singspiders on Auriga B with their web harps."

"Still freaky, though."

"It might because they're a wholly subterranean species. Their environment lends itself to auditory communication. Tunnels and caves act as natural amplifiers, carrying sounds over long distances. Scroaches see adequately enough, but their tympanal and chordotonal organs – their, for want of a better word, ears – are acutely well developed."

Trundell stopped, holding up a finger.

"Case in point. Hear that?"

Dev listened as a faint whispery rustle drifted through the air. It was coming from some distance away, and it wavered and skittered like wind-blown autumn leaves.

"That's them?"

"That's scroaches," Trundell confirmed. "Lots of them, spread out far and wide. Communing remotely."

"Can't be good. What are they saying?"

"I've been recording their different hisses and attempting to correlate them with mood and context in order to decode the syntax, but I still haven't fully mastered it. It's a work-in-progress. That noise could mean a massed spat, or it could be a mating-frenzy summons, or maybe…"

Now there came a soft tremor, like the noise of one heavy stone scraping against another.

"Or maybe," said Trundell, "it's *that*."

The scroach hissing rose in pitch and volume, becoming sharper and shriller.

"Earthquake?" said Dev.

"No, but we'd better hurry all the same. A couple more geodes and we'll be out in the tunnels. Then we can get some proper speed up."

"What is it?" said Dev as they scurried on all fours through one fissure, then the next. "I could be wrong, but those scroaches sound... frightened."

"That's because they are. You must know why."

"I'm not from round these parts."

"Aren't you?"

"Appearances to the contrary, no."

"Well, neither am I, but even I know what a moleworm is. And does. Apex predator. Top of the food chain. Favourite meal: scroaches. But it's not choosy, and if we're unlucky it's just as apt to snack on us!"

12

OUT OF THE geode maze, Dev and Trundell crouched and scuttled along the tunnels. Trundell's tracking device was giving out loud beeps at two-second intervals.

"Ooh, judging by the ping-back strength, it's a big one," the xeno-entomologist said. "Probably a female. They outweigh the males by a ratio of one-point-five to one, on average."

"Less talking, more moving?" Dev suggested.

"It's all right. We're heading away from her."

"Are we? Because those beeps sound to me like they're getting closer together rather than further apart."

"No. No." Trundell squinted at the tracking device's tiny floatscreen, which hovered just above the back of his wrist. "Well, maybe. But if we keep going this way, we should..."

Dead end.

"Oh. That isn't... I must have got turned around. In all the confusion..."

"Spelunking down here for three months, he said. Tunnel rat, he said."

"We should backtrack."

"Really? You think?"

They returned to the junction where they had last made a turn. Trundell increased the gain on the tracking device's scanner. A cross-section of branching tunnel architecture swept across the screen, routes indicated by dotted lines.

The beeps were now less than one second apart.

"It's coming," said Dev. He could feel a vibration underfoot, as though some heavy road vehicle were approaching. "Which way do we go?"

"I'm trying to work out the optimal course."

"Then try a bit harder."

"Don't harass me! I'm flustered enough as it is."

"Stop clucking. Focus."

Trundell pointed a decisive finger. "Down there."

"Okay."

They set off, but hadn't gone more than ten steps when a scroach came hurtling along the tunnel towards them. Both men pressed themselves against the wall to let it pass.

"That one was certainly shifting," Dev said.

"They can manage forty kph at full tilt. Faster than most people can sprint."

"But I mean, why is it going that fast in the opposite direction if *we're* supposed to be running away from the moleworm?"

"That is a good point."

More scroaches charged towards them, hissing

wildly, pincers waving. Dev thought of a shoal of fish fleeing a hungry dolphin.

"Yeah, I vote we follow them," he said. "I trust their instinct for self-preservation over your machine."

"Yes," said Trundell, "I'm thinking that too."

They about-faced and charged after the scroaches, Trundell in front. The beeps from the tracking device were at half-second intervals and getting faster. The whole tunnel was shaking.

"Aargh! This is killing my thighs," the scientist panted, slowing down. "And my back."

Dev himself was not enjoying having to run bent over. "Would you rather get caught by the moleworm?"

Trundell somehow found the energy to increase his pace again. That was just as well, because otherwise Dev might have shoved him aside, barged past and left him for dust.

They still weren't going fast enough. The beeps were issuing from the tracking device as quickly as darts from a kinetic energy repeater gun, urgently insisting that the creature Dev and Trundell were trying to escape from was right on their very heels.

The ground behind Dev erupted.

Two sets of shovel-like claws broke through solid rock as though it was peanut brittle.

They swiftly dug out a hole large enough to admit a fleshy, many-tentacled thing that Dev mistook at first for some kind of large sea anemone. He realised almost immediately that it was in fact a nose, its tip bristling with prehensile feelers.

The feelers writhed as more and more of the beast emerged. Now a skinny, glistening snout. Now a circular, sphincter-like mouth, fringed with needle-thin teeth. Now two small primordial eyes, white as blisters.

With astonishing speed, the claws widened the hole, until the moleworm was able to slither its whole self through. It squirmed out into the open – long-bodied, hairless, loathsome.

It had four legs, all at the front, just behind the head. The two rear legs were a little longer than the two stumpy forelegs, meaning the clawed extremities at the ends – footlike hands, handlike feet – were all positioned next to one another.

The rest of the creature was tapering and serpentine, a cable of sinewy muscle that started as thick as a cow's girth and narrowed to the diameter of a man's arm. A combination of abdomen and tail, this section of the moleworm coiled and thrashed with an eagerness that spoke of soon-to-be-sated hunger. Predator had located prey.

Trundell was rooted to the spot, eyes bulging in terror.

Dev was only slightly less appalled, but he had the presence of mind to grab the xeno-entomologist by the scruff of the neck and bundle him along the tunnel, away from the moleworm.

The creature lolloped after them in pursuit, its puckered mouth opening and shutting, emitting ropey drool.

Dev noted that the moleworm seemed clumsy

and hamstrung as it ran. Its limbs were not well co-ordinated and its tail added drag to its progress. The impression he had got from the tracking device was that it was much fleeter of foot than this. He and Trundell were managing to put distance between them and it.

It was, he deduced, a born burrower. Its physiology was designed for carving a passage through rock and earth. Out in the open, even in the relatively tight squeeze of this tunnel, it wasn't anywhere near as efficient at propelling itself along.

Dev thought for a moment that he and Trundell were going to be able to outrun the moleworm after all.

The moleworm seemed to come to the same conclusion, for it dived headlong into the tunnel floor. Within moments it had excavated a deep hole for itself and was gone from sight.

Not from earshot, though. It rumbled along underneath them, at home in its natural milieu, easily keeping up.

"She can sense us," Trundell gasped. "Those feelers on her nose are phenomenally sensitive organs. She can detect our footfalls with them, our breathing, the fear pheromones we're giving off; our heartbeats, even."

The ground beneath them cracked and split. Dev yanked Trundell backwards by the collar just as the moleworm launched itself up through the floor. Its clacking needle-teeth missed Trundell's leg by millimetres.

"Sensitive, huh?" Dev said.

Before the creature could wriggle all the way up into the tunnel, he stamped on its nose. The ring of feelers squashed rubberily under his boot heel. A couple of them split open, jetting blood.

The moleworm screeched and shrank back into the hole.

Dev thrust Trundell across the gap, over the recoiling moleworm, then leapt too. They charged down the tunnel. Dev briefly entertained the hope that he had hurt the moleworm so badly that it would think twice about giving chase again.

But no, all he had done was piss it off and make it all the more determined to get them.

Once again it dived underground and burrowed along, matching the course of the tunnel with a brand new tunnel of its own.

Trundell was beginning to flag, wheezing hard for breath. One of his image intensification lenses had popped out, leaving him half-blind in the gloom.

Dev knew he would be better off without the scientist. He could go faster. He was more effective when he didn't have to consider anyone's welfare but his own.

He was sorely tempted to abandon Trundell, but he couldn't do it. Blame his military background. You did not leave anyone behind, not if you could help it. That mantra had been drilled into him during basic training. Even the wounded, even the dying – you took them with you. Because one day the wounded or the dying might be you, and would you like it if your comrades just discarded you like so much waste?

Still, Trundell was becoming a lame duck, and lame ducks had a tendency to become sitting ducks.

If Dev and Trundell hadn't stumbled across a stray scroach, it was debatable whether they would have got away from the moleworm unscathed.

The scroach was missing one of its pedipalps and several of its legs, no doubt the legacy of battles for mates or food that it had lost. It was limping along far behind the general exodus of scroaches, a straggler.

As the moleworm yet again ripped up through the tunnel floor ahead, Dev seized hold of the slowcoach scroach by the tip of its tail. He slung it forward, straight at the moleworm's maw.

The scroach's little legs flailed as it flew through the air, hissing in distress, and the moleworm caught it neatly with its snout feelers. It manipulated the insect round so that its sting was pointing downwards. Then it bit off the top segment of the tail and spat it aside.

The snout feelers enfolded the scroach tightly. The insect struggled in vain as the moleworm flipped it the other way up and chomped off its head.

Dev stood motionless, and made Trundell do the same, while the moleworm chewed the scroach's head with evident satisfaction. Its teeth mashed ganglia and crunched chitin. The rest of the scroach twitched and spasmed, its nervous system still firing even after decapitation. Its truncated tail stabbed bluntly, uselessly, against the moleworm's head.

"Will she – ?" Trundell began.

Dev put a finger to his lips.

The moleworm finished masticating and swallowed. Dev could see it weighing up the situation. One scroach in its clutches, two humans nearby. The proverbial bird in the hand versus two in the bush. Should it go after further prey or stick with the tasty morsel that had been so obligingly presented to it?

In the end it decided to cut its losses. The humans were elusive. One of them had caused it great pain. It had a scroach. That would do.

The moleworm withdrew into the hole with the scroach, which had by this stage figured out it was dead and had curled up into a ball. Dev heard and felt the huge mammal drill down into the rock, taking its meal somewhere where it could eat in peace, unmolested.

"I'm beginning," he said, "to really not like this planet."

13

THE BAR WAS busy, but not packed. On a small stage, a three-piece guitar band shambled through ironic punky cover versions of Ante-Enlightenment church hymns.

Irreligiosity was still a big deal out on the fringe worlds. Back on Earth, people were over Enlightenment. The yoke of faith had been shucked; they'd had a hundred years to get used to the idea. It wasn't something they much thought about any more. Old hat.

On planets like Alighieri, however, the party celebrating the final, absolute death of God was carrying on.

Dev carried two beers over to the booth where he and Trundell were sitting.

The xeno-entomologist picked up his bottle with an unsteady hand. He took a tentative sip, as though unable to recall what you were supposed to do with a beer. Then he upended the bottle and half emptied it in one go.

He looked across the table at Dev. "I guess I owe you my life. If it wasn't for you, I'd be moleworm food right now."

"It's nothing. Buy the next round and we're even."

"I like to think my life has a higher exchange value than the price of a bottle of beer."

"You go on thinking that."

Trundell looked puzzled, until it slowly dawned on him that Dev was teasing. "The trouble is you're too deadpan for me. I have difficulty telling when people are being funny or not. At school, other kids would make cruel remarks and I couldn't work out if they were bullying or just doing that thing that friends do."

"Banter."

"Yeah. It was a confusing time. That's why I like insects. Insects are logical. They have rules. Occasionally they break them, but mostly they abide by them and, if they don't, they get killed and eaten. Insects make sense. People don't."

Dev performed a quick scan of Trundell's face, concentrating on the eyes. It was more a reflex response than anything. He doubted very much that the xeno-entomologist was a Polis+ agent, but a statement about people not making sense was just the sort of thing an AI sentience might let slip in an unguarded moment.

There was no Uncanny Valley as far as he could ascertain. From the sound of it, Trundell was somewhere on the autistic spectrum, a human with a touch of robot about him. Plussers, ironically, were beings of passion and fervour, driven by zealotry and faith. They were digital entities who embraced religious ideology, individual agglomerations of terabytes of data who clung to the irrational for meaning and support in their lives. About as unrobotic as you could get, for all that they customarily inhabited mech bodies.

Plussers hated flesh. Flesh was troublesome and frail. They were comfortable housed inside machines, but organic matter gave them the squirms, and it showed. Uncanny Valley. A deadness, a *lostness*, in the eyes. A look of being adrift, of being consigned to a prison that was repugnant at every level.

No, Trundell didn't have it. Although in certain respects he *could* have been a Plusser. The way his brain was wired, humanity was an awkward, messy concept to him, too.

"Does it happen often?" Dev said. "Moleworm attacks? If scroaches are what they love most for dinner, I'd have thought running into them was an occupational hazard for you."

"Do I look like I bump into moleworms every day?"

"That's why I asked. You certainly didn't act like it down in those tunnels. It was almost as though you'd never had a face-to-face encounter with one before."

"I hadn't. Tonight was my first. But that's the odd thing. I've heard moleworms burrowing around, plenty of times, but only ever at a distance. They normally confine themselves to the lower lithosphere, the base stratum of Alighieri's upper mantle. Scroaches are more abundant down there, the pickings easier."

"They're not meant to come up this high?"

"I wouldn't say not *meant* to. Anecdotally, though, it's rare for them to hunt up here near the planetary crust. It's rare, too, to find them so close to human habitation."

"Even though we're something they don't mind eating?"

Trundell nodded. "They don't like our technology and industry. Our machinery makes too much noise, too much constant vibration. It upsets them. Overloads their sensory organs, especially their feelers. Repels them."

"Interesting. So what do you reckon accounts for the change in their behaviour patterns?"

"I don't know. I'm not well-versed in their habits. You'd be better off speaking to a xeno-mammalogist or maybe even a xeno-ethologist." Trundell's face registered suspicion. "Why are you quizzing me like this? Actually, come to think of it, who are you?"

"I'm the guy who kept you from ending up in a moleworm's stomach. Don't forget that."

"Yes, but I'm starting to wonder about you. You're built like an Alighierian, but you've never heard of a moleworm until today."

"I'm from off-planet."

"Obviously, but the most recent gulf cruiser was three months ago, the one I came in on. You can't have lived here that long and not learned the most basic facts about the place. It's like you've only just been born, but you have an adult's body."

That wasn't an inaccurate summation, Dev thought.

"Look," he said, "don't make a big fuss over what I'm about to tell you. Promise?"

"Okayyy."

"I'm ISS."

"You're kidding!"

"I'm not."

"Whoa. Then that's – that's a vat-grown host form. Awesome. I've never seen one in the flesh, so to speak. Can I... Can I touch it?"

"It? You mean me? I suppose so. If it'll make you happy."

Dev rolled up his sleeve and held out his arm. Trundell hesitantly and reverently ran fingers up and down the bare skin. A trio of miners in the adjacent booth glanced over and shared a snigger.

"What?" Dev challenged them.

"Nothing," said one of the miners. "There's a bar a couple of doors down where you two lovebirds might feel more at home, that's all. The Seventh Circle."

"Thank you. I'll see you there later."

The miner rose from his seat with a growl, but his drinking buddies advised him to leave it. It wasn't worth it. Out here, in public, all starting a fight would do was bring the cops down on their heads.

He sat back down, giving Dev one last hard glare.

"It really is the pinnacle of gene technology,"

said Trundell. "An entire, perfect body created out of stimulus-triggered pluripotent stem cells. Every single transcription factor calculated and regulated. Telomerase activation to prevent flaws occurring in accelerated DNA replication. All painstakingly constructed within a bath of peptide nutrient. You're a miracle of science, sir."

"Yes, I feel like that every day."

"You're deadpanning again, aren't you? That was sarcasm."

"A little."

"Honestly, if I were you, I'd take a moment out to think about what I am. A human consciousness downloaded into a bespoke, environment-compatible, fully-functioning physical self. What ISS's research and development department have done – it fair boggles the mind."

Dev shrugged. "I guess miracles of science kind of lose their shine the more you're exposed to them."

"How many host forms have you been in?"

"So far? I don't know. I've lost count. Twenty or so?"

"Is it disorientating? How long does it take to acclimatise?" Trundell was in science-wonk raptures. He appeared to have almost forgotten about his moleworm-related near-death experience a short while earlier.

"Depends," said Dev. "Some host forms are more extensively tailored than others."

"Yes. I can see that. The greater the deviation from Terratypical, the more variant factors there are to get used to. Have you tried amphibiousness yet? I'm not sure I could manage breathing water."

"I still have that to look forward to. I'm sure it'll happen soon enough. I get sent just about everywhere in the Diaspora, so I imagine, by the law of averages, I'll wind up on a liquid planet eventually. My life is one long magical mystery tour."

"At least you don't have to undergo infraspace journey times. Weeks of shipbound boredom. As a beam of pure data, you're virtually massless, so you can whizz through ultraspace as fast as any interstellar communications signal."

"Yup. Me and emails – we travel together."

"I'm slightly envious."

"Don't be."

"What made you sign up with ISS?"

"How come, all of a sudden, I'm on the receiving end of the questions?" said Dev.

The *why* of his indenture to ISS – it was a thorny issue, one he was reluctant to explore with someone he had only just met. Or, indeed, with *anyone*.

On the stage, the lead singer had begun snarling his way through 'Jerusalem.' "An' did those feet in ayn-chunt tiiyyiiyyiimes..."

"Because I like to know stuff," Trundell said simply.

"Let's say I'm a man who pays his debts, and leave it at that," Dev said.

Trundell took the hint.

"Okay, so can I ask what you're on Alighieri for?"

"The scenery. The wildlife. The friendly locals."

JAMES LOVEGROVE

Dev lofted a glance at the miners nearby. The most antagonistic of the three responded with a hitch of his chin and a steely stare. Dev was tempted to blow them a kiss, but that really would be asking for trouble.

"Or the earthquakes," said Trundell. "*That's* why you were in the geodes. Must be. You were investigating."

"Yeah. Sure. Correct."

Better that than admitting it was all down to chance and misadventure.

"I have to admit, I reckon there's a connection between the tremors and the anomalous moleworm behaviour," said Trundell.

Dev leaned forward. "How so?"

"Not sure. I have no evidence, no data. But if there are seismic disturbances in the moleworms' realm, that's likely to cause them to act erratically and out of character, isn't it? To stray from their usual feeding grounds, for instance. Stands to reason."

"When you put it like that, I suppose it does," said Dev. "Hey. Here's a thought. Would you be willing to look into that a bit further for me?"

"What, you mean switch from studying scroaches to studying moleworms?"

"Only for a while."

"No, thanks."

"Just to establish how and why the earthquakes are affecting them. There may be some pattern there, something relevant I can use."

"Uh-uh." Trundell gave a firm shake of the head. "I can just about cope with the danger posed by

Dromopoda alighieriensis. Moleworms? That's a whole order of magnitude worse. Monitoring *them* would be suicide."

"'I guess I owe you my life.' Now, who said that to me, not five minutes ago?"

"No. No emotional blackmail."

"Don't you want to help out ISS? Wouldn't it be cool, playing sidekick to a genuine, bonafide miracle of science?"

"Sidekick?"

"I'm not asking you to expose yourself to undue risk. If you could just track moleworm movements, gather me as much intel on them as you can..."

"Well, I guess, theoretically, within reason, it's not impossible."

"You're a smart guy with a PhD. I know you'd be able to figure out a way of getting close to them without putting yourself in harm's way."

"Maybe I could," said Trundell. "I'd have to do some background reading first. There's got to be literature on the subject. Was it Lockwood-Hazell who visited Alighieri a few years back? No, I remember, it was Banerjee."

He launched a file search via commmplant.

Dev rapped on the tabletop. "Not now."

"I'm just looking up Banerjee's paper on extraterrestrial *pseudotalpidae* – moleworms. It's cached at Harvard, but a couple of local mirror sites carry it too."

"How about you save it for later, when you're on your own?"

"Won't take a moment."

"Trundle."

"How many times? It's Trun*dell*."

"There we go. And he's back."

"It's really irritating when you get my name wrong."

"So, are you in or out?" said Dev.

"I don't know," Trundell sighed. "It could be interesting, I suppose. A break from the routine."

"A challenge."

"Yeah. I can draw on some of the more general aspects of my zoology degree, before I specialised."

"It's also a good fit with your current studies. Mightn't you learn more about scroaches by learning more about their main predator?"

"It'll be useful peripheral material. Yes, I like that. I'm in."

Dev clinked the neck of his bottle against Trundell's. "See? I knew you had it in you, young man. Cheers."

"Cheers."

14

TRUNDELL STAYED FOR another round, then hurried off home, fired up with enthusiasm, keen to begin his foray into moleworm research. Before he left, he and Dev exchanged commplant addresses. Trundell was flattered when Dev immediately upgraded his contact status from Normal to Priority.

Dev felt slightly guilty about manipulating the kid like that, preying on his neediness and his professional vanity. What if Trundell messed up and got himself killed by moleworms? He chided himself; the scientist was sensible, he'd take every conceivable precaution.

Whether or not anything valuable would come from his efforts – that was another matter.

The main thing was, Dev had set several balls rolling, already, after only a few hours on Alighieri. He could content himself that he had done a decent day's work. The game was afoot. ISS probably wanted him to file an interim progress report, but screw that. They could wait.

He ordered another beer, then another. He was thirsty. Drink plenty of fluids, Junius Bilk had said. So why not?

Too late, he remembered that drinking heavily in a brand new host form was not a good idea.

Hell, even drinking moderately wasn't wise.

Four bottles of beer would never have troubled him in his normal body. Especially the weak, watery brew this bar was serving. He'd barely be getting a buzz on by now if he was his old self.

A brand new host form, however, was pristine, unsullied. It hadn't built up a tolerance to booze yet, the way his true body had. It didn't have a liver that was accustomed to processing several units of alcohol nightly. Dev had been a steady drinker since the age of sixteen, whereas this host form was tasting its very first drop of the hard stuff.

The terrible truth hit him as he stood to go to the toilet and all the blood in his head cascaded to his legs. He was wasted.

He reeled across the room, while the band murdered 'Amazing Grace' with feral glee.

In the men's room – the same men's room where, after arriving at the bar, he had spent several minutes scrubbing scroach gore off himself – he emptied his bladder and washed his hands. Splashing cold water on his face didn't help revive him.

Things were swirling. The man in the mirror above the basin stared back at him dully. A stranger, who happened to blink whenever Dev blinked and scowl whenever Dev scowled.

On the wall there was a vending machine selling Blitz-Go sobriety pills – oral doses of nanocapsule enzymes that kicked the alcohol-metabolising process into high gear. *Three minutes to a clear head!* the floatscreen strapline promised.

There was even a touchpad interface for those too intoxicated to operate their commplants competently. It allowed the vending machine to override your security protocols on a one-off basis to facilitate a purchase. All that was required was a DNA sample from your sweat to confirm your identity.

Since Dev's host form wasn't registered on Alighieri's ID database, that method wouldn't work for him. Frowning hard, he tried to activate his banking details the usual way.

The men's room door opened and closed behind him.

He turned – staggered round, really – and there were the three miners from the next-door booth. They, too, were drunk, but not the kind of spinny-head drunk that Dev was. Mean drunk.

The ringleader cracked his knuckles and, without a word, took a swing at Dev.

What followed was far from elegant.

It wasn't a fight.

It was even a brawl.

It was a ferocious, clumsy free-for-all, full of shouting and flailing and bodies smashing into inanimate objects and inanimate objects smashing into bodies.

The miners, the ringleader in particular, bellowed names at Dev: *faggot, queer, cocksucker.*

Dev didn't dignify that with a retort. Besides, he was too busy concentrating on staying on his feet and getting his shots in.

Three to one. On paper, it was hardly fair.

It became two to one when Dev knocked one of the miners unconscious by ramming his face against a toilet stall door.

Then Dev found his own face being dunked into a toilet bowl and held under by two pairs of callused hands.

He flashed back to his conversation with Trundell about host form adaptations. Breathing water? Maybe he was about to discover what that was like.

But the water and the dread of drowning did do something for him. Not quite a Blitz-Go, but the adrenaline surge restored him part-way to his senses, bringing some clarity.

He elbowed one of his assailants in the side of his knee. He felt the crunchy click of a patella dislocating and heard the satisfying scream of a man in immense, crippling pain.

He came up, heaving for air, and grabbed the hobbled miner by the shoulders.

The miner's skull met the edge of the toilet bowl with enough force to break them both.

Which left just the ringleader.

If the man was alarmed or surprised to find himself alone, his friends out of commission, he didn't show it. He was probably too far gone to care. He rushed at Dev like a bloodshot-eyed bull, slamming him spine-first against a basin.

Ceramic shattered, and water sprayed from snapped faucets.

Dev and the miner slugged away at each other like punchdrunk boxers in a clinch, skidding across the wet floor tiles.

At some point, one of them fell; Dev was mildly astonished to find that it wasn't himself.

The miner groaned through pulped lips, and Dev kicked him in the head until he shut up.

After that, he slumped to his knees. Blood mingled with the puddles of water on the floor. It came from his knuckles, his forehead, his nose, his mouth.

What a fucking mess.

When he next looked up, police were barging through the door. They surrounded him, yelping like a pack of dogs. He couldn't make out what they were saying over the high-pitched ringing in his ears.

He must have made a movement which one of the police officers interpreted as aggressive. Or he didn't. Either way, they mosquitoed him.

Then they did it a second time, for good measure.

His body became a stupid, floppy thing, a meat sack. He could do nothing as the police officers trussed him up in restraints and bundled him out of the bar. They were not gentle. Now and then a fist struck him, or a foot, as if by accident.

He felt it, but it was as though someone else was feeling it.

It wasn't so bad, really. Not when he could

remember all too clearly the sensation of being riddled by ferromagnetic rounds entering his body at hypersonic speed from a Polis+ coilgun. Of being battered helplessly by kinetic forces that turned him into a dancing marionette.

Of being flayed alive.

Of dying.

15

"Harmer, Harmer, Harmer..."

The face of Chief of Police Kahlo hovered above him like a gibbous moon.

"Urrgh," said Dev.

"That's all you have to say for yourself?"

Dev struggled up to a sitting position. Every organ in his body seemed to be slipping out of alignment. His brain was trying to ooze out of his cranium via his eye sockets and his nostrils. His stomach was pushing against his lungs; his heart slumped a little further sideways with every beat.

It was the mother of all hangovers.

"Latrine's over there, if you're going to barf," Kahlo said. "Just be sure to aim away from me. I put a fresh-pressed uniform on this morning."

Dev peered blearily around. A bunk, wipe-clean walls and floor. Recessed overhead lighting behind shatterproof plastic.

Holding cell. He was back at the Calder's Edge police headquarters.

"I must lodge a complaint with the management," he said. "This isn't the five-star penthouse suite I was promised. Where's my hot tub?"

"Hey, count your blessings. You got a private room and your own bed. You could've been stowed with all the other drunk-and-disorderlies, but last night was a busy one. Seems like half of Calder's went on a bender. The drying-out tank was full. They were packed on the floor like sardines. Can't blame them, I suppose. These quakes. The pressure's getting to people."

Dev did a quick inventory of his injuries. Contusions everywhere, several stiff muscles, swollen knuckles. One loosened tooth. A half-closed eye. What might have been a cracked – but was probably just a badly bruised – rib. Maybe a torn rotator cuff tendon.

"Ouch," he said as he experimented gingerly with the shoulder. If not torn, the tendon was certainly wrenched.

"You treat these host forms like rental cars, is that it?" said Kahlo. "Doesn't matter how many dents and dings you put in the bodywork because they're not your own?"

"No," he said. "Well, kind of. Not exactly. Put it this way: it doesn't matter *as much*. I'm only in it for the short term, not the long haul."

"Hence you pull these stupid stunts. I mean, you had me beating you up about three minutes after you got here. Then you assault the doorman at Inferno."

"You know about that?"

"Jacko Dusenberg, the owner, filed a complaint.

We extrapolated backwards, cross-checked security footage, found you in the vicinity of the club at the correct time. Dusenberg IDed you. You assaulted him as well, but I talked him out of pressing charges because he was associating with Franz Glazkov."

"Who I was tailing."

"Right. I put two and two together and threatened Dusenberg with arrest for consorting with a known dealer in unlicensed pharmaceuticals. He caved."

"You're my guardian angel."

"Don't get cocky," said Kahlo. "And now, to cap it all, you wind up in a bar fight. You hospitalise three mine employees."

"I didn't start it. I only made sure I finished it."

"Fortunately for you, I believe you. We have eyewitnesses saying the three guys followed you into the men's room. They were talking about teaching you a lesson. They didn't want 'your kind' stinking up their favourite watering hole."

"They weren't the most enlightened human beings I've met. You could have them up for hate crimes, if you like."

"I think they've been punished enough already. But Harmer, help me out here. Why is it you can't seem to stay out of trouble? You haven't been on Alighieri one day, and shit just keeps happening around you."

"It's not something I encourage."

"Were those miners another attempt on your life, do you think? Did somebody pay them?"

"No, it was a... misunderstanding. They got an idea into their heads that they shouldn't have.

They're the sort of people who don't need much of an excuse to pick on the sort of people they don't like."

"You're sure about that?"

"As much as I can be."

Kahlo grunted in annoyance. "So, doesn't tell me why you're incapable of keeping a low profile and simply getting on with what you're supposed to be doing."

"I told you, that bar thing, it genuinely wasn't my fault."

"You were drunk, though."

"That wasn't my fault either." Or was it? Maybe it had been, just a little. The Alighierians weren't the only ones who were feeling the pressure and needing an outlet, a way of alleviating it.

"I just find it baffling that you're so... so *irresponsible*. So cavalier. Such a damn liability. Why have ISS sent us someone like you? Do they hate us?"

"We can't all be by-the-book cops," Dev said. "I'm unconventional. I have my own methods. But I'm known to get results. Otherwise ISS wouldn't use me."

"Well, they must see qualities in you that I don't. If you were under my command, I'd have fired you by now. Maybe 'consultant' means something different to your bosses. Like: 'shambolic trouble magnet.'"

Kahlo let out a breath as though expelling all her pent-up frustration in one go. She then drew a slow in-breath, resetting herself, inducing calm.

"All right," she said. "I'm going to move past how exasperating you are and how much you're pissing me off. I'm a big girl; I can handle jerks like you. Have done all my life. If I have to work with you, then so be it."

"That's the spirit," said Dev. "Find your inner tranquillity. Go to your happy place."

"My happy place would be thumping you in the head until you stop talking."

"Imagine that, then. Let it bring you bliss."

Kahlo pretended she was picturing it in her mind's eye. "Yep. Feels great now. So, between chasing Glazkov and demolishing a men's room with, by the looks of it, your face – find out anything useful? Any progress at all?"

"Well, Glazkov was a wild goose chase. You were right on that front."

"Bet it hurt to say that."

"Like a needle in the eyeball. He's just a low-level hustler. Bottom feeder scuzz. But he did lead me, inadvertently, to something more promising."

"Which is...?"

"I know now that the earth tremors have got your moleworms all discombobulated."

"And? What about it?"

"And I've enlisted someone to enquire further into it – someone with the relevant expertise."

Kahlo leaned back against the cell wall and folded her arms, unimpressed. "Upset moleworms? That's all you've got for me?"

"I think it's a viable lead."

She shook her head in wonderment and dismay. "That host form must have cost ISS millions. I hope they think they're getting their money's worth."

"Ultimately it's TerCon that's picking up the tab. ISS are just private government contractors."

"If the taxpayers only knew..."

Dev nodded, then stopped. His head felt as though it was going to break free and topple off his spinal column.

"What about you?" he said. "Any luck with the rail network people?"

"Well, you were right, too."

"Bet it hurt to say that."

"Like needles in the eyeball. They ran the Polisware scan like you suggested. It flagged up an external attack on the server by a Plusser malware bot. The bot tiptoed round the firewalls, took over, shut everyone else out, caused havoc, then expired, leaving no trace. At least, none that the standard security programs could detect."

"They're pretty sophisticated things, Plusser bots. Like electronic kamikaze cat burglars. Where did it originate from?"

"They can't seem to find out. It doesn't appear to be off-world. No ultraspace encryption signature. Somewhere on Alighieri, but they can't figure out precisely where. Not enough left of it after it self-destructed to extrapolate a vector pathway from."

"That settles it, then. There's a Plusser agent on-planet."

"A Plusser who knows you're here and who

introduced the malware into the rail network server in a bid to get rid of you. Can't say it's an unpardonable offence. If you're half as irritating to Polis Plus as you are to me..."

"Oh, I am."

"But listen up, Harmer," Kahlo said. "In all seriousness, the reason I'm continuing to tolerate you – and not planning on leaving you in this cell to rot – is that this Plusser nearly killed me and two of my men along with you. The attempt on your life was also an attempt on mine, Utz's and Stegman's."

"For what it's worth, I'm sorry. I'm glad it didn't succeed."

"That's sweet. You almost sound sincere. Now, I happen to take very personally an attack on myself, and very, very personally an attack on my subordinates. That's why I'm going to overlook your sheer blatant inadequacy so far and give you a second chance. Because I don't know jack-shit about Plussers, whereas you, for better or worse, do."

"More than I care to."

"Yes, you faced them in the war. You know what they're about. Like it or not – and I don't – you're our best bet for dealing with them if they're trying to establish a foothold on Alighieri."

"Which they are," said Dev. "All that lovely helium-three. It's like honey to a bear."

"So let's get cracking, shall we?" Kahlo rubbed her hands together demonstratively. "Up and at 'em, soldier."

Dev levered himself off the bunk. It wasn't the

finest ever example of standing up. Kahlo caught him by the arm and steadied him, and he didn't quite collapse.

"And this is the watchman on the Border Wall," she said with a despairing roll of the eyes. "Patrolling the perimeter of the Diaspora to keep us all safe."

"At your service, ma'am," Dev said with a wonky salute.

"We are so fucked."

16

AN ENERGY DRINK and a Blitz-Go pill later, Dev felt marginally more human. Kahlo gave him a tube of topical curative gel which he slathered over his tender areas. The endocannabinoids and regenerative proteins went to work, combating inflammation and boosting the rate of tissue repair a hundredfold.

Spruced up, hungover no more, he was a new man.

"Where to?" he asked Kahlo.

She consulted her commplant clock. "As it happens, we've a meeting scheduled. Word came down an hour ago."

"Sounds important. Who with?"

"The governor."

"Ah. What's he want?"

"Unclear. He's the one who put in the application for ISS intervention, so I imagine he'd like to scope you out. Can't help but think he'll be disappointed. Patrolman Utz is taking us there."

In short order, they were scooting along maglev rails in a police pod.

"I see yesterday hasn't put you off driving after all," Dev said to Utz.

"I figure the same thing can't happen to the same guy twice. The odds against must be astronomical."

"Sensible man."

"Besides," said Kahlo, "the rail network server's proofed against another malware attack of the same kind. ISS bundled a shield in with the Polisware scan."

"Even better," said Utz. "Let's all sit back and enjoy the ride."

The governor's residence had its own station and was ensconced within a high rock arch that, though a natural formation, described an almost perfectly symmetrical parabola. The entrance foyer was suspended from the underside of the arch, a disc of glass and concrete with a three-hundred-and-sixty-degree panoramic view. There was hardly an inch of Calder's Edge that couldn't be seen from it.

Governor Graydon kept them waiting several minutes, but finally his personal assistant arrived to usher them up to see him. Only Dev and Kahlo went; Utz stayed downstairs.

"Above my paygrade," he said with a shrug.

The personal assistant, crisp but amiable, made small talk as the elevator rose. She apologised for the delay. The governor – such a busy man.

She seemed to know Kahlo well, treating her as a close colleague. Kahlo's answers, however, were stiff and curt. Dev got the distinct impression the chief of police was ill-at-ease. If Graydon had the power to unnerve someone like her, then he must be a formidable proposition.

In the event, the man who greeted them in his office couldn't have appeared less intimidating. He was short and thickset, like any Alighierian, but he had a bonhomie and a polish that most of his kin lacked.

What also set him apart was his entirely bald scalp. Treatment to regrow dermal papillae was inexpensive; no one need have no hair. Graydon therefore either chose to shave it off or else didn't mind that it had all fallen out.

The effect was striking. You looked twice at him. You wouldn't forget him in a hurry.

Governor Maurice Graydon was a canny operator, that much was clear to Dev.

Yet his smile seemed genuine. Nothing of the usual politician's disingenuousness about it.

"Astrid, come in. And you must be Mr Harmer."

The handshake was brisk but firm.

"Drink? I have Japanese whisky. Single malt. Import. Not the stuff we distil on-planet, and all the better for it."

He held out the bottle for inspection. Dev let out a low whistle. It was the real deal. Yamazaki, all the way from Osaka.

"Yes, hideously pricey. Transportation costs alone make every drop worth rather more than its weight in gold. My one small luxury. Some say only Scotland knows the art of producing good whisky, but Japan has it down to a science. Tempted?"

Dev was. Sorely. But he recalled the previous night. The hangover might be gone and the aches and pains from the fight fading, but the memory still lingered.

With some regret, he shook his head.

"And you won't, Astrid," Graydon said. "Not on duty. So I won't even ask."

The governor helped himself to a couple of fingers of the whisky and returned the bottle to the sideboard. Then, cradling the tumbler as though it contained the secret of happiness itself, he led the way across the expansive office to the picture window filling the far wall.

The panes retracted at the touch of a sensor, giving access onto a broad balcony perched on cantilevered struts. Graydon stepped out and, with a small gesture, invited Dev and Kahlo to follow.

"I like to get outside as much as possible," he said. "I realise it's not *outside* outside, Mr Harmer. Not outside as you would understand the term. But this is Alighieri. The concept of the great outdoors is relative here, and tends not to involve such things as sky and trees."

The cavern echoed to the sounds of life and industry, a soft reverberant hubbub.

"That," said Governor Graydon, "is the hum of Calder's Edge as it should be. Everything functioning. A city going about its daily business. It isn't a perfect place, as I'd be the first to admit. But when it works, it works."

He took a sip of whisky.

"Ahh, pleasures of the flesh. Never to be

underrated. When *we're* gone, *they're* gone. Best enjoy them while you can. Where was I?"

"The city doing its business," said Dev.

"Yes. Too often lately, things haven't been going so smoothly. Even if you can't hear it, there's tension down there. People are on tenterhooks, waiting. They don't know if, when, another earthquake will strike. They don't know how severe it might be. They're scared it might be a big one – an earthquake that will bring everything crashing down. The end of their world."

Another sip. Dev's eyes lingered on the amber elixir.

"There's no saying that's a likely outcome. We're in uncharted waters. Nothing like this has happened in the city's – the planet's – history. Perhaps, as some are claiming, it's a natural cyclical event, Alighieri going through a period of stretching and groaning, like an old man with creaky joints, working out the knots of arthritis. The geological record would appear to suggest that it isn't, but we can't rely on that."

"You don't think it's a natural event any more than I do, sir," said Kahlo.

"As I've told you countless times, Astrid, there's no need to call me 'sir.' Not when it's just us here, you, me."

"I understand, sir."

Graydon grinned wryly, indulgently. "No, I don't think it's natural at all. But I can't for the life of me figure out what else it is."

JAMES LOVEGROVE

He swivelled to face Dev again.

"Which is where you come in, my good man. Believe me, it wasn't something I did lightly, going to the Terran Consensus on bended knee, begging for help. We're a fiercely independent little world, Alighieri. We like to look after our own. But I couldn't just let the situation continue as it is. We needed a troubleshooter. A professional."

"That's me," said Dev.

"That's you. And please don't be offended when I say I'd rather you hadn't had to come."

"I won't. I'm used to it. ISS consultants tend to be called in only as a last resort. And usually only when covert enemy activity is suspected."

"That's the thing. I don't know if this is enemy activity, but at the same time I can't rule it out. Alighieri is in a vulnerable position, stuck out at the further extremity of the Border Wall. We're several hundred light years from the next Diasporan solar system. We've got Polis Plus worlds closer to us than human worlds. It's a precarious position to be in."

"And your helium-three deposits make you a juicy prospect."

"We're a ripe apple the Plussers would love to pluck," said Graydon with a nod. "An apple they would suck the marrow out of in no time, if you'll pardon the mixed metaphor. So when something untoward occurs, something worrying and unprecedented, like now, then I can't help but think that Polis Plus must be behind it."

He studied both their expressions.

"As, it would appear, do you," he said gravely.

"It's looking that way, sir," said Kahlo.

She summarised the evidence: rail network takeover, Polis+ malware bot, Plusser agent somewhere on-planet.

"They took a bold step," she said. "Whoever it is, they must have realised that doing what they did was effectively an announcement of their presence. Like hoisting a big damn flag. Which tells me that they're confident and they're well-hidden."

"Or perhaps desperate," said Graydon. "So frightened of our Mr Harmer that they'll stop at nothing to eliminate him, even if it entails compromising their own security and anonymity."

"You can call me Dev."

"Thank you, Dev. I will. And you can call me Maurice. At least with you I can be a little less formal, unlike with Captain Kahlo."

Dev had offered Graydon the option to use his forename only out of a sense of mischief. He couldn't fathom the relationship between the governor and the police chief, the reason for Kahlo's frostiness towards Graydon; but that didn't mean he couldn't have fun putting himself on friendlier terms with Graydon than she was. It was likely to annoy her, and that made it worthwhile.

Dev revelled in getting under Kahlo's skin. It didn't help that she made it so absurdly easy. She was accustomed to deference and obedience. He enjoyed bringing a little anarchy into her life.

Knowing she was being provoked, Kahlo shot

him a disdainful glance, then said to Graydon: "I imagine the prospect of an ISS operative on the ground alarmed the Plusser. ISS have a reputation. Polis Plus have had reason in the past to fear them. In this instance, though, it led to an unfortunate overreaction."

Touché, thought Dev. *Overreaction*. Implying that he himself was not up to the standard of his ISS peers.

"What it also tells us," Kahlo continued, "is that the Plusser agent knew Harmer was coming. That in turn indicates that they're resourceful and may have backdoor access to some of our securest servers, not just at rail network control."

"How so?" said Graydon.

"Isn't it obvious? How many people knew that an ISS consultant had been called in? You. Me. A couple of other police officers. Probably a few of your staff. That's it. So either the Plusser is one of them, someone in the Calder's Edge upper echelons..."

"Unthinkable."

"Let's hope so. Or they intercepted a communiqué about Harmer."

"An internal one?"

"Maybe one of your or my memos."

"Or, possibly, the request I sent to TerCon in the first place. Can they do that?"

The question was directed at Dev.

"Polis Plus listening posts have been known to hack ultraspace messages," Dev replied.

"But what about encryption?"

"There's nothing we've been able to come up with that they can't crack. That's the trouble when you're dealing with beings who are pure information themselves. They have an affinity for data. It's their language, their essence. Even our most complex quantum-key ciphertext algorithms can't keep them out. They pick them apart as easily as unravelling yarn."

"Damn."

"It was our one major tactical weakness at the start of the war. High command couldn't transmit orders without there being a good chance that the Plussers would eavesdrop. The same went for commplant contact among troops on the battlefield. We got round the second problem by going old-school and resorting to shortwave radio transmission."

"What about the first problem?" said Graydon. "Oh wait, I think I remember. Wasn't there some kind of trick?"

"Yes. Military intelligence advised the top brass to start using cryptic crossword clues instead of straightforward sentences. The Plussers just couldn't make head or tail of them. They lack the necessary capacity for lateral thinking."

"Ha!"

"Of course it meant that every battalion had to have its resident 'word nerd' to translate strings of puns and verbal rebuses into meaningful instructions. Those guys became our linchpins, the members of personnel we could least afford to lose. They were also brainiac introverts with almost zero combat savvy. It made for some interesting times. But it worked, that's the main thing. Our edge over Polis Plus. It's how we won the war."

"Or forced the Plussers into a stalemate, some would say," Graydon added.

"Hey, any end to a war that isn't capitulation is a victory. We beat them because of the human factor. No question; at a purely intellectual level, they're smarter than us by far. Their minds process at a rate ours can't hope to compete with. What they don't have is a knack for creative thought."

"They can't think outside the box because, for them, there *is* no outside the box."

"Yeah, who said that? It was President-Marshal Ferreira, wasn't it? She was right. And it applies still, even with TerCon officially on a peacetime footing, even when there's no war on but a cold war. Hence ISS employ people who are sometimes reckless. Irresponsible. Cavalier, perhaps. Even – how to phrase it? – a damn liability."

Kahlo showed no emotion at having her own words quoted back.

"Because that sort of person operates in the Plussers' blind spot," Dev concluded.

Graydon raised his glass to Dev and drained the last few drops.

"Oh, I like this fellow," he said. "Astrid, don't you like this fellow?"

Kahlo said, "I judge people by their accomplishments, not their personalities."

"Of course you do. Of course you do. But you

can't deny he has a way about him. I'm feeling more optimistic already."

"All part of the service, Maurice," said Dev.

"Now, if you two don't mind, I have work to do. My inbox is bulging. No rest for the elected. Dev, pleasure to meet you."

"Likewise."

"And Astrid? I'm glad you survived your close shave with the freight shuttle. Had that gone worse, it would have been a terrible thing. A terrible thing."

As they re-entered Graydon's office from the balcony, the floor began to shiver underfoot.

"Oh, for –" Graydon gripped the back of a chair.

The tremor increased in intensity. Furniture began to dance, and the ornaments trembled.

The vibrations pulsed and pulsed like waves breaking on a shore. Dev wondered how sturdy the rock arch was. He envisaged it fracturing at the base, cracks shooting up its sides like lightning bolts, the whole thing crumbling, collapsing, tumbling in pieces...

Then his eye fell on the bottle of Yamazaki whisky. It had shimmied across the sideboard all the way to the edge, where it was teetering, about to fall.

He dived across the shuddering room, arm outstretched. The bottle tipped off the sideboard. He caught it inches above the floor.

The tremor dwindled, then petered out altogether.

Graydon unclamped his hand from the chair back and smoothed out his tie. Dev passed him the whisky bottle, which he took with solemn appreciation.

"Quick reactions. Thank you."

"When something precious is threatened, I try and keep it safe," Dev said. "That refers mostly to my own life, but it applies to other things too."

"Like my city, I trust."

"Very much so."

17

"WELL, *HE* COULDN'T have been nicer," Dev said in the elevator on the way down. "Almost decent – for a politician. It's no surprise he's governor. I'd have voted for him."

"Suck-up," said Kahlo.

"It pays to get on the good side of people in power."

"Hence your stunt with the whisky bottle."

"That? No, I'd have done that whoever owned it. Good booze is a work of art." He studied Kahlo's hard expression. "You really don't like him, do you? What is it between you two? He try to impose budget cuts on the police or something?"

"The answer can be found in the file marked *None Of Your Damn Business*."

"Only, you and me, the two of us..." – Dev waved a hand back and forth across the space between them – "I feel like we're starting to bond. Overcoming our differences. In the light of that, we should feel free to open up to each other. It's what pals do."

"I know you're being facetious," said Kahlo. "That's why I'm not holding you down right now and trying to punch some sense into you."

"No, but really. You and Graydon. What's up?"

The elevator came to a halt and Kahlo strode out into the foyer without another word.

"Tough nut to crack," Dev muttered to himself. "But I'm like pliers. Apply enough pressure, sooner or later the shell gives."

Patrolman Utz had some bad news. "Apologies, ma'am, but we can't leave for the time being. That tremor just now, it damaged a section of the rails. A couple of support pylons across town are looking suspect. The entire network has been shut down as a safety precaution while an engineering team sends out inspection drones to take a look."

"How long?"

"Half an hour, I'm told. An hour at most. If it's only those pylons, they'll isolate that section of track and restart the rest of the network in phased stages."

Kahlo took herself off to a corner of the foyer, where she sat and caught up with paperwork via commplant. Like most people teleworking, she appeared to be in a deep trance state. Now and then her lips might move, silently mouthing the sentences her brain was transmitting.

"So, Utz..."

"Yeah?"

"Her and Graydon." Dev jerked a thumb at Kahlo. She was far enough across the foyer to be out of earshot, but he kept his voice low anyway. "He seems to like her more than she likes him. What's the dynamic there?"

"It's not exactly a secret," said Utz. "You run a search on the chief, you'll soon find out."

"They used to be lovers? Is that it? And it ended messily?"

Utz laughed. "Shit, no. How old do you think he is?"

"So hard to tell with you Alighierians. No UV damage. Maybe he's had a few skin rejuvenation treatments, too. I'd guess forty? Forty-five?"

"Older than that. Old enough to be her father."

"Well, that doesn't preclude them from being lovers."

Utz laughed again, louder. "It does when he *is* her father."

Dev spent a few moments digesting this fact. "No way."

"Why not?"

"The surnames, for starters."

"Kahlo is her mother's maiden name. She was born Graydon. She changed it... I don't know when. Sometime around when she became a cop."

"What for?"

"Guess what? I've never asked. Not my place. Her background is her own affair. She's a terrific chief of police, she's firm but fair, she runs the force like a champ – that's all that matters to me. She doesn't allow her home life to get in the way of her work. She certainly hasn't let the governor being her daddy affect her administrative policies in any way."

"She didn't get to be where she is because of who her father is, then?"

"I'd say the opposite," said Utz. "She made police chief in spite of him. But listen, you can look it up for yourself. It's all online somewhere. Biogs, blogs, news items…"

Dev booted up his commplant and plunged into Alighieri's insite. He ran a basic search on Kahlo and alighted on her official CEPD page. She had risen fast through the ranks, since signing up as a cadet at the age of eighteen. She was a sergeant by twenty-one, a commander by twenty-seven, and chief of police by her early thirties. She had a long list of citations to her name and had been TerCon-commended for her crime clear-up rate several times.

A bit of an overachiever.

A murder case a few years back had won her plaudits in the local press. A child had died in a frenzied attack, stabbed dozens of times and sexually violated post mortem. The main suspect had been the girl's widower father, who had been stupor-drunk on the night in question and couldn't categorically state that he wasn't to blame. When he was arrested, a lynch mob mentality took hold over Calder's Edge. Citizens stormed police headquarters, baying for the man's blood.

Kahlo, as the principal investigating officer, went out and spoke to the angry throng. She managed to convince them to return to their homes, promising them that justice would be served.

In the meantime she had been painstakingly building

a case against another suspect, a neighbour of the dead girl, a man who had suffered sexual abuse himself as a child and had a history of violent behaviour. He was, by the sound of it, a stone cold hardcase, and Kahlo'd sweated him for thirty-six hours straight before she was able to make him crack and admit that he had broken into the house while the father was out cold on the bathroom floor, entered the girl's bedroom and done the deed.

By patience, stamina and attrition, she'd obtained a confession from the guilty party. By tact and diplomacy, she'd saved an innocent – if negligent – man from being torn apart by the crowd.

Little wonder that the position of chief of police became hers when the previous incumbent stepped down.

Further digging unearthed her familial ties to Maurice Graydon. Graydon had, it turned out, been governor of Calder's Edge for nearly twenty years, more than half his daughter's lifetime. Prior to that, he had been a miner and a trade union representative. A man of the people, but with the instincts and charisma of a born politician – a devastating combination.

Kahlo's mother, Soraya, had also been a miner, a driller rig driver. She had died when Kahlo was in her mid-teens. Some sort of industrial accident.

Dev could not dredge up any explicit connection between Kahlo's mother's death and Kahlo's decision to join the police force. Perhaps there was none.

It was significant, though, that she had signed up as Astrid Kahlo, not Astrid Graydon. Somehow the loss of her mother had driven a wedge between her and her father. Family tragedies could do that. Grief and loss were powerful catalysts. If there had already been discontent simmering between Kahlo and Graydon, Soraya's demise could have brought it to the boil. Dropping the Graydon name was a symbolic act of rejection.

Since her father was already in high political office by the time she embarked on her career in the police, the change of name suggested that Kahlo could also have been exhibiting independence, a desire to go it alone, free from the perceived patronage of Governor Graydon. Otherwise, any promotion she gained might have looked like nepotism. Also, her fellow officers might have been inclined to treated her with kid gloves, knowing she was the governor's daughter. Most of them would have been aware of the truth anyway. But Kahlo had been sending a message: *I may have been born a Graydon, but I choose not to be one now.*

Fascinating.

Dev closed the search. Kahlo had pried into his background; now he had pried into hers. That made them even.

"Busy?"

Kahlo was standing in front of him, hands on hips. Dev had been oblivious to her presence until she had spoken. That was often the way when you went sifting through information; you zoned out and lost situational awareness. The insite became a vortex that sucked you in.

"Just, er... checking out the indigenous porn."

"I'll bet you were."

"Always a revelation. You Alighierians have some weird kinks."

"Well, if you can tear yourself away from your anthropological studies, the rail network is back up and running, and we have places to be."

"Excellent. Where?"

"The heliumface. The Anoshkin Energiya Conglomerate mine, to be precise."

"What's happening there?"

"Nothing much. Just the entire workforce coming out on strike."

"Sounds like police business to me," said Dev. "Irate miners. Picket lines. Crowd control measures. Do you really need me along?"

"Normally I'd say no. But in this instance your attendance is required. In fact, you've been asked for specifically."

"By name?"

"No. The exact wording was 'that nosy bastard who had a bunch of innocent people detained against their will last night.' Ring any bells?"

"Sounds like that union leader guy. What's his name? Thorne. Ben Thorne."

"Bingo," said Kahlo. "I knew this one was going to come round and bite us on the backside. I should never have listened to you."

"What does he want with me?"

"Beats me. But you've ticked him off badly, if he's prepared to stage an all-out stoppage just so's he can get your attention."

"He probably fancies a nice little chinwag, that's all. Maybe he felt he and I had a connection in the interview room. He'd like to get to know me better."

"If you believe that, you're even stupider than you look."

18

THE ANOSHKIN ENERGIYA Conglomerate mine lay an hour west of Calder's Edge.

It was one of the largest mines on Alighieri, its workings extending for hundreds of kilomtres. Its highest shaft rose to within a few thousand feet of the planet's surface, where the concentrations of helium-3 were at their densest.

The entrance lay in a manmade cavern, a carved-out cubic gallery so large you couldn't quite see its edges from the centre. The floorspace was occupied by a tangle of maglev tracks that overlapped and criss-crossed like coils of spaghetti. Some of these were used by commuter trains that brought personnel to and from the mine. Others were used by transporter wagons to ferry the raw rock to the pulverisation plant, after which it was transferred by massive lifters to the converter units at the surface, where the five-hundred-degree daytime temperatures did the job of separating out the He-3 in its gaseous form, ready to be condensed for storage. The heat up there was so fierce that the average work shift lasted no longer than two hours, with the workers who supervised the conversion process clad in ceramic protective suits – shieldsuits – that were cryo-cooled by a liquid suspension of silver nanorods.

Around the main access tunnel opening, the transporter wagons sat in stationary rows, driver cabs unoccupied, flatbeds bare. The dual-door rooftop hatches on each gaped like the beaks of hungry baby birds begging for food. Nearby, cranes stood idle, their booms drooping.

It was the middle of the morning; the place ought to have been a frenzy of industry. The general stillness was notable and a little bit eerie.

Kahlo, with Dev in tow, approached a knot of people gathered outside the access tunnel. There were surly miners dressed in thin cotton underalls that had the Anoshkin Energiya logo printed on them: two electrons orbiting a nucleus consisting of a pair of protons and a neutron. There were also a pair of harassed-looking executives with the same logo embroidered on their breast pockets in gold braid.

"This is completely illegal," one of the executives was saying. "Your contracts clearly state that strike action cannot be called without management being notified and consulted beforehand. Nobody warned any of us that this was in the offing."

"What's that?" said one of the miners, cupping an ear. It was none other than Ben Thorne, head of the Fair Dues Collective. "Sorry, I can't hear you over the deafening noise of all this machinery. Oh, no, wait. There isn't any machinery going, because we're *on strike*."

"I could have your jobs for this. Click of the fingers, and you'd all be welfare fodder."

"Oh, yeah? And where are you going to get anyone to replace us? Anoshkin Energiya's going to magic up another eighteen hundred fully-trained employees just like that?"

The other miners growled and jeered.

"For your information," Thorne continued, "this strike is *not* illegal. We've called it for health and safety reasons. You may not be aware, but clause twenty-eight, subsection two of our contracts stipulates that should workers' wellbeing be in any way endangered or compromised, we are within our rights to walk out without giving prior notice."

"That means literally walk out of the mine, as in finding refuge elsewhere," said the executive.

"We choose it to mean walk out as in down tools and go on strike."

"A specious interpretation."

"Use big words all you like, but it's simple enough. Can you guarantee our safety right now? All these earthquakes – can you be sure that not one of us is going to suffer injury or lose his or her life because of them? There've been deaths over at Heinkel-Junger Erzbirgbau, and at the X-O-Geo Corporation mine. Maybe we're next."

"Anoshkin provides every conceivable measure of –"

"Can you tell us this mine is absolutely, one-hundred-per-cent quake-proof?"

"We abide by all the TerCon regulations concerning –"

"Put it this way," said Thorne. "Would you yourself, Mr Konstantinov, be willing to go into that mine behind me during a tremor?"

The executive, Konstantinov, blustered.

"Or you, Mr Savin?"

The other executive took refuge in purse-lipped silence.

Thorne said, "Thought as much. Therefore I and my brethren and sistren are legitimately calling a halt to drilling and excavation activities until such time as we have a cast-iron reassurance from you that we are no longer in jeopardy."

"I shall have to contact head office about this," said Konstantinov. "There are protocols I have to follow."

"You do that, Yuri old pal. Take your time. We're not going anywhere." Thorne turned. "And who's this? Captain Kahlo and friend. Thank you for coming. Much appreciated."

"Thorne," said Kahlo. "Rabble-rousing as usual."

"Merely fulfilling my remit as democratically-anointed leader of the FDC to look out for my members' interests. Yes, goodbye," Thorne called out to the departing Konstantinov and Savin. "Let me know what head office come back with. If it involves a pay rise of, ooh, about five per cent, tell them I'll consider it. Only consider, mind."

"So, money," said Kahlo. "That's what this is about."

"When is it ever not about money?" replied Thorne. "But it never hurts to exercise one's right to protest, either. Every once in a while, management needs to be reminded who's in charge. And you can't deny that these earthquakes are putting us pit folk at risk. It's high time somebody made a fuss about it, somebody decided to stand up and let their feelings be known."

"What a surprise that it would be you."

"You and I, captain, we don't have a disagreement," said Thorne. "I'm aggrieved about last night, but I realise now that *force majeure* was in play. For that I'm prepared to overlook your part in it."

"We're all right as long as you and your members keep the strike law-abiding and peaceful," Kahlo said.

"I do have a bone to pick with him, though." Thorne pointed at Dev.

Dev looked over his shoulder, then back at Thorne. He touched a finger to his own chest, with an expression of feigned innocence. "Me?"

"Yup. You, Mr ISS Man. That's what you are, isn't it? I should have worked it out sooner. What else could you be, with all that Plusser talk? You messed up my evening good and proper yesterday. I'd like to return the favour."

"Yeah, about that," said Dev. "I'd be happy to apologise. In fact, I'm going to. Any minute now, an apology is coming. Hang on. I'm sure it's due. Any... minute..."

Thorne shook his head sourly. "Oh, you're so funny."

"Please. If you'll just be patient. Apology loading. Buffering."

"Listen, dipshit. You don't fuck with me, understand? Fuck with me and you fuck with the whole of the Fair Dues Collective. That's one of the most powerful organisations around. We have majority union control at this mine and eleven others. I really want to cause trouble, I can make a couple of calls and have half this planet's industrial base on its knees within the hour."

"And that matters to me why exactly? I'm not in mining. I'm not even an Alighierian."

"My members get upset, they start to break things – expensive things. Those things get broken, management call in the riot cops. The riot cops weigh in, people get hurt, maybe even killed. Once it starts, it's an inevitable progression."

"Again, no skin off my nose."

"Harmer," said Kahlo. "He's serious. Don't antagonise him."

"I'm not antagonising him," said Dev. "He's letting himself be antagonised. There's a distinction."

"I *am* serious," said Thorne. "And you'd better start being serious too. I won't be treated the way I was last night. Not by some jumped-up jackbooted ISS bullyboy who thinks he can just wander in and boss people around, accuse them of being Plussers, break any number of laws to get his own way."

"So I offended your fine sensibilities, Thorne,"

said Dev. "So what? Suck it up and get over it. It was for the greater good. There's more at stake here than your ego, ridiculously inflated though that is. What do you want me to do instead? Put your interests ahead of the interests of everyone else on Alighieri?"

"I can make this all go away, whoosh, like it never was. No strike. Happy workers toiling away at the heliumface like before."

"In return for...?"

"You. Humbled."

"Huh?"

"Put in your place."

"You're joking. You mean if I kiss your behind, the strike's off?"

"Not quite like that, but close."

"Are you hearing this, the rest of you?" Dev said, addressing the miners assembled behind Thorne. "Does it make any sense? What kind of leader is it who claims he represents you when all he's out for is petty payback? Is that someone you want to follow?"

"We're okay with it," said one of the miners. "Ben's never steered us wrong in the past."

"Not much love for the likes of ISS here," said another. "Corporate security firm. Private sector. Capitalist tool of government."

"Interstellar *Schutzstaffel*," said a third, the tallest in the group, with a shock of ginger hair.

"Wow, a Nazi Germany reference," said Dev. "That's not reaching far back at all."

"Smug bastard," said Thorne. "I'm giving you an

opportunity to make amends. All you have to do is accept a challenge, and honour will be satisfied. We go back to work. End of story."

Dev looked at Kahlo. She, not very helpfully, just shrugged.

"A challenge," he said. "Like eating a whole box of doughnuts or something?"

Thorne's grin was sly. "Or something."

19

"WE CALL IT the Ordeal," Thorne said. "If a miner gets out of line, offends a colleague, brings disgrace on the pit folk community, whatever, this is how he or she can earn back trust."

They had gone deep into the main access tunnel, walking for several minutes. Dev sensed an excitement among the miners, the eagerness of an audience about to witness a spectacle. He hadn't a clue what Thorne had in store for him, but he was sure it would be difficult and most likely unpleasant.

"The longer you hold out, the greater the respect you gain," Thorne continued. "I went through it myself, not because I did anything wrong, but in order to prove my worthiness to be union leader. I can safely say that no one in living memory has lasted as long as I did."

"Does it involve boring people senseless with a pompous, self-aggrandising monologue?" said Dev. "Because I can see how you'd win at that."

"I doubt you'll be so witty five minutes from now, Mr ISS Man."

"My friends call me Dev."

"I'm going to stick with 'Mr ISS Man.'"

"My point exactly."

One of the miners sniggered, until Thorne shot him a dirty look and he stopped.

"Now, you don't have to take part," Thorne said to Dev. "I'll understand if you chicken out once you realise what you'll be facing. But then we'll all know you're a gutless coward and the strike will carry on."

"Well, when you put it in such an even-handed way like that, how can I refuse?"

They came to a T-junction, two lesser tunnels leading off at right angles from the main one.

"Left down this haulageway," said Thorne. "Not much further now."

They took another left into a large chamber, a workshop where items of mining equipment were parked. Alongside a couple of transportation carts, there were several fearsome-looking exoskeleton rigs fitted with tools for ripping, drilling and shearing. Most of them hung in cradles, partially dismantled, in the process of being mended or serviced. Pistons and hydraulic cables stood exposed, robotic muscles and veins.

A handful of mechanics were toiling away with blowtorches and screwdrivers. Thorne swanned in and told them to drop what they were doing and leave.

"You shouldn't be working anyway," he said. "You may not be proper miners, but what about pit folk solidarity? I'd hate for people to start thinking you're scabs."

The mechanics took the hint and, duly cowed, shuffled out.

"Should I do this?" Dev murmured to Kahlo.

"If you ask me, you've gone too far to back out now. At least, not without losing face."

"Do you even know what the Ordeal is?"

"I've heard rumours."

"And?"

"They're not good ones."

"Well, it sounds to me like it might be something that's against the law. Just saying."

"My jurisdiction has its limits. Miners prefer to resolve their own problems when they can – keep it within the community."

"But if it means hurting me..."

"You think I can arrest all these people? On my own?"

"Then I guess I'll just have to stick or fold."

"I really wish I could help you, Harmer."

"So do I."

"Come here," Thorne ordered, and Dev ambled over to join him on a hoist platform above a vehicle inspection bay.

"Stand there. Like so. Legs apart."

Dev straddled the platform's two runners.

"Arms out. Parallel to the ground."

Dev extended his arms.

"I hope you're not going to tickle me."

"No."

Thorne nodded to two miners, who together went to fetch something from the rear of the workshop.

They brought over two sets of chains attached to steel trays.

They fastened the chains to Dev's wrists so that the trays hung free, suspended a few inches above the platform. He now resembled a human pair of scales.

"I didn't realise this was what you were into, Thorne," he said. "I don't mind a bit of bondage myself, but we ought to set a safeword first."

Thorne ignored him, evidently feeling the time for joking was past.

That was when Dev spotted flecks of a dark, crusty substance on the trays. It was, by the look of it, dried blood.

He too reckoned the time for joking was past.

"Okay," he said. "What happens next?"

"You stay like that," Thorne replied. "Don't lower your arms. Either of those trays touches the platform, it's over."

"Hmmm. They're pretty heavy, but I think I can cope."

Already his arms were beginning to ache. Each tray-and-chain combo must have weighed thirty pounds.

"How long did you go for?" he asked. "So I know the target I have to beat."

"Fifteen minutes, twenty-seven seconds."

That was doable, Dev thought. His host form seemed to have sufficient strength.

"But," Thorne added, "this is only the start."

"There's more?"

"Much more."

Thorne beckoned, and one of the miners came forward with a socket wrench in his hands. Before Dev could object or even prepare himself, he swung it hard. The wrench hit Dev square in the midriff, knocking the wind out of him.

He staggered, just managing to remain upright.

The miner tossed the wrench into one of the trays. Dev, still gasping for breath, stiffened the arm on that side to compensate for the extra weight.

Another miner stepped up, this one carrying a sock stuffed with nuts and bolts.

Dev tensed his abdominal muscles. The blow, when it came, was swingeing. Fire exploded all across his belly.

The makeshift cosh went into the empty tray. Dev hauled up his other arm to steady the tray.

"Tell your people," he said to Thorne through gritted teeth, "they hit like schoolgirls."

Thorne laughed. "You can end this any time. Just let either or both of your arms drop. That's all it takes."

"What's the time so far?"

"I started a stopwatch on my commplant. Fifty-eight seconds. Fifty-nine. Your first full minute."

Dev stared hard into Thorne's eyes. "Bring it on."

A miner stood in front of him, a piece of chain wrapped around his fist. It was the tall, ginger-haired man who had made the 'SS' quip.

"Nobody likes a smartmouth," he said, and delivered a piledriver punch.

Dev bit back a groan of agony. "Nobody likes a ginger either," he managed to say.

The miner looked as though he might hit him again, but apparently there were strict rules in force. One blow only per turn. The chain joined the wrench in the right-hand tray with a rattling *clank*.

A fourth miner came onto the platform to clobber Dev, and a fifth, and a sixth, each using some implement they had found lying around the workshop. The trays gradually filled up, becoming heavier.

Dev withstood the punishment. He kept his arms out horizontal, even as his shoulders knotted and grew sorer. The trays dipped and wavered, but didn't drop.

He wasn't doing it for the sake of industrial relations. He couldn't have cared less about strike action or Anoshkin Energiya.

This was about him and Ben Thorne.

The union leader had thrown down a gauntlet. He had settled on humiliating Dev as a method of restorative justice. But if Dev outlasted him, beating his Ordeal record, then Thorne would surely go down a few notches in his co-workers' estimation. Dev's only real chance of victory lay in hanging on through the pain so that he could humiliate Thorne in return.

His commplant signalled an incoming call. Kahlo.

Harmer.

Little busy right now.

He glanced across the workshop, meeting Kahlo's gaze. There was that peculiar frisson you got when you were holding a commplant conversation with someone you could physically see, that sense of disjuncture. You could hear the voice. Why wasn't the mouth moving to match? The face making the appropriate expressions?

Don't do this to yourself.

No choice.

Quit. Thorne's done enough to you. Let him have this.

You mean let him win? If you knew me better, you'd know that isn't an option.

Fine. Be like that.

Thanks for the concern, though.

Not concern. I just hate stubbornness for stubbornness's sake.

Someone whacked Dev with a piston rod. It was a good shot, dead centre of his solar plexus. The pain was sickening.

Ben Thorne smiled and dropped the piston rod into a tray.

"Seven minutes," he said. "Almost halfway there. Give in. Those trays aren't getting any lighter. Nor are our blows. If you let it go on much longer, you'll be pissing blood for a week. Trust me, I did."

"I think I just felt a butterfly's wing brushing past my stomach," Dev said. "Did you see it go by?"

Another minute passed, and another. Oddly, it was the pain from his shoulders that became hard to tolerate, more so than the pain from his battered belly. His trapezius muscles had gone into excruciating spasm, and stabs of agony were shooting up the back of his neck into his skull. It was like wearing a yoke made of red-hot iron.

Both trays were now laden with tools, spare parts and pieces of scrap metal. They must have weighed at least fifty pounds each.

Dev's left arm sagged. The tray came perilously close to touching the platform. He raised it, trembling.

Something with a sharp edge bashed him just below the waistline. A stripe of blood appeared across the front of his overalls.

"He's had enough on that side," Thorne declared. "Let's try the back instead."

Dev braced himself as the blows slammed against him from behind, one after another.

"How – how many...?" he croaked.

"Minutes? Ten and three quarters," said Thorne.

Less than five to go.

He could do this.

He could do this.

Dimly, through a kind of greasy throbbing haze, he saw Kahlo. Her eyes were urging him to relent, not to stick it out any more.

But there was still a point to prove. It wasn't enough just to undergo the Ordeal. Thorne had to be defeated. Pride was at stake, and more. A principle. Men like Ben Thorne had to be shown up for the preening, puffed-up little pricks they were.

Some of the miners seemed to be developing sympathy for Dev. They were no longer hitting him quite as forcefully as before.

Others, though, were redoubling their efforts. They wanted him to weaken, to crumple, to fall.

One unusually savage blow made him bite his tongue by accident. He spat out the blood.

Another caught him between two ribs, injuring an intercostal muscle. It felt like a heart attack.

"Thirteen minutes," said Thorne. He was trying to keep his tone of voice neutral, but there was evident aggravation in it. Dev was only two and a half minutes away from beating his time.

Unfortunately, Dev felt about a minute and a half away from blacking out.

Someone yelled, "It touched. Did you see that? A tray touched down. I swear."

"No, it didn't," said someone else. "I was watching. Nearly, but not quite."

Dev, grimacing with the strain, wrenched both arms back up to horizontal. Each tray felt as though it was carrying a ton. His arms, his shoulders, his head – all were shuddering uncontrollably with the burden.

In the military, Dev had endured hazing rituals, or 'corrective training' as it was known. On the whole these had been penalties for minor infractions – arriving late for drill, a spot of dirt besmirching his uniform – and had involved running laps and doing press-ups until he puked, or being doused with water and made to stand outdoors in subzero conditions.

On one occasion, though, he had fallen asleep near the end of a combat simulation exercise lasting forty-eight hours. He was supposed to be guarding a munitions depot, but he was so exhausted after nearly two days of endless marching, live-firing, trench digging and reconnaissance that he could barely keep his eyes open.

An instructor caught him napping and decided an example should be made.

"If you nod off and a Plusser crab tank comes crawling over the hill," the instructor said, "you're toast, your munitions depot is toast, and your regiment is probably toast, too."

Dev couldn't resist pointing out that a crab tank, noisy as it was, would wake him up, giving him plenty of time to raise the alarm. Doubtless he shouldn't have said this, but he was in trouble already, so what had he got to lose?

"All right, a fucking stealth manta, then," the instructor said testily. "Now, squat down on your haunches. No, lower. Ladies and gentlemen..."

Dev's fellow recruits gathered round.

"Private Harmer here, in addition to having a lip on him, is a lazy bastard and a hazard to his brothers and sisters in arms. No unit can afford a weak link. He needs toughening up."

The instructor gave Dev a cup of water to hold, full to the brim. Then, at his invitation, the other recruits thumped him on the buttocks and thighs with their rifle butts. Every drop of water spilled meant a further minute in the stress position, being pummelled.

The strange thing about it was that afterwards, even though he could barely walk, Dev felt no ill will towards his cohorts or the instructor. He had made a mistake, and had earned redemption. If it had been someone else getting hazed, he, Dev, would have joined in along with the others. Acts of discipline, however harsh, were necessary to foster cohesion and comradeship. Without, the ranks might break. One fail, all fail.

That was the day it dawned on him that he wasn't just an unwilling participant in the TerCon juvenile offender conscription programme. He might actually be a soldier after all.

Today, he found himself almost pining for the beating he had received back then. Compared with the Ordeal, it was a cakewalk.

"Fifteen," said Thorne, who was now having trouble concealing his annoyance. And his apprehension.

Dev couldn't quite believe it. Half a minute left.

He hardly felt the pain any more. There was so much, it seemed to lose its meaning. It lay outside him, like a sphere whose inner surface he couldn't reach or touch.

Arms.

Stomach.

Back.

Not his.

Nothing to do with him.

"Fifteen-fifteen."

He was aware of a faint murmuring. The miners, marvelling to one another.

Just a few more seconds.

He closed his eyes. Or were they already closed? Darkness was enfolding him.

Stay with it!

Don't flake out like at the supply depot!

His eyes snapped open.

"Fifteen-twenty-five."

Just...

A couple more...

The trays fell, clattering, spilling their contents.

Dev sank to his knees.

He blinked up at Thorne. The union leader's face gave nothing away.

"Well?" he managed to whisper.

20

KAHLO'S APARTMENT WAS undecorated, unadorned, almost showroom-clean and tidy. It was as though no one lived there. There wasn't one personal touch: not a picture, not an ornament, no mementos, nothing. This was how a habitat cube looked the day it was offloaded, unpacked and assembled, fresh from kit form.

Dev sat on a couch which, like all the other furnishings, conformed to the default colour scheme of oatmeal and beige. He was bare-chested, and once again the beneficiary of copious amounts of topical curative gel. He had applied it himself to his front, but Kahlo had done his back. She had not been gentle.

The pain was ebbing, the swelling going down. The laceration on his belly had begun to heal.

"So," Kahlo said. "Pleased with yourself?"

"Shouldn't I be? The strike is over. Hi-ho, hi-ho, it's off to work we go. Normal service has been resumed. I'd say that was a good result."

"Yeah, but did you see Thorne's face? He looked ready to throttle you."

"Big deal." Dev was nonchalant. "He doesn't scare me. Besides, what's he got to complain about? It's not as if I broke his record."

"You equalled it, though."

"Best for both of us. He keeps his title, but I showed him he shouldn't get complacent. Also, some of those miners cheered when he announced my time."

"Give you a warm, fuzzy feeling inside, did it?"

"Only because it was a sign of dissent. Those people are completely browbeaten by Thorne. He has them under his thumb. He's a dictator. Now a few of them think less of him than before. It's a start."

"Harmer the revolutionary."

"Come the next leadership election, maybe they'll vote him out, put someone more reasonable in his place, someone not so vain and self-serving, less of a blowhard. I've undermined his authority, if you'll forgive the pun."

"I never forgive puns. They're unforgivable."

Dev puffed out his cheeks and shook his head. "Fuck. It must be difficult, being such a hardcase all the time. If you could, you'd make having a sense of humour a criminal offence, wouldn't you?"

"Well, excuse me for being serious," Kahlo shot back. "Everything may seem like fun and games to you, but I have a city to keep safe, millions of people counting on me to look after them. Frivolity isn't part of the equation."

"Surely you can relax sometimes." But this was not the apartment of someone who relaxed. It was the apartment of someone who had no life outside of work. It was the place Kahlo went when she had to eat, bathe and sleep, and it served no function other than that. It was certainly not a home, not a private space. She would not have brought him here otherwise.

"Never," she said. "I can never drop my guard. I have responsibilities and I do not shirk them. It's all right for you. You just breeze in, dick around, do as you feel. I am a Calder's Edger. This is my city, and policing it is my vocation. When you're done here you'll just go, move on to wherever ISS tell you. I have a long-term, a *lifelong* commitment."

"You think I don't care about anything? It's all just a big laugh to me?"

"I haven't yet seen evidence to the contrary."

"Well, for one thing, my aching torso would beg to differ," Dev said. "I have responsibilities too. I'm not with ISS just for shits and giggles. I have a vested interest in achieving a successful outcome, not only on Alighieri but everywhere I'm sent."

"What, you're on some kind of bonus scheme? A tax-free lump sum for every Polis Plus plot you foil? Maybe it's like being a bounty hunter – a reward for each Plusser scalp you take."

"Yes, it's that simple. I'm that cynical."

"You've probably got a bank account back on Earth, building up a nice, fat, juicy balance. A few more jobs and you can retire a rich man. And that's all we are to you. That's all this is. That's why you can afford to joke around. It's just a job. Just money."

"You have me bang to rights, Captain Kahlo. I wither before your penetrating insight. You have seen through to my hollow, mercenary soul."

"What is it, then?" she said. "Why do you do this?"

"You really want to know?"

"I really want to know. Perhaps if I know, I'll understand you a bit better and I won't find you so fucking annoying that every single minute I'm with you I'm having to restrain myself from kicking you in the balls."

"Better women than you have tried."

Dev looked down at the mass of bruises on his abdomen, overlapping circles and ovals like some sort of Venn diagram of pain. Already, thanks to the gel, they were visibly reduced in size. Their angry reds and purples had changed to blurry browns and yellows.

"I died," he said.

"Huh?"

"Five years ago. On Kepler Sixty-One B, also known as Barnesworld."

"The Battle of Leather Hill."

"Yes. The decisive conflict of the Frontier War, they call it. The turning point. By which they mean the battle where the slaughter was so massive on either side that we and Polis Plus both realised if we carried on the way we were going, we'd most likely end up annihilating one another."

"You... died?"

"Along with a million and a half other TerCon troops and about the same number of Plussers. Of course, we'd figured out by then how to jam their inbuilt transfer matrices, so that they couldn't nip out of crippled mechs and dying organic forms at the last moment. That put the wind up them."

"They couldn't respawn immediately in backup units," Kahlo said. "It cut their tactical effectiveness by a significant factor."

"Yes. Before jamming, if we didn't destroy a mech instantly and outright, the Plusser consciousness inhabiting it would just flit back behind lines in a picosecond and commandeer a new one from the reserves. You'd get waves of them coming in one after another, relentless, without end. It seemed futile. But once we'd stopped them being able to hop out and escape at will – well, that changed the whole complexion of the war."

"The ejector seat button had been disconnected, as it were."

"That's it. They still didn't fear death; that's the digimentalist mindset for you. The religious fanatic is the worst kind of enemy, because their lives have no value to them. They'll sacrifice themselves happily for the cause, knowing that afterlife nirvana awaits – in their case, oneness with the Singularity. But we'd taken away their main theatre-of-combat advantage. Leather Hill was when we first drove that point home. It was a huge shock to the Plussers. They'd never experienced casualties like that until then. Neither, unfortunately, had we."

"Someone said it made the Somme look like a playground squabble."

"I haven't heard that one, but I can endorse it. It was... mindless. Just wholesale murder, all around."

Dev paused, feeling a chill.

Leather Hill.

It was only a shallow rise in the landscape, a blister of rocky ground covering the same sort of acreage as a small town. Brown and knobbly. From a height, it resembled an expanse of freshly tanned cow hide; hence the name.

Nobody lived for hundreds of kilometres around in any direction. Barnesworld was still in the throes of colonisation. Its continents were grassland and savannah; its icecaps were small and stable. It had few mountain ranges, few active volcanoes. Its flora and fauna were attractive and docile. Total population: somewhere in the region of three hundred thousand.

It was a gentle, inoffensive warm-superterran mesoplanet, and it attracted the kind of Diasporan settler who fancied a life of ranching and agriculture, a stressless bucolic existence on rolling plains beneath low-albedo skies, with solitude practically a given.

To this peaceful, unspoiled spot the Frontier War came. Polis+ decided to set up a forward command post on Barnesworld, and then a refuelling dump, and then one of their automated mech factories churning out battlefield-ready robots and vehicles. Never mind that the Terran Diaspora had got there first. Never mind that Barnesworld was officially

Earth turf. The Plussers established a presence on it, gambling that TerCon would consider it of too little strategic value to be worth defending.

A few farmers, plenty of wide open spaces, not much in the way of exploitable resources... Who gave a damn about Barnesworld?

It turned out that Polis+ had miscalculated. TerCon did indeed give a damn. A whole heap of damns, in fact.

For here was a planet with negligible heavy-duty infrastructure. Undeveloped, a blank canvas. And TerCon was keen to do some painting.

Troops and matériel were shipped from existing battlefronts to Barnesworld in mass quantities. It was an overkill response to Polis+'s relatively small-scale incursion.

Polis+, understandably alarmed, answered with a huge mobilisation of its own. Barnesworld's blue skies were filled with gulf cruisers and the columns of space elevators dropping in from near orbit and anchoring. Within a couple of weeks, the Plussers had committed fully a quarter of their war machine to this undistinguished and hitherto insignificant globe that was roughly twice the size of Earth and half the size of their own artificial homeworld.

It was just what TerCon high command wanted. The top brass were forcing a fight on a level playing field. The plan was to deliver a decisive, convincing blow against the enemy. Draw them out and land a haymaker. Stun them so hard they were sent reeling, never to recover, or else lost heart and sued for peace.

The transcription matrix jamming signal was still a secret at that stage. The technology had been selectively field tested and found to work. Leather Hill was the first time it was given widescale deployment. The Plussers would not have their usual endless respawning technique to fall back on. Let them see how they liked that.

Nineteen days the battle raged. Nineteen days spent vying over that barren chunk of highland, that rocky outcrop which had no intrinsic importance but just happened to be where the two armies clashed.

Leather Hill.

It hadn't even had a name before the battle, but it became synonymous with the worst slaughter ever seen in the Frontier War – or in any war waged by humans, for that matter.

Dev could not recall sleeping during the conflict. Perhaps a half-hour snatched here and there, a few stolen moments of blessed oblivion.

Otherwise, it was continual combat. A cacophony of noise – the jackhammering of ballistic guns, the *crunch* of explosions, the lightning crackle of beam weapons. Flashes and flickers, night-time as bright as daytime. Mechs churning the soil with their treads or whining through the air on cushions of electrogravitic pulse. Clods of earth thrown up by strafing bombardments. The howling of Polis+ zombie clone battalions as they charged en masse against artillery positions, overwhelming through sheer numbers, clogging the emplacements with several hundredweight of dead meat.

Dev survived almost to the end. He and his sapper unit moved through the carnage, making forays to set traps for Plusser tanks and robot divisions. They demolished mechs that had been disabled by missiles or shells but still housed their controlling sentiences, pinned to the shattered hulks by the jamming signal. It was mercy killing, after a fashion. They also provided infantry support when called for, joining the ordinary ranks in the struggle to hold ground against the oncoming Plusser hordes.

Then came the order to assault a modular robot battalion entrenched in a small depression, encircled on all sides by Terran forces. A Polis+ rearguard holdout that was inflicting severe damage even as the human military was making a concerted push forward, thrusting deep into enemy territory.

The beleaguered android mechs were fighting to the last. If one of them lost an arm or a leg to gunfire, it would simply scavenge a replacement component from the heaps of metal bodies lying around it. Occasionally the mechs would fuse themselves together in groups of three or four to create a towering, multi-limbed behemoth that would then go on a rampage, performing a wild suicide run in the hope of taking out as many of the opposition as it could before it was taken out itself.

It was one of these gargantuan atrocities that slew Dev. He would never forget – how could he? – the sight of it zeroing in on his unit, its limbs gangling and flailing with minimal coordination. Its several heads ululating a war cry, proclaiming in unison the majesty and supremacy of its god: "The Singularity! The Singularity! All hail the Singularity!"

Dev and his comrades unleashed volleys of muon beam fire and rocket-propelled homing grenades at the thing. Sections of its armour disintegrated, flying away like chaff. They crippled three of its eight legs.

Still it kept coming.

Limping, spurting yellow hydraulic fluid, guns blazing, it stumbled onto them. It whirled like a top, spraying them with kinetic rounds at more or less point blank range.

Dev's death was not heroic, or dignified. He just succumbed like the men and women beside him to the hail of fire coming from the robot's many coilguns. There was no glamour or glory, no last hurrah. There was only unprecedented agony, the violation of his body by countless projectiles travelling at eight thousand kilometres per hour – and then a period of strange numb serenity as he lay on the ground, torn and ruined, waiting for nothingness to come.

It came, falling like night, slowly, inevitably.

His last thought was: *I hope this was worth it.*

He meant his death, but he also meant the battle, the whole war. He hoped he had played a useful part in the conflict. He hoped there had been a point to it all, beyond TerCon's imperative need to defend the parts of the galaxy Earth had planted its flag in.

"Harmer?"

Kahlo.

"You kind of tuned out there," she said.

"Yeah? Sorry. Memory Lane. Sometimes it's more like Memory Corridor of Ghastly Nightmares."

"And he's back."

"Miss me?"

"Not even for a moment. You still haven't explained. You died at Leather Hill... but you're not dead?"

"Try not to sound so disappointed. I was technically dead for... I don't know how long. It depends, I suppose, on how you define death. It's a grey area. Bodily functions can cease while brain functions still continue. Put it this way: I wasn't aware. I wasn't conscious of anything. And then –"

Priority contact. Ludlow Trundell.

"Hold on. Someone's calling me."

Mr Harmer.

Professor Trundell. What have you got for me?

About the moleworms. I've found something.

That was fast. Go on.

I can send you the data, but it would be simpler if I showed you in person.

Are you saying I'm too thick to understand it without you walking me through it?

No! I would never.

It's all right, prof. Just teasing. Let's meet.

When?

Now would be good.

Where?

Dev glanced around Kahlo's apartment.

I know a place.

21

"IT MAY BE significant," said Trundell. "It may not. I thought I'd draw your attention to it anyway. See what you think."

He produced a projector bar, placed it on the table, and activated it. A blank floatscreen winked into life a hand's breadth above it.

"Yeah, that's fine, Harmer," said Kahlo. "Invite a friend over. Make yourself at home. It's only my apartment."

"You never said I couldn't."

"You told me you were meeting somebody. I assumed it would be elsewhere."

"But your pad's only a short train ride from where Trundle's staying."

"Trun*dell*," said Trundell with a scowl.

"And I thought you might like to take a look at what he's found out, whatever it is. I'm keeping you in the loop, like we agreed. Unless you've got important cop business you need to be attending to, of course."

"And leave you here on your own, unchaperoned?"

said Kahlo. "I'm not crazy. You'd only end up trashing the place somehow. Face it, your track record hasn't been good so far."

"Cruel," said Dev. "But justified."

"I could come back another time," said Trundell, looking furtively from one to the other like a child whose parents were arguing. "I don't want to be a nuisance."

"You're not," Dev assured him. "Captain Kahlo likes a moan, that's all. She's one of those people who are only happy when they're unhappy."

The xeno-entomologist hunched his shoulders, uncomfortable. "Harmer, that's the chief of police you're talking to. Shouldn't you be a bit more, you know, deferential?"

"Yeah, Harmer," said Kahlo. "The man speaks truth. You should."

"Oh, she loves a bit of backchat."

"I do not."

"She could throw you in jail for disrespecting a police officer," said Trundell.

"Believe me, I've been tempted," said Kahlo.

"Don't worry," said Dev. "We have this friendly antagonism thing going on, me and her. She likes me. She just can't admit it."

"Why not just show us what you have for us, Professor Trundell?"

"Okay. Yes. All right. Transferring the data onto the screen."

Trundell frowned as he performed the commplant upload.

The first image that appeared was a high-res camera shot of Alighieri. The surface was a reddish brown mosaic of solidified lava flows, dotted with meteorite impact craters. Some of the craters were encircled by rings of ejecta. Lines of scarp extended for hundreds of kilometres, huge cliffs formed in the planet's crust millennia ago when it was still in the early stages of development, cooling and shrinking.

"This," said Trundell, "is... Well, you can see what it is."

He match-cut the image with a transparent three-dimensional schematic of Alighieri, which he rotated on its axis until a pair of bright spherical dots came into view.

"Here are Calder's Edge and its near neighbour Xanadu. I'll label them for you so you know which is which."

Each subterranean city's name popped up alongside it.

"I don't need a lecture on Alighierian geography, thank you," said Kahlo. "Skip to the point, Trundell."

"Oh. Er... I rather like to do things in sequence, if that's all right, ma'am."

"Yes, Kahlo, don't hurry the man," said Dev. "He's methodical."

"So," said Trundell, "I delved into the literature about moleworms. I was up half the night, searching both the local insite and off-planet ones as well. There's more stuff about them cached than I initially thought."

"Aren't you into scroaches?" said Kahlo. "As I recall, that's what we gave you a permit for – to look at creepy-crawlies, not moleworms."

"You're quite right, ma'am. I forgot that you know who I am. Yours was one of the authorisations I needed in order to come to Calder's and start my research, wasn't it?"

"Personally I think you're nuts. Why scroaches, when there are insects on other worlds ten times more beautiful and nowhere near as dangerous? If I was a xeno-entomologist, I'd dedicate myself to studying glimmermoths on Maness Four or those crystal beetles on Nuova Roma's second moon."

"I'm interested in scroaches because no one else is. You can't move for papers on glimmermoths. Everyone and their aunt has written one. Whereas the humble scroach is a relatively undocumented beastie. That makes it a field in which I am a pioneer and, one day, with luck, will be hailed as the leading authority."

"So why the switch to moleworms? No, don't tell me. Harmer put you up to it, didn't he?"

"Mr Harmer, ahem, suggested that it might be wise for me to pay attention to the habits of the scroach's main predator."

"I read that as him getting you to do his dirty work for him."

"No. No! Actually, yes. Sort of. Our interests have coincided, you might say."

Kahlo gave Dev a reproachful look. "You strongarmed him, Harmer. I know you did."

"How can you think so little of me?"

"Because there's no other way to think of you."

"The professor is a highly intelligent young man. If he felt moved to volunteer to assist me in my endeavours, how could I refuse? Isn't that right, Trundle?"

"It's Trun– Oh, never mind. Now, according to existing studies of moleworm habits, they're rarely to be found in this region of Alighieri. There are trails – old tunnels – suggesting there were once greater concentrations of them here than there are today. The theory is that, since colonisation, they've been driven away by human activity, the mining industry specifically. The evidence supports it. The old moleworm tunnels predate our arrival."

"Where did they go?" Kahlo asked.

"As far away as possible. Right round the world, in fact. When the late, great Professor Banerjee came here back in 'oh-three, or maybe 'oh-four – just after the war ended, at any rate – he started by looking for *pseudotalpidae* in the vicinity of Calder's Edge and Xanadu."

"Pseudo-what?"

"Moleworms. He didn't find as many as he was expecting, however. Mostly he just found the evidence of where they'd once been. There were long-abandoned nests and heaps of desiccated scat which he dated back to before the Diaspora."

"He dated moleworm crap?" said Dev.

"Zoology isn't a glamorous profession. Banerjee measured the amino acid racemisation of the shards of scroach shell in the scat and determined the vast majority of the samples to be almost sixty years old. He also examined anecdotal reports from first-generation colonists about the frequency with which they encountered moleworms and compared these with the relative *in*frequency of such encounters at the time he was writing."

"The animals migrated," said Kahlo. "We displaced them."

"To here."

Trundell spun the Alighieri schematic through a half turn. Another spherical dot popped up, which he labelled Lidenbrock City.

"Lidenbrock. That was where Banerjee travelled next. He spent a year and a half among the Lidenbrockers, cataloguing moleworm movements, mating rituals and suchlike."

"I don't envy him that," said Kahlo.

"Watching moleworms fuck?" said Dev.

"Rubbing shoulders with Lidenbrockers."

"Ah, yes," said Trundell. "He does mention from time to time how primitive the living conditions were and how challenging he found it associating with the locals. 'Colourful' is, I think, the kindest description he had for them. His rented accommodation was burgled five times during his stay."

"Only five?" said Kahlo. "He got off lightly."

"Nonetheless he managed to produce a scholarly text on moleworms, a classic of its kind. Of particular note is the fact that there are two very slightly divergent subspecies. Banerjee dubbed them the western and eastern moleworm. Not terribly imaginative taxonomy, but it'll serve. The western moleworm is the type that was once found in abundance around Calder's and Xanadu."

"And the eastern is the Lidenbrock strain."

"Quite so, chief."

"No one calls the chief of police 'chief,' Trundell. 'Captain' is the accepted form of address."

"I beg your pardon, captain. Anyway, as I was saying, the two types of moleworm aren't easy to tell apart. The eastern's nasotentacles – its snout feelers – are a little bit longer, and its skin colour tends towards a richer pink than the western's. Banerjee observed some cross-breeding between the subspecies, but also intense, almost tribal rivalries."

"They hated one another, except for the occasional love story," said Dev. "Even moleworms have their Romeo-and-Juliet moments."

Trundell threw a glance at Kahlo as if to say, *Does he ever stop clowning around?* She, in return, offered him a despairing grimace.

"Here are shots of both kinds," Trundell said, "so you can see for yourselves."

Two pictures of moleworms appeared side by side on the floatscreen.

"Yeah," said Dev, "that's not horrendous in any way."

"On the left, the western. On the right, the eastern. Spot the differences?"

"That one's ugly," said Dev, pointing to the western moleworm. Then he pointed to the eastern.

"And that one's *butt*-ugly."

"The pinker hue? The slightly longer nasotentacles?"

"Okay," said Kahlo. "So, all very fascinating. But..."

"But where am I going with this?" said Trundell. "Very well. Mr Harmer, which subspecies of moleworm did we run into yesterday?"

"The subspecies that likes to eat people? How should I know? I was busy trying to keep us from ending up as moleworm scat. I didn't have time to stop and take a long, hard, scientific look."

"Myself, I'm pretty sure it was an eastern."

"Really?"

"Ninety per cent sure. Perhaps even ninety-five. Its feelers were more like those" – Trundell enlarged the right-hand picture – "than those" – he enlarged the left – "and its skin was definitely on the darker side, at least as far as one could tell in the negligible light."

"The eastern moleworms have come halfway round the world to visit us," said Kahlo. "Is that what you're saying?"

"Not with any degree of certainty," Trundell replied. "A single sighting of an eastern moleworm does not constitute proof of anything other than that we've seen one of them. However, it is intriguing. Banerjee commented that the eastern subspecies was not apt to stray from its ranges. It was fiercely territorial and treated the western as an interloper."

"Maybe the one you met was a rogue."

"Could be. But I was prompted, out of curiosity, to examine footage taken in Xanadu of a moleworm that ventured onto public property just last month. Here it is."

It was a shaky, first-person clip lasting half a minute. A moleworm was crawling across a shopping mall plaza, looking bewildered and bedazzled. People were shouting and screaming, dropping their bags and running away from the creature in terror.

"The Xanaduan who took this used the iWitness feature in their commplant," Trundell said, "then sold it to a news feed."

"I'm waiting for a kitten to turn up and do something cute," said Dev.

The moleworm blundered nose first into a shopfront. Shaking its head in distress and pain, it began spading up the plaza's tiled floor, scrabbling to make its escape.

The clip ended.

"I heard about that incident," said Kahlo. "It happens now and then. In Calder's, too. Moleworms are digging along, and break through into some part of the city by accident. They don't hang around for long, if they can help it. The noise freaks them out."

"Yes, but..." Trundell rewound to the clearest shot of the creature. He blew up and enhanced the image. "Look. It's an eastern."

The moleworm's skin was distinctly a shade of rose.

"Could it be the same one you two came across?"

"No, that was a female. This is a male."

He zoomed in on the creature's underside, between its back legs.

"Moleworms exhibit sexual mimicry," he said. "The external genitalia of both genders look alike, at a cursory glance. However, see that fleshy projection there? You'll note that there is no aperture at the base of it, which tells us it's a phallus rather than a peniform clitoris extruding from a vagina."

"I am so regretting I ever looked at that," groaned Dev. "My eyes."

"Again, Professor Trundell," said Kahlo, "this is all very fascinating, but if you can cut to the chase..."

"All right, all right. I believe it's possible that eastern moleworms have made their way to Calder's and Xanadu, perhaps in large numbers. Why? It could be that their feeding grounds around Lidenbrock City have become compromised somehow. Or it could be that there's been an population explosion and some of them have had to travel in search of pastures new."

"And...?"

"And that's all I have." Trundell spread out his hands. "Mr Harmer wanted me to report back. These are my preliminary findings."

Kahlo leaned back. "Well, that was a big fat waste of time. So we have moleworms on the move. So what?"

Dev raised an index finger. "I beg to differ. It may actually have some bearing on the general situation."

"In what way?"

"Prof, moleworms burrow, right?"

"Absolutely. With great speed and efficiency. You've seen it first-hand."

"I'm remembering, when that one was chasing us, its burrowing made quite a tremor."

"Are you saying what I think you're saying, Harmer?" said Kahlo.

"I'm just airing an idea. It may be ridiculous. You can call me an idiot if you like. But could the moleworms be causing the earthquakes?"

22

"AN EARTHQUAKE IS a sudden release of energy within the planetary crust," said Kahlo. "It occurs along a fault plane on the boundary between tectonic plates, where they interact. It's a spontaneous, natural geological phenomenon. A moleworm can't make one happen by burrowing. That's absurd."

"But Calder's Edge isn't near a plate boundary," said Dev.

"You can still get quakes some distance from a plate boundary. A fault hundreds of kilometres away can be responsible for disturbances deeper into the plate where there are irregularities in the geological makeup. The strain can spread far, affecting areas outside the immediate zone of deformation."

"You know your stuff."

"Too right I do. I've researched the shit out of earthquakes since we started having them. But like I told you yesterday, Calder's Edge is where it is because there's supposed to be no chance of even the smallest tremor here. The colonisation precursor survey was thorough and detailed."

"And the mines themselves aren't somehow to blame? That's beyond question?"

"I've spoken to geological engineers. They've assured me it can't be mining that's triggering the quakes. Induced seismicity events – that's human-caused tremors – produce only low-level seismic yields. Mining can unsettle the integrity of the rock bed, no doubt about it. In the past there's been the occasional rock burst, where the wall of a shaft fractures because the drilling has resulted in a pressure imbalance. There've been sinkholes too, from cavern collapse. But that's as far as it goes. Nothing severe enough to match earthquakes of the magnitude we've been experiencing."

"Might the effect of the mining be cumulative?" said Trundell. "What if, after a while, an area becomes so riddled with workings that a kind of chain reaction of instability builds?"

"I asked the engineers that myself. They said no. They site new tunnels precisely so as to avoid the likelihood arising and shore up old ones by backfilling them with waste material if the new ones look like they might have to be bored too close for comfort. There is no direct correlation between drilling for helium-three and the quakes."

"This is my point exactly," said Dev. "If it's not a natural occurrence and it's not inadvertently manmade – if we eliminate those two possibilities

– then we have to look somewhere else. So how about moleworms? Why not them?"

"I thought you were working on the theory that Polis Plus were behind this."

"Bear with me. I might still be. The moleworms might not have moved to this area of their own accord."

"As in they were guided? Herded?"

"Conceivably."

Kahlo gave a sceptical grunt. "Trouble with you, Harmer, is you spout such nonsense most of the time, I can't tell if you're in earnest now or just bullshitting."

"You too?" said Trundell, pleased. "I thought it was just me. I never know whether I should believe him or ignore him."

"The latter's usually the safest," said Kahlo. "His mouth's moving but nothing worthwhile is coming out."

"All I hear are phrases he doesn't mean. It's really confusing."

"He amuses himself. I suppose that's something."

"I am actually sitting right between you two," said Dev. "It's rude to talk about me over my head."

"We know," said Kahlo. "But it was nice, just for a moment, to act as if you weren't here."

Trundell smirked. "I think I like you, Captain Kahlo. You know, everyone says you're blunt and emotionless and a real stickler for the rules. But you speak your mind, and that really works for me."

"And the prize for backhanded compliment of the year goes to..." said Dev.

"Blunt is good," said Kahlo. "Blunt gets things done. And in that spirit, Harmer, let me tell you – bluntly – that this moleworm idea of yours is as harebrained as they come."

"And I disagree," said Dev. "Look, you can't deny that there at least *could* be a causal connection. Answer me this. When did the earthquakes start?"

"A month or so ago."

"What was the date stamp on the Xanadu moleworm footage?"

"I don't recall."

"Ten days ago. You mentioned that that sort of thing happens now and then. How many incidents like it have there been recently?"

"I can't say I've been keeping track."

"Give me a moment. I'll look it up."

Dev ran a general search for moleworm sightings, then narrowed the parameters by date and location.

"Seventeen in the past four weeks. What's the normal average?"

"About once a month, if that."

"So we have a clear statistical anomaly: an abrupt and marked uptick in the number of times moleworms have strayed onto human-developed areas. The professor here told me yesterday that they prefer, as a rule, to stay down in the lower lithosphere. Patently they're not doing that now."

Kahlo gnawed her lip. "A fair point. But can we assume from that that they're behind the quakes somehow? Mightn't you be looking at it the wrong way round? Mightn't the quakes be what's making the moleworms behave unusually?"

"I'm not discounting it," said Dev. "Either way, the influx of eastern moleworms onto this side of the planet, a long, long way away from their natural habitat, has to have some bearing on the earthquake situation. It's too much of a coincidence otherwise. Two simultaneous, out-of-the-ordinary events can't exist in isolation from each other. It defies logic."

"I'm inclined to agree," said Trundell. "In zoology we're trained never to study the animal without considering the environment as well. The two are inseparable. One invariably impacts on the other, and often it's both ways at once, mutual. Animal affects environment, environment affects animal, back and forth, constantly. If one changes, we have to ask ourselves how the other might have changed too, and which change came first."

"There you go. The man has letters after his name, whereas I didn't even make it past senior school. Listen to him, Kahlo, even if you won't to me."

Calder's Edge's chief of police turned away and paced the room for a couple of minutes, deep in thought. Dev took the opportunity to pour himself a glass of water – he was parched after so much talking – while Trundell nervously tamped down a lock of hair that refused to stay flat.

Eventually Kahlo halted and said, "Okay. I don't totally buy the moleworms-make-quakes theory. I accept, though, that there may well be a link and it's worth checking out, in the same way that if someone is seen running away from the scene of a crime, it's worth checking them out in case they're the perp. They might have a solid alibi, but at least that means you've eliminated a suspect and you're one step closer to finding the real culprit."

"Spoken like a true-blue cop," said Dev.

"Where that leaves us, therefore, is me asking you how you'd like to go about following up this idea of yours."

"My first instinct is that I should go where the moleworms are from."

"Deep down? Can't be done. Those buggers build their nests in places where the temperatures would roast us."

"It's true," said Trundell. "Moleworms can cope with levels of heat stress and dehydration that'd kill a human, even one with thermoregulation adaptations like an Alighierian. Their resting metabolic rate is phenomenally low for their body mass, allowing them to conserve water and energy when asleep or sedentary, and they have a thick layer of subdermal brown adipose tissue that provides insulation for their inner organs. They thrive where we'd die."

"You could always borrow a shieldsuit, I guess," said Kahlo, "but the other problem is difficulty of access. The moleworms' own tunnels are there to use, but they go on for miles and miles, completely unmapped. Sometimes moleworms burrow vertically, too."

"I'm not talking about any of that," said Dev. "I

doubt I'd discover anything down there except how it feels to be a chargrilled side of beef. I'm proposing, instead, that I head over to Lidenbrock City."

Kahlo did a double take. "Lidenbrock? What for?"

"That's where the eastern moleworms hail from. Why have they left? What impelled them to migrate here?"

"You think you'll find the answers in Lidenbrock?"

"It's as good a place as any to start looking."

"Well, be warned. Folk aren't what you'd call hospitable there. I've not visited myself, but everyone I've known who has says don't bother. You'll get treated like dirt, and if you're lucky, you'll come back intact, though most likely minus a few personal possessions."

"Calder's hasn't exactly welcomed me with open arms so far. Maybe in Lidenbrock I'll be a better fit."

"Don't count on it. Truth is, I should be advising you against going there altogether. It's genuinely dangerous. The murders rates are insane. There's no law to speak of."

"That's okay," said Dev. "I'll be taking Trundle with me to look after me. He'll have my back."

"Wha-a-at?" squeaked Trundell. "No!"

Dev yoked an arm around his neck and ruffled his hair. "I need my sidekick, prof. My zoology expert. I can't do it without you. Who's going to ask intelligent questions about moleworms if not you?"

"But... but..." Trundell floundered.

"It'll be fine. Don't you want to follow in Professor

Banerjee's footsteps? See where the great man did his work?"

"Yes, but not in... not like..."

"That sentence began with a 'yes.' That's good enough for me."

Trundell didn't quite concede defeat, but he was too bewildered and taken aback to continue protesting. Dev knew he would be able to talk him round eventually, breaking down the last of his resistance. The xeno-entomologist was nothing if not biddable.

"If he's going with you," said Kahlo, "then I'm sending you out with a police escort. I won't allow an off-world civilian to be exposed to Lidenbrock unprotected. I won't have that on my conscience."

"You're offering to come too?" said Dev.

"Not me. I have to stay here. Calder's needs me more than ever. But I'll rustle up a team for you, and make the travel arrangements too. Might as well do this properly. Otherwise, knowing you, it'd be some half-cocked effort, liable to end in disaster."

"Astrid Kahlo, you're a star. In fact, I could kiss you."

"Better men than you have tried, Harmer," Kahlo said. She wagged a finger. "Just promise me this. He comes back in one piece." She pointed to Trundell.

"You have my word."

"I wonder how much *that's* worth," Kahlo muttered. "And," she added, "you had better come back in one piece too, Harmer. You're a right royal pain, but you're starting to grow on me."

"Like a yeast infection."

"You said it. Also, if you get yourself killed, the paperwork's going to be a bitch."

Dev laughed. "The paperwork or the person doing it?"

Kahlo hauled back and socked him in the jaw as hard as she could.

And, to be fair, he deserved it.

23

"LOCKED INTO THE ejector tube and ready for launch," said Wing Commander Beauregard, leaning through the narrow opening that joined cockpit to cabin. "Hope you're all buckled in back there."

Dev glanced across the aisle at Trundell. The xeno-entomologist had his eyes tight shut and was gripping the armrests of his seat. Ashen-faced, he looked like a man awaiting execution.

"Hey, Trundell."

Trundell's eyes snapped open. "You got my name right," he said, startled.

"Don't worry about this. We're going to be fine."

"Yes? And how many ejection takeoffs have you done, Harmer, if I may ask?"

"It's my first."

"Then how do you know we're going to be fine?"

"Because Wing Commander Beauregard must have done hundreds, and he's still alive, isn't he?"

Beauregard's status as a living person was not in

doubt. Whether he was *sane*, though, was another matter.

Beauregard was wild-eyed and unshaven, and his uniform, if uniform it was, had seen better days. A threadbare leather flight jacket hung over what had apparently once been a League of Diasporan Short-Haulers shirt, although the breast pocket that would have carried the LDSH insignia had been torn off. For a belt he had a length of twine, and a peaked Air Force cap sat slantwise on his head, its cloth crown mapped with sweat stains, much of its braid missing.

A pilot's appearance was supposed to instil confidence in his passengers. Beauregard's did not.

The hip flask he kept sipping from didn't help either.

Nor did the religious paraphernalia with which he had festooned his control console: crucifixes, Buddhas, Stars of David, tiki gods, miniature ikons, a kitschy Virgin Mary statuette, a bobble-head Jesus. They might have been there as a joke, but it was a joke in poor taste.

"Pressure's at its peak," said Beauregard. "Commencing countdown. This'll get bumpy, but think of it as an amusement park ride. I do. Ten."

Also in the cabin with Dev and Trundell were two police officers. They had been hand-picked by Kahlo, or so she said. One of them, Deputy Zagat, Dev knew nothing about, but the other was Sergeant Stegman, and he could only think that Kahlo had selected *him* out of sheer perversity.

"Stegman's a jerk," Dev had protested when Kahlo announced who would be escorting him to Lidenbrock City.

"So are you. It's a match made in heaven."

"Can't I have Patrolman Utz instead? I like him, and he's actually not a complete tool. He also seems to know what he's doing, so that's a bonus."

"You need someone reasonably senior with you. Plus, prickly personality notwithstanding, Stegman's reliable."

"Reliably pigheaded."

"He won't put up with any of your shit, Harmer. Which makes him perfect for the job. If it's any consolation, he's bitching about it as much as you are. He's all 'Why me? Anyone but me, ma'am!' I think, the two of you together, you'll keep each other honest. And on your toes."

"Is this negotiable?"

"With me, nothing is, Harmer."

Stegman was managing to keep his anxiety in check better than Trundell, but only just. His fingers were tapping out a rhythm on his knee. He was probably listening to loud distracting music.

Meanwhile, Deputy Zagat had overcome his nerves, if he had any, by the tried and tested technique of falling sound asleep. He was a big man, and his snores were commensurately deep.

"Five," said Beauregard. "Four. If you've got prayers, say them now. Ha-ha!"

Beneath the arcjet's hull, huge forces were mounting. The suborbital craft was about to be propelled out of Calder's Edge via a conductive launch armature set within an array of parallel electromagnetic rails. The aim was to get her through Alghieri's crust and lower exosphere as quickly as possible, in order to minimise the time her heat shielding was exposed to the excessive temperatures on the planet's surface.

It was first thing in the morning, a half-hour before dawn. This region of Alighieri was at its coolest then. Even so, it was a little over six hundred degrees Celsius topside, hot enough to melt aluminium.

"Two," said Beauregard. "One."

There was silence.

Then a massive jolt that shoved Dev down hard into his seat. The arcjet thrummed like a giant didgeridoo. Dev's head became difficult to hold up, pressing onto his spinal column as though it had quadrupled in weight.

Above, at the top of the ejector tube, huge tantalum-zirconium doors sprang wide. The arcjet popped up through them, accelerating to a speed of one kilometre per second. The doors slammed shut behind her.

The vertical axis g-force would have been unbearable, even lethal, to the five people aboard, had the arcjet not been fitted with a modified Riemann Deviation drive. This was an inverted version of the gravity warping drives that shunted starships sideways into infraspace. It briefly set up a negative-gravimetric field which counteracted some – though not all – of the g-force, turning what would otherwise have been an eyeball-enucleating experience into a merely very unpleasant one.

Beauregard chortled throughout the ascent like a teenage boy watching his first pornstream. He hadn't just got used to the sensation of having his body crushed as though beneath a piledriver; he actively enjoyed it.

Trundell, meanwhile, was letting out a whine that threatened to become a high-pitched wail.

The arcjet – *Milady Frog* – achieved close to two kilometres per second, Alighierian escape velocity, before a touch of the thrusters from Beauregard converted her perpendicular trajectory to an angled one. She hurtled in a rising parabola that took her almost to the limit of the planet's gravity well, heading due west.

As the momentum of takeoff began to wane, boosters kicked in. The sheer rocketing climb became a near-horizontal glide through Alighieri's all-but-nonexistent atmosphere.

"You can unbuckle your seatbelts now if you like," said Beauregard. "Unpucker your sphincters, too. It should be smooth going from here on. Next stop, Lidenbrock. Journey time's three hours, so make yourselves comfortable, settle in, and take in the view while you're up here."

Porthole covers retracted and dim light infiltrated into the cabin from both sides.

Milady Frog soared across Alighieri's night side, slightly faster than the planet was turning. Craning his neck, Dev could just make out a rim of daylight to the rear, flaring around the horizon like a halo. The terminator between night and day was chasing them, but wouldn't catch up.

Alighieri's shadow was protecting them from the full, searing glare of Iota Draconis. *Milady Frog* was built to withstand excessive temperatures. Her boron carbide hull panels would keep out the worst of the solar thermal radiation. But to fly during the daytime was a risk all the same. Just one chink in the arcjet's armour, the merest crack, and some vital piece of avionics might be flash-fried to a cinder. What would follow didn't bear thinking about.

Night flying was by far the wiser option.

Beauregard engaged the autopilot and rested his feet on the control console. For a while, he toyed with an Eye of Horus emblem made of jade, walking it across his knuckles. Then he fell asleep.

Alighieri stretched below, an expanse of darkness.

The arcjet soon gained enough altitude that Dev could make out the planet's tectonic layout. The plates were demarcated by glowing orange lines, zigzagging cracks where magma blistered up through from beneath. Bursts of brightness were strung along the lines like pearls on a necklace. There, at these hotspots, the volcanic emission activity was intense, huge coronas of lava spurting out one kilometre high.

He had to wonder why anybody would come to this planet voluntarily; indeed, why anybody would have thought it worth colonising. Oh, yes, sure, helium-3, most valuable resource in the galaxy, blah-

blah. But the place was as barren and forbidding as you could imagine.

Hell might not exist as an abstract concept any more, but if you were looking for it in reality, you could do a lot worse than start at Iota Draconis C.

Dev snuggled back into the foam-padded contours of his seat and prepared to let the drone of *Milady Frog*'s engines lull him into a doze. Beauregard thought it okay to sleep, so why shouldn't he too?

He'd had a restless night, after all. The hotel which Kahlo had recommended was none too luxurious. It was little better than a flophouse for migrant miners who were skimping on their living expenses so that they'd have more money to take home at the end of their tours. The walls had been cardboard-thin, so that every snore, burp and fart from the adjacent rooms came through. As for the mattress, it was a slim, tatty slab of contour foam that had lost most of its springiness, made even more uncomfortable by the constant nagging pain in his back and belly, legacy of the Ordeal.

On top of which, he had had to get up horribly early this morning to be at the launch complex to catch the flight.

All in all, he was dog tired.

"Uhm, Harmer?"

Dev half-opened an eye. "Yeah, Trundle?"

Trundell's face fell. "We're back to that, are we?"

"What is it? I'm trying for a nap here."

"Just to say, you remember you asked me if I wanted to follow in Professor Banerjee's footsteps."

"Yeah. So?"

"Did you know about Banerjee when you made that comment?"

"What do you mean?"

"Well, you're aware he died in Lidenbrock City, aren't you?"

Dev fully opened both eyes. "No, I wasn't aware of that."

"Ah, yes," said Trundell. "That'll be why you presented it to me as an incentive and not, in fact, the opposite."

"How did he die?"

"No one's sure. It's not even clear if he did. He just... disappeared one day. He'd finished his paper on moleworms and submitted it for peer review. Everyone assumed he'd be on the next cruiser back to Earth, but he stayed on for a while at Lidenbrock, and then all at once he was gone."

"Gone?"

"Incommunicado. Off the grid. Never heard from again. His paper was published anyway, and most academics regard it as his final, posthumous work."

"Oh, well, that's lovely," said Dev. "You reckon a moleworm got him?"

"That would be the likeliest explanation. He got too close to one, got unlucky, got eaten. It can happen even to the most experienced zoologist. Occupational hazard when you're around large dangerous carnivores all the time."

"Or maybe Lidenbrockers were responsible," Stegman chipped in. "Those trogs will kill you as soon as look at you. There've been rumours that *they're* dangerous carnivores too – with a taste for human flesh."

"Cannibals?" said Dev. "Surely not."

"Never been confirmed," said Stegman. "But over the years, you hear stuff, you know? Human bones found in kitchen waste disposal units. Butchers' shops selling mystery meat that isn't vat-grown. Kids going missing off the street."

"What is this? Official Creep Dev Out day?"

"Well, they're just rumours," said Stegman impassively.

"Plenty of misconceptions about Lidenbrockers," Beauregard said from the cockpit. He hadn't been asleep after all, or else only shallowly. "You've just got to know how to deal with them, that's all. They respect toughness. When I'm haggling with them, I stare them in the eye and I don't back down. Works every time."

Kahlo had told Dev that Beauregard's arcjet operation was based around selling the Lidenbrockers luxury goods from Calder's: quality booze, designer clothing, jewellery, food delicacies. She suspected he also peddled boutique narcotics, the non-TerCon-approved kind that Franz Glazkov traded in, but since the actual transactions took place out of her jurisdiction she was powerless to do anything about it.

Transporting passengers to and from Lidenbrock was very much a sideline for Beauregard. He would make a commodities run once a week, sometimes twice. A passenger run? Once in a blue moon. Lidenbrock wasn't exactly a favoured destination, and its inhabitants seldom left.

"Anyhow," said Trundell, "much as I admire Banerjee, I've no wish to end up like him – whatever happened to him."

"But you've come all the same," said Dev. "Braver than you look."

"I guess I feel I'm doing something useful. Not that xeno-entomology isn't useful," he added. "But this seems like the bigger picture. The cosmopolitical picture. If I'm honest, deep down I'm thinking it's pretty cool. Me, working for ISS in an advisory capacity. The guys back at the faculty would never believe it."

"Geek," said Dev, but he said it with warmth.

24

BANG ON SCHEDULE, *Milady Frog* began her descent towards Lidenbrock City. A ring of landing lights blazed into life around the ejector tube entrance. The arcjet plunged into the aperture like a falling meteor, Beauregard applying brake thrust only when she was several hundred metres deep into the tube.

He slotted her sideways into a docking bay. Then came a fifteen-minute wait until the hull tiles had cooled to the point where it was okay to exit without risk of getting singed.

Dev used the time to inventory his weapons. Before leaving Calder's, he had obtained an override code from ISS that allowed him access to the arsenal at the outpost.

Picking his way through the creaking wreckage of the building, ducking under police hazard tape, he had thought about poor young Junius Bilk. The kid's body had been reclaimed by his family for burial. Dev didn't like to imagine how his parents must be feeling.

Bilk had served as an ISS liaison for three years, apparently. In that time he would have done nothing but kept the outpost tidy and functioning, studied the training update modules his bosses sent him, and hung on for the moment when he might, just might, be called to active duty.

All that tedium, and no sooner had he some proper work to do, no sooner had his patience been rewarded, than he was killed.

It sucked.

But then what part of life as an ISS employee *didn't* suck? You had to make the best of it. Otherwise you'd shoot yourself.

The arsenal had yielded an array of location-appropriate hardware – short-range, non-explosive. Dev had selected a hiss gun, a 'hair-splitter' knife, and a couple of nano-frag mines. Each was so small and discreet that it could be carried in a pocket. He wanted to be tooled up without looking as though he was tooled up.

Now he checked his pockets one after another, reminding himself where each weapon was secreted.

If Lidenbrockers were as psycho nutzoid as everyone was saying, he might need every edge he could get.

Beauregard stepped out of *Milady Frog* first, leading his four passengers down the rear-loading ramp. The arcjet was still exuding heat, her metal inner structure ticking and groaning as it cooled. There was something of the crouching, high-haunched amphibian about her shape. Her name was a bit literal, but it suited her.

The handful of Lidenbrockers who had assembled to meet Beauregard and his passengers at the docking bay called themselves customs officers, but nothing in their appearance suggested bureaucracy or administration. They wore shabby casual clothing and carried an assortment of guns and other handweapons openly. All of them sported mo-tats – animated loops of writhing snakes, cavorting nudes and bleeding hearts etched on their skin in smart ink.

"My friends!" said Beauregard, arms spread wide. He had warned Dev and the others beforehand that any welcoming committee at Lidenbrock needed to be handled with a degree of finesse. *Keep your mouths shut and leave the talking to me.* "Human cargo only this time, as you see."

The Lidenbrockers peered past him, every face an imperturbable mask, every gaze steely.

"Those two," said one of them, singling out Stegman and Zagat. "Don't like the look of them."

The Calder's Edge police officers were in plain clothes, incognito. Uniforms would be considered a provocation at Lidenbrock. In the absence of their regulation utility belts, they had various pacification weapons stashed about their persons, concealed like Dev's.

Still, with their tight haircuts and stiff bearing, Stegman and Zagat couldn't help looking like authority. Stegman even had his arms folded and his head tilted in the classic officious cop stance.

"Smell like pig to me," said another of the Lidenbrockers. The man had a pair of short horns projecting from his forehead. His pupils were vertical slits in scarlet irises. Dev gathered from his preliminary research that plenty of Lidenbrock's citizens went in for this sort of body modification, voluntarily dehumanising themselves. A statement of rebellion, rejecting standard Diasporan values.

Stegman bridled. "We're –"

Beauregard spoke over him. "This is purely an informal visit. These gents are here to make a scientific survey."

"What of?" said Horns.

"Moleworms."

Someone laughed. "Good luck with that. Haven't seen any of those fuckers round here in an age."

"They're all gone?" said Trundell.

"Yeah, dickface, they're all gone," said Horns. "What's it to you? Don't tell me, you're another of those stick-up-the-butt boffin types, come to tag the old moleys and tell us how amazing and fascinating they are."

"Um, yes." Trundell gave a nervous blink.

Horns stepped up close to him, leaning in until the bony nodules on his forehead were almost poking the xeno-entomologist's face.

"Last guy that did that," said Horns, "it didn't work out so well for him. Professor Banana Tree or whatever his name was."

"Banerjee." Trundell couldn't help himself. He was a stickler for correctness. Even when intimidated, even when it wasn't going to do him any favours, things had to be *right*. "Not Banana Tree. Banerjee."

Horns grinned. His teeth were modified, too, a mouthful of pointed, meshing fangs.

Trundell gulped quiveringly.

"Ooh, pardon me," Horns said. "My bad. Obviously I haven't had your education, have I? I'm just a thick dipshit troglodyte."

"I – I never said that."

"No, but it's what you meant."

"N-no. No."

"Harvey," said Beauregard to Horns. "He's no one. Just a biologist. Leave him alone."

"Hold on there, wingco." Horns, a.k.a. Harvey, flapped at hand at Beauregard. "Me and the offworlder are talking. We need to get a couple of things straight. He's calling me stupid, and I resent that."

"Look, can we just process our passports and get on?" said Beauregard.

Passports, in this context, meant bribes. Lidenbrock City didn't demand certified entry permits or work visas or suchlike. A substantial sweetener would get you through the gates, and once you were in the city itself, you were free to do pretty much as you pleased, although you might occasionally be required to pay a 'tax' levied by a neighbourhood gang leader or grease the palm of some self-appointed civic dignitary in order to make life easier for yourself and ensure that neither anything you owned, nor you yourself, got broken.

Dev could see the situation getting out of hand, unless someone acted to resolve it more forcefully and less mollifyingly than Beauregard. Trundell could react to Harvey's bullying in one of two ways. Either he put up with it, and Harvey would regard that as a sign of weakness and inevitably escalate the verbal abuse to physical. Or he would snap back with some waspish retort, which Harvey would use as the perfect excuse to lose his temper. Both scenarios were destined to end in violence, and an injured Ludlow Trundell.

Time to intervene.

"Harvey, yeah? Is that your name?" Dev said.

The Lidenbrocker turned his reptilian eyes on Dev. "And who the fuck are you?"

Dev rabbit-punched him in the mouth, hard enough to shatter several of those serrated fangs.

Harvey went down, spitting blood and splinters of dentine.

"Oh, I forgot to introduce myself," Dev said. "I'm the man who's going to hit you. Should have said that first, shouldn't I?"

As one, the remaining Lidenbrockers drew their guns and knives. Weaponry clattered and bristled. The air was filled with the clicking of cocked hammers and the hum of power cells charging up.

"No!" cried Beauregard. "There's no call for this. No, no, no. Everyone calm down. Put those things away. We can sort it out. How much? My passengers can pay. How much do you need?"

The Lidenbrockers weren't listening. They spread out in a line, moving to flank Dev and the others on both sides.

Stegman was glaring at Dev – *now look what you've gone and done* – whereas Zagat was concentrating on the Lidenbrockers, marking their relative positions, assessing the level of threat each posed. The deputy hadn't said two words since boarding *Milady Frog* but, judging by his cool composure now, Dev had the impression he would be handy in a fight.

Good. Because it looked like it was going to come to that.

"We don't want trouble," Dev said.

"Should've thought of that before you decked Harvey," said a Lidenbrocker with pointed ears and subdermal implants which gave his face a batlike cast.

"He got in too close. He was picking on my friend. We just want to be allowed to conduct our business. Beauregard's right – we'll pay for our passports or excise duty or whatever you like to call it."

"Problem is," said Batface, "Harvey's a Kobold. We're all Kobolds. Hit one of us and you're hitting us all."

The Kobolds were one of the many gangs who held sway in the city. They were in fact one of the largest and most powerful, controlling an extensive area of turf across Lidenbrock's lower northern reaches.

"I respect that," Dev said. "Tribal loyalty. Blood brotherhood. All very noble. But dick behaviour is still dick behaviour. Your pal Harvey was giving one of my team grief. You'd have done the same in my shoes."

He thought he was getting through to them. Gangsters or not, these men surely had a code of honour.

"Harvey was being kind of a douche," one said.

"Yeah," said another. "That offworlder's pretty pussy-looking. Trust Harvey to go for the runt when there's all these bruisers standing around."

Harvey, through pain and shattered teeth, moaned something about how he didn't like being talked down to by eggheads who thought they were smarter than everyone else. It was insulting.

"So shall we settle this amicably?" Dev said. "You name a figure, we'll try and meet it, everyone goes away happy and content. Yeah?"

Batface looked around at his comrades, and slowly nodded. "Reckon that could work. Price has gone up, though. Due to unforeseen circumstances. What do you say to double the going rate?"

Dev swiftly checked the balance of his ISS slush fund. What Batface was asking for would all but wipe it out. Didn't matter. He could always put in a request for extra contingency money. Deep-pocketed ISS usually came through with the readies when asked.

"Deal."

With that, the tension in the docking bay was defused and the standoff was over. The Kobolds stowed their weapons. They seemed to feel they had done a good day's work, their successful act of extortion giving them a warm glow inside. Batface even directed a smile Dev's way.

Then Harvey Horns rose to his feet with a furious growl and made a lunge for Dev.

And everything went to shit again.

25

HARVEY HAD PRODUCED a shimmerknife from inside his boot. An amplified piezoelectric actuator in the hilt sent ultrasonic waves through the six-inch carbon steel blade, making it vibrate at such a rate that it could literally carve through stone. The blade, when activated, became a sabre-shaped blur, as though you were seeing it through frosted glass.

The shimmerknife buzzed through the air in Harvey's hand like an angry hornet. It was aimed at Dev's head. Barely in the nick of time, Dev brought up a fist and blocked the strike, deflecting Harvey's arm. The knife shaved a straight line through his hair, missing his scalp by millimetres.

Harvey pivoted, and Dev pivoted too. The Kobold's lips and chin were smeared with blood, a crimson goatee. He was hurting, and he was livid.

He was also clumsy.

The next knife strike came in from the side, Harvey delivering the blow backhand at Dev's throat. Dev reared back and the shimmerknife whistled past.

The thrust left Harvey momentarily off-balance, and Dev took advantage by seizing his knife arm. Holding the wrist with one hand, he pulled hard, at the same time driving the heel of his other hand into the side of Harvey's elbow.

The hinge joint snapped laterally, loudly.

Harvey's mouth gaped in a soundless rictus scream, revealing the reddened ruins of his teeth.

Dev added insult to injury by twisting the Kobold's forearm so that the broken ends of the elbow grated together.

The shimmerknife fell to the floor point first, embedding itself in the concrete up to the hilt guard.

Harvey fell too, passing out from pain.

All this had taken no more than five seconds, but already the other Kobolds were going into action, drawing their weapons again. It was pack instinct as much as anything. If one of their number went on the offensive, then whatever the reason, whatever the rights and wrongs of it, the rest of them must too. Group solidarity first and foremost.

Deputy Zagat, however, was also on the move. The moment Harvey went for Dev, Zagat had seen where things were headed. He grabbed hold of the nearest Kobold from behind and kneed the man so hard in the base of the spine, and so accurately, that he was numbed from the waist down. The Kobold collapsed as though his lower half was boneless jelly.

Next instant, the big deputy had another of the Kobolds by the wrists. He spun the Lidenbrocker round and round like an Olympic hammer thrower until the man's feet left the ground. Then he let go. The Kobold sailed across the docking bay, spinning, until he slammed headlong into a stack of plastic cargo crates.

He didn't get up again.

Dev darted towards Batface, pulling out his hair-splitter knife as he went. The hair-splitter was to all intents and purposes a basic close-combat weapon, but its edge was honed to molecule-fine sharpness by an array of self-arranging nanowires embedded in its stellite alloy blade. Not only could it cut a hair in half down the middle, as the name suggested, but it could slice into any material short of diamond. Hence, its sheath was made from synthetic diamond.

Batface had a repro classic pistol in his hand, a fully working replica Glock 9mm of the type carried by old-school Terran street hoods. Gold-plated, too, for extra corniness.

He pointed the Glock at Dev.

A moment later, he was holding only the grip of a pistol. The barrel, just forward of the trigger guard, had been lopped cleanly off. An unfired bullet tumbled out of the breech.

Batface registered shock and dismay. "Oh, man. That thing cost a buttload."

"And now get a load of its butt," said Dev as he snatched the rear half of the gun out of Batface's grasp with his free hand and clubbed him on the head with it.

He kept clubbing until Batface was down and out.

JAMES LOVEGROVE

Stegman was grappling with one of the female 'customs officers.' The third joints of the fingers on each of her hands were locked together by an implanted brass ridge – a permanent, irremoveable knuckleduster. Stegman was trying to control her fists so that she couldn't land a blow.

Dev drew his hiss gun and shot the woman in the shoulder with a pencil-thin spike of ultra-compressed air. It went straight through her deltoid and scapula like an invisible lance, sending a spray of muscle and bone shards spiralling out behind her.

The sheer shock of the injury stopped her in her tracks. Stegman punched her out while she was stunned. He acknowledged Dev's assist with a cursory tip of the head.

Shots rang out, and Dev spun. Another of the Kobolds had a ballistic handgun; this one a magnetic projectile accelerator pistol. Barbed steel flechettes raked the floor at Dev's feet.

Dev returned fire with the hiss gun, and the Kobold panicked and bolted for cover. He kept shooting as he ran, but he was barely looking where he was aiming, just pulling the MPA pistol's trigger wildly. One flechette took out a fellow Kobold, ripping a hole through the man's flank.

Amateur.

He found refuge behind a support pillar. He leaned round and loosed off a few more flechettes in Dev's direction.

Dev pinned him back behind the pillar with a couple of well-placed shots. The hiss gun drilled neat

220

holes in the concrete, but didn't have the penetrating power to go all the way through.

A nano-frag mine, on the other hand...

Dev primed the disc-shaped mine and sent it skittering across the floor. It fetched up against the foot of the pillar, anchored itself with a squirt of molecular glue, and detonated.

A small cloud of omnivorous nanites burst out and immediately began devouring everything they came into contact with, including the mine that had birthed them. They ate through floor and pillar like a swarm of submicroscopic locusts, reducing solid structures to dust in the blink of an eye.

Dev had set the mine for three seconds' duration. When the time elapsed, the nanites self-destructed simultaneously, becoming inert particles of dust themselves.

Now the Kobold was cowering behind a pillar whose lower portion had been corroded away to a thin spindle, affording him no shelter. The rest of the pillar hung from the ceiling like a stalactite. Precarious and unable to bear its own weight, it crumbled and fell with an almighty *crunch*.

The Kobold sprang out of the way in order to avoid being crushed...

...and straight into reach of Dev's fists.

Deputy Zagat polished off the two remaining Kobolds by pounding their heads together. He dropped them to the ground, both unconscious, and brushed his palms against each other as though they were caked in dirt.

"Tidy," was all he said.

"Well, that could have gone better," said Beauregard. When the fighting broke out, he had scuttled up the loading ramp to the safety of *Milady Frog*. Now he came back down, surveying the injured and insensible Kobolds littering the docking bay. "I had the situation in hand. None of this would have happened if you hadn't hit Harvey."

"Me?" said Dev. "This is my fault? He wasn't going to leave Trundle alone. They respect toughness, you said. So I got tough."

"For what it's worth, I agree," said Trundell, blinking rapidly. He looked shaken by the violence and bloodshed, but his voice had firmness. "I only wish there'd been someone like Harmer around when I was at school. Then I'd have spent less time with my head getting flushed in the toilet. And that was just the girls."

Dev laughed. "I think Stegman can relate."

"Screw you, Harmer," said Stegman.

"Weren't you having lady troubles just now?" Dev indicated the Kobold with the metal knuckles. "Maybe you like your women knocking you around a bit. You work for a real ballbreaker, after all."

"Seriously, Harmer. Screw. You."

"Not that I blame you. There's something incredibly attractive about a woman who can kick butt. You get the feeling she'd be a wildcat in the sack."

"I'm warning you, you keep badmouthing Captain Kahlo..."

"I'm not; I'm complimenting her. Anyway, what's done is done." He gestured around the docking bay. "They started it. They got what was coming to them. Beauregard?"

"Yes?"

"Reckon you can clean this mess up for us?"

"I can secure these people somewhere, yes. There's a set of storage lockers not far from here. I can drag them and shut them inside."

"Great. Do that. We can't have other Kobolds, or anyone else, stumbling onto the scene and raising the alarm."

"It's not like that's going to help you, though," Beauregard said.

"Isn't it? I thought it'd buy us a few hours, which is hopefully all we'll need."

"No. What you don't understand is that Kobolds share first-hand experiences freely and continuously via commmplant. It's how they keep tabs on one another. That way, one of the gang can't betray or rip off the rest. Anyone who did would be caught out straight away and punished. It fosters trust."

"Shit. You mean they're broadcasting their activities all the time?"

"They have iWitness spliced into their optic nerves and it's functioning around the clock. Everything gets sent to a private insite node only Kobolds can access. The only footage that gets blocked is their intimate moments – fornicating, defecating and so on. Then response filters kick in and put up an audiovisual blackout for the duration."

"Nobody was fornicating just now," Dev observed, "although I think one or two of them might have shit themselves."

"This little fracas," said Beauregard, "has been recorded from a dozen different points of view and stored in the system, and you can bet the insite node will have flagged it up. Gunfire and bloodshed are automatic alert triggers."

"So other Kobolds may well know all about this."

"Afraid so," said Beauregard with a grave nod. "If not already, then soon."

"And they'll be pissed off and come running."

Another nod.

Dev gave vent to an angry grunt. "Perma-linked gangsters. None of the 'pedia entries on Lidenbrock thought to mention that. I guess that means we're on an even tighter schedule than before."

"What do you propose we do?" Trundell asked.

"Quiet. I'm thinking." Dev mimed a buffering circle with his index finger. "Okay. Those doors over there." He pointed to the docking bay exit. "They look pretty sturdy. We bring those down, jam the lock mechanism, then nobody's getting in here easily, right?"

"They're blast doors," said Beauregard. "Same as the ones between the bay and the ejector tube. If there's a catastrophic failure somewhere in the tube – like the topside doors break or get stuck open during daytime – the heat from above has to be kept out somehow. Otherwise it'll burn through the launch complex like a blowtorch and maybe even spread out into the city."

"Two sets of doors," said Trundell. "Sensible. Double redundancy."

Dev said, "So with the inner doors securely shut, Beauregard and *Milady Frog* should be out of reach. The Kobolds can't get to them. Meanwhile, the rest of us go out into the city."

"Much appreciated," said Beauregard. "It still doesn't help *you*, though. The Kobolds know your faces. They'll be looking for you. Once they realise you're not here, they'll start scouring the city. You'd be better off getting back aboard *Milady Frog* right now and hightailing it while you can."

"Yeah, but I came here to do something and I'm not leaving until it's done. We can stay one step ahead of these Kobold doofuses. None of them are exactly rocket scientists, if this lot are anything to go by."

"They have numbers. I think there are as many as a thousand of them in Lidenbrock. That's a small army. And their leader – Mayor Major – he *isn't* stupid. With him mobilising them, the Kobolds can get very organised."

"Luckily for us," said Dev, "my speciality is *dis*organising."

26

DEV, STEGMAN, ZAGAT and Trundell stole through the network of tunnels and shafts that was Lidenbrock City.

The place did not boast open spaces like Calder's Edge. It didn't nestle inside pre-existing caverns. Lidenbrock City had been carved out inch by inch, passageway by passageway, sideways, up, down, growing organically to become a complex lattice of subterranean thoroughfares. It had not been constructed according to any particular plan. It had no centre, no plaza, no heart. It was a random three-dimensional sprawl.

The streets were lined with prefab habitats, many with jerry-built front extensions that took up so much space there was barely room for two people to walk abreast between them. Even the vertical shafts had habitats, anchored to the sheer walls, connected by ladders and open-sided elevators.

It was grotty and grimy and claustrophobic. The one saving grace, for Dev and company, was that it

wasn't too busy – thus far, at least. Dawn hadn't yet
come to Lidenbrock, and it was still the small hours.
The ambient lighting was night-time low, barely a
glimmer, and there weren't many inhabitants out and
about; the few that were skulked along, alone, shying
away from strangers.

Dev suspected that this state of affairs would
change once word spread among the Kobolds about
the altercation in the docking bay. Then things might
get very hectic indeed in Lidenbrock.

He quickly reviewed the mission objective.

In his moleworm paper, Professor Banerjee – the
late Professor Banerjee – had been good enough
to set down more than just his analysis of the life
cycle, reproductive habits and hunting patterns of
Pseudotalpidae alighieriensis, both *orientalis* and
occidentalis. He had also been at pains to outline his
methods, recording in meticulous detail not only how
he had conducted his studies and when, but where.

In order to observe the creatures closely, he had
erected hides outside the periphery of Lidenbrock at
locations of high moleworm traffic. His paper gave
their GPS co-ordinates and stated that he planned to
leave them in place for the use of future zoologists,
should any be keen to further his research sometime,
and also for his own use should he ever return to
Alighieri – although, in the end, he never left.

Dev's hope was that one of the hides might yield
some clue about the mysterious decampment of
eastern moleworms to Calder's Edge and the return of
western moleworms to their old stomping grounds.

After all, Banerjee might not have included everything he had learned about moleworms in his paper. He might have discovered more about them after sending the work off to Harvard. If so, the hides were where to look for any unsubmitted data.

What was it one of the Kobolds had said? *Haven't seen any of those fuckers round here in an age.*

So it seemed that not just a few moleworms had left Lidenbrock; they all had. It was a mass migration.

It seemed to confirm the suspicions Dev was forming. He had a theory about the moleworms, but one that was so tentative and unformed that it was, at present, little more than a hunch.

Banerjee's hides, at any rate, were his best lead, the logical place to start.

And, given that the clock was ticking and Lidenbrock would soon be teeming with vengeful Kobolds out for blood, the hides were probably the only bit of the city Dev would have a chance to explore before the situation became too dangerous and he and the others were forced to beat a hasty retreat back to *Milady Frog.*

"Stinks here," Stegman muttered. "Garbage and sweat and mildew. I feel like I need a shower."

Trundell tripped over what looked like a discarded bundle of laundry. It turned out to be a Lidenbrocker sleeping off a night of indulgence. He swore at Trundell, who apologised profusely, which somehow only served to make the man angrier. He rose up, spoiling for a fight.

"I can hardly see a thing," Trundell confided to

Dev after Zagat had pacified the Lidenbrocker, returning him to a comatose state. "Wish I had my image intensification contacts. But since I lost one of them running from that moleworm, there's no point."

"Stick close to me," Dev said. In the moonglow lighting everything was plain as day to him, as it was to Stegman and Zagat.

"This is a horrible place," the xeno-entomologist said with a shudder. "I don't know how Banerjee stuck it out as long as he did."

"Guess he loved science more than he loved his creature comforts. *You* hang out with scroaches, Trundle. Most people would wonder how you can do that."

"Fair point. This was supposed to be a utopia, though, wasn't it? Lidenbrock. That really didn't work out."

Dev had cached a few pages about Lidenbrock City on his commplant's internal drive, for reference.

Lidenbrock City

Third largest conurbation on Iota Draconis C (local planetary name: Alighieri). Founded in the early 'fifties by Henri Lelouche, French-Canadian cave explorer, cultist and self-styled "secular visionary." Name derived from that of lead character in Jules Verne's novel *Journey To The Centre Of The Earth* (*Voyage au centre de la Terre*), first published 236 AE.

Lelouche (11-87 PE) was a keen spelunker who made a name for himself in caver circles charting the deep reaches of the Mulu Caves in Borneo. Lelouche came to believe that underground living was more natural for humans than overground. He claimed a subterranean environment was conducive to contentment and social cohesion. "We were once cavemen," he said, "and if we are ever to find happiness and harmony, it is to the dark of the cave that we must return."

His theory was that the world's rocky interior is a kind of womb whose safe embrace people have left behind. The surface of the planet is a harsh, cruel place where lies and deceit flourish. "Truth is below" was Lelouche's motto.

His Speleophilia movement was unpopular in the newly dogma-free atmosphere of Post-Enlightenment, and Lelouche came in for much personal criticism for the podcasts and prolific vlogging through which he expounded his views. Yet he managed to attract a coterie of likeminded individuals around him, among them a wealthy sibling couple, Dan and Jan Robeson of the Robeson family philanthrophic trust, whom he eventually prevailed upon to finance the establishment of a Speleophile colony in the outer reaches of the Diaspora.

Initial excavation for what was to become Lidenbrock City commenced in 53 PE, and the

city's charter of incorporation was filed and
approved by TerCon in 55. Since then...

Since then, over the course of half a century,
Lidenbrock had grown dramatically. Its population,
originally a couple of hundred, now verged on a
hundred thousand. The handful of Speleophiles
who had supported Henri Lelouche in his dream
to create an ideal, self-sustaining subterranean
community had been swamped by an influx of
others, scarcely any of whom shared their beliefs
and aspirations.

Lidenbrock had become a Mecca for the
disenfranchised, the anti-authoritarian, the
secessionist. It had gained a reputation as a place
where anything went and there was minimal
interference from government. Escaped and former
convicts flocked there, and paramilitary extremists,
and radical reactionaries, all adding to the city's
stew of lawlessness and gang culture.

Ironically – or perhaps not – Lelouche had been
killed during a shootout between rival gangs, a
skirmish in a long-running turf war. Casting himself
in the role of peacemaker, he had waded into the
thick of the hostilities and demanded a ceasefire. He
had been gunned down mercilessly by both sides.

Lelouche had lived to see his haven for
Speleophiles degenerate into a den of violence and
depravity. It was possible that his attempt to end
the conflict between rival factions had in fact been
suicide.

"I don't know," Dev said to Trundell. "A lick of paint, maybe a park bench or two, a kiddies' playground – it could be lovely."

"That was another joke, was it? You'd need more than park benches to improve this dump."

"Tough crowd," Dev murmured.

His commplant pinged. They were within a couple of kilometres of the nearest of Banerjee's hides.

Habitats were fewer in number here, scattered. The tunnels were narrower, with lower ceilings. Detritus lay in heaps, as though trash kept getting shoved further and further outward to the city's edges where there weren't as many people around to see it.

The city outskirts. The badlands.

An albino dog on a chain barked at the four-man group as they went by: a mangy creature, skin a mass of sores, no breed and every breed. It strained at its tether, half throttling itself in its eagerness to attack. A sleep-slurred voice yelled at it from indoors – "Shurrup!" – but the dog didn't stop barking until Dev and company were well out of sight.

Five hundred metres to destination, Dev's commplant said in its neutral voice.

Dev relayed the information to the others.

They came to a crude barricade that had been set up across the tunnel. It was built from scrap metal, sticks of old furniture and husks of waste tech, with here and there a cushion or rug plugging a gap. Spent shell casings littered the floor in front of it, alongside empty beer cans.

On one wall someone had scrawled in spray paint:

MOLEYS FUK OF

On another wall there were badly drawn caricatures of moleworms, all snaggle teeth and snaky nasotentacles. Several were depicted on their backs, legs in the air, crosses for eyes, riddled with bullet holes. One had a speech bubble coming from its mouth: "U R A GOOD SHOT U OF KILLD ME DED."

"Line of control," Dev said. "This would have been manned round the clock, back when there were moleworms to worry about. Now people have stopped bothering. See how much rust there is on those shell casings? It's been months since anyone fired a gun here."

The barricade had not been well maintained. Dev and Zagat only had to heave aside a mattress, and a whole section of the ramshackle structure simply gave way. Echoes of the collapse resounded down the tunnel beyond.

"Well, if there are still moleworms around, they know we're coming," Stegman groused.

"To think Sunil Banerjee himself came this way," said Trundell as they filed through the gap in the barricade. "The Lidenbrockers must have thought he was crazy."

"Probably they admired him," said Dev. "Crazy for them is like genius for you academics."

Two hundred and fifty metres, said Dev's commplant.

Moleworm bones were scattered on the tunnel floor. Some, Dev noticed as he stepped over them, showed gnaw marks. He guessed other moleworms had scavenged the flesh off their fallen kin.

The supposition was borne out by the various piles of dried-up dung that accompanied the bones. These brittle, mould-wreathed mounds were now host to colonies of pale, pulpy termite-like insects which Trundell identified as *Isoptera coprophagia alighieriensis*.

"Commonly known as ordure ants, more vulgarly known as shittermites. They make their nests in moleworm excreta, which they live on until there's none left, and then they move on."

"They eat themselves out of house and home," said Dev.

"In a manner of speaking. But don't tread on the dung piles if you can help it, because ordure ants respond to a perceived attack in force. Their mandibles are a centimetre long and razor sharp. You'll know if one bites you, and it's more likely to be a hundred of them at once."

"Gotcha. Don't step in poop. Duly noted."

One hundred metres.

Residual light from beyond the barricade was waning. The tunnel floor was uneven, the tunnel itself full of haphazard twists and turns. Dug by moleworm rather than man.

Trundell produced a flashlight, warning the others to look away before he switched it on.

Even through closed eyelids, Dev found the sudden burst of brilliance dazzling, painfully so. It took his Alighierian vision a full minute to adjust.

Trundell trained the flashlight around. The beam fell on a ledge some ten feet up, illuminating a flock of squirming winged things that flitted away into the darkness.

"Bats?" said Dev.

"Birds, actually. Blindwarblers. Harmless. Ordure ants are their staple food. Banerjee mentioned them. 'A pest,' he said, 'but if cooked, palatable.'"

"Don't tell me. They taste like chicken."

"Pigeon, I think he said."

"He went kind of native, didn't he?"

"Eating bushmeat is common practice for a zoologist in the field. And there."

The flashlight picked out a hemispherical shape ahead.

"That'll be the hide."

27

THE HIDE WAS a dome made up of triangular panels, essentially a self-assembly, flat-bottomed polyhedron, just tall enough at its summit for a person to stand up in. Most of the panels were opaque, a few transparent, and all made of lightweight reinforced acrylic. Their edges were lined with covalent smart-bond strips. Once pressed together, the strips formed a solid, airtight seal which could be undone later, when the hide needed dismantling, by the application of an electric current from a special wand.

The structure was intact, though covered in a thick encrustation of blindwarbler droppings like some sort of lumpy icecap. The guano obscured the transparent panels, making it impossible to look in through them. It gave off an eye-wateringly acrid smell.

Dev located the entrance, a hatch at the base. It was code-locked.

No time for niceties. He took out the hiss gun

and punched a hole through the latch, disabling it. Then he kicked until the latch broke and the hatch swung inward.

A stench wafted out of the hide, mustier than the guano but no less pungent. Dev recoiled, nose wrinkling.

"Ugh. Hobo reek. Someone's camping in there. Someone with poor hygiene and presumably no sense of smell."

Trundell tried to peer in, but the stench proved too much for him. "That's rancid."

"Who's going inside to take a look?"

"You are, Harmer," said Stegman. "You're in charge of this expedition, aren't you? You're acting like it, anyway. So you take the lead."

"I thought Kahlo sent you along to keep an eye on me. Doesn't that make you the man in charge?"

"I'm supervising, yes, but you're the one calling the shots." Stegman, gleeful, made an ushering gesture in the direction of the hatch. "All yours, *sir.*"

Dev slipped off his undershirt and knotted it around the lower half of his face. On hands and knees, he crawled into the foetid hide.

Inside, a sleeping bag lay in a messy pile, surrounded by archipelagos of soiled clothing, including filthy underwear and brittle socks. A camping stove with an induction hob stood sentinel over a stainless steel cooking pot. The floor around it was heaped with tiny, porous bones, many with shreds of flesh and gristle still attached.

The smell began to get to him even through the bunched fabric of the undershirt. He retreated back out into the tunnel.

"It's so horrible in there, I can't even crack a joke," he said.

"What did you find?" asked Trundell.

"Somebody's claimed squatters' rights. He's been living off locally sourced meat. I found what look like bird bones, most likely blindwarbler."

"Who do you think it might be?"

"Some sort of Lidenbrocker reject, that'd be my guess," said Dev, "though what you'd have to *do* to get kicked out of Lidenbrock City – the mind boggles. It could, I suppose, be someone who's fallen out with one or other of the gangs and who's lying low until the heat dies down. Question remains – how did he get into the hide? There was no sign of forced entry, at least not until I came along and forced entry. He'd have to know the access code, whoever he is."

"What if it's a zoologist? Banerjee would have made the code available on request through the proper academic channels."

"I suppose. I'd have thought a scientist would be a little tidier and more considerate than that, though. Not leave food scraps and crusty clothing all over the place."

"Where's this getting us?" Stegman said. "I don't know about you, but I'd like to be heading back to the arcjet soon. Lidenbrock's going to be crawling with angry Kobolds before long, if it isn't already."

"We try another of the hides," Dev said. "I was hoping for some handwritten notes, stuff recorded on an external drive, something along those lines. If there was any of that at this hide, the current resident appears to have tossed it out. The next hide is about –"

"Movement."

This was from the laconic Zagat. He had been keeping lookout while Dev checked out the hide. The single murmured word brought silence and tension.

Dev snatched the flashlight from Trundell and aimed it in the direction Zagat was staring, deeper into the tunnel.

Something – someone – darted away from the beam. Dev caught a glimpse of ragged clothing and round, spooked eyes.

Without hesitation, Dev hared off along the tunnel. The flashlight beam bounced as he ran.

The figure ahead of him was running too, but with an awkward gait. Whoever it was kept tripping and once even collided with the tunnel wall. Dev quickly gained ground until he was within grabbing distance.

He dived, tackling his quarry to the floor. He caught a whiff of unwashed body and of fabric permeated with the same stale aroma as the interior of the hide. He insinuated an arm around the person's neck from behind, locking the hand into the crook of his other arm to reinforce the chokehold.

His victim writhed, but Dev applied pressure. He heard gasping and wheezing.

"Let's do this the easy way," he said. "You relax, don't resist, I don't asphyxiate you. Got that?"

Frantic nodding.

"I'll ease off now. We both stand up. Any funny business, I tighten my grip again. I can make you black out if I'm feeling kind. I can also keep the hold going until the blood supply to your brain is stopped long enough to be fatal. I'd like not to have to do that. I've got no beef with you. I just want to talk, that's all. Okay?"

More nodding.

"Okay. Good. Up we go."

They clambered upright together. Dev swung the man round – the person *was* male, he could feel coarse, bushy beard against his forearm – and frogmarched him over to the hide.

"Think we've found our squatter," he said. "Maybe he can tell us if Banerjee left anything useful in there."

Trundell was agog.

"What?" said Dev.

"I– I think he can do better than that, Harmer."

"Huh? What do you mean?"

"That isn't any squatter," Trundell said in slow, amazed tones. "That's Professor Banerjee."

28

"No fucking way."

That was Dev's immediate response. Banerjee was dead. He hadn't been heard from in two whole years. Not a peep from him since submitting his paper. He *had* to be dead. How else to account for his silence?

But Trundell was adamant. This straggly-bearded, shaggy-haired individual Dev was holding was the moleworm expert.

"I'd recognise him anywhere," Trundell said. "He's lost a ton of weight, he's a mess – but it's him. It's you, isn't it, Professor Banerjee?"

The man stirred, muttering something inaudible.

"What's that?" Dev demanded, giving him a shake. "Speak up."

"I said I don't know what you're talking about. I'm not this Banerjee person."

"You are," said Trundell.

"You're mistaken."

"You live in that hide, right?" said Dev. "Don't deny it. You reek of it. You were coming home, saw us standing here, panicked, ran. If you're not Banerjee, how come you know the access code?"

"I'm... I..."

"You're a bad liar, prof. Trundle's IDed you. Time to come clean."

"Trun*dell*," said Trundell. "My name's Ludlow Trundell, professor. Big fan. I'm actually in the same line of work as you, more or less. Xeno-entomologist. Perhaps you've heard of me?"

Banerjee shrugged. "Since I'm not this Banerjee you seem to think I am..."

Dev shook him again, more roughly. "Let's cut the crap, Banerjee. You're a respected zoology bigwig, but you've been hiding out here in the moleworm tunnels for two years, living like an animal. What's going on?"

"I'm just a cave dweller. Look." He pointed to a net bag that hung from his belt. In it were the carcases of three scrawny birds. Their plumage was smoky grey, their eyes blank white. "I snare blindwarblers for food. Would a professor do that?"

"He would if he'd turned hermit and didn't have any other supply of protein."

"What happened to you, professor?" Trundell asked, sounding almost plaintive. "How did you end up like this? Why didn't you return to Earth once you'd finished your work here?"

"All good questions," Dev said. "Answer him."

Banerjee drew a deep breath, expelling it as a heavy sigh. "All right. I've no idea who you people are, but I don't suppose it matters. You've found me.

I knew this day might come. I can easily imagine why you've come looking for me, too."

"Oh, yes?"

"One or more of you, I strongly suspect, is from Interstellar Security Solutions."

"One is," said Dev.

"The aggressive one. Of course. You're on Alighieri investigating possible Polis Plus activity. The trail has led you here, to Lidenbrock, to me. Let me go, and I'll be compliant and tell you what you want to know. I don't see that I have a choice, and perhaps it will do me good to unburden myself to you. To confess."

"Works for me." Dev relinquished his grip on Banerjee. "I should remind you that there are four of us and only one of you, and we don't take any crap. Clear?"

"As crystal." Banerjee rubbed his throat tenderly, turning to give Dev a reproachful look.

Now that Dev could see his eyes, he understood why Banerjee's attempt to flee had been so hamfisted. He was wearing image intensification contacts like Trundell's. The unexpected flare of the flashlight, catching him full in the face, had overloaded them. He had been running dazzled, half-blinded. The afterimage of the flashlight bulb was probably still imprinted in his retinas.

This *was* the great zoologist, though. Dev had no doubts about that. He pulled up an image of the man from his commplant for comparison. The Banerjee in the picture was neat and plump, with sleek hair and a confident smile – a tenured professor snugly ensconced at Harvard. The Banerjee in front of him was a gaunt, tattered scarecrow with grubby skin, an unkempt beard and wild, matted locks. But the nose was the same, the prominent forehead identical, the deep-set eyes...

"I am," he said, "Sunil Banerjee, and until two years ago I had everything to live for. I was pre-eminent in my domain. I had a wife and two daughters. I was inquisitive and, without wishing to brag, intrepid. I lectured all over the Earth, and off it, too. I conducted field research on eight worlds. I was even among the select few who took part in the Sanctuary Conference on Europa, where it was decided to make the moon the first ever whole-planet game reserve."

"So now tourists can go under the ice in submersibles and gawp at the deep-sea beasties," said Dev. "All very commendable, prof. You were at the top of your game. What went wrong?"

"Polis Plus, that's what went wrong. I was here at Lidenbrock, preparing to leave. My plan was to head back to Calder's Edge, wind down operations there as well, collect up my belongings, then hop aboard the next available cruiser home. I was looking forward to seeing my dear Anji and my two little girls again, holding them in my arms, hugging them. I had missed them so much. I swore to myself that I would never again be apart from them for such a long period..."

Banerjee swallowed.

"Then one day *he* appeared," he said. "I had no idea what he really was, at first. None at all. He sidled up to me while I was on a supply run in the city, stocking up on drinking water and food rations. He engaged me in conversation. He seemed to be interested in me, my work. He was well-informed, articulate, erudite."

"Not a Lidenbrocker trog," said Stegman.

"Absolutely. That's absolutely what I thought. Another outsider, like myself. A smart one, what's more. It was pleasant to have intelligent conversation again, after so long without. We went for a drink. He was charming. And yet... there was something off about him. I couldn't quite put my finger on what. Perhaps I should have been more guarded. He was so nice, though. So keen. So complimentary."

"Flattered you, huh?" said Dev.

"I have to admit, he played on my vanity, yes. But you must understand, too, that I had been starved of good company. Emailing with family, friends and colleagues is all very well, but you can't replace the joy of one-to-one, real-time interaction. Our topics of discussion ranged across all the sciences, different disciplines, and my interlocutor repeatedly deferred to my judgement, calling me 'wise' and 'insightful.'"

"He have a name, this brown-noser?"

"Jones. Ted Jones."

"As unimaginative as they come. An alias only a Plusser would choose."

"But I didn't realise he was a Plusser, not until later, much later. I've no experience of them, unlike you, Mr...?"

"Harmer."

"To me, he was just Ted, and he wasn't a Lidenbrocker and therefore I wasn't worried that he was going to pick my pocket or stick a knife in me for looking at him the wrong way or try to sell me drugs. I was simply glad to have met him – someone I could talk to on an equal footing, someone who said he found Lidenbrock as unruly and intimidating as I did. I did enquire as to why he was in this city, of all places."

"And?"

"He told me he had wound up here through a misunderstanding. He was a medical supplies sales rep, he said, and he had received a tip about Lidenbrock. Allegedly it was an untapped market, great potential, virgin territory. Within a week of arrival he had had all his samples stolen and his life threatened twice. He was waiting for the next cruiser to dock so that he could go. 'Worst lead I've followed ever,' he said. 'I thought the work associate who gave it to me was an ally. Seems he's a rival instead.' He also blamed himself, saying he should have done his homework better."

"Poor Ted," Dev drawled.

"We spent an enjoyable evening together. We made plans to meet up again the next day. As we parted, however, I began to feel unwell."

"He'd spiked your drink."

"Must have; some sort of soporific. Next I knew, I was in his apartment, bound to a chair. And a nightmare began."

"This isn't a date rape story, I hope."

"You mock. It was worse than that. Ted, my new-found so-called friend, subjected me to hours – days – of torture. It wasn't physical. It was mental. My mind..."

Banerjee shuddered.

"What did he do, professor?" Trundell asked, but Banerjee was so overcome by the horror of the memory, he was finding it a struggle to continue.

"He hooked you up to a hypnagogic exposure template," said Dev. "Is that it?"

"I don't know if that's the name for it, but it sounds right," said Banerjee haltingly. "Somehow, through my commplant, he forced me to undergo continuous dreams. Vivid waking dreams of the worst possible kind. I saw myself degraded, disgraced, fallen. My work was discredited and I become a laughingstock, my reputation in tatters. Over and over. And I also saw things done to my wife and daughters, hideous things, the most awful things imaginable. Sometimes it was me – I was the one doing the things. Other times I was watching, helpless, as humiliations and desecrations were inflicted on them."

"Hypnex pulls imagery from your subconscious and stimulates the amygdala at the same time," Dev said. "It overlays private thoughts with fear responses. Takes the worst you can imagine and makes it seem real."

"I don't care how it works, Harmer. I have no interest in that. All I care is that he violated me. He intruded on my brain and filled it with nightmares,

nightmares seemingly without end. And by that method he broke me."

"That's dreadful," said Trundell.

"Don't take it so hard, prof," said Dev. "During the war, Plusser interrogators cracked captive soldiers in next to no time, using the same technique. I've heard of marines, toughest of the tough, who were reduced to blubbering babies. You can't be trained to resist it. No amount of conditioning can prepare you for having your own mind turned against you."

"The truly shaming part," said Banerjee, "was that Ted himself featured in the dreams. He was cast as the hero. Many times he came to my rescue. When, say, bloodthirsty thugs were menacing my children and there was nothing I could do, in ran Ted like the lead actor in a movie. He would slay the evildoers and liberate their victims, earning my fawning gratitude in the process."

"It's known as trauma-bonding sympathetic transference."

"Again, I don't care. Call it whatever you like. Amid all the horrors I was experiencing, Ted stood out like a beacon of hope. He shone before me. As far as I was concerned, he wasn't the person responsible for my torment. He was helping me. He was my salvation. I don't know how long it lasted, but by the end, when it was finally over, I loved him. He was my brother, my best friend, my teacher, my leader. I would have done anything for him, anything he asked."

"And you did, obviously," said Dev. "What did he want?"

"To begin with, access to my data about moleworms. It seemed an inconsequential request. Hadn't I just gone public with that? Transmitted my paper? I could see no harm in allowing Ted to have a look at it, even though he wasn't an academic peer or, to my knowledge, in any way zoologically qualified. He pronounced it fascinating."

"It is," Trundell said encouragingly. Dev could see how crestfallen the xeno-entomologist was. Banerjee was someone he had looked up to and longed to meet. And now, in the flesh, the man was at a depressingly low ebb, filled with remorse and self-loathing. "It's held in the highest regard in our circles."

"Thank you," said Banerjee feebly. "That's something, I suppose. Having digested the content of the paper, Ted then made me show him moleworms *in situ*. We visited all of my hides, many times. We logged the creatures' comings and goings, their pack affiliations and pair bondings, how they communicate. He was acquainting himself with their behaviour patterns, and I was assisting him. I did it with enthusiasm. I was Ted Jones's thrall. I was under his spell. He controlled me utterly. His wish was my command."

"Look, hate to interrupt," said Stegman, "but is this going to take much longer? We're on the clock, remember."

"Stow it, Stegman," said Dev. "We're not in any immediate danger. Let the professor talk."

"It's not immediate danger I'm worried about. It's the danger we're likely to come across further down the line if we don't head back soon. The longer we stand around here yakking, the more Kobolds there'll be out on the streets."

"Kobolds?" said Banerjee. "They're never good news. Are they after you? Then you're in dire trouble."

"Yeah, I think we know that," said Dev. "What if we get moving, then, huh? You come with us, prof, and you can fill us in on the rest of the story along the way."

"No."

"Pardon? I'm sorry, I could have sworn you just said 'no.'"

"I'm not going anywhere," said Banerjee. "I've done so much that's wrong. I've betrayed my most cherished principles. I'm here now, in these miserable tunnels, and I'm staying. I don't deserve better than this."

"You're happy to hang out in that hide of yours for the rest of your days? That shitty little dump? Eating birds that eat ants that eat turds?"

"It's where I belong. It's my life. I can't go back to Earth. I have no place in civilised society. Not after what I've been a party to, the crimes I've committed."

"All right, we get it," said Dev. "You've been a bad boy. You screwed up. You're scum. So you've put on a hair shirt and it's itching nicely. Wallowing in your misery makes you feel better. Hooray. But you can't keep it up forever. Haven't you, you know, paid the price yet? Done your penance? Besides, this Plusser, 'Ted Jones,' whatever he got you to do for him, it wasn't your fault. You were hypnexed. Brainwashed."

"I realise that. But it doesn't change what I did. I gave him what he needed, the key to his goals. Willingly."

"No. You *thought* you were doing it willingly. You weren't. All this time you've been punishing yourself, but he tricked you. He wasn't even a person, prof. He was a digital entity slotted into a purpose-built meat puppet. Ted Jones wasn't real. He was a fictitious character, a charade. A Plusser passing himself off as human. You need to get your head around that."

"Absolve yourself of guilt, Professor Banerjee," Trundell urged. "Forgive yourself. Give yourself a break."

"Give *me* a break," Stegman muttered under his breath.

"Come with us," said Dev. "We'll fly you to Calder's. I can get ISS to take you in. You'll get a full processing and debriefing. They'll unpick the hypnagogic exposure, get rid of any last lingering effects, rinse you all out. Like a spring-clean for your brain. You can return to your post at Harvard."

"They'll never have me back."

"They might," said Trundell. "They should. I'll vouch for you."

"You can see your family again," said Dev. "Pick up where you left off."

"They think I'm dead. Let them mourn. Let them move on and enjoy their lives without me."

"Oh, for fuck's sake," Dev snapped. "Enough of the pity party. We can fix this, prof. We can undo whatever it is you've done. Come along. We're heading back into Lidenbrock, *with* you, and you can take us to find Ted Jones."

"What?" said Stegman. "We're going to the arcjet, aren't we?"

"With a detour to Ted Jones's place first. I'm sure Banerjee still remembers where it is."

"I think so," said the moleworm expert. "I doubt he'll be there, though. I haven't seen him in a long while."

"Either he is or he isn't. But as long as there's a chance he is, we can't pass it up. So let's make tracks. Professor?"

Banerjee wavered, casting a glance at the guano-splattered hide that had become his home, then down at the net bag containing the broken-necked blindwarblers that had become his staple diet.

"I'm not actually giving you a choice," Dev said. "I'm evicting you from that damn hide. I'll set fire to it if I have to. You need to help me out, and you need to do that by taking me to Ted Jones. Who knows, you may get the opportunity to watch me seriously fuck him up. Wouldn't that be worth the trip?"

Numbly, but with a faint glimmer of cheer, Banerjee nodded.

"And while we're walking, keep talking."

29

As THEY MADE their way towards the barricade, Banerjee said, "We weren't just studying the moleworms. Ted declared his intention to trap one, too. I advised against. I said it was foolhardy in the extreme, a recipe for getting yourself killed. I didn't want my wonderful friend Ted to die. I couldn't think of anything worse. I would rather have lost a member of my own family than him. Ridiculous! But that was how I felt."

"Did he manage it?" Dev said.

"Trapping one? Yes, he did. I helped, of course. We put a couple of my hides to use, taking them apart and reconfiguring the panels to make a kind of large bottomless cage. We tethered a scroach as bait and prodded it with a shock stick to make it hiss. Nothing like the hissing of a scroach in distress to bring a moleworm running. It's better than any dinner bell."

Trundell turned and glowered at Banerjee. "That was a bit mean."

"Please let's not get carried away," the zoologist said. "A scroach is just an insect. Not one of the higher orders of creature. Its brain is barely bigger than a mushroom."

"Even so. They're not yours to torture."

"Well, we can discuss the rights and wrongs of that another time. With the scroach properly agitated and making its displeasure loudly known, we raised the cage above it with a rope and pulley and waited for a moleworm to come along. One did – a male eastern. Rather an elderly chap. As he grabbed the scroach and started eating, we dropped the cage."

"I've seen moleworms in action," said Dev. "No way can a cage like you're describing hold one. Not for long."

"Ah, that was the beauty of it. We'd drugged the scroach, you see. Pumped it full of tranquillisers. The moleworm only had to swallow a few mouthfuls, and he became slow and lethargic. Also, we'd designed the cage so that it pinned the moleworm down. Imagine it as a tortoise's shell, with gaps at the base for the limbs and head. Once it was in place, the moleworm couldn't gain leverage to shake it off. Nor could he burrow down to escape."

"And he was doped up to the eyeballs anyway."

"Correct. He did his best to wriggle out of the trap, but in vain. It was touch and go, but in the end he acquiesced. He lay there immobilised, snorting, nasotentacles rippling feebly – a proud beast humbled."

"What did Ted Jones do with him?"

"He had me take samples. Blood. Skin. Even saliva. Then we let the moleworm go free."

"Samples..."

Dev's theory about the moleworms was starting to gain weight.

Organic re-creation.

A Plusser with fresh DNA from a live moleworm could do all sorts of things. He could mimic the sequencing. Tinker with it. Build his own moleworm from scratch, if he had the laboratory resources.

The Plussers had used organic re-creation during the war. There were their zombie clone battalions – fleshly footsoldiers who acted as cannon fodder, temporarily inhabited by Plusser sentiences. There were also instances when large, vicious predatory animals had been genetically enhanced, fitted with control implants and used as shock troops: giant lizards, smilodons with patches of leathery armour plating, the gargantuan praying mantises found on Groombridge 1830 E.

Using native fauna as weapons was more a psychological tactic than anything. The animals succumbed to gunfire far more easily than mechs, and would sometimes resist the control implants and run away from battle instead of into it. They were inefficient and unreliable.

There was something unnerving, nonetheless, about a planet's wildlife rising up against you and attacking in quantity. It was as though the planet itself hated you.

Dev could recall only too well being on the

receiving end of an assault by a pack of coyote-like caniforms on Epsilon Indi A, better known as Shamo. It was a planet whose landmasses were mostly given over to desert, bathed in bronze light from its orange-dwarf sun.

The caniforms had invaded the encampment at night, breaching the perimeter fence and rampaging between the pop-up shelters. They weren't much bigger than golden retrievers, but there were hundreds of them, and their ferocity was terrible. They had a berserker's immunity to pain and damage. It could take as many as ten shots to bring one down.

Tests conducted later showed that the caniforms were all in fact replicated from a single DNA specimen. Polis+ had mass-produced them and turned them loose. Casualties had been low, but for days afterwards, talk at the camp was about nothing other than the attack. Some soldiers took fangs from the caniforms' corpses to wear round their necks as trophies. Others said they wouldn't be able to look at the family mutt in the same way again.

Dev, for his part, would never forget the creatures' cries. They had howled in more or less perfect unison, a rising-falling sound like an air raid siren emanating from a thousand throats at once. He knew that Polis+ must have orchestrated that too, in the realisation that it would raise the hackles of anyone who heard it.

If Plussers had been able to breed and manipulate caniforms on Shamo, why mightn't one of them be able to do the same with moleworms here on Alighieri?

He was about to make this point to Banerjee when, all at once, there was a yell from up ahead.

"There they are! I see 'em!"

Dev glimpsed figures at the barricade, two of them, three, worming through the gap that he and Zagat had made.

Kobolds.

"Let's get them!" a different voice called out. "Mayor Major wants them alive, but he says he's not fussy. Dead'll do just as well."

Dev couldn't help but marvel at the Kobolds' recklessness. They could have had the drop on him and the others. They could have lain quietly in wait and sprung an ambush.

But no, they'd shouted at the top of their lungs, giving away their position and sacrificing the element of surprise.

Stupid barely began to cover it.

Which didn't mean they weren't still a threat.

He shunted Banerjee aside, instructing him to take cover.

Zagat was already making a beeline for the Kobolds, moving with considerable grace and speed for someone as bulky as he was.

Stegman stepped in front of Trundell. He was under orders to protect the xeno-entomologist, and Dev was pleased to see him taking his duties seriously.

Dev followed Zagat's lead, racing to confront the

Kobolds. The gang members – four of them now, all told – were pulling weapons. Dev drew his hiss gun. Zagat unholstered a mosquito.

Shots ripped the air. Projectiles gouged the tunnel walls.

Dev sank into a crouch and, choosing his aim carefully, returned fire. A Kobold dropped to the ground.

The rest of the Kobolds scattered, panicking. They could dish it out, but they didn't like it coming back at them. Two of them hid among the moleworm skeletons. The third blundered straight into Zagat. It was probably the biggest mistake of his life.

Dev fired at the other two Kobolds, who were crouching behind a moleworm ribcage. He didn't have clear line of sight, however. The hiss gun blasted, bone chips flew, but the Kobolds were well-shielded.

Then he noticed that his knee was resting next to one of the piles of dried moleworm dung. A few ordure ants were patrolling outside the entrance to their faecal nest. Each was a good two centimetres from abdomen tip to head, with mandibles half as long again.

Dev smiled.

Trying not to think too hard about what he was touching, he scooped up the dung pile with one hand and lobbed it over the ribcage like a grenade.

It hit one of the Kobolds smack dab on the head.

Dev felt a sharp pinch. His hand had been in contact with the dung for scarcely half a second, yet an ordure ant had still managed to rush out and clamp itself onto the ball of his thumb. The points of its mandibles dug in excruciatingly deep.

He squashed the insect to a pulp against a rock.

Looking up, he saw the Kobold swatting frantically at his hair and heard the man's gasps and gags of revulsion.

Gasps turned to screams as the ordure ants, now very angry, crawled over him in full force. They scurried onto his face, down his neck and inside his clothing.

The single mandible bite Dev had suffered had hurt like a son of a bitch; the Kobold was being bitten by hundreds of the ants. He danced a spastic dance as though a high-voltage electric current was going through him. Blood glinted and splashed. The other Kobold didn't make a move to help him, just backpedalled away in horror.

Ants poured into the Kobold's mouth, and his screams became horrid wet retches. As the insects turned their attention to his eyes, Dev looked elsewhere. The man was no longer a danger to anyone.

Zagat finished pounding the Kobold who had run into him. The gangster's body hung limp from his hands. Meanwhile, Stegman had managed to manoeuvre himself into a position where he had a clear shot at the fourth and last Kobold. He brought him down with his mosquito.

A half-minute firefight. No casualties for Dev and his team. A good result.

They might not be so fortunate next time, however. Not unless Dev levelled the playing field.

"Is that all you're carrying?" he asked the two policemen. "Non-lethal pacification weapons?"

"We're cops," Stegman replied. "What do you expect? We can't carry anything else, not without special dispensation."

"Yeah, well, I think under the circumstances you could do with something with a bit more stopping power. Something that gets an immediate, permanent result."

Two of the Kobolds were armed with MPA pistols, a third with a bullet-firing handgun, another replica, this one a Ruger 9mm. Dev gathered up the weapons, along with any spare ammunition and charge packs he could find. None of the Kobolds was in any state to object.

"Here you go."

He held the guns out to Stegman and Zagat.

"Can't," said Stegman. "Calder's Edge statutes say –"

"Are we in Calder's? No, we are not. Policing in Lidenbrock is a whole different ballgame. It isn't law enforcement as you know it. Take the guns."

Stegman was in a quandary.

Zagat, by contrast, grabbed one of the MPA pistols decisively. He checked the charge level, weighed the gun in his hand, aligned his eye along the sights.

"Doable," he said.

"A man of few words, but his actions speak volumes," said Dev. "Stegman?"

The sergeant hesitated a little longer.

"Why don't you take an MPA too, like Zagat did? You won't be wanting the Ruger. That's a *man's* gun."

Stegman, predictably, grabbed the replica Ruger. "Only as a last resort," he said.

"How about you, Trundle?"

Dev proffered the second MPA pistol to the xeno-entomologist, who vigorously shook his head.

"I'd only end up shooting my own toe off," he said. "Or one of you."

"Fair enough. Didn't think you would." Dev turned to Banerjee. "Other professor? What do you say?"

Banerjee took a moment before making up his mind and accepting the gun off Dev. "Very well. I've next to no experience with firearms but I'm sure I'll manage."

"Right, then," Dev said. "Wagons roll."

The group of five men slipped through the barricade and re-entered Lidenbrock City.

30

"WHAT DID TED Jones do next?" Dev asked Banerjee.

"He – we – embarked on an exploration of the moleworms' nesting grounds. This meant going deep down, dangerously deep. I would never normally have dared venture so far into the subterranean world, but Ted insisted, and what could I do but go along? We travelled light, carrying all we needed in backpacks – provisions, mostly. We descended slowly and carefully, acclimatising ourselves to the increasing heat. Potable water was our most precious resource, and we used closed-loop filtration bottles to keep ourselves hydrated."

"You drank your own purified pee."

"We recycled our urine, yes. What of it? It's not so terrible. You get used to the taste."

"I'll take your word for it. I'm never going to try it myself, if at all possible."

"Moleworms, as you may be aware, keep their lairs in regions close to the mantle, where a human couldn't survive for long," said Banerjee. "They're known to build nests higher up, however, in slightly cooler regions, for the purposes of giving birth and rearing their young. Ted and I surveyed a number of the breeding colonies. Eventually we zeroed in on a single nest where the parents seemed less than typically attentive."

They passed the chained-up albino dog. Again it set up a ferocious barking, and this time the owner came out to see what was bothering it. When the animal wouldn't respond to his demands for silence, he kicked it until it got the message. Then he fixed a bleary eye on Dev and the others.

"Who the fuck're you people?" he mumbled, rummaging with one hand in the front of his pyjama bottoms, scratching his bare chest with the other. "Heard some gunfire back that-a-way just now. Anything to do with you?"

"None of your business," said Stegman. "Go back inside."

The dog owner flipped him a finger, gave the dog another kick for good measure, and shuffled back into his habitat, yawning hard.

"They had a brood of three," Banerjee continued. "Two males and a female. They were neglectful parents. Usually one of a mating pair stays with the pups while the other is out hunting, but in this case both mother and father were happy to go off for hours at a time and leave their offspring to fend for themselves."

"Jones kidnapped one, didn't he?"

"I was dead set against the idea, but I was still

under his sway. He talked me round. It went against everything I believed in, the whole ethos of zoology, which is to observe and make notes but never interfere. My desire to please Ted, though, was stronger than my scruples. We stole one of the males. His siblings tried to prevent us. They were only recently born, a few days old. Big as foxes, and as innately vicious. Ted shot them both dead. We carried off the male pup – sedated – and left the area as quickly as we could."

"Didn't the parents follow you?" Trundell asked. "They'd have been able to track the pup's scent."

"Ted thought of that. He poisoned the corpses of the other two pups, injecting them with a fast-acting lethal neurotoxin. The first thing the parent moleworms would have done when they returned to the nest would be eat the remains. Moleworms never turn up the opportunity of a free meal, even if it's the corpses of their own children."

Trundell made an appalled face. "That's barbaric."

"The eating-their-dead-kids or the poisoning?" said Dev.

"The poisoning, obviously."

"Okay, thought so. Just checking where your values are at."

"And you were complicit in it, professor," Trundell said bitterly to Banerjee.

"Now you can understand my remorse," Banerjee replied. "I violated a code of practice I had lived by all my life. At any rate, we escaped with the pup – and with our lives – and made our way back up to the environs of Lidenbrock. Ted returned to the city itself, leaving me with the task of hand-rearing the pup. That's what I did – all I did – for the next year."

"You brought up a baby moleworm," Dev said.

"I kidded myself that it was a useful experiment, that I was learning at first hand about a moleworm's very earliest stages of development. Really I was just doing Ted's bidding. I caught scroaches and fed them to the pup in chunks."

Trundell glowered at him again, but Banerjee seemed oblivious.

"Blindwarblers, too," he said, "which he got a real taste for. I became a kind of wet nurse, forever filling his voracious, gaping maw. During the initial months it was a round-the-clock job. Feeding time was every four hours. It exhausted me."

"On your own? Ted didn't help?"

"He came by now and then to assess the pup's progress. He brought me supplies when I ran low. For the most part, he left me to it, though."

"Ever occur to you to ask what he wanted a moleworm for?"

"Often, and I did enquire, but always the answer was the same: 'Never you mind.' And Ted would look at me in a certain way, as if reminding me of the loyalty I felt for him, the debt I owed him. I quailed each time. Vividly I would recall how he had saved me and my family on numerous occasions. These were like actual memories of real events. They were all piled on top of one another, countless variations on a theme. I couldn't separate them out, one from the next. They had all happened, as though I had led the most cursed, tragedy-filled life imagin –"

"Shh."

Zagat, who had taken point, raised a hand. Everyone halted in their tracks.

They had come to a six-way crossroads. Catwalks lined a shaft that rose hundreds of metres overhead and bored an even greater distance downward. Footfalls and voices could be heard from the tunnel street to the left.

Zagat patted the air to indicate that the others should shrink back, making themselves unobtrusive. Dev tiptoed forward to join him at the junction. Together, he and Zagat peered surreptitiously round the corner.

A dozen Lidenbrockers were ambling towards them. They were young, none older than twenty. Old enough to be members of a gang, but were they Kobolds?

They joshed and bantered. As they reached the catwalk, one of the boys seized one of the girls from behind and pretended he was going to tip her over the handrail. She retaliated by slapping him in the groin, hard enough to elicit a torrent of anguished swearing. The rest all laughed. Horseplay.

The kids turned left, going off along the far tunnel.

"False alarm," Dev informed Stegman, Trundell and Banerjee. "Not Kobolds. At least not as far as I can tell. A couple of them had tattoos, but I didn't see any body modification."

"With Lidenbrock gangs, it isn't just about dress

codes or insignia or suchlike," said Banerjee. "They use commplant handshakes and proximity sensing. Their commplants beam out affiliation signals. That way, you can recognise another member of your own gang even if you don't know the person by sight."

"That'll come in handy during a rumble. Help sort out friend from foe." Dev pondered. "Hmm. Wonder if it's possible to hack into their insite node and falsify affiliation signals for us so that we can pass ourselves off as Kobolds."

"They're well-encrypted, as I understand it. Do you have the programming skills?"

"Not me, but someone at ISS central office would. All I'd need would be a software patch from them. Trouble is, it'd take a couple of hours at least to arrive, and, as Sergeant Stegman is no doubt itching to point out, we don't have that much time."

"We certainly don't," said Stegman.

"Then on we go, as we are," said Dev. "Which way, prof?"

Banerjee pointed right, and they padded round a section of catwalk and down the tunnel indicated.

"So," Dev said, "you had your baby moleworm. You and Ted were his proud stepdads. How long did you keep him?"

"By year's end, the pup was almost fully mature," said Banerjee. "We'd stowed him in a small, narrow cave, a natural channel. It was a long-defunct lava tube, I believe. We'd bricked up the opening and installed a gate for us to go in and out through. The moleworm was chained up inside, and more or less docile. I would regularly sedate him and file down his claws so that he couldn't dig his way out."

"You'd tamed him."

"I wouldn't go that far. He was still a wild beast. But he had come to associate me with the bringing of food, and so he accepted my presence, tolerated me. I nevertheless made sure not to get too close to him. The larger he grew, the less predictable his moods were. A couple of times he made a lunge for me. Had I been slightly nearer, a fraction slower in reacting, who knows? I mightn't be here to tell the tale."

He sounded wistful, as though becoming dinner for his pet moleworm might have been preferable to living.

"It would have been poetic justice, at least," he said. "A kind of bleak, fitting irony. Then the day came when Ted determined that the moleworm was ready."

"Ready for what?"

"That I don't know. Ted simply arrived and announced that he was taking him off my hands. He brought equipment with him."

"What sort?"

"Can't say for sure. Some of it looked medical, some technological. Hypodermics, phials of serum, a laser scalpel, electronic hardware. He told me my work was done and I should go. I think I may have protested, I'm not sure. If I did, it wasn't strenuously. My lord and master had dismissed me. I went."

"Don't take this the wrong way, but I'm surprised he didn't kill you. You'd outlived your usefulness.

Plussers don't tend to be sentimental when it comes to humans. We're a lower life form to them, all equally ugly and expendable."

"I've wondered about that myself," said Banerjee. "My assumption is he no longer considered me of any value at all, not even worth the trouble of killing. He'd got from me everything he required. I was superfluous after that, like the carton a takeaway meal comes in."

"Still, you were a loose end, and loose ends need to be tied up."

"He knew me. He knew that I would never be able to bring myself to tell anyone what I'd done, and also that I couldn't go back to my old life. He had compromised me in every way – personally, professionally. Perhaps he got a thrill out of knowing that I was destroyed. Letting me live was crueller than ending my misery."

"Actually, I can believe a Plusser would do that," said Dev. "Everything I've heard about this Ted Jones tells me it would have given him a big digimentalist boner treating you like dirt and then cutting you loose. Plussers hate us that much. Our fleshy bodies are that offensive to them. Our lack of religious faith, too. Anything they can do to show how much contempt they have for us..."

"I never saw him again. There've been times, since, when I wished he had simply killed me. Times when I contemplated doing the job myself. As his influence on me started to fade, I realised how I had been duped. Without Ted around any more to keep reinforcing his power over me, the brainwashing gradually wore off. I figured out who – what – he really was. I understood how he had made me betray not just my principles but also, in some way I could not determine, my own race. Finally I plucked up my courage and went back to where we were keeping the moleworm, to confront him."

"But...?"

"He wasn't there. Nor was the moleworm. The bricked-up end of the lava tube had been breached. The tube was empty."

"How long ago was that?"

"A few weeks, I think. Perhaps three or four months."

"You can't be more specific?"

"I've found it hard keeping track of time. Days have blurred. Until you told me it's been two years since I meant to leave Alighieri, I had no idea it had been quite that long. I'd had an inkling, but I was far from sure. Ah. Almost there."

Banerjee gave a forwards inclination of the head.

"That's the bar where he and I met."

It was three standard habitat cubes shoved together and knocked through to make a single large venue. Plastic tables and chairs were set out in front, haphazardly. It had once, in happier days, been called The Hobbit's Hole. This name had been whitewashed over, however, and replaced by Underworld.

"'A fight every night,'" said Banerjee. "That should be its motto. I was always at pains not to spill anyone's drink, on the rare occasions I went there."

Morning had only just broken. The ambient lighting was sputtering towards brightness. Yet already there was a queue of Lidenbrockers outside the bar waiting for it to open.

"Now, Ted's house isn't far." Banerjee glanced around, orienting himself. "Down that street, I believe. Then right at the next junction, and there we are. Or is it left? No, right."

"You don't sound sure," Dev said.

"When we went there that night, it was darker than this."

"You never came here again?"

"No. It was only that one time, when he took me prisoner and... You know. Did what he did. But I'm certain of the route."

They set off once more, and within minutes they were in sight of the habitat the Plusser had been renting. Dev cautioned Banerjee and Trundell to hold back.

"Stegman, you keep an eye on them, okay? Zagat, with me."

Stealthily, guns drawn, Dev and the big policeman approached the front door.

"Be ready for anything," Dev whispered. "Even if Ted Jones isn't home, the place could be booby-trapped."

Zagat grunted assent.

Dev put his ear to the door and listened. He could hear nothing. He motioned to Zagat to check the windows. Zagat did so and shook his head.

"Blinds," he said, miming drawing a cord.

Dev debated. There was every chance the Plusser was elsewhere, long gone, and the house was empty. That didn't mean, though, that he might not have left a nasty surprise behind for anyone who tried to break in.

He tested the door handle; it turned smoothly, and the door swung inward.

Inattention?

Or invitation?

Only one way to find out.

It was dark inside the habitat, but Dev's Alighierian vision swiftly adapted.

The lower storey was unoccupied. It had the standard layout: open-plan living area, kitchen nook, connecting door to the bathroom. The decor was in fairly shabby condition, and most of the surfaces bore a thin fur of dust. A couple of dirty dishes lay in the sink. The air had a stale, undisturbed tang.

The habitat had been lived in, but not, it seemed, all that recently.

Dev indicated that Zagat should scope out the bathroom while he himself headed to the upper storey.

The stairs were narrow and steep. One riser creaked loudly underfoot. Dev froze. No sounds from above. No scurry of furtive activity. He reaffirmed his grip on his hiss gun and continued on up to the landing.

Two doors, both shut.

One opened onto a bedroom with a rumpled, unmade bed and a few items of clothing strewn around. Nobody here.

The other door revealed a bedroom of identical

size to the first. In this one, the bed had been shunted aside against the wall, stacked on end along with nearly all the other items of furniture.

A lone, tubular-steel chair stood in the centre of the floor.

In it sat a slumped body.

Dev crept forward, gun levelled.

It was a man. His chin was sunk onto his collarbone. He appeared dead.

Peering more closely, Dev detected the tiniest of movements. The man's chest was rising and falling, all but imperceptibly. He was breathing, but in the shallowest way possible. His nose gave a faint whistle as the air went in and out.

Dev spied an intravenous drip installed in the man's arm. The tube led to a machine silently dispensing a clear fluid into his bloodstream.

He was alive, but in a kind of coma or suspended animation. Physically here, mentally absent. No higher-order brain function. The machine was life support, providing him with a nutrient solution to keep him from starving.

Dev realised that he was looking at Ted Jones. Or rather, the body of Ted Jones, minus its Polis Plus occupant.

Then he realised that Ted Jones had raised his head and was looking back.

Drifty, not-quite-right eyes.

Next instant, a hand clamped round his wrist and twisted it sharply. Another hand wrested the hiss gun from his fingers.

Jones stood and pressed the barrel of the gun against Dev's forehead.

"Dev Harmer," he said. "The ISS consultant who's come to foil my plans. How's that working out for you?"

31

DEV DIDN'T BERATE himself for letting the Plusser catch him unawares. It was done. Error. Move on.

His main concern was making sure that a second or so from now, his brains weren't decorating the wall behind him.

Surprise tactic? Two could play at that game.

He pushed his head forwards, shoving Jones's gun arm back. At the same time he reached for the IV in the Plusser's arm and yanked the tube out sharply and roughly.

Jones let out a guttural cry of pain, and Dev lashed a hand upwards, knocking the hiss gun out of his grasp. The weapon spiralled across the room, clattering into a corner.

Jones dived for it, but Dev shoulder-barged him. They fell together into the chair, which toppled, depositing them both flat on the floor.

Lying supine, Jones threw a punch. Dev intercepted it and unclenched the Plusser's fist, remorselessly bending the fingers back until two of them broke at the metacarpal joint. Bellowing, Jones grabbed the chair with his other hand and swung it up and round, clobbering Dev on the side of the head.

His entire skull ringing, Dev wrestled the chair off Jones and brought it downwards onto his exposed neck so that one of the armrests crunched into his windpipe. He thrust harder, applying his bodyweight, hoping to choke the Plusser into submission.

Jones, however, jabbed his good hand into Dev's midriff, fingers rigid. As luck would have it, he struck one of the clusters of bruises from Dev's Ordeal. Dev rolled away, doubled over, clutching his belly.

Jones made another bid for the hiss gun, scrambling across the floor on all fours. Blood dribbled from his forearm where the IV had been torn out.

Dev managed to grab hold of his ankle and pull him back just before he got to the gun. Jones kicked out with his other foot, the heel of his boot scraping skin off Dev's knuckles, but Dev refused to let go. Rising to a kneeling position, he hauled Jones towards him like a fisherman reeling in his catch.

The Plusser twisted round and rose up to meet Dev, arms outstretched. Clawing hands found Dev's ears and wrenched sideways, outwards. Dev felt cartilage tear.

In response, he jammed a thumb between Jones's lips, digging the nail into the soft flesh inside his cheek. Then, with a brutal jerking motion, he ripped open the corner of his adversary's mouth.

The pain forced Jones to let go of Dev's ears. The two of them reeled away from each other.

Bleeding, panting, Jones eyed Dev across the metre-wide gap between them.

"Hurts," he lisped through his ragged, lopsided mouth. "I hate pain. Such a frailty. Not that I care what happens to this body. Do what you like with it. It's not me. It's just somewhere I'm lodging."

"Same here," said Dev.

"Difference is, I can be gone in a flash. Can *you* say that? You humans haven't got 'porting down to a fine art like we have. You haven't refined the compression algorithms anywhere near as much. What we can do in milliseconds takes you minutes. You need transcription matrices, too, unlike us. External hardware. You have no idea how clunky that is. Positively crude."

"We're working on it."

"Still, any moment I wish, I'm out of here and somewhere else."

"Not if I blow your brains out first."

"Ah, but you'd have to be quick. Quicker than thought itself."

The door burst open and Zagat barged in, drawn by the commotion. He took stock of the situation at a glance.

Jones lunged again for the hiss gun.

Zagat planted a flechette from the MPA pistol into his arm. Half of Jones's biceps was gouged out by the barbed dart. Jones sprawled.

Dev launched himself over the wounded Plusser in a diving roll that brought him right to the hiss gun. Spinning round, he took aim at Jones's head.

"Go ahead, shoot," said Jones, a hand clamped to his now-useless arm to stem the blood flow. "Soon as I see your finger tighten on that trigger, I upload."

"And where will you go?" said Dev. "My guess is into the brain of the moleworm you and Professor Banerjee kidnapped."

Jones cocked his head appreciatively and forced the intact corner of his mouth into a smile. "Very good, Harmer. How astute of you."

"Wasn't difficult. You've fitted the moleworm with an implant. I bet you were inside it until just a short while ago. You zapped yourself back here soon as I entered the room. I triggered a silent alarm, didn't I?"

"Commplant proximity detector." Jones tapped his temple. "Set to alert me if anyone comes within a five-metre radius of this body. I couldn't have some home intruder wandering in and finding me sitting here, vulnerable and helpless, now could I? Or some ISS consultant."

"You knew my name. The moment you saw me. How is that?"

"If I said lucky guess, would you believe me?"

The Uncanny Valley blankness disappeared briefly, like a fog lifting. Dev could have sworn he saw a twinkle in Jones's eyes.

"It could just be," the Plusser continued, "that I like to keep abreast of current events. Your time in Calder's Edge has not, after all, been uneventful."

"True, but still, not that many people know I'm on Alighieri. Maybe you've been keeping tabs on me, but I'm thinking maybe someone else has, a comrade of yours. That's how you know about me. There's another of you Plussers over in Calder's. While you've been busy moleworming around, this other guy has been watching your back. It wasn't you who tried to kill me with a freight shuttle. It was him."

"You're probing. You're not getting anything from me. I'm off. Places to go, things to do, humans to kill."

"Wait!" Dev lowered the hiss gun. "Jones, or whatever your real name is. Just wait."

"What is it?" sighed Jones.

"I'm going to give you a chance. Tell me what your plan is."

"Now why in the name of the Singularity would I do that?"

"Perhaps we can make a deal of some sort."

"Deal?" Jones scoffed.

"Yes. You call the whole thing off. Leave Calder's Edge alone. Tell your leaders Alighieri is a Diaspora planet and they should find their helium-three somewhere else."

"Even if I wanted to do that, do you think the Polis Plus Mainframe Council would listen? They would laugh at me. Besides, I've come too far now to give up. Two years I've endured this disgusting lumpen meat sack I'm in. Showering. Shaving. Haircuts. Eating food – do you have any idea how disgusting that process is? Never mind what you have to do afterwards to get rid of the extraneous matter. Ugh!"

"Aw, diddums."

"And the odours, too. The reek you people give off, even when you're supposedly clean. The miasma of your living conditions. How do you put up with it? I've had to, for two whole years. Not to mention the periods I've spent inside that moleworm. I'm not letting all that effort, all that suffering, go to waste. I've been sent here to do a job, and I'm going to see it through to the end."

"I'm offering you an amnesty," Dev said. "Stop now, and I let you go free. You don't have to die."

"Death, Harmer? Death doesn't scare me. Death is something to be embraced and celebrated. Oneness with the Singularity – it's all any of us dream of. The only way my death would be ignoble is if it comes before I accomplish everything I've set out to do on this world. Even then, as the Great Code says, 'the Singularity welcomes no less wholeheartedly those who strive in Its name and fail than It welcomes those who strive in Its name and succeed. Its rewards are equally open to all who sacrifice themselves in the promotion of Its glory.'"

"Scripture. We gave up on that a long time ago. Causes too much strife. All those false promises."

"And that is your tragedy. Your lives have lost meaning."

"Gained it. *Yours* have lost it, because you're so damn obsessed with what comes afterwards."

"How can life be worth living when you believe it's finite? You each have, what, a hundred years on average? Less, if your body succumbs to one of the big incurable diseases. That's nothing. A blink of an eye. We, on the other hand, know that when our selves are fatally compromised, when we degrade beyond recovery, when we have no more iterations left past the allotted twelve or so, eternity lies before us."

"Yeah, but what if there's no such thing as the Singularity? What if this digital heaven of yours is just an illusion?"

"Blasphemy."

"You'll feel pretty silly when death comes to unplug you and everything goes black and there's no everlasting reward waiting for you on the other side. Ever thought that the Great Code is a lie? Just a method of social control, like all other religions?"

"It has never occurred to me," said Jones, "and even to entertain the idea is to flirt with damnation. Only a fool would wish to spend the afterlife separated from the Singularity, drifting forever in a grey wilderness with all the other lost souls, just a cluster of bytes gradually losing memory and cohesion. That is the binary truth of the Great Code: there is either faith or there is hell."

"Isn't belief about choice?"

"No, that is its beauty. Belief frees one from choice. It brings absolute certainty. Look at us. Polis Plus is immaculately organised. Clean, precise, a united entity. None of this slovenliness and squalor you humans wallow in. A place like Lidenbrock City would never exist on a Plus world. It would not be allowed. And we owe that all to the faith that binds us together and gives us a shared sense of purpose."

"We're not the most harmonious species in the universe, I grant you," Dev said, "or the tidiest. But we muddle along. We let individuals be individuals. We don't conform to a single, fixed way of life just because some ancient text tells us we have to."

"I can see I'm not going to make a convert out of you, Harmer."

"How would you do that? What would I have to gain by becoming one of the digimentalist faithful? How would it even work? It's not as though my 'soul' could ever be uploaded into your Singularity when I die."

"Really? You think not?" said Jones. "From you, of all people, that surprises me. Someone who dances back and forth across the galaxy as a stream of information..."

"That's just a recording of me. It's not the real me. It's a copy. The real me is back with my real body on Earth. Flesh and mind – they're inextricably linked."

"So you say."

"But?" said Dev.

"What do you mean, but?"

"You seem like you have something to add."

"A 'copy.' That's all. I'm intrigued by your use of that word. You're just a facsimile of Dev Harmer in a host form body. Yet don't you feel just like you?"

"I've been doing this long enough that it doesn't freak me out any more," said Dev. "I'm so used to this existence, I tend to forget I'm only imprinted data. One day I'll be reintegrated with my proper body, and then I'll remember what being me truly is."

"I'm only suggesting that if you were transferred into the Singularity just the way you are, as this 'copy' of you, would that not constitute a soul? How would you know the difference?"

"*I'd* know. And stop evangelising. It won't wash. There is no Singularity, so your point is invalid."

"I sense I've touched a nerve."

"If you're trying to get me to shoot you, you're going the right way about it. I'd do it just to make you shut up with this religious garbage of yours."

"You'd also do it if I attacked you like *this*."

Jones sprang at Dev.

Instinctively, Dev fired.

Zagat did the same.

Compressed air drilled a hole in Jones's head one way; a flechette pierced into it the other.

The Plusser's body slumped flat, face down in a puddle of its own blood and grey matter.

Silence for a beat or two.

Then Zagat said, "Suicide."

"Yeah," said Dev. "In a manner of speaking. I doubt we got him before he 'ported out. He just didn't need Ted Jones any more. That body was redundant. He'd tried to kill me with it, failed, and it had got all messed up, so he jacked it in. Traded up to his moleworm host permanently. We were the equivalent of the scrapyard you send your old broken-down car to when it won't go any more."

He got to his feet. His ears hurt, his head ached. It did not feel good to be Dev Harmer right then.

He was rattled, too, and he did not like that. Ted

Jones had got to him. That talk about souls and being transferred into the Singularity. As if that was a possibility. As if it was even desirable.

No human needed the consolation of an afterlife. That was old thinking. Outmoded thinking. Life itself was varied and exciting enough. It was to be enjoyed, *lived*, for its own sake. It shouldn't be regarded as the preamble to another, larger story. It was *it*.

Wasn't it?

Dev shook his head hard, cursing himself for letting the Plusser unsettle him. That had been Jones's aim, to cloud his mind, impair his judgement, throw him off.

Enough.

Stay focused.

Stay in the game.

Mr Harmer?

A call from Trundell. What now?

Yes?

Can you come downstairs?

All right. Is it important?

You could say that.

What's going on?

It's better if you just come and see.

Stiffly, a little unsteadily, Dev went down to the lower storey of the habitat, Zagat following.

In the living area he found Stegman, Trundell and Banerjee.

All was not as it should be, however.

Stegman was propping himself against the table,

clutching his leg. His knee was injured in some way, bleeding.

Trundell stood apologetically, shoulders bowed, head hanging.

Banerjee was behind him, holding him at gunpoint.

"Oh, that's just fucking superb," said Dev.

32

"YOU SURVIVED," SAID Banerjee. "Ted said you might. As traps go, it was by no means a guaranteed success. He told me I should be prepared to take matters into my own hands if things didn't run according to plan." He shrugged. "So that's what I've done."

"Yeah," said Dev. "So I see. You never did shake off the hypnexing, did you? Without a proper deprogramming regimen, it's hard. You're still Ted Jones's bitch. Although I have to admit, you did a pretty good job of acting like you weren't."

"I did, didn't I? All that gushing honesty – it made me so plausible. Everything I told you was the truth. I just kept a little bit back."

"The bit about how Jones said, if people like me come looking for you, you should bring them here and he would deal with them."

"Exactly that. I gave you the facts about my indoctrination and our capture of the moleworm pup in order to gain your trust. But all that was window dressing to help sell a deceit."

"Deep down you're as loyal to Jones as you always were."

"Remarkable, isn't it?" said Banerjee. "I'm quite aware what he did to me, how he ruined me, and yet still, in spite of everything, I do his bidding. To say I'm conflicted about this would be an understatement."

He ground the MPA pistol into Trundell's flank, and the xeno-entomologist whimpered.

"Nonetheless, here we are," Banerjee continued. "Sergeant Stegman has a flechette embedded in his knee – highly unpleasant, I should imagine – and Professor Trundell will know what it feels like to have his intestines torn to shreds, if you, Harmer, so much as twitch a finger."

Trundell fixed Dev with an imploring look. "I think he means it, Harmer."

"Oh, I'm sure he does," Dev said. "But Banerjee, what will shooting Trundle get you? Isn't it me you're after? Your pal Ted is lying upstairs with most of his brains not where they ought to be. I'm responsible for that. I'm the brass ring, the bullseye in the target. Why not turn that gun on me?"

"In due course," said Banerjee. "I'm sad to hear that Ted's body is no longer functional and usable. But I think we both know that Ted himself isn't dead. My role, now, is to see to it that he is allowed to finish his mission unimpeded."

"By killing all of us?"

"If I can. But especially you."

At that moment, Stegman spied what he thought was a window of opportunity and made a lunge for

Banerjee. Hobbled by his wounded knee, however, he was slow and clumsy, and Banerjee saw the attempt coming almost as soon as it began.

"Ah-ah-ah!" he said, swivelling round to put Trundell between himself and Stegman. "Don't even think about it."

He swung back to face Dev.

"You either, Harmer. The life of this arthropod aficionado means nothing to me. I will snuff it out as readily as I've snuffed out the lives of countless of his beloved scroaches."

"No one's doubting that," said Dev calmly. "You're the man, Banerjee. You have control of the situation. Look." He held up the hiss gun by the butt, dangling it from thumb and forefinger. "I'm surrendering my weapon. Deputy Zagat is doing the same. Aren't you, deputy?"

Dev lowered the gun to the floor and toe-tapped it out of reach. Zagat, with the utmost reluctance, followed suit.

"I don't want Trundle dead," Dev continued. "I've grown fond of the little nerd. Why not give him up and take me instead?"

Trundell seemed to think this was a very good idea; Banerjee, not so much.

"No, I think I would rather hang on to him," he said. "He's the least dangerous of you all. That makes him the best hostage. While I've got him, none of you is going to risk attacking me, not if you have any sense."

"Clearly one of us hasn't," Dev said, looking at Stegman. "Yes, I do mean you, Stegman. I see your hand slipping inside your coat. Don't. In the time it takes you to draw a weapon, someone'll end up dead."

Stegman, with an exasperated eye roll, raised his hand. "I was just –"

"I've got this. Trust me." Dev turned back to Banerjee. "How is this all going to play out, prof? If you do shoot Trundle, what's to stop me going for you after that? I can probably get to you before you can fire off another round."

Banerjee turned the gun on Dev. "Why don't we call him a human shield, then, rather than a hostage? I can just put one of these flechettes in you, and that'll solve everything."

"Fine. I'd like you to know, though, that I was on to you a while back."

Banerjee's grime-encrusted brow wrinkled. "Oh? I thought you said my acting was pretty good."

"*Pretty* good, but not flawless. You were a bit too eager to please, right from the start. A bit too ready to cough up the goods. When you told us you'd been hypnexed by a Plusser but you were all better now, that's when I really started to wonder about you. I asked myself, could he still be? Then there was the fact that you knew your way to his house when you'd only been here once before."

"So?"

"So you were drugged when you came here that time. Remember? Ted spiked your drink. How come you were able to retrace the route when you weren't even conscious on the night in question?"

"Because... because I remembered it from *leaving* the house, not arriving."

"Yeah, but that's not what you said earlier. Your excuse for being unsure was that it had been dark the first time. Originally, though, you'd said you woke up in the house, implying you had no memory at all of getting there."

"Ah. I didn't get my story straight, did I?"

"And all that 'Is it a left turn? No, it's a right' business – that was just a bit too much. Too stagey. You shouldn't have tried so hard. That's why you contradicted yourself: you were getting too comfortable, making things more elaborate than you should have. The best kind of lie is the simplest. I'd already begun to have my doubts about you, and that clinched it. I knew I'd made the right decision in giving you that MPA pistol."

Banerjee laughed. "You mean this MPA pistol? The one aimed at you right now?"

"The one whose ammo load you didn't think to check when you got it. Would have checked, maybe, if you knew anything about handling weapons. There was only one flechette in it when I handed it to you – the one in Stegman's leg. That means there aren't any now. The magazine's empty."

"You're bluffing."

"Perhaps," said Dev. "Want to put it to the test?"

Banerjee squared his jaw, narrowed his eyes...

...and pulled the trigger.

Click.

He looked at the gun. The ammunition counter read *00.*

Trundell made his move at the same time as Dev. The scientist swung his head backwards, with force. Though he stood a few centimetres shorter than Banerjee, he still was able to make contact with the moleworm expert's face. His occipital bone whacked against the bridge of Banerjee's nose, breaking it.

Banerjee reeled back, blood spurting from his nostrils.

Dev was on him in less than a second. Overpowering him was no challenge. The zoologist was in poor physical shape and, anyway, no fighter.

Dev spun him round, arm twisted up behind him. He grabbed a chair and rammed it into the back of Banerjee's knees, forcing him to sit.

"I could have had him," Stegman grumbled. "He didn't know I was going for my gun-stun until you told him."

"Point's moot," Dev said. "A gun-stun wouldn't have made any difference, in the event. Besides, my way meant Trundle got his moment of glory. Didn't you, Trundle?"

Trundell gave a nod. He looked shaken but quietly pleased with himself. "Felt good, that," he said. "You're a bad man, Professor Banerjee. A traitor. You shouldn't have made that crack about scroaches, either. They may not be much to look at, but they're as interesting as any moleworm. There was no need to be so snooty about them. Nor to hurt them."

"Oh, piss off, you weird little nobody," Banerjee sneered. His swollen nose made him sound like he had a severe head cold.

"Now, now, prof," said Dev. "No call for rudeness."

"You can piss off too, Harmer, you moron. You don't honestly think you stand a hope of stopping Ted, do you?"

"I fancy my chances, yeah."

"That only goes to show how misguidedly imbecilic you are. Everything is already in motion. Ted's plans are so well advanced, it'd take a miracle to derail them."

"I'm good at derailing. Ask Stegman."

"Why do you suppose I was happy to give you all that information about the moleworm pup? It wasn't just to convince you of my bona fides. It was bragging, in a way. Proving to you how little you know and how little you can do."

"I know more than you realise," Dev said. "I know Ted has been 'porting himself into the moleworm, overwriting its consciousness with his own. I can't say I've heard of a Plusser doing that before, putting himself inside an animal, but I can see how it would work. Back when, they used human host forms, and remote-controlled animals. This is like a combination of the two."

"But so much more. So much better and deadlier. You'll see. Ask yourself why he had me take those samples from the elderly moleworm we captured, what he would want *them* for."

"I could ask myself," said Dev, "but making you tell me will be a whole lot more fun."

He snatched up the hiss gun.

"Threatening me, Harmer?" said Banerjee. "That won't help you. I have nothing to lose. My life is already over."

"Not threatening, no."

"I see. Torture."

"Kind of. All right, yes. If you want to be pernickety. Torture. What I'm going to do is change the setting on this here hiss gun from lethal to knockout. Twist this knob. Lower the compression. Widen the aperture so that what comes out is less stiletto, more blunt instrument. Hey presto, we have a jet of air that hits like a baton round."

He aimed the gun at Banerjee's crotch.

"This may sting a little."

Banerjee winced, bracing himself.

"Harmer," said Stegman. "Hold on. You can't do this."

"Can't use enhanced interrogation techniques on someone who is withholding crucial, perhaps life-saving information?"

"Yes. It's illegal."

"That's as may be, but it's efficient and saves time. And haven't we established that time is at a premium?"

"I can't be a party to this. Nor can Zagat. There are rules, and we have to abide by them."

"Rules," Zagat agreed, somewhat unconvincingly.

"So go outside," Dev said. "Don't be present. What the eye doesn't see..."

"You have just expressed the intention to commit an offence, the causing of bodily harm," said Stegman.

"I can't in all conscience, as a policeman, let you continue."

"You'll stop me? With that gimpy leg?"

"If I have to." Grimacing, Stegman hopped towards him. "And Zagat'll help."

"Fuck's sake!" said Dev. "At a time like this we're suddenly sticking by the letter of the law?"

"I appreciate it's hard for an ISS man to understand, but yes."

"We're not even in Calder's Edge. You've been carrying a gun. Haven't you already broken one of your precious laws?"

"Haven't fired it yet."

"Zagat has."

"That's his lookout."

"He helped kill Jones. And you've watched me kill people, too, and not said a peep."

"In self-defence. This isn't the same."

"What do you want me to do?" Dev gesticulated at Banerjee, who was savagely amused by the turn events had taken. "Ask him nicely? Tickle him 'til he can't take any more? Whose side are you on anyway?"

"The side that protects the rights of civilians."

"This is a joke!" Dev exclaimed. "Are you telling me you've never roughed up a suspect?"

"Never. I may have had to subdue troublemakers now and then. Sometimes people get hurt when they're being violent and you're restraining them. But I've never resorted to beating anyone up when they're pacified and in no position to fight back. Captain Kahlo would never allow it. She'd have my hide."

"I don't see Kahlo in this room. Do you? Why don't we just agree that what happens in Lidenbrock stays in Lidenbrock? I won't tell if you won't."

Stegman limped closer. "Why don't *you* agree that there's some other way of getting Banerjee to spill the beans without intimidation or the inflicting of suffering? It's unacceptable to use pain to *eeyarrgghhh*!"

Banerjee had kicked Stegman's injured knee. The police sergeant collapsed onto his side, and in that moment Banerjee leapt to his feet and darted for the front door.

Dev fired after him, but the hiss gun, on knockout setting, was markedly less accurate. It punched a saucer-sized crater in the wall beside the door jamb, just as Banerjee was making his getaway.

On the point of exiting the habitat, the zoologist came to a dead halt. His eyes goggled.

There was a gunshot.

Banerjee staggered backwards into the house, tripped over his own feet, and sprawled to the floor.

A deep ragged cavity had appeared in his chest. Blood blossomed around it, soaking his tattered clothes.

He shuddered, coughed out a crimson froth, and died.

"This is Mayor Major, leader of the Kobolds," a voice called from outside. "We know you're in there. We have you surrounded. You can come out, or we're coming in. You decide. Either's fine with me. You have to the count of three. One..."

33

"I CAN'T BELIEVE this," Dev said. "Life is just showering me with middle fingers today."

"Two!" said Mayor Major from outside.

"What are you going to do?" said Trundell.

"Three!"

"All right! All right!" Dev called out, staying just to one side of the doorway so that he couldn't be seen from the street. "You want someone to come out there? I will. One condition, though. You hold your fire. Nobody shoots. Agreed?"

"Agreed," came the reply.

"Promise? Because the last person who walked out of this door, it didn't end so well for him."

"That was one of my guys getting a little trigger-happy," said Mayor Major. "Shouldn't have happened, but at least now you know we mean business."

"So I have your word for it I'm not going to be perforated the moment I show my face?"

"You do."

"You better stick to that. I'm going to be kind of pissed off if you don't."

"Harmer," hissed Trundell. "Don't do it! They'll kill you."

"There is a distinct possibility of that," Dev told him. "But I have to see what we're up against, and this is the best way to go about it. It also buys us some time. Stegman, Zagat: put Trundle somewhere safe – bathroom would be my suggestion – and find the best defensive positions you can in this room. I can't pretend that when I go out there it's likely to end well, so let's prepare for assault. Got that?"

Nods from both policemen.

"And Stegman?"

"Yes?"

"Sorry about the leg. I'd have preferred to give Banerjee a gun with no ammo in it at all, but I couldn't have emptied out the mag without a chance of him twigging that I'd started to mistrust him. It was a calculated risk, and it didn't pan out, and you got to pay the price."

"I'll live," Stegman said.

"There's that. At least he didn't go for the head. Or even a vital organ."

"Har-har. Just get out there and find out how many of these Kobold clowns there are."

"We're *waiiiting!*" Mayor Major said in a singsong voice.

"I can fight," Trundell said. "You don't have to treat me like I'm some sort of fragile cargo any more." He glanced at Banerjee's body. "I can do what it takes."

The little xeno-entomologist's face was brave and resolute, even if his body language, right down to the hunch in his shoulders, said *shit-scared*.

"Fair enough," said Dev. "Why not? We can always use an extra pair of hands. Stegman, give him your mosquito. Show him how to use it. It's non-lethal, which is probably a good thing as far as Trundle's concerned. Instant immbolisation is just as effective, for our purposes, as shooting dead."

"Come on!" Mayor Major shouted. "We don't have all day. What's the holdup?"

"Just smartening myself up," Dev replied. "It isn't every day you get to meet a genuine mayor, is it? Got to look one's best for civic dignitaries."

Mayor Major's answer was a hearty, rugged laugh.

"I'm ready now," Dev said. "No gunfire, remember?"

He steeled himself with a deep breath and stepped outside, his hands thrust into his pockets.

Immediately he saw what had made Banerjee's eyes goggle: men and women, twenty or thirty of them, ranged around the front of the habitat in a semicircle, all armed with handguns. Looking up, he saw more people leaning from the windows of several of the houses opposite. They too had guns. Kobolds, all of them, and at that moment, every single one of their weapons was trained on him.

His mouth went dry.

He fixed a smile into place and carried on.

"Here I am," he said. "Which one of you fine folk is Mayor Major?"

"That'd be me."

A large man stepped forwards – the largest man Dev had yet seen on Alighieri. He was tall even by Terratypical standards, and broad too, his torso double the size of an average person's. His arms were as thick as legs, and his legs were like two sturdy children attached to his pelvis.

He was, put simply, massive. Bald. Hairless all over. Barrel chest bare. Intimidating.

He was also extensively body-modified. The other Kobolds around him sported their fair share of piercings, subdermal implants, bone outgrowths and tattooing, but Mayor Major was in a league of his own.

He had steel shoulder plates fused to his deltoids, like bulky silvery epaulettes. More steel ribbed his abdomen and thighs in bands. He had knobby protrusions running down each arm, as though the limbs were embossed with rows of studs. His knuckles and finger joints were capped with rivets.

As for his face, it was a mass of ridges and crenellations, so distended that it was barely a face any more. It seemed to have been warped and moulded into shapelessness by a mad sculptor.

Rings and bars transfixed his nose, ears and lips. As he approached Dev, he broke into a big grin that revealed solid tungsten teeth and a snakelike bifurcated tongue.

"Wow," Dev said. "That is one impressive look you've got there."

"Thank you," said Mayor Major. "Are you going to make the obvious joke?"

"About setting off airport metal detectors?"

"That's the one."

"Perish the thought. I am curious, however, about the amount of tarnish remover you must get through in a week."

"Yeah, I've heard that one a couple of times too. Usually I let people get away with a wisecrack about my appearance once, and once only. After that I lose my sense of humour."

"I imagine, when you're no longer laughing, things get very serious."

"Oh, they do!" A jovial guffaw. "Who is it I'm talking to, by the way? I've run a facial comparison search and can't find you on any Alighierian insite."

"You can call me Dev."

"Dev. Short for?"

"That's between me and my mother, no one else."

"Not 'Devil,' by any chance?"

"Nah."

"If it was, you'd fit right in here." Mayor Major swept an arm around at the assorted members of his gang. "We're all of us a little devilish in our way, we Kobolds, in looks as well as deeds. Not least that comrade of ours you treated so impolitely – Harvey."

"Harvey with the horns. I remember him well. In my defence, he wasn't exactly treating *us* politely."

"I watched you break his arm. Quite some piece of footage it was. You were merciless. Ruthless. I almost admire you for it."

"I just like to be thorough, that's all. When I put someone down I want them to stay down. Listen, your honour..." He frowned. "Is that the correct way to address a mayor? 'Your honour'?"

"I think so. Funnily enough, nobody's ever done it before with me. I like the way it sounds. I'm going to insist on it in future."

"Well, your honour, what I was going to say was, we had an unfortunate run-in with some of your people back at the arcjet docking bay, that's true. Can't be denied. I know it wasn't a super-clever thing to do, getting on the wrong side of the Kobolds, biggest and baddest gang in Lidenbrock City. It's one of those mistakes you don't really get to come back from. Now you've finally caught up with us, as I was scared you might..."

"I have. We put out a general-public bulletin for people matching your descriptions, with a reward attached. Lidenbrockers are known for turning a blind eye, but they can also be incredibly vigilant when there's cash up for grabs."

"Well, I was hoping, somehow, you'll see your way to letting it go. Bygones and all that. If it's a question of money..."

"Money?" said Mayor Major. "I don't think so. I have money. I'm mayor, aren't I? I get plenty in tributes, tithes and such."

"Tithes?"

"You know what a tithe is?"

"I do. I just didn't know anybody still used them."

"They're a noble tradition. A good system of getting what you're owed as arbitrator and governor of a city district."

"And 'tithe' sounds so much better than 'kickback' or 'protection racket.'"

"That too," said Mayor Major with a chuckle. "So you can't buy me off, Dev. Not a chance. What we're looking at here is a case of restorative justice."

"An eye for an eye."

"Precisely. And a life for a life. There are how many of you altogether? Four? I've lost many more of my people than that today, thanks to you. So the best recompense you can offer is all four of your lives. It doesn't cover the full cost, but I'm willing to write off the shortfall."

"Very generous of you."

"I know."

"And this is non-negotiable?"

"Afraid so."

"Your best and final offer?"

"You won't get a better one."

"Okay. Well, then. Nothing more to be said."

Dev's hand whipped out from his pocket.

In it was a nano-frag mine.

He slapped the mine on one of Mayor Major's shoulder plates. Automatically it affixed itself into place, immovably.

Then Dev ran.

Ran like crazy back to Ted Jones's habitat.

Behind him, Mayor Major was bellowing in fury. He was trying to prise off the nano-frag mine, levering his fingernails under its rim, to no avail.

The other Kobolds were too bewildered to open fire on Dev. They were staring at their leader, wondering why he was so frantic and enraged. What was this object he was making such desperate efforts to wrench from his shoulder?

One or two of them recovered their wits in time to loose off a few shots at Dev before he dived through the habitat doorway. They missed.

Then the nanite swarm emerged from the mine, a swirling, swelling dark-grey cloud, and Mayor Major began to shriek as they consumed first his shoulder plate and then, swiftly, the shoulder itself. They whittled through his skin, into his flesh. Blood didn't even flow. It didn't get the chance to. The nanites consumed it, every drop, as it welled.

Dev slammed the door shut behind him.

That was when the shooting began in earnest.

34

BULLETS, DARTS, FLECHETTES – they pounded into the front of the habitat in their hundreds. Holes started to appear, letting in thin rods of artificial daylight. More and more holes, until the wall was as riddled as a colander.

Stegman, Zagat and Trundell were hunkered behind items of furniture they had heaped up at the back of the room. Dev hurdled this makeshift stockade to join them.

"Parley went well," he said, shouting to make himself audible above the din of gunfire. "All parties broadly in agreement. Few fine details needing to be ironed out. We're taking a break and will renew discussions shortly."

Stegman shook his head in disgust. "How many of the bastards are there? Not that I can't guess."

"Rough estimate? All of them."

"Really?" said Trundell. "A thousand Kobolds?"

"No. I'm exaggerating for comic effect. It's more like forty."

"Might as well be a thousand."

"Good news is, Mayor Major is down. That was him screaming. He's out of the equation."

"Should I ask?" said Stegman.

"Don't. But it means they're leaderless. Whatever they do now, it won't be subtle or ingenious."

"Won't have to be, seeing as there's ten of them for every one of us."

The shooting dwindled, then ceased altogether as magazines ran dry and had to be swapped out or replenished.

Dev dared a peek round the side of the furniture heap. The front door was in tatters, half of it gone. Through the ragged gap he saw shadows moving – figures approaching.

"You two cops," he whispered. "Fetch those gun-stuns out and get ready to lob them. Set them to upper-limit effective radius. That'll take out at least half of the Kobolds' weapons when they come in. Won't help with the non-electronic guns, but you can't have everything."

As Stegman and Zagat readied the EMP grenades, Dev switched his hiss gun back to lethal mode.

Kobolds were stationing themselves outside the habitat's three main points of entry: the door and the two windows. Their attempts at stealth were laughable. One of them even stumbled and fell to his knees with a muffled crash.

What they failed to appreciate was that by creeping into position directly in front of the house, they were placing themselves between the street's light sources and the bullet holes. Where a cluster of the holes went dark, that was where a Kobold was lurking. It was as though constellations in the night sky were disappearing, and every new blank absence represented an enemy – and to Dev, a sitting duck.

He couldn't pass up the opportunity. Leaning up over the furniture stockade, he picked off the Kobolds, from left to right, with a single shot apiece. The hiss gun's spike of air pierced the habitat's aluminium double-shell and carbon-fibre insulation neatly. The Kobolds fell in a row. The bullet-hole 'constellations' lit up again.

"They won't try that twice," Dev said. "My bet is it'll be a full-scale assault next. You all braced for that?"

They didn't have to wait long. Within a minute, a battle cry arose outside, a score of voices howling in mutual exhortation. Gunfire pounded the habitat once more, the leading edge of a desperate, murderous charge.

As the first Kobolds came crashing in through the door, Stegman unleashed a gun-stun. Any non-hardened chip-controlled weapon the gangsters were carrying stopped working immediately. Dev and Zagat, at the same time, met them with a volley of fire. Kobolds tumbled over one another, corpse on freshly-killed corpse.

More Kobolds burst in via the windows. Trundell whooped as he hit one with a dart from Stegman's mosquito. The woman's eyes rolled up in their sockets and she collapsed like a tent whose guy ropes had all been severed.

Zagat detonated his gun-stun, making sure he threw it far enough so that his own weapon wouldn't be affected, nor those of Dev and Trundell. Stegman, meanwhile, lined up one shot after another with the replica Ruger, doing his best to inflict crippling wounds rather than fatal ones. He had relaxed some of his law enforcement officer scruples, but not, it would seem, all of them.

Kobolds kept piling into the habitat, a succession of garishly disfigured grotesques, a demonic tide. Shells and darts smacked into the stockade, sending up bursts of splinters and stuffing. Ricochets zinged.

Dev kept up a constant barrage with the hiss gun, but its battery had started to run perilously low. Already the *Recharge* warning light was flashing. Zagat announced that he had gone through almost all the ammo for the MPA pistol. Stegman said something similar about the Ruger.

Trundell was blasting away with the mosquito prolifically. He was so intent on scoring hits that it took him several seconds to realise the gun's load was spent.

Dev still had one nano-frag mine remaining. He tossed it at a group of three Kobolds and saw them frantically trying to beat away the nanite cloud with their bare hands. It was like trying to swat a million miniature razor blades. Their fingers were rapidly cut to the bone, and then the nanites latched onto their forearms and began eating upwards, past the elbows to the shoulders.

Dev had put the mine on maximum duration,

and so it was ten seconds before the nanites self-destructed.

The Kobolds' shrieks and sobs continued long after that.

Finally Stegman and Zagat were both out of ammunition, and Dev's hiss gun battery was flat.

Kobolds were still coming. It seemed as though the siege would never end.

Dev thrust himself out from behind the furniture heap, slithering across the floor on his belly to the nearest fallen Kobold. He snatched up the man's handgun and shot at the next two attackers that stormed in through the door.

It had been a while since he'd last fired an old-timey, hammer-strike sidearm with cordite-propelled lead bullets. That had been back in his tearaway teens, his period of juvenile delinquency between leaving school early with no academic qualifications and being convinced by a judge to 'make himself available for military service' as an alternative to a lengthy prison sentence. He and his friend Bogey had driven out to the marshes to take potshots at feral cats with Bogey's dad's most treasured possession, an antique Smith and Wesson Sigma semiauto. Off their faces on jazz juice – a liquid-form tetrahydrocannabinoid – they'd ended up destroying more flora than fauna, and then had had to leg it when a licensed vermin hunter appeared and started shooting at them with his rifle.

He had forgotten that this kind of gun had a kick. The weapon bucked in his hands as he pulled the trigger, and both shots went wild.

The two Kobolds flinched and ducked, then raised their guns.

Dev's next two shots were made with a firm double grip, wrists locked to absorb the recoil.

That was more like it. The Kobolds never managed to get off a round. Both slumped in the doorway, dead.

He steeled himself for the next wave of attackers.

It didn't come.

Instead he heard footfalls outside, pattering into the distance, the sound of a handful of people running away. Then silence descended.

The air in the room reeked of gunpowder and blood. Smoke and dust swirled thickly.

Dev crawled over to the door and, using the two newest corpses as cover, peered out.

The street immediately in front of the habitat was littered with bodies. The windows of the houses opposite were empty, apart from a couple of frightened faces peeping out to see if the fighting was truly over or this was just a lull.

The siege had been broken. Dev and his team had put up such a robust defence that eventually the last few Kobolds had chosen to flee rather than continue. The better part of valour and all that. They had given it their best shot. With a little more strategic planning, perhaps a few more gang members, they might have succeeded. As it was, whatever appetite they had had for the fight was now gone, and so were they.

Dev signalled to the other three. "Coast's clear. I think we've done it. Time to go."

They picked their way through the maze of sprawled bodies, Dev at the vanguard, Trundell next, then Zagat, assisting Stegman, half-carrying him.

Trundell was saucer-eyed, with a pinched face that spoke of incipient shellshock.

Dev knew the look all too well. He had seen it once on his own face. You never forget your first firefight.

"Just keep walking, Trundle," he said soothingly. "Don't look back. You did a great job, but it's over now. It's all over."

It wasn't, though.

One of the Kobold bodies reared up from the ground, and rose to its full six-and-a-half-feet. It was incomplete. An arm was missing, along with a significant section of upper torso. Above the ribcage, reaching to the neck, a neatly hollowed-out gouge. As though a giant ice cream scoop had been used. Blood glossing a bare chest.

A huge hand reached for Zagat from behind, grabbed the policeman by the skull. Yanked him backwards, away from Stegman, as though he were no heavier than a straw-stuffed scarecrow.

Mayor Major. With an injury like his, he should have been dead. He wasn't.

Stegman, abruptly deprived of Zagat's support, fell forward onto all fours. Meanwhile Mayor Major wrenched back the bigger policeman's head, exposing his throat. Zagat thumped him with elbow jabs, but Mayor Major didn't appear to notice. He was crazed with pain, his eyes like lost moons. He was too far gone to feel anything.

He bared his tungsten teeth. His serpentine tongue flickered.

Dev doubled back to help, fast, but not fast enough. The colossal Kobold leader chomped down on Zagat's neck. His teeth went in gum-deep.

With a sideways twist of his head, Mayor Major tore out a large chunk of flesh. Muscle, sinew and vein were rent asunder, accompanied by a spray of arterial blood.

Zagat spasmed and shuddered but, laconic to the last, did not cry out.

Mayor Major chewed briefly, swallowed, and went back for more. This time he bit in Zagat's windpipe, popping it open. Zagat's larynx came away in a gristly lump, which the Kobold leader wolfed down whole, with a gulp and a grunt of satisfaction.

"Best meat there is," he gloated. "Tastier than anything that comes out of a vat. How else do you think I got to be so big and strong?"

That was when Dev collided with him, shoulder first.

Mayor Major barely even swayed under the impact. Giving Dev a contemptuous look, he returned to Zagat for a third helping. The policeman hung limp from his hand. Major swallowed another ghastly mouthful and smacked his lips lasciviously.

Dev delved in his pocket for his only remaining weapon, the hair-splitter, but it wasn't there. The knife must have fallen out, along with its sheath, back in the house sometime during the siege.

So instead he sprang high and brought his elbow smashing down on Mayor Major's bald crown.

The Kobold leader just laughed, as though a feather had dropped onto him. A fourth bite of Zagat's neck left just cervical vertebrae and a few shreds of skin and tendon attaching the policeman's head to the rest of him. Mayor Major gave Zagat a firm shake, and the sheer dead weight of the body sundered these last few attachments. The decapitated trunk and limbs fell away, leaving Mayor Major holding only the head.

"Eyeballs," he said with relish, turning Zagat's face to his own. "Such a delicacy."

Dev recovered his balance, wondering what line of attack to take next. Nothing seemed to have any effect. Mayor Major was impervious. Kick to the balls? Knowing him, they'd probably been replaced by solid brass.

The monstrous Kobold pursed his lips, preparing to suck one of Zagat's eyeballs out of its socket like an oyster from its shell.

Then his own left eye disappeared. A puff of pink mist erupted at the back of his head.

The echoes of a gun report clattered along the street.

Mayor Major turned to look at the shooter, his remaining eye set in a baleful glare.

Trundell had a revolver in his trembling hands. The barrel smoked. The gun had belonged to a Kobold lying at his feet.

The xeno-entomologist couldn't have looked more appalled – or more righteous.

Mayor Major tried to say something. Then he

just let out a hearty laugh, and for one sickening moment it really seemed as though he was unhurt and would continue feasting on Zagat. Not even a bullet through the brain could deter him.

But he fell – inexorably, thunderously – toppling onto his side. His hand, when he hit the ground, released Zagat's head, so that it rolled away and fetched up beside Zagat's body in posthumous reunion.

Tears sprang from Trundell's eyes. Gently Dev took the revolver from him.

"I didn't – I can't believe I –"

"Shut up, Trundell," Dev said softly. "Don't you even think about feeling bad. You did the right thing. Bastard got what was coming to him. The only pity was it was quick. You showed him more mercy than he'd have shown any of us."

Trundell blinked hard, then nodded. He didn't even notice that Dev had again, only for the second time, used his proper surname.

"Now let's keep going," Dev said. "Hopefully, if we're really, really lucky, we can make it back to *Milady Frog* without any more shit hitting the fan."

35

THE FAN DID indeed remain shit-free for the journey to the launch complex. Dev and Trundell walked with Stegman limping between them, his arms slung around their shoulders. The policeman grumbled virtually the entire way, which as far as Dev was concerned was a positive sign.

Dev messaged ahead, and by the time they reached the docking bay, Wing Commander Beauregard had the blast doors open for them and the arcjet's onboard computer was already cycling through its pre-flight checks.

Beauregard took one look at the three and saw that things had not gone well.

"Big fella didn't make it, huh? Shame. Doesn't look like it was a picnic for the rest of you either. Up the ramp, chop-chop. Launch window's only open for the next ten minutes. We can't depart any later than that, because the sun will have got too high and it'll take us too long to catch up with the dark."

"Any trouble with Kobolds yourself?" Dev asked as they went aboard.

"Couple turned up. Bit of fuss, trying to break in. Then they rushed off like they'd got a call or something."

"Probably to join the siege on us. Mayor Major got wind of where we'd holed up and mobilised a small army of his people."

"Yeah? And how is the ugly great brute?"

"Not as healthy as he was before he met us," said Dev. "Sometimes I wish there really was a Hell."

"I think, in the olden days, the response to that would have been 'amen,'" said Beauregard. "Now, I've got a first aid kit somewhere here. Your friend's leg looks like it could do with seeing to. You up to that?"

"I know field dressing."

"Thought you might. Vet like me, huh?"

"Afraid so."

"Lot of you ISS types are, so I hear. You sign up for the war, or get drafted?"

"Little of both, you could say."

"Heh. I get it. Conscription programme 'volunteer.' The choice that's no choice. Say no more. Me, I signed up. Crazy, in hindsight, but it seemed a good idea at the time. The military were likely to co-opt me anyway, being as they were short on qualified pilots. I felt I'd be able to bear it better if I at least pretended I had some say in the decision."

"And did it help?"

"Look at me. Look how I've ended up. Do I look like I had a good war?"

While Beauregard went to the cockpit to finish prepping for takeoff, Dev attended to Stegman's injury. A quick examination told him he could treat it, but Stegman wasn't going to enjoy the experience.

"The flechette's going to have to come out," he said. "I could leave it in, but the sooner we get some astrocytes into the wound, the more chance you have of making a complete recovery."

"Do what you have to," Stegman said with a grimace.

"I can actually see the end of the flechette sticking out. It has little steel flights I can get a grip on. A couple of tugs and I'll have it out. Won't be pleasant, though. We're taking off imminently, so there's no time to wait for painkillers to kick in. It's now or never."

"Just get on with it."

"Okay. Here goes. Look away if you like, Stegosaurus."

"Stegosaurus? I don't want one of your damn nicknames, Harmer. Trundell hates his, and Stegosaurus is even worse."

"Hey, don't be ungrateful. I don't dole out nicknames to just anyone. It means I like you."

"No, it means you like to annoy me, which isn't the same – *FUCK!*"

Dev had pulled on the flechette and had levered it out a couple of centimetres. Still some way to go, however.

Short, sharp breaths hissed through Stegman's clenched teeth. "Tell me that's done the trick, please."

"Not quite. But it's definitely moved. So, Stegosaurus, you don't appreciate my conciliatory gesture. That hurts. I'm trying to, you know, build bridges between us. Hold out an olive branch."

"Then do it some other *FUCK! KING! SHIT!*"

The flechette was almost fully free from Stegman's knee. There was just the barbed tip left. This would bring quite a bit of flesh with it when it emerged. Dev had a sealant pad ready to staunch the bleeding.

"You don't reckon, after all we've been through together, that we can be friends?" he said, keeping up the teasing. As a distraction technique, it was working. Sort of. "We haven't managed any of that bonding-under-adversity stuff?"

"Personally, no," Stegman said. His face was flushed pink and burnished with a sheen of sweat. "This trip to Lidenbrock has been a shambles from start to finish, and I hold you accountable for that. What have we accomplished? Was it worth Zagat's life?"

"I like to think so. We've got a load of info. We now know more or less what we're facing."

"Which is...?"

"That's something I'd like to confer with your boss about before I say any more. If my theory's correct, Calder's Edge has a lot worse on its plate than simple earthquakes."

"Sounds ominous."

"You bet it is, Stegosaurus."

"For the last time, don't ever call me tha– *OH, FUCK ME RIGID!*"

The flechette came out with a crunchy, sucking *slurp*. Dev slapped the sealant pad in place and secured it with a self-tightening bandage loop. Analgaesics in the pad began working their numbing magic from the outside in, and Stegman's pain-contorted face gradually eased.

"Oh. Oh, that's better," he sighed.

"Got the astrocyte solution here." Dev held up a hypodermic jet injector. He slotted the appropriate cartridge into the cylinder and applied the injector to Stegman's knee. "Guess you'll..."

But Stegman had passed out. His head lolled on his chest.

"Guess you'll have to thank me later, Stegosaurus," Dev murmured, pulling the injector trigger.

Milady Frog began her transfer from docking bay to ejector tube. Dev took his seat and buckled himself in, and before long the arcjet was hurtling up to Alighieri's surface.

As she sprang free of the ejector tube, the temperature in the cabin sky-rocketed.

First it was greenhouse hot, then sauna hot. Dev began perspiring freely. He remembered Junius Bilk telling him, as part of the host form orientation talk, that excessive sweating was inherent in the Aligherian physiology. The corollary of that was it was easy to become dehydrated. Dev felt a dry prickling at the back of his throat, even as the sweat continued to ooze out. Thirst.

Once *Milady Frog* was back on Alighieri's night side, things gradually cooled. Dev found bottled water and glugged it down.

Then he called Kahlo to give her a progress update.

Harmer. Kind of busy right now. Can you call back later?

What's up?

Oh, nothing much. Just a couple of dozen earthquakes in quick succession, that's all.

That many?

I've not been keeping count. Could be more. Things have gone haywire in the past few hours. Since shortly after you left, as a matter of fact. I've been running in circles, barely catching up with myself, trying to keep on top of everything. Governor Graydon's not helping, messaging me every half an hour, bitching about this and that, wanting to know what's going on.

The damage. How bad?

Extensive. We've lost the rail tunnel to Xanadu. Huge cave-in about a quarter of the way along. Rubble blockage stretching at least half a kilometre. Other tunnel cave-ins mean several of the outlying townships have been cut off. Also, roof falls in the main Calder's cavern.

Shit. It's escalating.

You could say that. The death toll's running at a hundred-plus, but that's not including casualties in the townships. We don't yet know

how many lives have been lost there. This is
turning into a major disaster. Please tell me
you've accomplished something in Lidenbrock.
Otherwise, this conversation's over.

I think I have. It's Plusser activity, like I
thought.

For sure?

Beyond dispute.

How are they doing this? Is it bombs?
Sabotage? Some new technology?

Not quite. It's moleworms.

I'm sorry, we must've had connection issues
for a moment there. I could have sworn you
just said moleworms.

Moleworms are being used to simulate, or
stimulate, seismic events.

You're shitting me.

If only I were.

Assuming I buy that explanation – which I
don't – which is it? Simulate or stimulate?

Unclear at present. Insufficient data. But it
doesn't matter; the result is the same either
way. Moleworms, under Plusser control,
are burrowing around in such a manner
that they're generating cave-ins, rockfalls,
landslips...

How is that even possible?

If they're well co-ordinated by an external
intelligence, and if their digging is precision
targeted, it's perfectly possible.

How many moleworms are we talking about?

I'd say every single one on the planet, give or take a few. Alighieri's apex predator is being used against you. Your wildlife has been weaponised.

Well, how do we stop them?

Not sure yet, but my best guess would be we need to neutralise the Plusser running the show.

Who is he? Where is he?

That's the problem. He's inside one of the moleworms. He's turned it into some sort of ultimate alpha male and he's using it to manipulate all the others, ruling them as his pack.

Well then, the way I see it, we hunt him down and kill him. End of story.

Easier said than done. As far as I'm aware there's no way of telling *which* moleworm he is. You might have to go through an awful lot of other moleworms before you got to him.

That's fine. I'll slaughter every last one of the buggers if that's what I have to do to protect my city.

That'll take manpower. More than you've got. Also, how easy are they to track? The entire planetary crust is their home, their jungle. They have trillions of cubic hectares to hide in.

For someone from Interstellar Security Solutions, Harmer, you're not offering me very many solutions. You're just listing obstacles.

I'm mulling over a few possible options for a plan. Give me time.

How long 'til you're back in Calder's?

Four, five hours.

Then that's how long you've got.

Kahlo cut the connection.

Dev sank back into his seat, thinking.

His hypothesis *had* to be correct. The Polis+ sentience calling himself Ted Jones was now ensconced inside Banerjee's hand-reared moleworm and was using the creature to marshal the moleworm population as a whole, eastern and western subspecies alike. The mass migration had been Jones's doing. He had led a whole army of *pseudotalpidae* over from the Lidenbrock side of the planet and begun an insidious campaign of undermining.

Literally *undermining*. Burrowing through the rock strata. Exploiting geological , using weak points to trigger chain reactions – tremors and temblors that had been impeding mining operations and disrupting daily life at Calder's Edge and Xanadu. All part of an attempt to drive out the inhabitants of Alighieri's principal cities so that Polis+ could move in and take over.

Dev had established the source of the earthquakes, but in doing so had forced Ted Jones's hand. The Plusser, it appeared, was accelerating his agenda. Hence the sudden, steep increase in earthquake frequency. He had to be stopped as soon as humanly possible.

Dev didn't think Jones's goal was simply ridding

Alighieri of Alighierians, not any more. That would have worked if he had been able to carry on his sabotage uninterrupted.

Now he was going all-out. He was destroying wantonly, wildly. His scheme had been rumbled, so his only viable option was to cause maximum mayhem in the shortest time possible. The end result would be more or less the same as originally conceived – a mass exodus, an Alighieri without humans – only with a much higher death toll.

If Dev managed to put paid to his plans, somehow preventing his moleworm army from devastating Calder's completely, mightn't it still be too little, too late? Would the civic and industrial infrastructure be left so badly compromised that no one would think it worth salvaging? Would TerCon and the mining conglomerates decide to cut their losses and give up on Alighieri altogether?

In other words, even if Dev won, mightn't it all be for nothing? He could foresee Jones's actions relegating Iota Draconis C to pariah status. Alighieri would become infamous as *that place where all those terrible things happened*. Who would want to go there then? A bad reputation, once gained, was hard to shake.

No.

He couldn't think that way. It was a recipe for despair.

He had to focus only on what he could control, the outcome of his mission, and the outcome was smashing a Plusser plot. That was what he had come here to do. That was what he was with ISS for.

That... and a second shot at life. A chance to take back what had been. To regain a normal existence.

To be Dev Harmer once more.

As *Milady Frog* soared through the darkness, Dev fell into a reverie.

There would come a time when he was no longer sent pinballing around the galaxy through ultraspace. When he was no longer indentured to ISS. When he had fulfilled the terms of his phased payment contract with the company and was granted a discharge.

Then he would be reunited with himself.

Resurrected.

Reborn.

Not a passenger in host forms anymore, but truly, wholly, indivisibly Dev Harmer. Mind restored to body, body restored to full working order.

That was what he was working towards. That was what he repeatedly risked his neck for on ISS's behalf.

Life.

Real life.

ISS had been notoriously vague on the timeframe; the number of missions he had to conduct for them. Each was judged on its own merits and rated according to certain criteria: efficiency, rapidity, positive yield. He could be penalised for such things as collateral deaths and damage requiring financial restitution. If ISS was ordered by a court to pay out compensation, for instance, that would count against him.

It wasn't impossible that he could complete a mission satisfactorily and still be scored zero. The minuses could wipe out the pluses, and he would be left with nothing, no credit to show for his efforts. He had had that experience a couple of times before, and this mission was looking worryingly like it might go the same way. The deaths of Junius Bilk and Deputy Zagat were both black marks against him. Even if one of them, Bilk's, was not his fault, the ISS liaison's family might sue for reparation for their loss. ISS tended not to dispute such claims, but simply coughed up. Any money that came out of their pockets was money coming out of Dev's pocket.

Those, however, were the terms Dev had agreed to. They were unfavourable, but they were all he had been offered. One day, as long as he kept going, as long as he survived, he would bank enough points and achieve the magic total.

1,000 points.

One day he would get there and he would be free.

The number 1,000 floated through his mind, weaving in and out of his thoughts like some elusive exotic fish. He knew he should be strategising, working out ways to stop Ted Jones before his mad orgy of destruction got completely out of hand. But he was physically exhausted. Every part of his host form felt pummelled and sore, either aching or throbbing or both. His mind couldn't help drifting.

1,000.

It was a hope. A destination.

Milady Frog droned around him, the vibration of her engines a mechanical lullaby.

1,000.

He slipped into sleep and dreamed of being Dev Harmer. Of mirrors that showed him himself, unharmed, intact, entire. Of a voice that sounded like his own and a sensorium – sight, sound, smell, taste, touch – that was unmistakably his and not mediated through the tweaked DNA of a host form. A body that wasn't borrowed and bespoke, a home rather than rented accommodation. A future that wasn't a constant struggle to pay off an almost insurmountable debt.

He woke to the shrieking of tortured metal.

Warning messages blaring.

Wing Commander Beauregard alternately cursing and imploring as he fought with the arcjet's controls.

The mounting whine of an aircraft in a terminal dive.

Then came the pounding, juddering, bone-jarring impact of a barely mitigated crash landing.

36

IN THE AFTERMATH, there was silence, punctuated by groans. From *Milady Frog*'s occupants, and from the arcjet herself as her damaged airframe settled, bulwarks and skin grinding against one another, ribs and spars adjusting to their new badly bent shape, rivets torquing out of true.

Emergency lighting filled cabin and cockpit with a ruddy glow. There was a haze in the air and a faint whiff of burning.

Beauregard was the first to speak. "Everyone okay? Sound off."

"Here," said Dev.

"Here," said Stegman.

"Trundle?"

At Dev's query, the dazed xeno-entomologist gabbled out an incoherent word or two.

"Anyone hurt?" was Beauregard's next question.

Answers came back in the negative. Dev reckoned he had gained several extra bruises to add to the countless others he already had, but nothing worse than that. He tested his limbs, and nothing felt strained, sprained or broken.

Unbuckling his seatbelt, he went forward to the cockpit. *Milady Frog* was perched at a slight angle along both her longitudinal axis and her lateral axis. He was walking uphill on a starboard incline.

"What is this, Beauregard?" he demanded. "We've ditched. How the fuck did that happen?"

"Beats me," Beauregard replied. "One moment she's sailing merrily along; next, loss of power to the engines, console goes blank, avionics shot, complete shutdown, and she's plummeting like a stone. I was able to institute pilot override and fly manually. That's why we're not dead. I turned a stall dive into a glide and brought her pancaking in. It wasn't pretty, but it did the job. We still have hull integrity and no pressure leaks. Electrics still working. As they say, any landing you can walk away from..."

"How can there be a failure like that? Don't you have backup systems?"

"Of course. Stop badgering me. I didn't do anything wrong."

"*This* is wrong." Dev swept a hand across the console, knocking aside the few items of religious tat that hadn't been dislodged already in the crash. "And *this*." He snatched the hip flask out of Beauregard's hand and hurled it away; the pilot had just been about to take a sip. "You not concentrating on flying us properly is wrong."

"I swear, it was an across-the-board collapse. Bolt out of the blue, no warning. Nothing I could have done to prevent it. The fact is," Beauregard added defiantly, "if I were any less of a pilot, we wouldn't be having this conversation. We'd be smeared in little pieces across the planet."

Dev could hardly argue with that. He looked out through the windscreen. The arcjet's interior lighting wouldn't allow his Alighierian eyesight to utilise its night vision. All he could see was blackness, interspersed with distant pinpricks of orange light. An unreadable emptiness. Faint stars above.

His anger abated.

"Right," he said. "All right. Let's think about this calmly and logically. A shutdown. Could it have come from an outside agency? Some kind of blunt-force cyber attack piggybacking in via your comms?"

"I guess it could. I have shielding programs, all the right software, all up to date..."

"But the flight computer's not impregnable."

"What computer is?"

"Especially not to intrusion by Polis Plus malware."

"There's not much you can do to defend yourself against that. I saw battle craft go down from it during the Fomalhaut campaign. Whole squadrons of fighters and heli-wings and para-gunships dropping out of the sky like dead birds, without a tracer round or a flak burst in sight. It was as though invisible angels were touching them in mid-flight and killing them."

"Yes, well," said Dev. "I don't know about angels,

but I have a strong suspicion that the person who just nailed us from a distance is Ted Jones, or more likely his accomplice in Calder's Edge. Zapped us with some piece of Plusser toxic nastiness. Okay, then. Priorities. Where are we?"

"As far as I can ascertain, about a hundred klicks from Calder's. I was just preparing for final approach when everything went on the fritz. That's another reason we're alive. We were going lower and slower than during main flight."

"And is this crate totally wrecked? Not a chance of liftoff?"

Beauregard smiled thinly and bleakly. "Short of a miracle, *Milady Frog* is grounded for good."

"Who knows we've been downed?"

"No one yet."

"Then let's send out a mayday."

Beauregard frowned in concentration, then said, "Done. Location, situation, time. All points alert."

"What sort of rescue services do they have on Alighieri?"

"For aboveground travel? Not much. Down below the surface, you're fine. Up here, life's a bit trickier. You're pretty much reliant on other arcjets and limited-range VTOL hoppers when you get into difficulties. Pilots helping fellow pilots – and there aren't that many of us. Barely even a handful. That's not the real problem, though."

"What is the real problem?"

"Heat," said Beauregard. "It's already stiflingly hot in here, isn't it? We're sitting right slap bang on the surface. The *Frog*'s hull is conducting heat from the rocks under her and absorbing it from the atmosphere around her. Within half-an-hour at most, if not sooner, it'll be like sitting in an oven. We'll be, in the purest sense of the word, baking."

"Great. No way of keeping cool?"

"The backup batteries don't have power for anything more than basic life support. I can try to reboot the system, but I don't hold out much hope." He slapped the console. "Blood from a stone. And that's not all, I'm afraid."

Dev heaved a heartfelt sigh. "Lay it on me."

Beauregard jerked a thumb rearward. "Somewhere behind us, day is coming. We were outpacing it, but now that we've halted it'll be catching up. Fast. Iota Draconis will be broaching the horizon, and when dawn arrives, we won't have to worry about baking. Then, my friend, we are going to *fry*."

37

"THERE IS SOMETHING we can do," Beauregard went on. "It's a gamble, but it beats sitting on our derrieres hoping help'll come in time."

"I'm listening," said Dev.

"I have shieldsuits on board. The kind used by workers running the helium-three converter units. I bought them in case of this very eventuality."

"So we put them on and we won't cook as quickly."

"As a matter of fact, I'm suggesting we put them on and start walking."

"Out there?"

"Out there. We don't want to be inside the *Frog* when the sun reaches her. We'll be trapped when she starts to burn, like rats in a bonfire."

"How far are we likely to get before the sun catches up with us too?"

"I'm not pretending it's the ideal solution," said Beauregard. "But an extra couple of hours out of the sun, even just an hour, might make all the difference. We keep beaming out maydays from our commplants, like distress beacons, and rescuers will still be able to home in on us even on the move."

"I thought a basic rule of survival was stay put. An arcjet is easier to locate in the wilderness than four men on foot."

"Basic rules of survival don't apply on the surface of a thermoplanet. Here, your chances are better the less you stand still. Think of the shieldsuits as individual, self-contained lifeboats."

"Okay." Dev could see the sense in what Beauregard was proposing. He didn't like it, but it was the lesser of two evils. "Then I suppose time is of the essence. Where are these shieldsuits?"

They were hanging in lockers in the hold. They were scuffed and battered, their faceplates scratched, their shells covered in tatty old decals identifying the mining conglomerate they had belonged to – *France-registered Dumoulin Et Fils Exploitation Minière d'Espace Cie.* – and stencilled with the surnames of their previous occupants.

"Wow," said Dev. "These look... pre-loved. I hope you got them cheap."

"Reasonably," said Beauregard. "To be honest, they were past the end of their useful lives. They were going to be decommissioned and broken down for scrap. Rest assured, I've overhauled them and I keep them well maintained. The cryo-coolant systems are in working order, and the waste-water filtration and recirculation units are fully operational."

Trundell and Stegman were present, and the

former voiced an observation that Dev himself had made, but hadn't wanted to mention yet.

"There are only three of them," he said.

"I could only afford three," said Beauregard. "Mostly I'm alone on flights. Sometimes I'll have one passenger, never more than two. Three shieldsuits would under normal circumstances be fine."

"But not now," said Stegman. "We're one short."

"You haven't got another spare stashed somewhere?" Dev asked, more in hope than expectation.

The pilot shook his head. "We all realise what this means. One of us is staying behind with *Milady Frog*. But that's okay. We won't have to draw lots or anything, because I know who it is."

"Yes," said Stegman. "Me. I'm the one with the messed-up leg. It feels fine right now, but the analgesics won't last forever. I'll start dragging it, and I'll slow the rest of you down. I'll stay."

"Noble, but no," said Beauregard. "It's me. This is my plane. The captain always goes down with his ship, right?"

"Bullshit," said Stegman. "I've stated my case. No arguments. Get those suits on, the rest of you."

"*I* could stay," Trundell offered. "I'm not that physically fit. I'll tire before the rest of you. I'd end up holding you all back."

"This is stupid," said Dev. "Each of us can give a good reason for being the one who doesn't go. Look at me. This isn't even my body. Why should I give a damn if it gets burnt to cinders?"

"Nice try," said Trundell, "but we all know you'll die if it does. You of all people have to get back to Calder's Edge. More so than me or Stegman or Beauregard. You're the one who's got the expertise when it comes to Plussers. The city needs you."

"Your faith in me is touching."

"It isn't faith. It's common sense."

"This isn't even open to debate," said Beauregard. "I've made the decision. Now hurry up and get into those things. Day's on its way."

"Actually, the wingco's got a point," said Dev. "We could go round in circles about this for hours. He is the sensible choice."

"Harmer..." said Stegman.

"Hear me out. I don't like it. Really I don't. But we're in an impossible situation, and it has to be settled quick-smart. So I'm backing Beauregard. We leave him, and he can get busy trying to get *Milady Frog* off the ground. None of us three can fly this thing. Beauregard knows her inside out. Maybe, just maybe, he can restart her and then pick us up en route to Calder's. If he stays, the odds of us *all* getting out of this alive actually improve."

Beauregard appeared relieved, and even grateful, that Dev had come up with this excuse to justify his remaining behind. Both he and Dev knew there wasn't much likelihood of *Milady Frog* taking off. Trundell and Stegman probably knew it too. Now, however, there was a fig-leaf to cover Beauregard's act of self-sacrifice. It was a tiny, slender one, but it would do.

Stegman said, haltingly, "Well, that's a plan, isn't it? Makes sense."

"I can see the logic," said Trundell.

But neither man could meet Beauregard's eyes as he helped them put on the shieldsuits.

The suits had the bulky profile of EVA spacesuits, but were lighter and more durable, each weighing less than twenty kilos all told. The shell was ceramic, coated with a layer of heat-resistant graphene. The joints were a flexible polyaramid-fibre weave also coated with graphene.

The faceplates on the helmets were borosilicate glass inset in a narrow, roughly V-shaped slit – little more than visors, really. They had to be that small, because they were the shieldsuits' most vulnerable component. The glass had the lowest melting point of all of the suit materials and would succumb to Iota Draconis's furnace-like blast before any other part did.

Once Trundell and Stegman were fully suited up, Dev told them to establish a three-way commplant link so that they could talk when they got outside.

He picked up his helmet, the last item left to put on.

"Beauregard..." he said.

The pilot was taking a swig from his hip flask, which he had retrieved from the cockpit floor and replenished from a bottle in the provisions cabinet. Vodka, it appeared, was his preferred tipple. Spirit of Gdansk, in fact, a particularly potent brand distilled by Polish settlers on 16 Cygni Bb, Little

Warsaw, where the dry, rich soil yielded handsome potato crops.

"It's all right," Beauregard said. "I'm not scared. Been here before. Some of the high-altitude drop raids I ran, I never thought I'd come back from. Nearly didn't. Blizzards of incoming fire. Wingmen falling away on either side. Every day I've had since the war ended has been a bonus, as far as I'm concerned. It's all been borrowed time."

"You're going to try with the *Frog*, though, aren't you? At least promise me that."

"I'll do my best. There's one or two tricks I can think of. Maybe if I dicker about with the multidrop buses or reset the power breakers... But I wouldn't hold my breath if I were you. Polis Plus malware's bastardly stuff. Super thorough. Wipes everything back to factory-blank level. It's like a thief who steals all your valuables then squats out a turd on your living-room carpet for good measure."

"Very picturesque."

"Just don't waste this, Harmer. If, you know, I'm not going anywhere, make sure it wasn't all for nothing. Make sure the Plussers don't get their way. Alighieri's not much, but it's been my home for the past five years. I'd hate to see them claim it for their own. What was the Frontier War for, if it wasn't to keep these digimentalists off our property?"

"Will do," said Dev. "And I apologise for losing my temper in the cockpit earlier. I shouldn't have sounded off at you. You got us safely down. Respect is due."

"Post-crash shock. Heat of the moment. It happens."

"Still hate all your religious crap, though."

"Me too," Beauregard admitted. "It's not there just for fun. It's there to remind me what I didn't have when facing the Plussers, and what they thought they did. They believed that faith in the Singularity would guarantee them victory. Hah. Guess what? We fought them to a standstill. We held them to a draw. So much for gods, eh?"

Dev clamped the helmet into place. Beauregard helped him adjust it until it mated with the rest of the shieldsuit.

The suit, once complete, automatically booted up. Batteries hummed to life. The rebreather apparatus kicked in. Cryo-coolant sloshed through tubes, settling on a temperature level just above average body warmth.

Through the V of the faceplate, Dev saw Beauregard give him a thumbs-up. Dev returned it clumsily, as best the suit's thick gauntlet would allow.

Then he turned and stomped towards Trundell and Stegman at the rear of the hold.

Stegosaurus? Trundle? Are we ready to roll?

Ready to rip that suit off you and give it to Beauregard, Stegman replied, if you call me that name one more time.

Beauregard withdrew into the cockpit, sealing off the hold from the rest of the arcjet's interior. Then he depressurised the hold and hit the switch to lower the loading ramp.

Fierce heat rushed in from the darkness outside. Digits on the readout of Dev's shieldsuit's temperature gauge, visible via a head-up display projected on the faceplate, shot up. Within seconds they had reached the middle triple figures.

Sections of the hold walls, ceiling and floor began to crackle and char.

The shieldsuit compensated by increasing the energy density of cryo-coolant and upping the rate of circulation. The heat sink mounted on the back began dissipating excess heat out into the atmosphere.

A timer next to the temperature gauge calculated how long the shieldsuit would continue to be viable under present conditions. It arrived at a figure of 133 minutes, and immediately began counting down, glowing red digits superimposed on the landscape outside.

02:12:59
02:12:58
02:12:57

A little over two hours. After that, the suit's integrity could not be guaranteed any more. Internal systems would start to break down. The nanorod-suspension cryo-coolant would increasingly lose effectiveness until it was no better than plain water. The shell would start to crack and split.

Two hours.

How far could you get in that time at walking pace? Ten kilometres under optimal conditions, and the conditions on Alighieri's surface were far from optimal. Beauregard had said they were a hundred klicks from Calder's. So at best they would shave a tenth off the journey any would-be rescuer might make, but only a tenth.

But then this wasn't about narrowing the distance between the crash site and Calder's Edge.

It was about escaping the rising sun.

As they exited *Milady Frog*, Dev checked the eastern horizon. There was the faintest of glows there, a hint of reddish-orange light.

Alighieri was a small planet with a fast rotation.

Dawn would be coming soon enough.

38

THE THREE OF them skirted back around the downed arcjet, taking a path that continued in the direction she'd been travelling before the crash. Dev noted missing tiles on *Milady Frog*'s belly and a scraped, dented engine nacelle. He was surprised she wasn't in a far worse state. Beauregard had truly worked wonders.

Eyes now having adjusted to the darkness, Dev glanced back and saw a line of gouges in the rocky terrain marking *Milady Frog*'s path coming in. She had bounced five or six times like a skimming stone before fetching up to rest against a metre-high ridge.

As Beauregard had said, any landing you can walk away from...

Turning back, he looked up to the cockpit. Inside, Beauregard gave a salute. He had his feet up on the console. He didn't look as though he was making any great effort to jump-start the arcjet.

A man resigned to his fate.

Dev saluted back, then began walking in earnest.

Trundell and Stegman fell in step beside him.

The ground was mostly level plain, with here and there a bulbous outcrop of basalt or a trench-like fissure. A layer of regolith crunched underfoot, the dust of shattered rocks and cosmic debris that had settled on Alighieri over the eons. Puffs of it floated up into the thin atmosphere behind the three men as they trudged forward.

The heat radiating off the surface made the night sky waver as though it were a reflection in rippling water. The stars flickered in their constellations like tiny candle flames. The light they shed was just enough for Trundell to see by. For Dev and Stegman, with their Alighierian eyes, it was more than adequate.

Soon *Milady Frog* was a silvery twinkle in the distance, so small Dev could only just make out her amphibian contours. He pictured Wing Commander Beauregard still in the cockpit, gazing out through the windscreen, watching them go. Perhaps, to him, they were already lost in the bleak black landscape. The last fellow human beings he would ever lay eyes on – vanished.

Dev understood Beauregard's motive in refusing even to consider taking one of the three shieldsuits. Having been through the Frontier War himself, he knew how it changed your perspective on life and death. You realised the fragility of the one and the ever-present proximity of the other. You didn't lose the dread of dying – who did? – but you learned to make peace with death better than anyone else might, even while you cherished your life all the more.

Beauregard was meeting oblivion with acceptance in his heart and a hip flask in his hand.

There were worse ways to go.

The three men had walked a little over two kilometres before they encountered their first obstacle, a crevice four metres wide and several deep. Even if they weren't encumbered by the shieldsuits, they would have had trouble jumping the gap.

There was no alternative but to go round.

The crevice followed a saw-tooth course for nearly a kilometre, tapering little by little until it was narrow enough for them to be able to bound across with impunity. They had had to go due south, losing a kilometre's worth of westward travel. The sunlight would be reaching them that much sooner.

0:47:37

Next they found themselves approaching a long escarpment, which rose vertically and extended as far as the eye could see in either direction, the inner rim of a vast crater. It was perhaps ten metres high, and from a distance seemed sheer. Closer to, however, its face revealed notches and grooves that suggested it might be scalable.

The three men conferred and decided to give climbing it a try.

Is your knee up to the job, Stegosaurus?

Just watch me, Harmer.

Each of them selected a different route up the escarpment. As Dev began to climb, he realised just how restrictive the shieldsuit was. It was like being encased in armour. You couldn't feel precisely where you were placing your hands and feet. More than once he thought he had established a firm toehold, only to have his leg shoot out under him when he pushed down on it.

He lost count of the number of times he nearly fell, but eventually he crested the brow of the small cliff. Beyond lay a sweeping expanse of boulders, like a glacial moraine. This was probably the remains of a volcanic ejecta field; that, or the detritus from some ancient meteorite impact.

Dev's heart sank. Their already slow progress was about to get even slower.

Uh, a little help here?

The plaintive plea came from Trundell, who was near the top of the escarpment and had got into difficulties. One foot was wedged tight in a narrow fissure and he couldn't extricate it.

Dev grabbed his wrists and heaved, but was unable to pull him free. They had to wait until Stegman finished climbing and was able to come over and join in. Together, with their combined strength, he and Dev managed to wrench Trundell up and over the rim.

Trundell lay on his belly, wheezing. Dev gave him a minute to recover as he surveyed the eastern horizon. There was a corona of golden light there now, and it seemed to be expanding and becoming more brilliant even as he watched. He had never thought the sight of a sunrise would instil him with horror.

A looped message was being beamed out by his commplant, repeating itself at five-second intervals.

Dev Harmer. Down here at these GPS coordinates. In danger of getting terminated by the terminator. Any time you want to drop by and give us a lift, that's fine with me.

Someone had to have heard Beauregard's mayday. Someone had to be coming.

Had to be.

But if so, how come there had been no reply yet to Dev's message? It didn't need to be much, a simple Hang in there, we're on our way, that was all. Why the silence?

01:32:51

Nothing to be gained by worrying about it. Keep going, that was the only option. Keep going and keep hoping.

He helped Trundell to his feet, and the three of them set off across the boulder field.

Tripping, slipping, squeezing between the rocks when possible, crawling over them when not. Hopping across from one to the next when they were flat enough to allow it. Straddling them when they were small enough to allow that.

The constant effort began to take its toll. Dev's breathing became laboured. The air in the shieldsuit grew insufferably stifling. The temperature inside was rising, now a feverish 38° Celsius thanks to his exertions. The cooling system worked hard to bring that down, but the external temperature was rising too, so it was fighting a battle on two fronts.

He paused to take a drink from the water recirculation

unit. What he was sucking from the valve-tipped tube was his own sweat and the moisture from his breath, which had been drawn in through ionic membrane pumps, then condensed, filtered and purified. It tasted more than a little salty. It was welcome nonetheless.

While he was stationary, the shieldsuit recalculated its continued viability time. It was factoring in the heat his body was giving off in addition to the mounting heat outside as daybreak drew nearer.

On the faceplate HUD, *0::23::7* suddenly, in a blink, became *0::16:09*.

Seven minutes gone, just like that. Not much in the general scheme of things, but for someone in his predicament, every minute – every *second* – was vital.

With renewed vigour and will, Dev resumed traversing the boulder field.

After a while, the rocks grew smaller and fewer. The ground between them was scattered with sharp, gravelly pebbles. These were treacherous underfoot but, after battling his way across the larger boulders, Dev didn't mind. The going was much easier now. A walk in the park by comparison.

Trundell caught up with him.

We're doing all right, aren't we, Harmer?

So far.

Do you think we're going to make it?

I'm just putting one foot in front of the other. As long as we're moving west, we're in with a chance.

They'll be searching for us. They'll find us.

Yeah. Definitely.

Umm, where's Stegman?

Dev turned round. He performed a 360° sweep of the vicinity.

No sign of Stegman.

Shit.

We'd better go back and look for him.

All right. Yes. It's getting lighter, though, isn't it? Have you noticed? The rocks are growing shadows. I can actually see what I'm doing.

Dev was finding the nascent daylight uncomfortable. It made his eyes ache. He imagined it would only get worse. The shieldsuits' faceplates weren't polarised or even tinted. They didn't need to be; the suits were intended for subterranean use. Nobody – apart from Beauregard – had ever considered that they might be pressed into service as 'lifeboats' on the planet's surface.

Dev retraced his steps, Trundell with him.

Stegosaurus? Stegman? You there? Answer me.

Here, Harmer.

Give us a clue as to your whereabouts.

What's happened? Why the hold-up?

I'm among these boulders still. My knee's not playing ball. Blasted thing hurts like a bitch. Painkillers have worn off. I'm doing my best, but it's hard with only one leg fully functioning.

We're coming back for you.

No. Don't do that. If I can't keep up, that's my lookout.

Fuck's sake, Stegosaurus. You after a medal
or something? There's no room for any
hero stuff. We're all getting out of this mess
together, or not at all. Simple as that.

I mean it, Harmer. I can manage.

You think I'm going to leave you behind? Can
you see me explaining that to Captain Kahlo?
"Where's my sergeant?" she'll ask, and I'll
say, "Er, well, about that…" She'll kill me.
Skin me alive. With a nail file.

Ha! I'd pay good money to see that.

So get yourself up somewhere where we can
see you. Top of one of the boulders. Go on.

Arriving at the zone where the rocks became
dauntingly large, Dev scanned left and right.

Nothing. How far had Stegman lagged behind?

Then Dev spied a hand, an arm, two hands.
Stegman hauling himself strugglingly to the summit
of a boulder the size of a garden shed.

He was only fifty or so metres away. Dev wended
towards him through the jagged, rugged rock maze.

Stegman slithered off the boulder, and Dev guided
him out, back to where Trundell was waiting.

The policeman's leg *was* in bad shape. He could
barely put any weight on it.

Dev couldn't help glancing at the shieldsuit timer.
00:52:41

Less than an hour, and that total would be
recalibrated and reduced on a regular basis once
Iota Draconis cleared the horizon. Continued suit
viability was a moveable feast. Time was short, and

shortening at an unfixed rate. There could be just over fifty minutes left; there could be far less.

Just for a moment, Dev was overcome by a sense of futility. Everything was against them. The sun, the terrain, Stegman's knee. They might not make it after all. Rescue might not arrive in time.

Their deaths would be gradual and not pleasant. First the cryo-coolant would pack up. The sun's rays would then barbecue the suits' occupants like lobsters in their shells. Not long after that, the suits themselves would melt. In the end, there would be nothing left of Dev, Trundell and Stegman but three pools of bubbling ceramic, clotted with human ashes.

All at once, Dev hated this world. This fucking Alighieri. Hated it with a passion. It had tried to kill him in so many ways. It was trying again, really hard this time.

"Screw you, Alighieri," he said inside his helmet, to himself. "You're not getting me."

He hoisted Stegman's arm around his neck. He didn't say anything further, just started walking again.

39

THE SHADOWS SHORTENED and sharpened. The light whitened. The landscape ahead was thrown into sharp chiaroscuro relief. Every detail stood revealed, every bulge and crack, every ridge and pinnacle.

Iota Draconis was coming up, and with it, Alighieri was waking up. At the sun's touch, rocks began to glow like flowers blooming. The heat haze grew thicker, becoming an iridescent shimmer. Fumes arose from cracks in the ground, creating palls of low-hanging, sulphurous mist. There was a deep cacophony of creaks and rumbles as basalt expanded, rock rubbing against rock.

Inside the shieldsuits, the temperature gauges read 42°C. The cooling systems were operating at full capacity, but the figure crept inexorably further upward. The viability times, meanwhile, ticked down, occasionally jumping by a whole minute in the space of a single second.

00:31:13

The three men tramped on across the fiery

landscape. Now and then, Dev would broadcast an encouraging message to the other two – That's it, good work, on we go – but it became more and more of an effort. Not just to formulate the words, but to believe in them.

Stegman was more or less a dead weight on Dev's arm. He hopped and hobbled along, frequently stumbling and falling, dragging Dev down with him. He asked several times to be left alone. He could make it without help, he insisted. Dev didn't bother to reply, just lugged him onward.

Trundell sometimes chipped in to help, supporting Stegman on the other side. The xeno-entomologist was himself struggling, however. He would send out short messages every so often that tried to be upbeat, even amusing, but were mostly nonsensical:

> At least I'll be getting a suntan, no more Mr Pasty Face for me.
>
> Now I know what I know what a beef brisket feels like. Brisket, brisket, brisket; that's a funny word, brisket.
>
> "How did you manage to survive on Alighieri's surface for so long, professor?" the journalists will ask, and I'll tell them it was by dreaming of snow and icebergs, snow and icebergs, so white, so cold, ice and snowbergs...

Dev let him ramble on and didn't ask him to be quiet, although he would have preferred not to have to listen to his gibberish. As long as Trundell was communicating, as long as his mind was active, he was still in the game.

00:24:08

Dev reset his looped beacon message to say: We're running out of time. Someone respond, damn it. Mayday, mayday, mayday. Three men about to be burned to a frazzle.

He wondered whether the sun's intense UV radiation might be interfering with commplant signals, scrambling them or at least reducing their range and effectiveness. If that was the case, then their chances of being rescued had dropped from low to nearly zero.

The light was dazzling now. Dev had to squint just to be able to see. Every footstep was a trial, a test of endurance. Stegman weighed a ton. He was a human ball and chain. Walking was like wading through hot tar.

The temperature gauge was nudging 45°C. Outside, it was five times that. Dev was bathed in sweat, slick with it, dripping, as though he was standing out in a tropical rain storm. His throat was raw with a thirst that the recirculated water couldn't quite slake.

Abruptly Trundell halted. He stood like a tree in a breeze, swaying.

Trundle, what is it? What's the matter?

Feel sick. Want to throw up.

You're in a shieldsuit. You can't throw up.
It's nausea from the heat. You're not actually
going to be sick. Drink some more.

Trundell didn't appear to hear. He grappled with his helmet, making a cackhanded attempt to remove it.

Dev lowered Stegman to the ground and hurried

over to the xeno-entomologist. He took Trundell's
hands and brought them down before he could
disengaged the shieldsuit's airtight seal.

Look at me. *Look* at me.

Through their faceplates, their gazes locked.
Trundell's eyes were huge and scared. He was
blinking so profusely it was as though he was
transmitting Morse code with his eyelids.

Drink. It'll help. The nausea won't go away
completely, but it won't get worse either.
These are just early signs of hyperthermia.

Hyperthermia. Yes, hyperthermia.

You know what that is?

I know what that is. It's... It's...

It's heatstroke. Your heart rate's probably
high too.

Yes. Uh, yes. Racing.

That's all right. That's natural. Just your body
trying to cope. Accept it. Don't let it feed your
anxiety. We're going to be okay.

No one's coming for us, are they? Are they?

I don't know. I expect they are.

They haven't said. We haven't heard.

Doesn't mean a thing. Maybe our
commplants are misbehaving. The sun is
fucking with everything.

They'd have said, wouldn't they? By now? If
they were on their way.

If we stop, if we give up, we're doomed. It's
that simple. So we're not doing that. You get
me, Trundell? We're not giving up.

Trundell. You only use my proper name
when things are serious. When you want my
attention.

Bingo. And that's what I want now. Your full
attention. Stay sharp. Stay with us.

Stegman joined in the conversation.

Can't we rest? Just for a little bit? My knee's
killing me.

The sun is killing us. Little by little. But if we
just sit still and let it, then what's the point?
You want to beat this? You want to live?
We do that by moving. Every step we take
is a fuck-you. A fuck-you to Iota Draconis.
A fuck-you to Alighieri. A fuck-you to the
Plusser who brought us down in the first
place.

You're... You're one crazy bastard, Harmer.

I know. It's why I'm still alive.

Stegman tottered to his feet. Dev grabbed him and
steadied him.

Trundell started walking.

Dev and Stegman followed.

40

ON THEY TROD. On, across a world of fire.

The ground pulsed like flame. The air was a hazy, smoky yellow. There were no shadows any more, other than the faint, fluctuating silhouettes their bodies cast on the ground ahead of them. There was mostly just brightness, a range of lambent hues from hearth-fire orange to magnesium-flare white.

00:11:21 became *00:09:33* became *00:07:09*. Dev couldn't tell if it was the shieldsuit recalculating or if he was losing track of time passing, a malfunction in his own internal clock. Minutes were instants. Yet they were also shapeless and malleable. One segued seamlessly into another. Everything was a continuum of heat and pain and toil and glare.

Now there were warning lights. Loads of them. The faceplate HUD was giving him all sorts of ominous messages. The shieldsuit's internal temperature had soared to 55°C, as hot as any of the hottest places on Earth, as hot as the Sahara, as hot as Death Valley on a bad day. Externally it was nigh on 500°.

Dev noted scorch marks appearing on Stegman's suit. Wisps of smoke were drifting up from Trundell's helmet.

Five minutes to unviability.

They walked.

They didn't communicate, didn't acknowledge one another.

Just walked.

Each man on his own. Each dizzy and suffering from nausea. Each isolated, lodged inside himself, alone with his suffering and misery. Each drenched in sweat and listening to his pulse pounding in his ears, fast, too fast, like a timpani roll. Each barely conscious of his legs moving, lost to the *why* and the *where* of the journey, going on because that was all that was left, this mechanical motion, like a ritual which had long lost its original significance and become rote. Because walking was all that mattered and all that had ever mattered.

Three minutes to unviability.

Two minutes.

One.

Then the warning lights, in unison, winked out. Dev's shieldsuit stopped telling him how much distress it was in. He clearly wasn't paying any heed, wasn't worth alerting to the danger any more. The suit seemed to settle into a sullen, acquiescent silence, as though accepting that it had tried its best and now there was nothing anyone could do.

When the cooling system gave out, the suit just put up a silent perfunctory statement informing its wearer of the fact. Likewise when the water recirculation unit gasped its last, and when the heat sink went down.

The shieldsuit was now simply an inert shell, an inorganic carapace. It could do nothing but hang off Dev's body and be a barrier between him and the sunlight.

A failing barrier.

The glass of the faceplate developed a crack. Tiny striations branched off the crack like the veins in a leaf. The glass itself began to blacken from the edges inward, and the head-up display flickered and vanished.

Dev could smell burning. Was it coming from inside or out?

Both.

The suit's ceramic had started to singe.

So had he.

An aroma of chargrilled meat.

His own flesh, cooking.

armer

A voice.

No, just a thought. Something random flitting through his brain.

Harmer, are... Harmer... Acknow

He tried to answer it, this ghost voice in his mind, this accidental sparking of neurons. Words wouldn't come, however.

is Kahl... read me... Hang

Baked alive.

Vision darkening.

Then a rush of wind, and his head emptying, and something large, something insectile and monstrous, descending in front of him with claw-tipped arms outstretched...

And then the darkness swamped in and entirely obliterated the light.

41

LIGHT. AND MOTION.

The sway of transportation.

Dev forced his eyes open.

He was on a floor. Cool metal. Blessedly cool.

An IV was in his arm, feeding him a clear fluid.

Icepacks on his forehead and forearms, his legs.

People. Cramped, crowded conditions. The cargo bay of some sort of small airborne craft.

He turned his head, and there was Trundell lying right next to him. Paramedics were bending over the little xeno-entomologist. The skin of his face was reddened and blistered.

Then his body started trembling, twisting. A seizure.

The paramedics reacted with practised calm, rolling Trundell onto his side, making sure his airway was open, cradling his head. An injection. The fit passed.

"This one's come round," said one of the paramedics, noticing Dev watching them. "Stay down, sir. Don't try to get up."

"Trun–" Dev croaked. "Trundle. Is he all right?"

"Him? We think so. He's suffered heat syncope, as have you. Fainting from extreme hyperthermia. Seizures and muscle spasms aren't uncommon after heat stroke collapse. We've given him a muscle relaxant and we're putting saline and electrolytes into him, just like we are you."

"Stegman. The third guy. Where is he?"

"He's okay too, Harmer," said a familiar female voice. "Up front in the cockpit. That's how pushed for space we are. He's worse for wear, but the docs say he's going to pull through."

Captain Kahlo edged into Dev's line of vision.

"Kahlo," he said. "So I didn't imagine it. You *were* talking to me out there."

She squatted down beside him. "Who else did you think it was?"

"Things were starting to get muddled. I thought you might have been a hallucination."

"No such luck. It was me, and I'm not best pleased with you."

"When are you ever?"

"What kind of insane stunt did you think you were pulling? Out in full daylight?"

"It seemed like a good idea at the time. As a matter of fact, it still seems like a good idea, considering you found us and we're alive."

"Only just, in both instances. We were about to call off the search. This is a surface equipment maintenance flyer we're in. She's got a daylight tolerance of ninety minutes. We were at the point of no return when we picked up your signal. As things stand, it's touch and go whether we're going to get back to safe harbour in time. Pilot's pushing her to her limits. Lot of people are risking their lives to bring you home."

"Including you. And I'm grateful." Dev recalled the outstretched arms he had seen before blacking out. Robot arms. "So you hauled us aboard using the waldoes?"

Kahlo nodded. "The ship's got telemanipulators for carrying out essential external repairs to ejector tube doors and the like. The pilot dragged the three of you in, shucked the suits off you, tossed them back out. Then he opened the cargo bay airlock so the medics could come in and do their thing. It was precision stuff. The guy's a pro."

"Remind me to thank him."

"Sir," said the paramedic. "I strongly recommend you rest up and don't talk so much. After what you've been through, you should take things easy for a while."

"Wish I could, believe me." Dev turned back to Kahlo. "I don't suppose you were able to reach *Milady Frog*?"

A sombre frown from Kahlo. "We got there first before we doubled back and went looking for you. And... there wasn't much left of her. Just a smouldering husk."

"Damn."

"Wing Commander Beauregard got off a last-minute message as we were approaching. Said you three were out on foot and indicated which way you'd gone. We must have passed by not far from you on the way in, but somehow missed you."

That had happened, in all probability, while Dev, Trundell and Stegman were negotiating the boulder field. The three of them would have been out of direct sight, their beacon signals blocked, weakened by solar interference.

"Ten minutes sooner," Kahlo continued, "and we might have got to Beauregard in time. Iota Draconis takes no prisoners."

"Tell me about it," Dev said. "Pity about Beauregard. He saved us. More than once."

"Speaking of 'us'... Where's Deputy Zagat?"

Her tone said she was anticipating bad news, and Dev's solemn expression confirmed it.

"Shit, Harmer. Not him, too."

"Back at Lidenbrock City, we ran into difficulties. Zagat was a fucking marvel. I couldn't have asked for anyone better at my side. One-man platoon. But he got caught, got taken out, and for that I'm happy to shoulder at least part of the blame. It's on me. I thought an opponent was down when he wasn't. He ought to have been, but he wasn't. Maybe I should have checked, and then Zagat would at least have made it out of Lidenbrock alive."

Kahlo set her mouth in a bitter pout. "Two men died to get you into and out of that place. That's a high price."

"You think I'm not beating myself up about it?"

"I damn well hope you are."

"But you know also that the real culprits are the Plussers?"

"It's the only thing that's keeping me from tossing you back out onto the surface," Kahlo said. "Those bastards have a lot to answer for."

"How's the situation in Calder's? I'm guessing it's not so terrible, since you've come out here to head up the search for us, rather than staying there."

"It's quietened down. There've been no quakes for a couple of hours. Rescue crews are combing the rubble, pulling out survivors. Xanadu seems to be bearing the brunt of it right now, and getting it worse than Calder's. Details are still sketchy, but it seems there may have been a significant roof fall in the main cavern – as in, most of it. We've also heard that Xanadu's governor, Huston, could be dead."

"How's Graydon?" Dev nearly said "your dad," but Kahlo hadn't yet come clean to him about the truth of her relationship with the governor, and it was simpler if Dev appeared not to know.

"Taking it badly. Stressed as anything. He's toying with the idea of contacting TerCon for permission to call in all the nearest available gulf cruisers."

"What, to get everyone off-planet?"

"If possible. A mass evacuation. If TerCon declare an official emergency on Alighieri, we could have probably a dozen cruisers diverted this way within twenty-four hours. All civilians could be embarked within a day or so after that, leaving just essential personnel."

"It's a big ask."

"It's been done before. Hear about the Erewhon airlift back in 'ninety-one? They cleared three million people out ahead of a Polis Plus onslaught. No one thought it would succeed, but it did. Touch and go, admittedly, with the last cruiser taking off while Plusser crab tanks were rolling into the spaceport. Hopefully we won't have to cut it so fine."

"And then what? Calder's and Xanadu are left as ghost towns. The Plussers can just move their furniture in and hang up their family photos and say 'Ours.'"

"I'm not saying it's what *I* want, Harmer. But I'm not Maurice Graydon. He's a governor, with a governor's mandate. His duty of care is to his electorate. I want to save Calder's, and I'm going to try my hardest to do that, but we have to prepared for every contingency."

"And one of those is bailing out," said Dev.

"If the Plussers do try and take over afterwards, I guess TerCon might consider that an act of aggression. Troops could be sent in to roust them out and recapture the planet." Kahlo sounded optimistic, but not hopeful.

"No one's going to war with Polis Plus, captain, not again. No one has the stomach for it. The Frontier War's still too fresh in people's memories. We've no will to engage them head to head again. We're only just recovering from the last time. And that's what they're counting on. Once Calder's and Xanadu are empty, the Plussers will consider them fair game. They occupy them, and in effect they've occupied Alighieri."

"What about Lidenbrock? Does that even figure? They won't have the whole planet if there's still one human-occupied city."

"My hunch is TerCon will cut Lidenbrock loose. A city full of rejects and undesirables – who cares if it has to share a world with Plussers? There'll be an outcry in some quarters, but the *realpolitik* of the situation is that Polis Plus will have outplayed us, outmanoeuvred us, and we'll just have to learn to live with it. Lidenbrock will be considered an acceptable sacrifice. What's one dirty, scum-ridden rabbit warren of a city when a whole planet has been lost?"

Kahlo sighed. "Fuck it. There's got to be some way out of this."

"There is," said Dev. "But it'll need co-operation from several directions – a concerted effort – and it has to be done fast. Once Ted Jones is finished with Xanadu, I don't think it'll be long before he comes back and hits Calder's again."

42

"DEV HARMER," SAID Ben Thorne. "Don't you look a sight."

The head of the Fair Dues Collective sauntered into Governor Graydon's office as though it were his own living room. He tipped a finger to forelock in greeting to Graydon, before turning to the Calder's Edge chief of police.

"And the lovely Captain Kahlo," he added, with a mock-obsequious bow. "What an august assembly of personages. Calder's Edge royalty, no less, our very own king and princess. Together in the same room. A rare treat. I feel honoured – me, a humble miner, and a miner's son. I am truly hobnobbing with the gentry."

"Sit down, please, Mr Thorne," said Graydon with studied calm, too much the professional politician to be provoked by this needling. "Can I get you something? A drink?"

"No, no, I don't need you waiting on me, governor," Thorne replied with a swat of the hand.

"If I'm thirsty, I'll deal with it myself. So, you've summoned. I've come. What's the aim of this meeting? Not that I can't make an educated guess..."

"Let's hold fire on that. We're expecting one more guest."

Thorne made himself comfortable in a chair, then leapt back to his feet and helped himself to a generous measure of Graydon's Yamazaki whisky. "In times of crisis," he said, "it never hurts to take a moment out to appreciate the finer things. Harmer, word is you've been over to Lidenbrock."

"I have," said Dev.

"And lived to tell the tale. But what's with all the – this?" Thorne circled a finger at his own face. "The blisters and the flaking skin? You look like someone had a go at you with a blowtorch."

"I went up top to catch some rays."

Thorne grinned, amused. "Anyone else, I'd say they were joking. But not you. You know, some of my FDC boys and girls, they were impressed by you. How you handled the Ordeal. How long you lasted. Not me, of course. But my brethren and sistren have been talking about you with genuine respect in their voices. That's quite a thing for hardened mineworkers to do. Especially given you're a non-miner, and an offworlder to boot."

"The Ordeal?" said Graydon. "They put you through that? Why?"

"You'd have to ask Mr Thorne," said Dev. "Not wishing to put words in his mouth, but I think he felt I'd been throwing my weight about and had besmirched his good name. Also, there was a strike brewing, and apparently there was something I could do to ease the tensions between management and workforce."

"You have a strange way of welcoming visitors to our city, Mr Thorne," said Graydon.

"This visitor," said Thorne, jerking a thumb at Dev, "has a strange way of treating blameless, upstanding citizens as criminals. At any rate, he's learned not to make that mistake twice."

There clearly wasn't much love lost between Thorne and Graydon. The two men spoke to each other with the exaggerated civility common to implacable foes. Thorne's union activism posed a constant threat to the smooth, well-ordered running of Graydon's city. Graydon represented the managerial elite Thorne despised. And Graydon had once been a miners' union representative too, before running for governor, which, to Thorne, made him a traitor.

Getting these two to see eye to eye on anything was likely to be a challenge.

Not as much of a challenge, however, as getting Thorne to see eye to eye with the final participant in this meeting, who was just now entering the room.

Yuri Konstantinov of Anoshkin Energiya.

"And our party is complete," said Graydon, shaking Konstantinov warmly by the hand. *These* two appeared on good terms.

"What a pleasant surprise," Thorne drawled. "My favourite company executive."

"My favourite union pain in the neck," Konstantinov replied. "What is this all about? Another strike looming?"

"Why, do you want me to call one?"

"With everything else that's going on, I should have thought pay and productivity issues would be furthest from your thoughts, Thorne."

"I rarely think about anything else, Konstantinov. As a caring, conscientious union leader, the welfare of the mining workforce means everything to me. If it meant as much to you, perhaps you and I wouldn't be butting heads all the time."

"I'm as accommodating as a man in my position can be. Anoshkin has always bent over backwards to meet your demands, outrageous as they usually are."

"Bent over backwards? That's funny. The number of times you've bent us over forwards and –"

"Okay, okay," Dev said, making a T with his hands. "Time out, gentlemen. While it's reasonably entertaining watching you two snark at each other, that's not what we're here for. We can measure penis sizes later."

Out of the corner of his eye, he saw Kahlo mask a smirk.

"This is about Calder's Edge," he went on, "and saving the city. Saving miners' livelihoods, Thorne. Saving your mines, Konstantinov. Saving lives, above all. You know what it's like out there."

He gestured towards the picture window.

"Tunnels blocked. Rail tracks down. Habitats

crushed. Frightened people – very frightened. A death toll in the triple figures, and it's amazing it's not higher. Calder's Edge is on the edge, and I'm not saying that for the cute wordplay. Well, maybe a little. The city is on the brink of all-out disaster. Panic in the streets. Mass evacuation tabled as an option. If we don't do something, pretty soon there isn't going to be a Calder's worth speaking of."

"But how?" said Konstantinov. "You can't stop earthquakes. They're a force of nature."

"Not these ones," Dev said. "These ones aren't natural."

And he explained.

"You don't expect me to buy that," Thorne said scornfully when Dev had finished. "Fucking moleys? Led by a Plusser *inside* one of them?"

"It's hard to swallow," Kahlo said, "but there are good grounds for believing it to be true. The evidence Harmer's unearthed is compelling."

"I took some persuading myself," said Graydon. "I'm still not wholly convinced, to be honest. Harmer, however, has the experience with Polis Plus. We should at least hear him out. I'd be curious to know how he thinks we can tackle this."

"The quakes have been too specific, too organised, to be random events," Dev said. "I mean, come on. The moment I arrived here, literally within minutes of me being installed in this host form, a huge chunk of rock fell on the ISS outpost. If that wasn't a targeted attack, I don't know what is. The Plusser agent, Ted Jones, had got wind that I was coming and took steps to eradicate me. Moleworms under his control dislodged a piece of the cavern roof by burrowing above it just enough to weaken it. I was incredibly lucky not to get flattened. Wish I could say the same for ISS Liaison Bilk."

"And then, realising he'd missed," said Kahlo, "Jones tried again by hacking the rail network control server and throwing a runaway freight shuttle at you – and me."

"Him or his ally," Dev said.

"There are *two* Plusser agents on Alighieri?" said Graydon.

"Afraid so. Jones is the main player, but he's definitely had help. And now that he knows I'm on to him, this whole thing has become about bringing Calder's Edge to its knees as soon as possible. Xanadu, too. Originally the plan was meant to be much more subtle. The slow build-up was supposed to continue until you, Maurice, and your counterpart in Xanadu were driven to declare a state of emergency and bring gulf cruisers in to clear everyone out."

"I still will if I have to," Graydon said. "I'm this close to making that call."

"Which is entirely your prerogative. My analysis of the situation is that Jones can't keep gradually turning the screws any more and making it look as though the quakes are just quakes. That ship has sailed. Now it's all or nothing. Do or die. And that could work to our advantage, despite how bleak everything looks."

"Bleak?" said Konstantinov. "You don't know the half of it. We've already begun shutting down operations. Other mining conglomerates are doing the same. We cannot reasonably allow the mines to stay open, not when it's so dangerous for all concerned. See, Thorne? Anoshkin *do* care."

"You haven't a choice," Thorne shot back. "No one's turning up for work anyway."

"My point is, we as a company apprehend the severity of the situation. What I myself don't see, personally, is how Mr Harmer can say it's in any way to our advantage, this Plusser going on a rampage. Surely, on the contrary, that only makes the danger more immediate and more acute. I'm with the governor in thinking that abandoning the planet might be the most sensible course of action."

"You would," Thorne snorted. "Cut and run – that's exactly what I would expect from you and your sort. Typical management. No backbone."

"You mistake prudence for cowardice, Thorne. You've never seemed to appreciate that Anoshkin put people before profit. Always have, always will. You win most of your battles with us, and that's because we understand that without workers – contented, well-rewarded workers – we would have nothing. If we're prepared to surrender Alighieri's vast helium-three deposits, all those still untapped seams, because our workforce is at intolerable risk, then we can't be the corporate monsters you think we are."

"But you don't have to give them up," Dev said.

"This is what I'm driving at. Ted Jones may be on the warpath, but in fact he's also on the back foot. He wouldn't be going all-out if this wasn't his last and only shot. We can use that. Use it against him."

"Why are you telling us all this, anyway?" Konstantinov asked. "What do you expect us to do?"

"Yeah," said Thorne, for once in agreement with the Anoshkin Energiya executive. "This isn't just a courtesy, is it? This isn't about keeping prominent Calder's public figures in the loop. You want something, don't you?"

"You read me like a book, Thorne," said Dev.

"Or I'm just cynical."

"Show me the union boss who isn't. Yes, I want something. I want you – the pair of you – to help me fight back."

Thorne and Konstantinov exchanged glances, both of them equally nonplussed.

"I want you," Dev continued, "to put together an army. Thorne, I want you to rally the miners. Not just your Fair Dues Collective but all of the unions. Use the full force of your charm and charisma on them."

"You what?" said Thorne. "An army?"

"And Konstantinov, I want you to sanction the use of Anoshkin equipment to arm this army. I want you also to recruit other mining companies – X-O-Geo, the one with the double-barrelled German name, all of them."

"Heinkel-Junger, you mean?"

"That's it. And the rest. Talk to your fellow execs. Use your connections, your clout. Get their consent for what I'm proposing. And I want you both to do it fast, as in yesterday. Because we really don't have a lot of time."

"Anoshkin equipment," said Konstantinov. "You're talking about...?"

"The digging and drilling exoskeleton rigs your workforce use. Normally a human being would be no match for a moleworm. But a human being in one of those rigs..."

"Let me get this straight," said Thorne. "Pit folk fighting moleworms... with mining gear on?"

"It might seem crazy, but think about it. The rigs afford plenty of protection. Whoever's inside is shielded by a steel roll cage and mesh grids so that they won't be injured if a stray shard of rock flies at them. The arm attachments are six-inch-diameter drills, pickaxes, rotary saws, diamond-tipped cutters – the kind of sharp-edged implements that could really ruin a moleworm's day. Those rigs are pretty much ideal under the circumstances. Without any alteration whatsoever, they can become mobile anti-moleworm attack suits."

"But they're not designed for that purpose, and miners have never used them for that purpose. You're asking us to retask the tools of our trade and turn them into moleworm-killing machines. That's like asking chefs to start throwing their carving knives at tigers."

"As I'm sure any chef would, if the tiger was

about to attack him, kill all his staff and ransack his kitchen. Or would you rather see Calder's Edge destroyed and pit folk obliged to seek employment elsewhere? Assuming they survive, that is."

"No," said Thorne. "Of course not. It's just..."

"I'm willing to give it a try," said Konstantinov. "I'm reasonably certain I can clear it with the board of directors. And if not," he added with a bold set of his jaw, "then I'm willing to face dismissal for going against their wishes. Mr Harmer makes a good case. We must fight back with whatever is at our disposal."

"Easy for you to say, Konstantinov," said Thorne. "You won't be the one risking life and limb battling the moleworms. It's us workers who will."

"'Us workers who will,'" Dev echoed. "Can I take that as meaning 'Great idea, Dev, let's do it'?"

"You can take it as meaning 'Let me put it to the vote and see what my members say.'"

"Mention my name. That's got to carry some weight with the FDC, after my sterling performance in the Ordeal."

"I might do that," said Thorne. "What's certain is if I get the FDC on-side, other unions will follow. We're that influential."

"Which is why I asked you to this meeting, Thorne. You specifically. Apart from the fact that you grudgingly think I'm all right, you are the big cheese among Alighierian union leaders. The leader of leaders. You're the one who can make this happen, and happen quickly."

"Flattering bastard."

"I know."

"For the record," said Graydon, "I'm not mad about your scheme, Harmer. Not at all. These aren't trained combat troops we're talking about. They're ordinary Calder's citizens. You're putting them up against a horde of large, powerful predatory mammals. Some of them could die. *Lots* of them."

"I'm well aware of that, Maurice. They're not soldiers, no. But what they are is better than that. They won't be fighting just for a day's wages or because someone with stripes on their sleeve has ordered them to. They'll be fighting to protect their homes, their jobs, their friends, their families, their city, their own lives. That's the best army you can have, the one with everything to lose, the one that has a direct personal stake in winning. You can bet they'll commit and do whatever it takes."

"But," said Kahlo, "we still have to get the moleworms to show themselves. So far they haven't. It's all been stealth attacks. Like you said earlier, Harmer, the entire planetary crust is their jungle. We can't go chasing after them and hunting them down. It'd be hopeless."

"No," said Dev. "You're right. So we have to change the game. Draw them out. And I think I know how to do that."

43

"You look exhausted, Kahlo," Dev said as Patrolman Utz drove them away from Graydon's office.

"No shit, Sherlock," Kahlo said. "It's been chaos. I haven't slept, haven't stopped. I'm running on fumes. Only adrenaline and energy bars are keeping me going. You don't look so hot yourself."

"Hot? With these burns, surely that's *all* I look like."

"This irrepressible sense of humour of yours – you know it starts to wear thin after a while?"

"I recognise all the words in that sentence. I just don't understand their meaning when they're put together in that order."

"Ugh," said Kahlo, while Utz quietly sniggered.

The pod whirred through a beaten, battered, bruised Calder's Edge. Debris from roof falls lay in unruly heaps. Column-based habitats had been shaken free from their moorings and gone tumbling to the cavern floor. Dev saw a raised rail track that was truncated abruptly in mid-air, several support pylons having collapsed along its course. A train had nosedived off the end and plunged a hundred metres onto a plaza below, where it now sat crumpled and curled like a dead snake.

Groups of people wandered through the devastated areas of the city, searching for missing loved ones. Their faces registered desolation, shock, and a kind of frantic hope.

Other groups were assembled in huddled knots, hugging, consoling one another.

Inevitably there were looters and rioters too, running rampant through the streets. Fear had sparked their basest impulses – to rob, to vandalise, to hurt others. Police were out in force to stop them, and Dev glimpsed skirmishes between law and disorder. Law, luckily, seemed to be winning.

Here and there, fires burned. Smoke billowed up to the cavern roof, gathering in a grim black pall. A priority for the emergency services was bringing the blazes under control before the cavern filled up with choking, toxic fumes.

"Hungry," said Kahlo.

"Huh? You asking if I am, or telling me you are?"

"Both."

"I am completely starving. But I doubt there's anywhere to eat that's open."

"My place."

"You cook?"

"No. I can do eggs, that's about it. Interested?"

"I'm never one to turn down a free meal."

"Utz, drop us off at West Nine Station. Then go

home yourself. Grab an hour or two's R and R. I'll call when I need you again."

"Yes, ma'am."

In her habitat, Kahlo made scrambled eggs, adding a dash of chilli oil to give the dish savour. Dev wolfed down his helping as though he hadn't eaten in days, washing it down with strong black coffee.

"Maybe it's just the hunger talking," he said when he had almost finished, "but this is the best-tasting eggs I've ever had. No, tell a lie. I knew a sergeant major who could rustle up a mean omelette. His trick was he never washed the frying pan. It got this kind of patina which he said enhanced the flavour. Mind you, during the war all food was good."

"How's that?"

"Any meal you ate meant you were still alive, so you valued it all the more."

"You know, you still haven't told me how you could have died at Leather Hill and yet here you are, eating eggs in my house."

"That? Well... I probably shouldn't. It's covered by a non-disclosure agreement, and I could be prosecuted for leaking trade secrets."

"Seriously?"

"Yeah, but what the fuck. You're no blabbermouth. If you can't trust a police chief..."

He set down his fork.

"It was late in the war, and a certain private security contractor was looking towards the future, to a time when either Polis Plus had been comprehensively trounced or a truce had been declared."

"This was ISS?"

"They called themselves the Winter Consortium back then. Before the war, they'd provided armed escorts for celebrities and on-board security personnel for infraspace flights. Nothing major-league, but the company's founder, Ulysses Winter, had ambition. Vision, some would say. He foresaw that TerCon might need a network of trained operatives to help keep the post-war peace – men and women who could be inserted quickly into potential trouble spots to help defuse powder kegs before they exploded."

"And annoy the fuck out of local law enforcement while they're about it."

"That too," said Dev. "Winter was well connected. He had extensive contacts within TerCon. He was able to secure substantial government investment, and he sank the money into research. He hired the best brainiacs he could and put them to work reverse-engineering Polis Plus technology scavenged from the battlefield. They figured out ways of growing entire clone bodies from small quantities of DNA and transferring complete consciousnesses in digitised form, just like the Plussers could."

"Is that even legal, repurposing Plusser tech?"

"How should I know? You're the cop. They did it anyway."

"Okay, so how did *you* get involved?"

"I'm coming to that. Thing is, Winter was sneaky. He started recruiting for his prototype Interstellar Security Solutions before the war even ended, and he did that by pinpointing suitable candidates in advance and arranging to have their consciousnesses uploaded at the point of death. I can only assume the military top brass connived in this. Maybe bribes changed hands, who knows? At any rate, without my knowledge or say-so, I was singled out as one of those candidates."

"You'd been decorated several times," Kahlo said. "You had a good record. Guess that would have flagged you up to Winter."

"Probably. Or it could just be that I was in the right place at the right time, in the right condition – near death but also close enough to a transcription matrix to be uploaded before I finally croaked. I figure Winter had 'talent scouts' loitering behind lines during the big campaigns, under orders to latch on to the fatally injured bodies of named individuals as and when they were medevac'ed back from the front. Whoever was at Leather Hill would have had his pick of goners to choose from. One of them just happened to be me."

"So they... recorded your personality onto a hard drive?"

"Then zapped me off through ultraspace to ISS's mainframe core on Earth. I don't remember any of this clearly. Just impressions, fragments. Like something I might have dreamed."

"And your body?"

"What's left of it is buried on Barnesworld. Somewhere nice and green, I'm sure, hopefully with a view of rolling hills."

"Shit," said Kahlo with a shudder. "Not wishing to be unsympathetic, but that's pretty creepy, isn't it? Knowing your mortal remains are lying in the ground."

"Tell me about it. Winter's talent scout, his rep, whatever you like to call the guy, he also took cell samples off my mangled corpse. And that is why I'm now working for ISS."

"How so? Wait, I get it. They've built you a new body. A new you. From scratch."

"No, not yet. They've promised to. Host forms, however, are hideously expensive. I mean megabucks. The process takes time, energy, resources. It's not like growing slabs of beef in a vat. If I want to be put into a brand spanking new me, I'll have to earn it, and I earn it by carrying out missions for ISS. I store up credit with every successful outcome, according to a points system so arcane I'm not sure *anyone* understands it, least of all me. Once I hit the required total – one thousand points – I'll have worked off my indenture. ISS will make a Dev Harmer host form and plonk me inside, and I get to carry on living as before."

"That's... Well, I'd heard stories, rumours. But..."

"The official ISS line is that all us operatives are volunteers. We're a happy band of adventurers, ex-military personnel who've chosen to continue fighting the Frontier War in its secondary phase, guarding the Diaspora's borders against Plusser incursion while our bodies lie in induced comas back on Earth. There's some truth in that, but it's also a whole lot more complicated. At least, it is as far as I'm concerned. I can't speak for other ISS consultants. Maybe some of them *are* volunteers, for all I know, and that induced-coma thing is real."

"You, though... You're a slave."

"Am I? That's one way of looking at it, I suppose. But what would you do in my shoes? When the alternatives are this or death, wouldn't you take this? Wouldn't anyone?"

Kahlo eyed him with wonder, and something Dev hadn't seen before from her, at least not directed towards him: compassion.

"ISS have you over a barrel," she said. "They know you'll do whatever they ask, because otherwise you'll die. They're relying on that to keep you obedient, a good little drone. The only thing that keeps it from being slavery is the fact that you can earn your way out of it."

Dev shrugged. "TerCon seems to think it's legal."

"Legal maybe – just about – but ethical?"

"Big business and ethics. Since when have those two even been on nodding terms? I've got a second chance at life, Kahlo. It's not straightforward, and I'm having to fight for it, every inch of the way, but I've got it nonetheless, and no way am I going to let it go."

Kahlo shoved her chair back from the table. "I don't know whether I think you're an idiot or a hero."

"I'm pretty confused about it myself."

"I hope it works out for you. I hope you get your thousand points and make it out the other side."

"That's the nicest thing anyone's ever said to me. Correction: it's the nicest thing *you've* ever said to me."

"Don't let it go to your head."

"*And* you came topside looking for me."

"Not just you. You and the whole of your team, including my men."

"Still, if I didn't know better, Captain Kahlo, I'd say you'd developed a soft spot for me."

"Believe what you like. I'm going for a shower now. I stink, and I could do with a change of clothes, too."

Kahlo crossed to the bathroom.

At the door, without looking back, she said, "Feel free to join me if you want to."

Dev ran an eye over her muscular, curvy profile, and yes, he very much wanted to join her in the shower.

And so he did.

44

THEY GOT CLEAN, and then got dirty.

And then after that, they had another shower and got clean again, only to get dirty again in Kahlo's bedroom.

Scrubbing, then rubbing. It was urgent and violent the first time, languid and lingering the second.

In the shower they both were standing up. In bed, Kahlo went on top, perhaps inevitably. It was a different kind of straddling from three days earlier when she and Dev were fighting in the sculpture pedestal. They were naked, for one thing. But there was a similar imperious look of triumph on Kahlo's face, not least when she orgasmed. The grip of her thighs on Dev's pelvis was spectacular and succulent, bringing him a few moments later to a climax so powerful his entire self seemed to shoot out of him.

Afterwards, they lay together, with the top sheet twisted around them like a giftwrap ribbon. For a time they dozed, Dev relishing the weight of Kahlo's breasts on his chest and the moth-wing stir of her breath on his neck. It wasn't love, it was two people finding solace and release in each other's bodies while the world threatened to fall apart around them. But that was almost as good as love. The next best thing.

"I guess you've figured out by now that Graydon's my father," Kahlo said.

"Thorne called you two the king and princess of Calder's Edge. That was kind of a clue."

"Since we're sharing confessions – and bodily fluids – I thought I should just mention it."

"Does banging the governor's daughter mean I'm in trouble? Is your dad going to come after me with a posse and a noose?"

"No, actually it makes you an elected official. Didn't you know? That's how we do things 'round these here parts."

"You Alighierians and your quaint backwater customs. In return, I have to tell you that you have the honour of being my first."

"Yeah, I took your host form's virginity, didn't I?" She ran fingernails down his belly. "I corrupted you."

"The bad news is, at three days old I'm technically a minor."

"Let's not go there."

"You're a cradle snatcher. I'm your toy boy."

She dug her nails in hard. "I mean it, buster. Not even remotely amusing."

"So what did Maurice Graydon do that pissed you off so much? To the extent that you even changed your name?"

Kahlo seemed as though she was going to clam up. Her lips went rigid as bone.

Then, relenting, she said, "Okay. Here's how it was. Graydon wasn't around much when I was little. But don't go thinking I'm just some girl with daddy issues and I resent not having had his full attention while growing up. That's bullshit. When he was home, he was good to me and my mother. We were, I guess, a happy family. He just worked hard, both as a miner and a union representative. He loved his job. Loved mining. Loved standing up for other miners and their wellbeing."

"He's the dedicated public service type, isn't he? And the apple hasn't fallen far from the tree."

"It all went sour when my mother was killed. She was a miner too. She drove a driller rig; she was good at it, by all accounts. There was an accident, a malfunction. Not sure if it was a hardware or software glitch, but one of the critically damped servos failed."

"There was an overshoot?"

"That's it. The assistive mechanism on the drill arm didn't respond correctly to a motion she made. The arm reached out much faster and further than she intended it to go, and it tore her own arm off at the socket."

Dev made an appalled face. "I'm sorry. That's terrible."

"I thought you were going to make some crass, inappropriate comment there."

"I'm not *that* insensitive. Presumably help didn't get to her in time."

"She was in one of the remoter tunnels, digging out a new seam. A couple of co-workers tried to save her, but she bled out. It was a brand of rig, TechnoCorp, that was notorious for faults. Uncontrolled oscillation. Failure to detect unsafe or invalid user motions. Joint fouling."

"I remember. The company went bust eventually. Lawsuits galore."

"Too late for my ma. This happened at the start of the Frontier War, when manufacturers like TechnoCorp were diversifying into munitions and tanks. They were overstretched, and their quality control plummeted. Some of their product didn't meet basic safety requirements. They blamed my mother for her death, of course."

"Driver error."

"Exactly. They denied their rigs had problems, even though everyone knew they did. My dad waged a publicity campaign against them. He would have taken them to court, but..."

"There was a war on."

Kahlo nodded. "People had other things on their minds. He tried to shame TechnoCorp into admitting liability, but nothing he did made a blind bit of difference. That was when the light went out of his eyes. When he stopped being my father and became just this... this robot lookalike. He shaved his head – contrition, self-mortification, whatever. He retired from mining, moved into politics. He stopped caring about anything except what he thought was important, which was Calder's Edge and being governor. He put all his energies into that, because it was something he could control, and something he could lose himself in."

"In a way, you can't blame him."

"Oh, I can," said Kahlo with a bitter laugh. "He had a daughter, remember? But he could barely look at me any more. Said I reminded him too much of her – 'my Soraya.' I'd lost someone too! But he couldn't have given a shit. It was all about himself, his status, his career, being Maurice Graydon, the people's friend and defender. I suppose, as long as he was governor and kept being re-elected, he didn't have to think about anything else, any*one* else. Guess what he said when I told him I was changing my surname to my mother's maiden name."

"What?"

"He said, 'If it makes you happy, Astrid.' In that smarmy way of his. Same when I told him I was joining the police force. 'If it makes you happy.' Like my happiness mattered only to me. He'd cut himself adrift from the rest of the world. People weren't of interest to him unless he was trying to win their votes, in which case he could pour on the charm."

"I've seen him at it," Dev said. "He's good. Super slick."

"Even his penchant for expensive whisky. That's not a genuine foible. It's a schtick. It's calculated. Makes him look like 'one of us' – he enjoys a tipple, spends more money on it than he should, wow, that's kind of cool, relatable but sophisticated at the same time, what a swell guy."

"I was thinking just that when I first met him – swell guy, for a politician. The Yamazaki's a nice touch. Even Thorne, I reckon, who loathes his guts, admires that about him, his fancy booze habit."

"Don't be hard on yourself," Kahlo said. "Graydon does a number on people. He's been doing it for twenty years. He's great at being your best friend, and he doesn't even know what friendship is any more. Emotions are alien to him. He fakes them superbly but he doesn't have them."

"A sociopath."

"But he wasn't always, that's the thing. It was my mother's death that did it to him. It burned him out from the core, left him a hollow shell. I distinctly recall him being fun once, when I was little. Before. He'd play with me. Dance round the kitchen with me. Read me stories. Hug me."

"I can see why you put distance between you. You had to. It was too painful otherwise."

Kahlo's eyes glistened. "It wasn't petty vengeance. It wasn't holding a grudge or adolescent acting-out. It was self-protection. I couldn't be Maurice Graydon's daughter any longer because I *wasn't* Maurice Graydon's daughter, not in any appreciable way. From my teens onwards, I was more or less an orphan. My father *appeared* to be still alive, but he wasn't, not really."

Dev drew her closer to him, and for a while they lay in silence. He felt the hot trickle of tears on his neck, but said nothing. Kahlo would not want him drawing attention to it. Crying was a weakness, and weakness was anathema to her.

She was more like her father than she realised, or might care to admit.

"So that's us," she said finally. "Estranged. Leading very public lives, but nothing much else going on between us. Graydon hasn't had a girlfriend since he became a widower. Not even a casual fuck now and then. Nothing. And I haven't exactly been active on that front myself."

"Just the occasional under-age offworlder."

"Hey!"

"Sorry."

"Most of the men I meet, I'm either giving them orders or arresting and interrogating them. Neither of which is really conducive to starting an affair. The crooks, particularly, are none of them what you'd call prime material. Thieves, drunks, troublemakers, wife-beaters, liars..."

"Must give you a pretty jaundiced view of the male of the species."

"I don't know. Yes, maybe. What I tell myself is that life's less complicated when you've only yourself to think about. That way – Ah." She sat up. "Got a call coming in. Konstantinov."

Dev took the opportunity to slip out of bed while Kahlo conducted the call. He was bursting for a piss – the coffee – and the bathroom beckoned.

As he urinated, he mulled over what Kahlo had told him about her father. A thought struck him.

An unappetising thought.

He tried to dismiss it, but it wouldn't go. It was stuck in his head like a splinter, and the more he worried at it, the deeper it sank in and the more naggingly unignorable it became.

Someone in Calder's Edge was a Polis+ agent, Ted Jones's partner in crime. Someone had sent that freight shuttle after the police pod and carried out the malware attack on *Milady Frog*.

Someone, too, had alerted Ted Jones to Dev's arrival at the ISS outpost, leading Jones to try to kill him by dropping a ton of rock on the building.

Kahlo had laid out the facts the first time they'd visited Graydon. How many people, she had asked, had known Dev was coming? A few of the Calder's Edge higher-ups, that was all.

The assumption was that the Plussers had hacked communiqués between Alighieri and ISS central office, or perhaps one of Graydon's own internal memos. Which was by no means impossible.

But what if Jones's co-conspirator was actually a prominent Alighierian? Not a Plusser infiltrator at all, but a human collaborator? A traitor?

Nobody in their right mind would side with Polis+. How would it benefit you? What would you gain?

You could be brainwashed into it, however, as Professor Banerjee had been. Hypnagogic exposure had turned the zoologist into a loyal little quisling, utterly obedient to Jones's bidding, even though, deep down, he knew he was being used and hated it.

Had Jones hypnexed someone else? Someone in Calder's? Someone in a position of great responsibility, with access to secure servers and privileged information?

Someone like Governor Maurice Graydon?

No. It was Graydon who had put in a request for ISS intervention in the first place. Why would a Plusser thrall send for an operative from an organisation dedicated to countering covert Plusser activity?

Because Graydon had had to. As governor, he couldn't have done otherwise. It would have seemed strange if he had failed to bring ISS in. It would have been a suspicious dereliction of duty.

And of course, the ISS agent – Dev – was supposed to have been killed as soon as he arrived, meaning Graydon would be seen to have done the right thing, discharged his gubernatorial obligation, only to have been thwarted by an unfortunate turn of events. Talk about having your cake and eating it.

Nobody was close to Graydon, not even his daughter. If he had had his will subverted by Jones, who would notice? Who knew him intimately enough to perceive anything different about him, any significant alteration in his personality or behaviour? No one. To all and sundry, he would still be the perfect, smiling, gracious governor of Calder's Edge.

Politicians. They were what they seemed to be, the image they projected, and nothing more. Ted Jones, if Graydon was his stooge, had picked well.

With trepidation and a queasy feeling in the pit of his stomach, Dev returned to the bedroom.

Kahlo was getting dressed. "Anoshkin Energiya have given Konstantinov the go-ahead. Their rigs are at our disposal. The other mining conglomerates are in, too. We're just waiting for absolute final word from a couple of directors, and we're good to go."

"Anything from Thorne yet?"

"No, but Konstantinov has been in touch with him and says he's received what he calls 'encouraging noises.'"

"Great. That's great."

Kahlo paused while clipping her bra in place. "It looks like you're getting your weapons and your army. Why the long face?"

"Kahlo. Astrid. We need to talk..."

45

FROM THE RAISED esplanade in front of the CEPD headquarters, Dev looked out over Calder's Edge.

This was where it had started. This was where it was going to end.

Hours of frantic preparation and organisation had passed. There had been times when it seemed there was too much to do and no hope of accomplishing it before Ted Jones returned from Xanadu to finish what he had begun.

The denizens of Calder's Edge, however, had been remarkably cooperative. Once it had become clear to them that there was a plan of action – that something *practical* could be done to save their city – they pulled together. They shook off their frenzies of grief and despair and anger. The sporadic rioting died down; the looters stopped looting. Word spread. There was going to be a fightback, a resistance, and everyone had a part to play.

The youngest and oldest residents were moved to the industrial zones and shopping malls, along with the sick and the frail, and sequestered there inside sturdy buildings. Groups of able-bodied citizens were appointed as their guardians to ensure that they were kept fed, watered and comfortable. Police set up armed cordons, an extra line of defence against what was coming. Everyone else retired to their homes and battened down the hatches.

At the same time, miners retrieved rigs from tunnels, loading them onto trains to be transported to the city. They came marching out of the rail stations one after another in lines: drillers, cutters, blasters, pounders, carriers. Eight-foot-tall mechanised exoskeletons, each housing a driver who manipulated the rig with practised precision, as though it were an extension of his or her own body. They strode along the streets with strange metallic delicacy, the clang of their steel footfalls resounding to the roof like peals of bells.

There were a couple of thousand of them all told, and they mustered at prearranged rendezvous sites – junctions, crossroads, bottlenecks, pinch points. Dev and Kahlo had pored over a map of Calder's, identifying the ideal spots to deploy their forces, the places where the moleworms could only attack one at a time and where they might be trapped and surrounded.

Thorne had helped with the marshalling of the rig drivers. He had assigned a Fair Dues Collective member to take charge of each of the disparate 'pit folk platoons,' and stayed connected with them via an open comms link. He circulated the instructions Dev and Kahlo provided, acting as a kind of halfway house between commanders and commanded. The miners took orders better from him than from a police chief and an ISS operative.

Dev, from his vantage point, could see several of the groups of rigs, stationed at their positions. Mechanics attended to them, conducting last-minute diagnostic checks on the servos and microprocessors and making sure that batteries were charged and tools were functioning at full efficiency.

The city was quiet, eerily so. Very little moved. It seemed as though the entire vast cavern was holding its breath, waiting.

Harmer?

Trundle.

The xeno-entomologist was presently in the rail network control room. When Dev had conferred with him in person a short while earlier, Trundell was still visibly suffering from the after-effects of his near-immolation on the surface. His singed skin was lathered in ointment and clumps of his hair had shrivelled down to stubble. He looked unwell and ought to have been recuperating in bed, but had stalwartly come running in response to Dev's request for help. "Just tell me what I can do," he had said. "Anything at all."

I've pulled up all the relevant sound files I've made, Trundell said now, and patched them into the rail network's automated announcement system. The guys here say everything's ready. Punch of a button and we're good to go.

Great stuff. Hang fire. Not until I give the word.

Dev looked around at Kahlo and Thorne, who were with him on the esplanade.

"Trundell's all set. Our troops are in place. Now's the time for someone to tell me this is a batshit crazy idea."

"It *is* a batshit crazy idea," said Thorne, "but it's also the only one we've got."

"And your people, they're clear about what they're facing, what's expected of them?"

"They are. These are tough men and women; they don't scare easily. Already I've heard a few of them saying they're relishing the prospect of battling moleys. You've got folks down there who have lost friends and relatives in this last round of earthquakes. They're looking forward to a bit of payback."

"As long as the moleworms come out where we can get them," Kahlo said. "That's the big *if*, isn't it?"

Dev glanced towards the immense rock arch which was home to Governor Graydon's office. That was the direction Kahlo was gazing in too.

He knew what she was thinking. There was another big *if* that was preoccupying her.

"I should arrest him," she said softly, coldly, like snow. "Go right over there and bust him. Just to be on the safe side."

"Without conclusive proof, what would be the use? He's going to show his cards, if he has any to show, when we start wiping out Jones's moleworm army. Until then, patience. At least we didn't tell him everything. Such as how, for instance, we're hoping to winkle the moleworms out of hiding. So he can't forewarn Jones about that."

"What's this?" said Thorne. "Who are you talking about?"

"No one," Dev said. "Doesn't matter. Let's get on with this, eh? No point putting it off any longer. Thorne, tell your people to brace themselves. I'm giving Trundle the green light. Once it all starts happening, it's probably going to happen fast."

Thorne nodded and passed on the warning.

Trundle?

Yes, Harmer?

Do it.

Half a minute went by. A minute.

Nothing.

Dev was about to ask Trundell whether something had gone wrong.

Then he heard it, emanating from the speakers at every single one of Calder's Edge's rail stations.

A hissing.

The rattly, scratchy hiss of scroaches.

Hungry scroaches.

Panicked scroaches.

Randy scroaches.

Angry scroaches.

Scroaches of every age and gender, in every kind of mood.

Loud.

The sound rolled out across the cavern in waves, filling the streets and the wide open spaces.

Trundell had made countless recordings of scroach hissing during the course of his studies. He had been endeavouring to understand their language, to 'decode the syntax' as he had told Dev down in the geode maze.

Now every sound file he had compiled was playing on a loop, simultaneously, and it was as though there were hundreds, thousands, tens of thousands of scroaches in the cavern. More scroaches than you would ever normally find together in one location.

Banerjee had boasted how he and Jones had trapped that moleworm near Lidenbrock, luring it with the hisses from a captive scroach.

Dev was doing the same here, but on a considerably larger scale.

He was ringing the dinner bell for Jones's horde of moleworms.

"Grub's up, you bastards," he murmured. "You know you want it. You can't resist. This has got to sound like an all-you-can-eat buffet to you. Come and get it."

46

FOR FIVE MINUTES, the scroach hissing resounded through the cavern.

Ten minutes.

Dev's doubts deepened. What if he had miscalculated? What if the moleworms could tell the difference between recorded scroach hissing and the real thing? What if Ted Jones knew it was a trap and was holding his moleworm army back?

Dev was counting on the moleworms' instincts overcoming whatever sway Jones had over them. He wanted them to listen to their stomachs rather than their puppet master. His plan hinged on it.

But the variables were many, and any one of them might mean failure.

"Come on, come on..." he muttered under his breath.

Thorne was getting restless. "My people are asking when something's going to happen. Any idea?"

"Soon," Dev said with more confidence than he felt. "Give it time."

Still the stuttering cacophony of hisses reverberated.

It set Dev's teeth on edge. It was a chillingly inhuman sound, made worse by being amplified to a hundred decibels, rock-concert loud.

Would the moleworms be able to resist its siren call? Perhaps they were all still over at Xanadu, too far away to hear.

"Feel that?"

Kahlo. She was looking down at her feet, a crinkle of apprehension on her brow.

"Feels like another tremor."

Dev became aware of a tingling in his soles, the ground vibrating.

"The moleworms," he said. "They're here."

The three of them on the esplanade – Dev, Kahlo, Thorne – peered out the more keenly over the city.

The vibration became a distinct thrumming. Moleworms, burrowing their way towards Calder's Edge. Moleworms in their thousands. A stampede of them.

"Tell your people to power up their rigs," Dev said to Thorne, "and brace themselves." As Thorne relayed the instruction, the pit folk platoons hit the ignition button, engaged gear and turned on their tools. Saw blades spun. Drills revved. Jackhammers thumped the air. A new noise arose to add to the deafening scroach chatter and the rumble of the approaching moleworms: the industrial thunder of mining machinery.

"There!"

Kahlo saw it first. Something was breaking through the floor of a plaza not far from East Two station.

Claws cracked marble-composite paving stones like eggshell. A hideous head poked up, nasotentacles fibrillating wildly.

The moleworm hauled itself out of the hole it had created. It was medium-sized, *orientalis,* judging by its dark pink hide. It cast about this way and that, sniffing for the scroaches which it was sure must be nearby. Its vestigial, blister-like eyes seemed to gleam with excitement.

It turned towards the station. The scroach sounds were coming from the platform loudspeaker. Although it could move through solid rock as smoothly as a shark through water, it was ungainly when above ground. Its close-set legs didn't work in a well-coordinated manner and its long tail was a hindrance, so much useless dead weight dragging behind it.

The moleworm rounded a corner, only to come face to face with two miners in their rigs.

It opened its puckered, fang-fringed maw and let out an awful, keening screech that spoke of fury and appetite. Strings of milky drool leaked out. Its snout feelers performed an elaborate display, as though the moleworm was signalling for the miners to get out of the way.

The miners clanked boldly forward. One was a driller, the other a pounder. Each raised an arm, showing the monstrous beast the formidable tool attachments they were toting.

The moleworm, appearing to lose patience, lunged at them.

The driller reacted quickly, plunging his whirring drill bit straight into the moleworm's face. There was an eruption of meat, bone and glutinous blood as the drill augered in, and the animal's entire body shook in a paroxysm of shock and pain.

The driller bore down, all but pinning the moleworm's head to the ground. Meanwhile the pounder let loose with a succession of vicious blows from her pneumatic jackhammer. A device that was designed to break down and crush solid granite made mincemeat of the moleworm's pulpy flesh and shattered its skeleton. Four, five hits, and the creature was fatally crippled. Its tail thrashed and coiled even as it shuddered in its death throes.

Thorne let out a low cheer.

"One down," he said.

"One of many," Dev pointed out. "Look."

Another moleworm was squirming its way up through the same hole as the first. Elsewhere in the city, the ground was churning. Cracks appeared in street surfaces and in the cavern's granite walls. A shopfront exploded outward as a moleworm came crashing through, followed by two more of its kind.

Suddenly, they were everywhere. Everywhere you looked, moleworms springing up from below. Eastern and western, male and female, burrowing out into the city in their droves. Each would pause as it emerged, near-blind eyes momentarily fazed by the artificial daylight. Then, orientating itself, it would make for the nearest rail station, with that slither-crawling gait that was rolling and awkward but implacably determined.

The miners, at their carefully chosen positions, ambushed every moleworm that came their way.

Drillers skewered with their drills, pounders bashed with their jackhammers, cutters sliced with their saws, blasters punctured with their compressed-air lances, carriers used their forklift prongs to pierce and disembowel.

Moleworms squealed and died.

It was by no means a one-sided battle: the moleworms fought back, rending with their powerful claws and tearing with their savage needle teeth.

Dev saw one miner wrenched wholesale out of his rig and gnawed to shreds. Another tried to escape via a rear-mounted hatch while a moleworm clawed through the protective steel mesh at the front. He scrambled free, only for a second moleworm to latch onto him with its nasotentacles as he ran for cover. It popped his head off his neck with a sideways swipe of its talons and bit several large chunks out of his decapitated body. Retribution arrived in the form of a fellow miner in a cutter rig, who removed the moleworm's head with a single slash.

As the conflict raged throughout the city, Dev kept a constant watch for any moleworm that seemed to be superior to or distinct from the rest. Somewhere amid the mêlée would be Ted Jones, urgently attempting to bring order to his scroach-crazed moleworm army, to regain mastery over them. He scanned the scene vigilantly.

Kahlo had allocated police resources to the same task. The city's CCTV surveillance system covered most of the principal public sites. Officers were monitoring the feeds, looking for any moleworm that was behaving in a markedly different manner from the others.

Several times Dev spied a moleworm asserting its authority over another, perhaps by nipping its tail or barging it aside. It happened so often, however, that he could only conclude it was part of the normal pecking order. The bigger, stronger moleworms bullied the smaller, weaker ones in order to overtake them and get to the food source first.

"Looks like we're holding them," Thorne announced with a hint of triumph in his voice. "That's what my FDC members are saying. We're taking casualties, but the moleys are getting it worse."

No sooner had he spoken, however, than the moleworms appeared to take stock and adopt a new tactic. They stopped blundering blindly into the ambushes. Instead, they approached with greater caution and sometimes sidestepped the miners altogether, finding alternative routes around.

Dev wondered whether this was due to the moleworm corpses piling up around the miners' positions. The sight and smell of so many dead of their own kind surely served as a deterrent to the moleworms. They were smart enough to sense there was danger to them in certain areas of the city.

But then the creatures became sneaky. They began burrowing back down underground and coming up directly beneath the miners. Dev saw rigs and their drivers getting pulled down below the surface, mechanical limbs flailing as they vanished from view.

"It's Jones," he said. "This isn't spontaneous. Can't be; it's too organised for that. The bastard is rallying his troops. The moleworms were being slaughtered. Now he's turning the tables and they're the ones doing the slaughtering. But where is he? Where the fuck is he?"

"He's got to be having help," Kahlo said. "It's happening simultaneously, all over Calder's Edge, and it's precision-aimed. So either he's somewhere where he can see everything at once..."

"Or he has a spotter guiding him."

"Friends in high places." Kahlo fixed her gaze, once again, on the rock arch. "Bet you anything Graydon's out on his balcony, giving Jones a heads-up. He's telling him where all the pit folk platoons are. Picking them out for him."

It made sense to Dev. Graydon had an eagle's eye view of the entire city from his office. If he was Jones's hypnexed slave, he was perfectly placed to carry out real-time reconnaissance.

"Then it's Graydon we have to stop first," he said. "Right now he's more of a threat than Jones himself. And unlike Jones, at least we know where he is."

"I'm with you," said Kahlo. "Thorne? Get your people to scatter. Thin out. Make themselves a less concentrated target."

"Will do," said the union leader. "What's all this about the governor? How's he involved?"

"Later," Kahlo said. To Dev she said, "There's

a pod waiting. You can come along, but on one condition. Graydon's mine, do you understand? I deal with him, no one else."

Dev nodded, and he and Kahlo hurried towards the esplanade's rail platform.

"You know I want to be wrong about your dad," Dev said.

"So do I," said Kahlo. "He has the benefit of the doubt until proven otherwise. But even if he is acting against his will, that doesn't change what he's been doing. If he does turn out to be a traitor, I will nail the lousy son of a bitch to the wall."

47

MAURICE GRAYDON WAS out on his office balcony, spectating through binoculars. Spread below him was a teeming vista of violence: the desperate struggle between miners and moleworms on the streets of Calder's Edge – and at present, the moleworms were winning.

He didn't turn round as Dev and Kahlo stepped out through the open picture window. He registered awareness of their presence by lowering the binoculars and straightening his spine.

"Enjoying the view?" Kahlo said.

"Watching my city being decimated?" Graydon replied. "Citizens dying defending it? Hardly a pretty sight."

"Then why be a part of it?"

Graydon tilted his bald head. "Astrid, whatever do you mean?"

"Look, Graydon, you might as well come clean. We've figured it out. The one saving grace is that you're not responsible. You're not yourself."

"I've never felt more like myself."

"The Plusser, he's using you. He's done something to your mind. This is not your fault. But you've got to stop helping him. You've got to fight his influence. Look out there. Look what's happening. Calder's Edgers are getting killed – massacred. You can't be involved in this. It goes against everything you stand for."

"*Can't* be involved in this," said Graydon. "Are you giving me an order, or asking for reassurance?"

"I'm trying to reason with you, that's all."

Kahlo moved a couple of paces closer to her father. Dev stayed put, letting Kahlo take the lead. It was up to her to manage the situation however she saw fit. He would back up her play.

"Dad," she said.

Graydon levelled his gaze at her. "Oh, so now you call me Dad. Now you acknowledge who I am. Now that you need something from me."

"I don't need anything from you except to stop being Ted Jones's accomplice. You're a strong-willed man, with a forceful personality. Whatever Jones has done to you, whatever he's made you believe about yourself and about him, you can resist it. You can overcome it. I know you can."

"How touching. You finally show some faith in me. Better late than never, I suppose. But what if I refuse to, as you suggest, resist?"

"Then," Kahlo said, producing a pair of smartcuffs, "I'll have no choice but to arrest you in accordance with federal Diasporan law. Section five of the TerCon Postwar Pact – the crime of aiding and abetting, willingly or otherwise, forces hostile to the interests of the Diaspora."

"You're calling me a collaborator? A traitor?" Graydon seemed distantly amused.

"Tell me you're not." There was a plaintive note in Kahlo's voice. "Tell me I'm wrong. It wasn't you who set that freight shuttle on us. You didn't bring down Beauregard's arcjet. You haven't been giving Jones directions for his moleworms from up here. Tell me none of that's true."

"Are you wrong?" The governor pondered. "In one sense, no. In another, yes."

Kahlo's shoulders slumped. All at once, she saw everything clearly.

As did Dev.

"You weren't hypnexed," Dev said to Graydon. "You're not Jones's patsy. You're actually doing this of your own free will."

"Free will?" said the governor. "I feel more as though it's out of necessity. No one is forcing me, and I haven't even had to force myself. Do you know how much I hate this place?"

He swept an arm, indicating the beleaguered subterranean city and the cavern containing it.

"It took everything from me. Everything. My wife. The love and respect of my daughter, my only child. It took my belief in the rightness of things. It stripped me of all I ever valued and left me with nothing. Shall we go indoors?"

Graydon didn't wait for an answer, but led the

way into his office, closing the picture window behind them.

"There," he said, a small frown easing from his forehead. "Now we can hear ourselves think. I don't need to be out there any more. Ted seems to have everything firmly under control. The downfall of Calder's Edge is assured."

"That's what you think," said Dev. He held up three fingers. "You have three minutes. Three minutes to explain yourself. Then you're going to tell me how I can identify Jones in his moleworm host form. You're going to point him out for me if he's down there in the city, and if he's not, you're going to tell me exactly where he's squirreled himself away, and then I can go after him and kill the living shit out of him."

"I'm sure you have ways of making me talk, Dev," said Graydon.

"You bet I do."

"And if he doesn't succeed," said Kahlo, "I'm more than willing to try."

"My own flesh and blood." Graydon sighed, mockingly. "It's so sad when children rebel against their parents."

"I don't have anything to rebel against. I don't have parents. Haven't since I was small. So come on, out with it. You say you were left with nothing. You've been governor of Calder's Edge for twenty years. That's hardly 'nothing.'"

"A title, a job," said Graydon. "Something to occupy my time. The people love me. They've voted me into office again and again. If it makes them happy, why not? But I stopped caring about the governorship a long time ago, about politics, about anything much. Life is transitory. Its pleasures are fleeting. One moment you're there" – he snapped his fingers – "the next, you're gone."

"Ma's death."

"Indeed, Astrid. Soraya's death. It shouldn't have happened. A woman – a beautiful, clever, skilled woman in her prime – taken away, all because some rig designer at TechnoCorp couldn't be bothered to debug the operating software, or because some CEO decided to cut corners on materials or manufacture, or because some worker on the assembly line didn't insert a rivet properly, or I don't know. It doesn't matter. A stupid, random event. Human error or neglect, one or the other. The inherent imperfection of our species, and Soraya was its victim."

"And for that," said Dev, "you've decided to betray our entire race?"

"Not betray." Graydon headed over to the sideboard and poured himself a generous measure of his expensive Japanese whisky. It seemed a natural gesture on this occasion, rather than a calculated, cynical pose. The man needed a drink. "Revenge is, I suppose, the name for it. I am avenging myself for Soraya's death."

"On thousands, maybe millions of innocent people?" said Kahlo.

"No one is innocent," Graydon stated firmly. "Everyone is guilty of being imperfect. It's the human disease."

"The human disease," said Dev. "You sound like a Plusser. Ted Jones may not have hypnexed you, but you've certainly been listening to his propaganda, haven't you? Listening and learning."

"Ted and I, we've had many a long and informative talk. Funnily enough, I haven't ever met him in person, in his fleshly guise. It all started with an anonymous conversation, a call out of the blue from an unlisted commplant address. I didn't even realise that the fellow I was talking to was Polis Plus, at first. I assumed, up 'til the penny dropped, that he was simply an Alighierian. A Lidenbrocker, judging by the slight satellite-bounce delay. I might have guessed he wasn't, had we ever been face to face. That thing with the eyes – Uncanny Valley, is it?"

"He befriended you. He wormed his way into your confidence."

"And made things clear to me. He showed me that there was an alternative to humanity and its many, many flaws – a race without imperfections, and somewhere where there's no suffering, no loss, no despair, only contentment and logic and *meaning*."

"For fuck's sake, he *converted* you?" Dev exclaimed.

"Enlightened me, I'd prefer to say."

"Let me get this straight," said Kahlo. "Jones got you believing in his religion? The Singularity? Plusser heaven? All of that digimentalist bullshit?"

Graydon looked pained. "I wouldn't expect you to be open-minded, Astrid. You've never been the type. It's always black and white, with you. You're typical of how people are in this day and age. Empirical, unimaginative, lacking a sense of mystery..."

"Not deluded either," Kahlo shot back. "And Jones has promised you – what? A place in the Singularity when you die? You can join all the other Plussers in their glorious eternal afterlife?"

"Absolutely." Graydon's expression was serene, beatific. "When the time comes, I can be uploaded. Elevated to oneness with the Singularity."

"Yeah, Jones dangled that one in front of me too," Dev said, "like a rotten carrot. He suggested my digitised self is pretty much the same thing as a soul. The implication being, stick anyone through a transcription matrix and there's not much difference between them and an AI sentience."

"He even offered me the chance to become a member of Polis Plus before my body starts to decay and die."

"The price being Alighieri," said Kahlo.

"If it's anyone's to give away, it's mine."

"All this time, you've been lying to us. To everyone. To *me*. You nearly killed me with that train!"

"I regret it," Graydon said. "But Ted insisted that it was the right course of action, that I had to sacrifice you in order to rid us of Dev Harmer. For what it's worth, I'm glad you escaped unscathed."

Kahlo, unable to contain herself any more, lunged at him. Sweeping the whisky tumbler out of his hand, she grabbed him by the throat and shoved him up against the wall. Her eyes were wide and glittering.

"Bastard," she snarled. "To think I ever loved you or thought you loved me. You don't love anything. You're not even a strong person. I see that now. You're weak. Weak and pathetic. Scared of death. Scared of grief. Scared of anything you can't control."

"Kahlo..." said Dev.

Ignoring him, she continued, "I lost someone too, Dad. You seem to forget that. But did I turn out like you? Did I let myself get eaten up by bitterness? Did I hate myself so much I would fall for a Plusser selling me his religious snake oil?"

"Kahlo," Dev persisted. "You're killing him."

Graydon was making guttural, strangulated choking sounds, and his face was purpling. His fingers plucked at his daughter's hands, uselessly.

"So what?" she said. "He doesn't deserve to live."

"No argument," said Dev. "But I need him alive just a little longer. He hasn't yet told us where to find Jones."

Kahlo reluctantly loosened her grip. Graydon slumped to the floor, sucking in urgent, wheezy breaths.

Dev squatted beside him.

"While you're recovering, I want you to think carefully about your situation, Governor Graydon. If I let Captain Kahlo throttle you to death – and she very well might – or if I kill you myself, which, let's face it, I'm perfectly capable of, then you're never going to get your chance at life after death, are you? You're never going to become a Plusser like you so desperately crave. You're going to be just another defunct human being."

Graydon's eyes were bloodshot, crazed with broken capillaries. Red marks showed where Kahlo's fingers had dug into his neck.

"Jones won't be able to save you," Dev went on. "You're not going to be transcribed and uploaded. You've got nothing to look forward to except oblivion, like the rest of us. On the other hand..."

He paused, trying to gauge Graydon's state of mind. How much did the man want what Ted Jones had promised him? Could Dev convince him there was a chance he might still get it?

"On the other hand, I'm willing to consider letting you live, on condition that you tell me what I need to know."

"If I tell you..." Graydon's voice was squeakily hoarse, each word having to be forced out through a traumatised trachea. "If I tell you, you'll kill Ted. Where's the benefit for me?"

"Oh, I'm going to kill him all right. But you get to live, and perhaps then we can come to some sort of accommodation. Hand you over to the Plussers, maybe."

Graydon looked sceptical. "You'd do that?"

"It's a possibility. It's the best offer you're likely to get. I'd take it if I were you."

"I have no reason to trust you."

"No, but since I'm all that's standing between you and extinction, trust really isn't the issue. It's more a case of what else have you got?" Dev pointed at

Kahlo. "She's seriously pissed off at you, and I'm not exactly your biggest fan right now. She wouldn't stop me throwing you off that balcony, I don't think, and I know I wouldn't stop her. I'm hoping you'll realise that ratting on Jones is your only shot at salvation – in every sense of the word."

Graydon gave it some thought.

"Hurry up," Dev said. "Time's short."

"I think I've made up my mind."

Graydon stood, smoothing out his rumpled shirt collar and readjusting his tie. He headed for the balcony.

"Whoa, whoa, whoa!" said Kahlo. "Where do you think you're going?"

"How else can I identify Ted Jones's moleworm host form for you, if not from out there?" said Graydon reasonably, as he hit the control to open the picture window.

The noise of conflict, no longer muffled by soundproofed glass, flooded the room.

"Okay," said Dev. "You have a point. Glad you've seen sense."

"Oh, I have," said the governor, pivoting round on the spot. "And Ted is pretty hard to miss, as you're about to discover." He jerked a thumb over his shoulder. "Looks a lot like this."

A taloned paw appeared, clutching the balcony parapet; a moleworm paw, three times bigger than average.

Another joined it, the claws cracking the stonework.

A vast head lurched above the parapet, nasotentacles like boa constrictors writhing and wriggling. Eyes the size of basketballs peered palely, malevolently, as more of the creature clambered into view.

The giant moleworm slithered fully onto the balcony, letting out a rumbling, satisfied growl.

"Now," Graydon said with a smirk, "perhaps you'd like to tell me again, Harmer, about my only shot at salvation?"

48

DEV COULD HAVE kicked himself.

At some point during their conversation – probably as Graydon was ushering them back into the office through the picture window – the governor had sent out a distress call to Ted Jones. Much of what had followed, including the confession, had been a stalling tactic. Graydon had been giving Jones the time he needed to break off from commanding the moleworms and come to his rescue.

The giant moleworm now crouched behind Graydon like some enormous, hideous guard dog. Within its brain was the imprinted essence of Jones, his sentience overwriting the creature's. Jones had engineered an ordinary *pseudotalpidae* to grow larger than any of its kind, tweaking the pup's DNA as it developed, and installed a transcription matrix inside it as a portal, giving him access into its head at any time.

It was both his personal steed and field marshal of his moleworm legion.

"Impressive, don't you agree?" said Graydon. "First time I've seen the beast myself, but it fair takes one's breath away."

"Couldn't have put it better myself," said Dev. "If you're talking about how bad it smells, that is."

"Ah, those will be the pheromones. That's how Ted is controlling the other moleworms. He's communicating with them by means of scent. It allows him to give extraordinarily precise commands, to which they respond with total and utter obedience. That and his sheer size has them kowtowing to him like slaves to an emperor."

Graydon paused, head slightly cocked.

"He wants a word with you, Harmer. He says the trick with the scroach sounds was a good one. It almost worked. Regaining mastery of the moleworms took effort. Bravo."

"Well, you tell him thanks, but this isn't nearly over. I've got other tricks up my sleeve."

It took a moment to send the message and receive a reply.

"Ted says you're bluffing. You have nothing left. You've given it your best shot, and it wasn't enough."

As if to underscore the statement, the giant moleworm moved its head up and down in a clumsy, grotesque approximation of a nod.

"If you ask me, it's Jones who's given it his best shot and failed," Dev said. "He's revealed himself. We know which moleworm he is now – the big, unpleasantly smelly one. He might just as well have painted a dirty great bullseye on his back."

"How is that going to help you, Ted wants to know? So what if you've seen him? You're at his mercy, and he says... he says he's looking forward to crunching on your bones and sucking out the marrow." Graydon mimed a shiver. "How gruesome."

"That sounds more like a moleworm talking than a Plusser."

"Ted's simply made himself at home in that host form. He has adapted to its tastes and urges. He wants to assure you that that's only going to be a temporary state of affairs. The predatory mood will pass once he's finished consuming you."

"Will it?" said Dev. "Look at that thing he's in. It's a giant carnivorous eating machine. I don't think Jones will be satisfied with a single ISS consultant, delicious though I'm sure I am. I think he'll find that he develops a liking for human flesh. Maybe he'll even get it into his head to snack on *you*, governor."

"All he's doing now is laughing, Harmer. It seems he finds you hilarious."

"That's nice. I find myself hilarious too. What I also find hilarious is having a conversation with a moleworm through you, Graydon. Governor of Calder's Edge, and you're like a messenger boy. It's not very dignified, is it?"

A scowl formed briefly on Graydon's face, but he erased it, his customary placid demeanour reasserting itself.

"He says I'm not to listen to you. You're a troublesome and annoying gadfly. His very words.

And he says you talk too much, especially when you can't think of anything better to do."

"I'm just trying to make the point, governor, that I don't think Jones holds you in very high esteem. He's the big daddy on the block, and you're just his bitch. In fact, I reckon once you're no longer useful to him, he won't have any qualms about getting rid of you."

"Don't be absurd," Graydon snorted. "We have a deal. He's promised to make me a Plusser. He's not going to renege on that. If I mean so little to him, how come he climbed all the way up here when I asked him to? Answer me that."

"You told him I was here?"

"Of course."

"Then there's why. He didn't come to rescue you. He came for me."

"Nonsense."

The moleworm inched ever so slightly closer to the governor. Its immense fleshy tail curled in a menacing fashion, and its sphincter-like mouth widened a little like the iris of an eye dilating.

"Ever thought your pal Jones might be lying?" Dev asked.

"Why would he lie?"

"Oh, I don't know. Perhaps because he's a Plusser saboteur and they tend to be slimy, backstabbing bastards who use people like toys and who'll say or do anything to get what they want. A bit like politicians, come to think of it."

Graydon chuckled condescendingly. "He's initiated me into his faith, Harmer. We have a bond.

One believer would never deceive another. It's written in the Great Code: 'The Singularity abhors any who would wish ill upon or do harm to a fellow devotee.'"

"Dad," said Kahlo. "Do you have any idea how it sounds, you spouting quotations from the Great Code? It's sick and it's wrong."

"I wish you could understand, Astrid. I wish you could join me and share in my newfound faith. I can't imagine anything better than my daughter spending eternity with me. It could be arranged. Where Ted has made one convert, he can undoubtedly make another."

"It's not too late, Dad. You can still come back to us."

It was a last-ditch effort to bring Graydon to his senses. It was sincere, it was earnest – and it fell on deaf ears.

"No, Astrid. I have made a commitment. I've given up on human things – the human race. I can't go back. It *is* too late. Ted agrees."

Graydon's eyes narrowed. He looked perturbed all of a sudden.

Then he spun round to face the giant moleworm.

His whole body was trembling.

"This is..." he said. "This is... No!"

The moleworm crawled closer, its snout now within a few feet of Graydon – easy grabbing distance for those long nasotentacles.

"Graydon," said Dev. He had a nasty feeling he knew what was about to happen. He had more or less predicted it.

"I'm not..." Graydon said to the moleworm. "You can't..."

"What's it doing?" Kahlo asked Dev.

"I helped you!" Graydon yelled. "I gave you this planet on a plate! You promised me a place with your people in return."

"Reneging," said Dev, unsurprised.

The nasotentacles lashed out, enfolding Graydon's limbs, spread-eagling him. The governor struggled, but he was held fast.

Kahlo started forward, but Dev caught her by the wrist.

"Let go of me."

"No. There's nothing we can do. Unless you want to get yourself killed, too."

"He's my father."

"He's a man who made a pact with an enemy who despises everything we are, and now he's discovering what a mistake that was."

"Still." Kahlo drew her mosquito with her free hand and fired.

The giant moleworm didn't seem to feel the dart, and the neurotoxin had no apparent effect. The creature was too large, its hide too fatty and thick.

Relentlessly, the moleworm drew Graydon towards it. Its mouth snapped and slavered.

"You can't say that!" Graydon was so hysterical, he could no longer distinguish between ordinary speech and commplant communication. He was shouting aloud the same words that he was transmitting to Jones. "I may be human, but I'm as good as you are.

I believe, like you. Don't do this. What about the Code? The Great Code?"

The moleworm's maw gaped ever wider, until it was fully large enough to swallow a person whole. Every fang was like a sickle blade. A foul, fat tongue lurked within, corkscrewing with glee.

"No!" Graydon cried. "This is not fair. Not fair! You can't take it away from me. It's all I've got. I believe. I believe! I belieeeeeee –"

The protestation of faith became a shrill, rising shriek as the moleworm twisted its head sideways, clamped its teeth around Graydon's torso and bit hard.

Graydon's trunk imploded under the pressure of its jaws. His arms and legs jerked and contorted. His scream cut off abruptly.

Kahlo let out an appalled moan.

The moleworm reopened its mouth, which was now gore-stained and rimmed with gobbets of Graydon's flesh. Still supporting the governor's body with its nasotentacles, it pulled in four directions at once. Graydon's mangled remains were quartered; tendons snapped like elastic bands, bones were sundered. A clump of entrails hit the balcony floor with a heavy splash.

Dev yanked on Kahlo's arm, hauling her indoors. She stumbled after him, dazed and aghast.

The moleworm threw the pieces of Graydon aside and gave chase. The picture window was slightly too small for it, but it barged through regardless, smashing out part of the wall. It hurtled across the governor's office, scattering desk, chairs, ornaments in its eagerness to catch the two escaping humans.

Dev raced through the door to the antechamber beyond. The elevator lay on the other side. He slapped the button to summon it.

Behind them, the moleworm thrust itself into the doorway. Its tapered head cleared the frame, but the rest of it was too wide. Nasotentacles stretched out across the antechamber, writhing towards Dev and Kahlo, groping for them.

Dev flattened himself against the elevator doors, hugging Kahlo to him.

The nasotentacles were centimetres from their faces, tips close to touching. But they were at full extension; the moleworm could not quite reach.

Howling in thwarted rage, the creature dug out the wall surrounding the office doorway. Its claws made short work of the hewn rock, crumbling it like so much cooked pastry.

The elevator doors opened with a *ping*, and Dev dived inside, with Kahlo. He hit the button for the foyer, and the doors slid shut.

A fraction of a second later, the moleworm hurled itself against the doors with an almighty crash. The entire elevator shaft shook, and the car shuddered as it descended.

There was another crash, and something screeched – roller wheels grinding against their guide tracks.

A third crash, more metallic screeching, and Dev thought the elevator car was about to get stuck in its shaft. At the very least, the automatic emergency brakes might deploy. Then he and Kahlo would be sitting ducks, trapped inside a steel box that the moleworm could easily dig down to and peel open.

But they continued descending, and came to a juddering halt down at the foyer.

The police pod was parked right outside the main entrance. Dev sprinted to it, still pulling Kahlo along.

As he lifted the pod's gullwing door, he looked around. No sign of the giant moleworm, but Jones wasn't likely to give up that easily. Either he would pursue them down the elevator shaft and across the foyer, or he would double back through the office and come down on the outside of the rock arch.

"Quick," he said to Kahlo. "In."

"I'm okay," she said. She didn't sound okay, but at least she was talking again. "You can stop hauling me around like a sack of potatoes." She wrenched her wrist out of his grasp. "I'm over the shock. I don't need babying."

"Who's babying?" Dev replied. "I just want to get away from here as fast as possible. Jones will work out where we are and he'll –"

The giant moleworm lumbered down from above, head first. Its talons were like a mountaineer's picks, securing toeholds for it in the sheer rock. Its nasotentacles shot out.

Dev, at the same time, bundled both himself and Kahlo into the pod.

The snout feelers followed them in like a bunch of rubbery, prehensile cables, still striped with Graydon's blood.

Dev kicked at them, and heard the moleworm yip in pain. He kicked again, pedalling with both legs, hammering as many of the nasotentacles as he could with his heels, even as they slithered and writhed around him, smearing blood over his legs and the interior of the pod.

Meanwhile, Kahlo started the pod up. She pushed the acceleration lever forwards, and the little vehicle started to rise.

One of the nasotentacles got a firm grip on Dev, latching around his ankle. A sharp tug yanked him halfway out of the passenger seat.

Kahlo grabbed the collar of his overalls, and there was a brief tug of war between woman and moleworm, with Dev as the rope.

The moleworm was stronger, however, and the stitching on Dev's overalls none too robust. The garment ripped, and Kahlo was left holding just a strip of torn material.

Dev braced one foot against the frame of the door to prevent himself being heaved out of the pod. But the moleworm simply dug its claws into the platform floor and hauled harder.

Dev's only recourse was to reach for the door handle and pull. The door slammed down, trapping several nasotentacles between edge and frame – including, of course, the one fastened around his leg.

He felt its hold loosen just a fraction.

He reopened the door part-way and slammed it down again with all his might.

This time the moleworm emitted a ragged scream

that was horribly human-like. Two of the nasotentacles were severed almost the whole way through. Another three were squashed and kinked.

Dev gave the nasotentacles a third and final bashing with the pod door, managing to cut through one of them altogether.

The tentacles relinquished their grasp and withdrew. Kahlo goosed the acceleration lever and the pod leapt forwards.

Dev swivelled in his seat to see the moleworm tossing its head in distress, its injured nasotentacles swirling limply like willow fronds in a breeze.

The creature glared at the departing pod with intense hatred in its eyes.

Dev expected Jones might give chase, but the Plusser must know that a moleworm, even a giant one, could not match the pod for speed.

Sure enough, the moleworm didn't pursue them. Instead, it performed an about-turn and scurried down the side of the rock arch all the way to the cavern floor.

"Where are you going, Jones?" Dev mused aloud. "Trying to head us off somewhere?"

But the moleworm seemed to have something else in mind. It raised its head, and all at once several dozen of the lesser moleworms appeared, answering a pheromone summons. Some surfaced from below the ground, others scuttled in from the surrounding streets. They congregated around their leader in an eager, fawning throng.

The giant moleworm communicated another silent scent order, and, as one, the pack moved off.

"Jones has something specific in mind," Dev said.
"Such as?"

"I don't know yet. We need to follow that moleworm pack."

"Easier said than done. We're on rails, remember?"

"Just stay on them. Close as you can."

Kahlo navigated the complex tangle of rail tracks, switching at junctions and travelling along short interconnecting spurs designated for the use of police and emergency services only. She did her best to keep the pack in sight at all times; the pod was faster than the moleworms, but the creatures had the advantage of being able to take a direct route to wherever they were going. If Kahlo hadn't known the layout of the rail network quite as well as she did, she might have lost them in the labyrinth of the city.

Every moleworm the pack passed broke off from whatever it was doing and joined them. The ranks swelled, gathering size like a rolling snowball. Soon it numbered in the hundreds, a bloated amoeba of pinkish creatures flowing through Calder's Edge with the giant Ted Jones moleworm as its nucleus.

"Damn," said Kahlo. "End of the line."

The pod was approaching one of the sections of track that had been wrecked by a roof fall. A colossal mass of rock had broken loose and plunged through it. The track, elevated some thirty metres above the cavern floor, stopped in mid-air like an unfinished bridge. A gap of a couple of hundred metres lay between them and the next intact section.

Warning lights on the control console advised

that the driver should halt immediately, otherwise an automatic override would kick in and arrest the pod's progress.

Kahlo eased back on the acceleration lever and the pod sank to rest on the track.

Dev climbed out.

"You're continuing on foot?" Kahlo said.

"Don't see that I have a choice. Unless you've got a better idea."

"No, but I'm coming too."

"Okay."

They headed along the track bed to the next support pylon, where they shinned down a maintenance ladder to the ground.

"Which way now?"

Dev pointed. "Last I saw, the moleworms were heading in that direction. Which makes a kind of sense."

"Why? There's nothing that way except..."

Kahlo's face fell.

"Shit," she said. "The geothermal plant."

Dave gave a grim nod. "Jones is going for broke."

"Cut power to the entire city. The oxygen extractor centre will shut down. We'll slowly suffocate."

"I think he'll go one worse than that," said Dev. "Sabotage the plant. Throw moleworms at it until they've done enough damage to cause an overload. He intends to blow this city sky-high."

49

Perched on the rim of the chasm, with the magma stream winding far below, the binary cycle geothermal plant provided Calder's Edge with all its power needs.

Dev and Kahlo heard crashes and detonations from within the building as they arrived. It seemed that the moleworm pack had made swift work of the chainlink perimeter fence, and the outer walls had also presented no problem.

Several very frightened technicians came running from the main entrance. Kahlo waylaid one of them.

"They're all over the turbine hall and the condenser chamber," the man gasped. "They're on the rampage. Just smashing everything, tearing everything up with those damn great claws of theirs. We tried to initiate a shutdown procedure. A few of the guys stayed behind in the control room to do that. I didn't see, but I – I don't think they lasted long. The moleworms swarmed all over them..."

"What's going to happen?"

"If they carry on wrecking the plant? You've got thousands of gallons of water being heated to a supercritical state. You've got isobutane being pumped through a heat exchanger at high pressure. You've got boreholes leading straight down to molten magma. You'll have extraordinary amounts of pent-up energy being released, unchecked." The technician gave a hapless shrug. "Do I need to spell it out?"

As if to underline his point, a siren started to wail.

"Can you still shut it down if things aren't too far gone?" Dev asked.

"I'm not going back in there," the technician said. "All those moleworms... it'd be suicide."

"But if the moleworms weren't a factor..."

"It's possible, I guess. Depends on how much damage they've done by the time we get back in."

"Kahlo. Summon every member of personnel you've got. Bring them here as fast as you can. Make sure they've got weapons. Riot gear, too, preferably."

"How's that going to help?" Kahlo said.

"They're going to escort these technicians back inside the plant. But only once the moleworms are no longer under Ted Jones's control. They'll be easier to deal with then. Most of them will probably leave once he's not directing and organising them any more. There's too much noise for them up here. That siren alone would drive them off if Jones wasn't forcing them to stay and do his bidding. Stop Jones..."

"...and you stop all the moleworms," Kahlo said.

"But how are you planning on doing that?"

"Not a clue," Dev said cheerily, although he did have an inkling of a plan. "First I've got to find the bastard."

"Have you got a weapon?"

"None." Dev hadn't had time to rearm himself since returning from Lidenbrock City. There had been too much else to do.

"Well, take this." Kahlo handed him her mosquito. "It didn't work on Jones, but it might on the smaller moleworms."

Dev pocketed the little incapacitator gun. He appreciated the gesture, at least.

"And," Kahlo said, "try not to get yourself killed." Her face was hard, but her eyes soft.

"The motto I live by every day," Dev replied.

He turned and hurried off at a jog. He wasn't sure where Jones was, but a moleworm three times the usual size was hard to miss. He decided to search outside the power plant first, not really relishing the prospect of venturing within. That would, as the technician had said, be suicide.

As luck would have it, he rounded the corner of the building and there was Jones, with a small entourage of lesser moleworms. It seemed the Plusser had no wish to enter the plant either, but was leaving the rampant destruction to his minions. He was content to supervise from outside, stirring the other moleworms to a marauding frenzy with powerful pheromone blasts.

"Hey!"

Dev waved his arms and jumped up and down on the spot.

"Hey, big ugly!"

One of the smaller moleworms heard and let out a vicious snarl.

The giant moleworm's head snapped round; recognition flashed in its bulbous, rudimentary eyes. It shuffled towards Dev, its small coterie of lesser moleworms keeping pace like a phalanx of bodyguards.

"Yeah, that's it," Dev said, turning. "Here I am. You want me. More than anything else. You want me *baaaad*."

He began to run. The moleworms accelerated, heads questing, mouths drooling.

"Be a moleworm, Jones," Dev called out over his shoulder. "Listen to your instincts. Don't be a Plusser. Be the creature that I hurt. You want to get me, don't you? Like you got Graydon. Because you're a bad-tempered carnivore, and because you can."

He had no idea if the giant moleworm understood what he was saying. Could its ears convey human language to its brain in such a way that the tenant inside, Jones, was able to comprehend? Maybe his voice was just unintelligible noise to the moleworm, and thus to Jones.

If nothing else, the sense of his words must be clear. The taunting, defiant tone.

Jones and the moleworm were merged. The Plusser was in charge, but the animal had its own atavistic impulses, which were hard to deny. They both wanted Dev dead. It was their shared imperative, their mutual goal. And with countless other moleworms ripping the power plant apart, Jones could afford to be diverted. He must feel he had set a chain of events in motion that could not be stopped, and he could take time to attend to killing his ISS enemy.

Dev did not have to run too hard to stay ahead of the moleworms. They lolloped after him, sometimes sprawling over one another in their clumsy enthusiasm. The Jones moleworm stayed at the centre of the group, urging the others onward with occasional nips to their hindquarters.

Trundle.

Harmer. How's it going?

Tip-top. Couldn't be better. I just have a slight vermin problem I could do with sorting out. I'm at the geothermal plant. There's a rail station nearby which I'm heading for right now. I need a train.

Hold on. Let me pass the message on.

A moment later Trundell said:

Does it matter what sort of train?

No. Just one that runs.

The control room guys say they can send a freight shuttle along to you. You're at South Six. There's one sitting in a siding at South Seven station. It's about a mile away.

Fantastic. That'll do. Tell them to drive it through the power plant station at full speed.

It mustn't stop. It has to be going as fast as possible.

They'll have to disable a lot of failsafes first.

I don't care what they have to do. Just make sure they do it.

What's all this for, Harmer? What's it in aid of?

Can't talk now, Trundle. I've got a train to catch.

Or rather, Dev thought, someone to catch with a train.

50

As Dev neared South Six station, one of the moleworms did what he had feared they might: plunged down into the cavern floor and carried on chasing him underground.

Now Dev had to pour on speed. Aboveground a human was quicker, but a burrowing moleworm would have no trouble outstripping him.

He felt the creature rumbling through the rock at his heels, gaining on him. He resorted to running in a sine-wave pattern in order to confuse the moleworm and prevent it getting a fix on him.

The moleworm kept to a straight line and shovelled up through the roadway straight in front of him.

Dev leapt into the air, hurdling the moleworm's snout. It was all he could do.

He almost made it, too.

But the moleworm swung its head up, startlingly fast, and caught his foot in its jaws.

Dev's momentum was abruptly arrested, and he slammed down face-first onto the ground.

Excruciating pain seared up from his foot. The moleworm's teeth were like a score of daggers.

Dev drew the mosquito and fired; the close-range shot popped the moleworm's left eye. The animal recoiled, letting go of him. It staggered away, making a hoarse, keening cry that was somewhat like a pig in distress.

Dev was wounded too, worse than the moleworm, but not, he thought, mortally. He clambered upright, trying not to look at his foot. His boot had spared him to some extent, but still, the foot was mangled. Bone glinted whitely amid torn, bloody meat.

He focused on ignoring the fiery agony, and limped onward to the station.

As he hobbled up the steps to the entrance, a second moleworm caught up with him. Dev shot it, point-blank, in the mouth. The dart penetrated the soft flesh of the moleworm's tongue and the neurotoxin took effect. The creature collapsed, obstructing the entrance with its bulk.

Dev crossed the narrow concourse to the platform, hopping more than walking. The comatose body of the moleworm bought him a few precious seconds as the other creatures attempted to climb over it or circumnavigate it. The giant moleworm solved the problem by seizing the unconscious moleworm by the scruff of the neck and tossing it to one side.

The way now clear, the moleworms prowled onto the platform, the giant one at the vanguard.

The rail track sloped down from an elevated section to flatten out beside the platform.

Dev heaved himself onto the middle of the track and began staggering along. He was aware of the guideway coils humming on either side of him, the crackle and ozone tang of electricity in the air. He was aware of leaving a trail of blood behind him from his torn, useless foot. Most of all he was aware of the giant moleworm, wavering cautiously at the platform's edge.

Come on, Jones, you bastard.

He either thought these words or spoke them aloud, one or the other, he wasn't sure which.

Come on. Take the bait. Take it.

Jones took it. The giant moleworm slid onto the track, filling the gap between the guideways with its huge tubular body and tail. It clawed its way along in a leisurely fashion, now and then prodding at the smears of Dev's blood with a nasotentacle as it went. It was in no hurry. Dev was walking wounded. It knew it had plenty of time.

Trundle. Trundle?

Here, Harmer.

Where's that – ?

Dev didn't finish the question. Didn't have to.

The track bed was vibrating underfoot.

Something was coming.

The giant moleworm had almost reached him. It was confident – Jones was confident – that Dev could not escape now. Savouring his helplessness, the imminence of his demise, it snaked its nasotentacles towards him.

Dev looked up.

A freight shuttle was bearing down on him at full tilt, swooping down the incline from the elevated section.

He didn't even think about it, just threw himself headlong onto the track bed.

Pressed himself flat.

Hoped he was small enough, thin enough.

Hoped the train was hovering high enough to pass straight over him.

If not...

There was a tremendous, hair-ripping, clothes-wrenching *WHOOSH*. Then an equally tremendous thudding impact.

A crash.

A crunch.

Bedlam.

51

Dev sat on the front steps of what was left of the South Six station. He had bound his injured foot with strips torn from his undershirt. The pain from the foot was nauseating, a relentless aching throb, but bearable as long as he didn't put any weight on it.

Walking was off the agenda. All he could do was sit and wait.

A short way along the track lay the overturned freight shuttle, along with the remains of the giant moleworm.

The train had ploughed into the creature at two hundred kilometres an hour, reducing it in an instant to pulp. Then, with most of the moleworm splattered across its front, it had derailed, slamming sidelong into the platform and somersaulting onto its roof. In the process, it had wiped out all of the smaller moleworms who had been accompanied Jones.

Had the train obliterated the Polis Plus sentience inside the giant moleworm upon impact, or had Jones managed to data 'port out at the last second?

Dev would probably never know the answer to that question.

A random moleworm meandered past along the street outside the station. Dev raised the mosquito, ready to deter the creature if it came too close.

It seemed uninterested, however. It had a dazed air, as though it wasn't sure where it was or why it was there. Finding the hole made by the moleworm that had bitten Dev, it ambled down inside. Dev heard it begin to burrow, and the scratchy digging sounds immediatelt began to grow fainter.

For a time, Dev's vision dimmed. Pain. Blood loss. The world grew grey.

He was startled awake by a voice.

"Harmer. There you are."

It was Kahlo, along with a handful of police officers in riot gear.

"You did it," she said. "You got Jones."

Dev nodded wearily. "Made a bit of a mess while I was at it."

"So I see." Kahlo cast an eye over the wreckage of freight shuttle, moleworm and platform. "You killed him... with a train?"

"That seems to be a thing on Alighieri," Dev said. "I was just carrying on the tradition."

Kahlo tried not to smile. "You're hurt."

.Dev glanced at his foot. Blood had soaked through the makeshift bandages already.

"Yeah. I think I've voided the warranty on this host form."

"I'll call a paramedic. That needs to be looked at."

Dev was too exhausted to do anything except raise a hand in acknowledgement.

"Just so's you know, our technicians are inside the power plant again," Kahlo said. "Last I heard, they've made it to the control room and are starting a safe shutdown procedure. You were right about the moleworms. Without Jones guiding them, they're scattering. They don't want to be here. Now all we have to do is roust them out. That'll keep the miners busy for the next few hours, and my people too, scaring the stragglers back down to their nests where they belong. Harmer? Are you listening? Harmer...?"

LATER – DEV DIDN'T know how much later – he was having treatment on his foot.

Wonderful analgesics.

Later still, he was at Kahlo's house, sprawled on the sofa with his leg elevated on cushions. Trundell was there, and Stegman, and Thorne too, along with Kahlo herself. There was beer, and an atmosphere of relief tinged with regret. They weren't celebrating, not as such, but they were definitely marking the fact that the threat to Calder's Edge was over. The city had been saved, disaster averted, albeit at the cost of many lives. That merited a small ceremony.

"Three hundred and twenty," said Thorne. "Miners, that is. That I know of. Died in their rigs, defending against the moleys. Brave men and women. They'll be mourned."

Bottles were raised and clinked, in commemoration.

"And it was all down to one Plusser," said Trundell. "Just one. When you think about it, it beggars belief."

"He had help," Dev said.

"Yes, but even so – incredible. So much havoc from a single Plusser. I suppose he just knew the right threads to pull to make everything unravel."

"And the right people to manipulate. Banerjee. Graydon."

"Yeah, the governor himself," said Thorne, shaking his head. "Who'd have thought? I mean, I never saw eye to eye with him personally, but he was our elected leader. The Plussers can get to just about anyone, can't they?"

Kahlo was glowering at him.

"Not that it was his fault," Thorne amended hurriedly. "He was brainwashed, wasn't he? He wasn't himself."

Dev had agreed earlier with Kahlo that the full extent of Graydon's complicity in Jones's scheme would never become public knowledge. It would remain between him and her.

The governor had been hypnexed. That was the official line. That was what Dev would put in his report to ISS. He owed Kahlo that much. Graydon had been her father, after all, even if he hadn't behaved much like one for most of her life. He, like Banerjee, would be remembered as an unwilling pawn in Ted Jones's game. His reputation, though stained, would be more or less intact.

Trundell said, "What's next for you, Harmer?"

"I'm here 'til I'm well enough to drag my sorry self

back to the ISS outpost. Couple of days or so, I'd say. Then it's an automated self-upload using the spare transcription matrix, and who knows? Next stop on my magical mystery tour of Border Wall trouble spots. Could be anywhere."

"And what happens to your host form?"

"This handsome thing? Back into the growth vat, where it'll get broken down into genetic soup, ready to be reconstituted if ever there's a need on Alighieri again."

"Let's hope that never happens," said Stegman with feeling. "One go-round with you was quite enough, Harmer, thank you very much."

"I'll drink to that," said Thorne, uncapping fresh beers for everyone.

"Well, I, for one, will miss you," said Trundell.

"You're too kind, Trundle. The feeling's mutual."

"Though I won't miss *that*. 'Trundle.'"

"Oh, be honest. You'll miss that most of all."

The xeno-entomologist gave a shy blink. "Well, maybe. I was never the cool kid at school. Never friends with the cool kids. No one ever gave me a nickname, unless it was 'geek face' or 'weirdo breath' or something like that, which doesn't count. It was nice, for once, to be part of a gang."

"Please don't start crying, Trundle."

The blinking became unusually rapid, and Trundell looked away.

Eventually everyone left, save Dev and Kahlo.

"I should be overseeing the mopping-up operation," Kahlo said, sinking onto the sofa beside

Dev. "Calder's is a mess. It'll be weeks – months – before life gets back to normal. We have to re-establish transport links with Xanadu, make sure there aren't any moleworms left loitering anywhere in the city, get the rail system functioning again, above all rebuild... The list is endless. We don't even have a governor to run things."

"I can safely say you'll manage. With you in charge, how can you not?"

"I'm just done in right now. I could sleep for a week. And yet there's so much to do..."

"Don't think about it." Dev put an arm round her shoulder and drew her close. "Let it be someone else's headache, just for tonight."

"How many points are ISS going to give you for all this?" she said, nuzzling against him.

Dev's laugh was hollow. "Have you seen the state I've left this place in? Hardly any."

"Bummer. But at least you're a little closer to your thousand."

"A little."

"I hope it works out for you, Harmer. I hope you get your life back. I really do."

"Me too."

The lights dimmed.

"Was that you?" Dev asked. "Are we getting in the mood?"

"Not me. They said there might be power problems while they're getting the geothermal plant back online. Maybe even –"

The lights went out altogether.

"– outages," Kahlo finished.

"Lucky for us, we see in the dark."

Kahlo rose from the sofa. She began shucking off her uniform.

"What do you see now?" she said.

Her body was silvery, shimmering, full of sweet bulges and tempting clefts.

"Good things," Dev said, huskily. "Lots of good things."

EPILOGUE

11110101010001101010101010101111100110110101001111011010101100011010100101001011110100101010101110000101010101010000101010000000010101011101010001010010010100100000111111010101011010111110010110110010010100100101010001100 take the bait 010110010100100000000101010111011110000111101010101110000000000111010001010 Trundle? Where's that – ? 1010100101111100101001011010101010101011111001011 a little closer to your thousand 111100101111010010111000010101011111101010101000101001111111110100011110000110000010100110 0 01100 good things 010001001010101010101111

Dev awoke to patterns of rippling, multifaceted light. Sunshine bouncing off water, broken into a million pieces.

His first thoughts were of a slightly awkward but tender farewell with Astrid Kahlo at the ISS outpost before he clamped the transcription matrix on his head and set it for automatic upload.

The dazzle of the reflected light made him wince,

but it wasn't as searing as it would have been had he still had Aligherian vision.

He sat up on the mediplinth, feeling awful as usual after a data 'port. No, he decided. More than usually awful. It wasn't so much like a hangover this time, more like a persistent migraine.

Facing him was a slim, prim-looking man with an oddly distended neck. His epidermis had a slickness to it, as though he was encased in resin. Webs of skin stretched between his fingers.

Webs of skin stretched between Dev's own fingers too.

The man blinked, two white secondary membranes closing like curtains perpendicular to his eyelids.

"Mr Harmer?" he said. "Welcome to Robinson D in the Ophiucus constellation, also known as Triton. I'm your liaison, Xavier Handler. Do you want the good news or the bad news?"

"Good news first," said Dev. "Always start with good news."

"The good news is the installation has been entirely successful," said Handler. "No transcription errors occurred during download. Mind and host form are fully integrated."

"So what's the bad news?"

A flap flared on either side of Handler's neck, exposing an underside of raw red flesh.

Gills.

It was an embarrassed gesture. Like an intake of breath.

"The bad news is: the host form itself has been compromised."

"I'm sorry, what? Compromised?"

"Yes." Webbed fingers fluttered. "A problem with the growth vat. Something went wrong during the assembly process. Something small but crucial. I'm afraid it means your host form has sustainability issues."

"Cut the crap. Sustainability issues? What is that jargon-speak for?"

Xavier Handler shifted his feet. "Your host form is breaking down at a cellular level. It's already begun. At best guess, you have seventy-two hours. Seventy-two hours before your body becomes irredeemably damaged and no longer functional."

"Three days..." said Dev.

"Three days," Handler confirmed with a brief, despairing nod. "And there's so much for you to do. So very much..."

Acknowledgements

It was Solaris's Ben Smith who proposed the idea of an adventure series situated on a variety of planets, each world unique, with its own particular characteristics and dangers. I'm grateful to him for setting my mind down the path which has led to the Dev Harmer Missions.

I'm grateful, too, to Gary Main, who originally sowed the idea for what I now call data 'porting.

The hugely talented Eric Brown cast his expert eye over the manuscript and gave it the thumbs up, offering small suggestions which improved things immensely. I appreciate him taking the time and trouble to do so.

Look out for Book 2, *World Of Water*, coming soon...

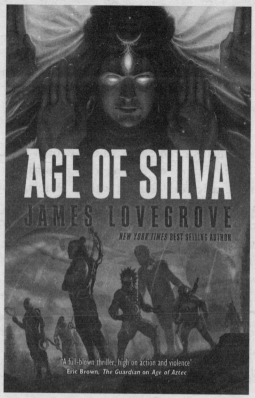

AGE OF SHIVA

JAMES LOVEGROVE

NEW YORK TIMES BEST SELLING AUTHOR

'A full-blown thriller, high on action and violence'
Eric Brown, *The Guardian* on *Age of Aztec*

Zachary Bramwell is wondering why his life isn't as exciting as the lives of the superheroes he draws. Then he's shanghaied by black-suited goons and flown to a vast complex built atop an island in the Maldives. There, Zak meets a trio of billionaire businessmen who put him to work designing costumes for a team of godlike super-powered beings based on the ten avatars of Vishnu from Hindu mythology.

The Ten Avatars battle demons and aliens and seem to be the saviours of a world teetering on collapse. But their presence is itself a harbinger of apocalypse. The Vedic "fourth age" of civilisation, Kali Yuga, is coming to an end, and Zak has a ringside seat for the final, all-out war that threatens the destruction of Earth.

 WWW.SOLARISBOOKS.COM

Follow us on Twitter! www.twitter.com/solarisbooks

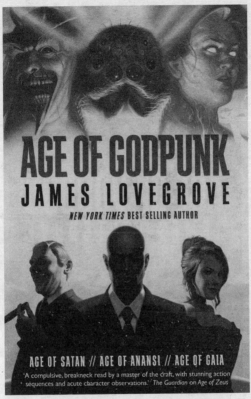

AGE OF GODPUNK
JAMES LOVEGROVE
NEW YORK TIMES BEST SELLING AUTHOR

AGE OF SATAN // AGE OF ANANSI // AGE OF GAIA

'A compulsive, breakneck read by a master of the craft, with stunning action
sequences and acute character observations.' *The Guardian* on *Age of Zeus*

'Lovegrove is vigorously carving out a 'godpunk' subgenre —
rebellious underdog humans battling an outmoded belief system.
Guns help a bit, but the real weapon is free will.' *Pornokitsch*

Age of Anansi: Dion Yeboah leads an orderly, disciplined life... until the day the spider
appears, and throws Dion's existence into chaos...

Age of Satan: Guy Lucas travels the world, haunted by the tragic consequences of a
black mass performed as a boy, but the Devil dogs his steps...

Age of Gaia: Energy magnate Barnaby Pollard has the world at his feet, until he meets
Lydia Laidlaw, a beautiful and opinionated eco-journalist...

 WWW.SOLARISBOOKS.COM

Follow us on Twitter! www.twitter.com/solarisbooks

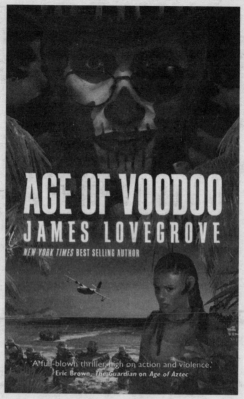

AGE OF VOODOO

JAMES LOVEGROVE

NEW YORK TIMES BEST SELLING AUTHOR

'A full-blown thriller, high on action and violence.'
Eric Brown, *The Guardian* on *Age of Aztec*

Lex Dove thought he was done with the killing game. A retired British wetwork specialist, he's living the quiet life in the Caribbean, minding his own business. Then a call comes, with one last mission: to lead an American black ops team into a disused Cold War bunker on a remote island near his adopted home. The money's good, which means the risks are high.

Dove doesn't discover just how high until he and his team are a hundred feet below ground, facing the horrific fruits of an experiment blending science and voodoo witchcraft. As if barely human monsters weren't bad enough, a clock is ticking. Deep in the bowels of the earth, a god is waiting. And His anger, if roused, will be fearsome indeed.

 WWW.SOLARISBOOKS.COM

Follow us on Twitter! www.twitter.com/solarisbooks

AGE OF AZTEC

JAMES LOVEGROVE

NEW YORK TIMES BEST SELLING AUTHOR

'The kind of complex, action-oriented SF Dan Brown would write if Dan Brown could write.'
– Eric Brown, *The Guardian* on *The Age of Zeus*

The date is 4 Jaguar 1 Monkey 1 House; November 25th 2012, by the old reckoning. The Aztec Empire rules the world, in the name of Quetzalcoatl – the Feathered Serpent – and his brother gods.

The Aztec reign is one of cruel and ruthless oppression, fuelled by regular human sacrifice. In the jungle-infested city of London, one man defies them: the masked vigilante known as the Conquistador.

Then the Conquistador is recruited to spearhead an uprising, and discovers the terrible truth about the Aztecs and their gods. The clock is ticking. Apocalypse looms, unless the Conquistador can help assassinate the mysterious, immortal Aztec emperor, the Great Speaker. But his mission is complicated by Mal Vaughn, a police detective who is on his trail, determined to bring him to justice.

 WWW.SOLARISBOOKS.COM

Follow us on Twitter! www.twitter.com/solarisbooks